Soolie Beetch and the Binding Blood is a work of fiction. Names, characters, places, and incidents are the product of the author's imagination and are used fictitiously. Any resemblance to actual events, locales, or persons, living or dead (or undead), is strictly coincidental.

Copyright © 2023 by Skelly Harrington

Published in the United States by bridge city coven press.
https://www.bridgecitycoven.com/

ISBN- 9798860988699
Printed in the United States of America

www.sooliebeetch.com

skelly@sooliebeetch.com

Cover Design by Cassandra Koehler
Author Photo © Jackaldog Photography

Foreword

Dear Reader,

You and I have built a world together that is both mine and uniquely yours, and now you hold the end of that world in your hands. If you have read Soolie's story up to this point, then we have already been through a great deal together, and I want to thank you for trusting me with something so precious as your time, perhaps even a corner of your mind and heart. To read a book, is to allow someone you may have never met to craft memories for you of things you have never done. There is an odd intimacy and a witchcraft to it, and I can say in all truth that by reading this, you have become precious to me.

Thank you for allowing yourself to care for things that never were, and never happened, in a world that only exists for those of us who choose to imagine and remember it.

See you at the end of the world,

Skel

Foreword

Content warnings can be found at the back of the book.

for the laser swords my wife wanted and never got

Some say the world will end in fire,
Some say in ice.
From what I've tasted of desire
I hold with those who favor fire.

— Robert Frost

Prologue

The ship's sails glowed white in the morning sun and cast a cold shadow over the dead girl and her monster. They clung to one another, Dog's railbone legs churning to keep them afloat as the broad side of the vessel slid towards them, rocking them in a heaving swell and folding the last scummy detritus of the Constant Fortune under the waves.

A rope ladder scrolled down.

Soolie could sense his fear, but the boy monster did not falter. He swam up and grabbed hold, waiting for her to wrap her legs around his waist before beginning to climb, hoisting them from the ocean and delivering them into the hands of his former master, the Dead Man.

As they neared the top rail, scores of living hands reached over to help them, and as their feet touched the boards, dozens of people dressed in white surrounded them. A fluffy blanket wrapped around Soolie's shoulders and many hands took her hands, leading her aft, while others pulled Dog in an opposite direction.

"STOP!" she shouted. The hands pulled, insisting, and she shucked them off. "He stays with me."

They laid hold of her again, more firmly this time, and she smacked them away, dropping the blanket to the deck. They picked it up and tried to wrap it about her, and she snarled, and the people stepped back.

"Mistress?" Dog's black bedraggled head bobbed in a retreating clutch of white bodies.

"Dog!" She lunged, shoving them aside, and grabbed his cold taloned hand.

The people closed a watching circle, just out of reach.

Dog was shivering, and she gripped his hand tighter. She didn't know what the Dead Man was going to do with either of them, but she'd be fucked if, after all the horrors they had faced together, they got separated by a crowd of *living* people. She was a single aggravation away from killing them all.

"Do any of you speak?"

They looked back, blankly blinking and breathing. They were short and tall, wide and thin, in all living colors from rust to wheat and bone to coal, and all wearing the same simple tunic, as if they'd been outfitted to be a part of the ship, just like the rigging or the sails.

Dog whined.

"Where is the Dead Man?" she asked. "Do you have somewhere to take me?"

A wall of hands rose to reach for her.

"You will not separate us."

The hands lowered. The people waited.

Soolie whispered to Dog, "What are they?"

"Servants, Mistress."

"But why are they alive? Doesn't the Dead Man prefer corpses?"

"The Master is served by many, Mistress."

This ship wasn't anything like the black-sailed ship they had seen, full of the hungry desiccating dead, its wooden bones fused to the body of a rotting beast. The deck beneath their feet was clean and honey-sealed. Rigging ropes tented down from five masts and multiple nests. This was a vessel tended and guided by the living. If it wasn't for the fact that she could sense the Dead Man's presence nearby, she might be tempted to think she and Dog were the only dead things on board.

Okay, she thought to Dog, *stay with me.*

She took one step, and the people stepped back. She took another step, and the wall of bodies began to part. Slowly, Soolie advanced in the direction they had tried to drag her before, and silently, the people accompanied, keeping pace. As she reached the aft-cabin door, they surrounded on three sides, watching.

She turned the latch, and the door opened to a dim hallway. Soolie and Dog stepped in and the people piled after, filling the left corridor and leaving the way to the right open. She was being herded. The people ushered them down the hall to a door with no knob or latch.

"Is any of this familiar?" she asked.

"No, Mistress."

The door swung in easily. When Soolie and Dog stepped through, the people didn't follow, and the door closed behind them.

They stood in sunlit room with windows on two sides. There was a dressing table and cabinet, and a four-post bed heaped in silver-gray furs. On the bed was a tidy stack of white clothes topped with a crisp white envelope.

Compared to what she had been expecting, it was downright luxurious.

She let go of Dog's hand and tested the door they had just walked through. It didn't budge, which wasn't a surprise, but now she knew for sure.

Dog stood quivering, clutching his hands to his chest and dripping seawater on the rugs. Maybe he could sense the Dead Man too.

Soolie picked up the envelope, tossed the clothes on the floor, and walked over to one of the many windows. Far below, the ocean was rushing by. The ship was already on the move, carrying them to the Southern Lands.

The envelope was sealed with white wax that had been pressed with a round, unmarked signet. She cracked it, flipped the flap, and pulled out a folded piece of paper. Inside were ten words in tidy black script.

Welcome, dead girl. I will see you in the morning.

DOG PACED the room and eyed the door. His arms were tucked to his chest like the plucked wings of a hen, and his talons click-clicked as he twisted his hands together. Soolie decided against commanding him to stop and lie down. It wouldn't make him feel any better. There was nothing for them to do except wait.

She curled cold under the pressing heap of covers and watched him trying to wear trenches in the moonlight. He was still pacing when she finally closed her eyes.

~

THE SOUL HUNTER stood in a void, wearing the form of a young girl with nutmeg skin, long black hair, and golden brazier eyes. "You have destroyed the world, Soolie Beetch."

Soolie snorted. "Oh, spak. Again?" She was surprised to see it. It hadn't spoken to her since she learned to feed herself from living souls.

"You will not find what you seek with the Dead Man. We are one being. Nothing can separate us."

"Well, we're about to find out."

"You have delivered me to the one who stole the source of my strength, who traps the souls of the dead in the realm of the living." Its distress was a comfort to her. "I was created by the Ancients to return the Lost Souls to the Eternal Realm."

"And then you let some corpse-fucker rip out your Heart, and pinned all your hopes of getting it back on possessing a human girl. If one of us is to blame, I think we both know it's not me."

"You are my greatest error, Soolie Beetch."

"Yeah. You fucked up."

Its image flickered, and its golden eyes went wide. "He is coming."

She could sense it too. Even before they boarded the ship, she had felt his presence like a wind at her back, compelling her toward him. It made her nervous, but also a little bit excited. After all this time, she was finally going to meet the Dead Man the Hunter was so afraid of.

HE IS HERE, it said.

And maybe, just *maybe,* he would set her free.

HE IS HERE, SOOLIE BEETCH. RUN.
The Hunter's eyes filled with blood.

∼

Sunlight warmed her eyelids, and she stretched languid under the covers. Her foot pushed against something that shouldn't be there. She sat up.

There was a man sitting on the edge of the bed.

"Good morning," he said.

"Who the fuck are you?"

He laughed, tossing a mop of dark curls sun-gilt with red-gold wire. His skin was ruddy bronze, and a light umber tunic hung loose and pleasing over a chest that was both well-muscled and well-fed. The bridge of his nose was knotted as if it had once been broken, and his eyes were sable, large and crinkling with merriment. He looked like he belonged in sunlight.

"Who do you think I am?" he asked.

She didn't understand, but she could sense it. The Dead Man. Yevah. The first ghost. The Soul Hunter's enemy. He looked very, very alive.

"I thought . . ." She scooted back against the headboard, tucking her legs.

"You expected to find a ghost."

"Why do you have a body? Doesn't that put your sand in a time-glass?" She looked around the room. "Where's Dog?"

"You have many questions, and I am prepared to answer them." He extended the same warm-blooded hand that had reached out to her in her dreams, inviting *come and see*. "Will you trust me?"

Relief washed over her as she trusted him immediately. She accepted, and his hand was calloused, but soft, strong, and warm. "You are different from what I expected."

"I'm glad we can surprise each other."

He stood, and she pushed off the covers to stand with him. The power of the Hunter's Heart called to her, and he felt like home.

"Where is Dog?" she asked as he led her to the door.

"Getting reacquainted with old friends," he said.

He led her into the sunlight, up a set of stairs to the deck above the cabin. Wind tousled his curls and whisked the bare dome of her head. Across the ship, men and women in white worked side by side, washing the deck, mending the sails, climbing the rigging.

He pointed to the horizon where dark sea met pale sky. "In a few days, land will be visible. Then it is only a few days travel inland, and we will be home."

She missed home. She had been traveling for so long. The stitch of the horizon twisted and bled, and he put an arm around her, and his body was warm and smelled like cardamom and sweat.

"We should talk," she said. She was feeling fuzzy. She was feeling good; like how she was supposed to feel. No . . . . She corrected that thought. "We should talk," she said again and stepped out from under his arm.

"What about?"

She backed away until she hit the transom and gripped it to stabilize herself. "You promised to help me get rid of the Soul Hunter."

"I will help you," he said, taking his place at her side, leaning against the rail.

Even without touching, she could feel his heat. The washing sound of the ocean and the flap of the sails soothed her. After all the pain and the fighting and the struggle, she finally had someone to take care of her. She looked up into his eyes, and he smiled down at her, and she wanted to please him.

"Good," he said, "because I can do *better* than remove the Soul Hunter. We can use it."

"No . . . ." She stepped away. "I want to get rid of it. I don't care what you do with it once it's out, but I want it *out* of me. You said you would help."

"I will help," he said.

She believed him. He wanted to help her, and she wanted to help him. The horizon bled more and more, as if someone sawed the sea from the sky with a jagged blade.

"Where is Dog?" she asked.

"There he is, behind you."

She turned, and Dog stood by the ship rail looking out. His black eyes gleamed red in the light of the wounded sky.

Dog, come here, she thought, and he didn't move.

The Dead Man rested a hand on her shoulder. "You don't need to be afraid."

She wanted to sink into his arms, so she turned and plunged a knife into his chest.

She looked up with both her hands on the handle, and his eyes met hers. A wave of sorrow for having hurt him washed over her, and she screamed and shoved the knife deeper, cracking his ribs and pinning the orange cloth between the soft mounds of his breast.

"Even if you resist me," he said, "I *will* help you. It doesn't have to hurt."

She was panting from the effort. "I'd rather have my pain than your lies."

"They are only lies if you choose not to believe them."

His blood ran down the knife that she had created and down her forearms and dripped from her elbows and into the sea and into the sky and turned the world to blood.

"I want to wake up," she said.

"I can't let you do that," he said.

She woke up.

She was on her back in a dark room. Her arms were strapped down at her sides, her legs restrained, her head locked in a cage. She could sense Dog somewhere nearby and hear the creaking of wood and the brush of the sea. They were still on the boat.

Red-raw eyes gleamed down at her in swinging lamplight. "You never had to see this."

"You're not trying to remove the Soul Hunter, you're trying to use me to control it." She struggled against the straps, rattling the cage.

"I want to set you free."

"You want to *control* me."

"If you stop resisting," he said, "I won't have to."

"Keep your fucking thoughts out of my head," Soolie snapped.

"We can try something different," the red eyes retreated from view, "but I don't think you're going to like it."

"What?" Soolie strained to see. "What are you going to do?"

"Have you *always* been this defiant, Soolie Beetch?"

Chapter 1

"It looks like a dog's mouth."

"Soolie!"

"It does!" She crouched next to Papa and pointed at the birthing wound between Mama's legs. "The top is the lips and whiskers. The hole is the mouth. And the bottom is where another dog shook it *real hard*. GRRRRAwrrrarrrrarrrrr!"

"Soolie, go sit on the workbench."

"I want to help!"

"NOW."

"NNNOOO!"

"Silas, let her stay." Mama's face was damp and gray, but her eyes were clear and kind. "She may not have many opportunities left."

Soolie grinned and settled back down. If Mama wanted her to stay, she got to stay. Mama got everything she wanted, because Mama was dying.

"You know I hate when you say things like that," Papa said.

He twisted the washing cloth, and water spilled into the bowl, rolling steam in the light of the evening fire. Soolie leaned in to watch as he folded the cloth over his fingers and reached up to dab Mama's torn flesh. The wound winced, but Mama didn't make a sound. She sat on the edge of the bed, knees wide, her chest sagging between the sharp points of her shoulders. Every time Soolie looked up, Mama's eyes met hers and one side of Mama's mouth turned up a little more than the other.

Papa dipped the cloth back in the bowl, softly swishing. Now, the wound looked rumpled, sad, and meaty. Private parts tended to look like butcher scrap on the best of days, but Mama's slit was always ragged and raw. It reminded Soolie of the way the edges of the room bled and pulsed, just out of sight.

Stay back, Soolie thought.

"*Stop resisting me,*" Papa said.

"Can I try?" she asked.

"Why don't you give her the cloth, Silas."

"Pleeeeeaaase, Papa!??" Soolie squirmed her butt on her heels. Papa wanted to keep Mama's care all to himself. "I won't mess it up. I promise."

"Her hands aren't clean," he objected.

"Yes they are!" Soolie bounced. "I washed them with soap when you did. I haven't touched *anything*."

"Silas." Mama closed her eyes. "Let her."

"Yes!" Soolie scooted forward, and Papa reluctantly handed her the washcloth.

"Rinse the cloth in the bowl," Papa said, "and wash gently around the upper vaginal opening...."

"And don't go near the spakhole yet," Soolie interrupted, swishing the cloth and squeezing out the water.

"Soolie!"

"Like washing a baby. Don't get spak in the *vaginal opening*." Those last two words were funny.

"That's right," Mama said.

"She gets that coarse language from your sister," Papa muttered.

Soolie scrunched her face in concentration and pet the furry top lips with the warm cloth. It didn't smell like much, even close up. Kind of sourish, but that might just be Mama. Papa washed Mama every day to stave off infection, but the sicker Mama got, the more she didn't smell right.

The slit wasn't very long, and Soolie had a hard time imagining her head fitting through that hole, but Soolie also had a hard time imagining herself fitting inside Mama's belly. At this rate, if Soolie kept growing and Mama kept shrinking, there would come a day when Soolie could swallow Mama in one gulp and carry her around in her *own* belly. That way, Soolie's body could heal Mama's body the way Mama's body couldn't heal itself. It was a nice, but very silly thought.

The seams of the room throbbed raw and wrong.

"Stop resisting," Papa said.

Soolie ignored him. She knew she was doing a good job. She swished the cloth again and wrung it out. "I'm going to wash the lower parts now." She wiped down and away between Mama's cheeks. "Does it hurt?"

"Pain loses color when it never goes away."

Soolie nodded. Mama liked to speak in parcels that needed to be unfolded to be understood. Soolie could probably talk like that if she wanted to, but she didn't have the patience for it. "Like a smell that you can't smell any more?"

"Sometimes." Mama's smile sagged on both sides now. She was getting tired. "There are many different kinds of pain. Some are shallow and some run deep. The wounds you can see are shallow pain."

"The wounds I can't see are why you are dying?"

"That's right."

"That's enough." Papa's voice was sharp. He stood. "Mama needs to lie down."

"But I'm almost done!"

Soolie scrambled up as Papa stepped in to drape Mama's nightgown back over her knees. He put an arm around Mama to help her to the top of the bed, and Soolie grabbed the water bowl out of the way.

"You shouldn't fight each other," Mama was saying.

"I don't like how she treats you," Papa said, positioning Mama's legs. "She acts like she doesn't care that you could die."

Mama rested her head in the pillows, and Papa rearranged the nightgown and lifted the covers up to her waist. Soolie stood in the middle of the floor with the bowl in her hands, while the edges of the room throbbed. Exploratory tendrils tickled the shores of her sight.

GO AWAY. She pushed back extra hard, and the rawness receded to the shadows.

Papa took Mama's hand. "Caring for you is sacred. It should be an act of love, and sometimes I worry that our daughter acts a little . . . like she's approaching your care with the same attitude as a dead possum she wants to pick apart, and I don't like anyone treating you that way."

"She's eight-years-old," Mama said.

"Old enough to act like a loving daughter," Papa said.

Soolie scowled, and her hands tightened on the bowl. Papa wasn't being fair.

He kissed Mama on the forehead. "I'll fetch the Doc."

"Mmmmm," Mama murmured, her eyes closed.

Papa laced up his boots and threw on his coat. Soolie didn't look at him. She set the bowl on the workbench, walked to the bed, and took Mama's hand. It was cool and limp.

"I love you both very much." Papa turned the latch, opened the door, and was gone.

Finally. Soolie plopped down on the bed. "Papa is stupid, and I don't like him."

"Don't tell him." Mama didn't open her eyes, but her hand squeezed Soolie's back. "Just love him."

"He acts like I don't love you," Soolie scowled. "He's the one who's making everything hard. He's the one pretending you're not dying."

"Your Papa was born tender, and life has been very cruel to him. He is fragile."

"Then he's a bad Papa."

"No, Soolie." Mama opened her eyes. "He may not be as courageous and strong as you are, but he loves you very much. You must be patient with him."

Soolie kicked her bare feet against the side of the bed. "Okay."

Mama was dying, so Mama got what she wanted. The rawness at the edges of the room pulsed. Soolie should behave and do as she was told. The rawness crawled out from the shores and the shadows. But she still didn't think that *loving* someone and being *good* for them were the same thing.

"I *mean it*, Soolie."

"I know."

"Don't resist me," Mama said.

"I'm not."

Mama's grip tightened. She wasn't smiling at all any more. *"You are."*

STOP IT. "No I'm NOT!" Soolie tried to pull away, but Mama held on with welded strength. "FUCK OFF!"

Mama's eyes were fixed on Soolie, unblinking. *"Stop fighting."*

"FUCK YOU!" Soolie tried to jump off the bed, but was unable to stand, unable to move, unable to turn her head.

The rawness grew twisting paths that snaked towards them, forming a ring that turned and turned, closing in.

"You will never be free of the Hunter until you STOP RESISTING."

"I'M NOT."

The ring moved faster, tightening like a snare, and she still couldn't move, and it reached the bed and consumed the covers until Soolie and Mama were all that was left.

Mama's eyes filled with blood. *"YOU ARE."*

Blackness swallowed, and Mama was gone. All that remained was a set of red eyes watching through a ring of moving blood.

She screamed, and she was awake in the dark room of the ship. Raw eyes gleamed in the lamplight, and the writhing ring of blood settled into a crown that seethed in the Dead Man's hair.

"You are divided, and so you fight me as you fight yourself."

"Let me go," Soolie hissed. Her throat was rough with unremembered screaming. How long had she been in this room?

"Have no fear, little dead girl. I only need to find *one* moment of submission. We will find it together, and then you will never need to fight again. Our ship has reached the shore. The next time you wake up, you will be home."

Chapter 2

Papa's face spattered with her blood.

Papa's body in the dirt, barely breathing.

Papa no longer fighting. Water spilling from his mouth. Gruel blocking his airway so that she had to swipe her fingers at his slimy slack tongue and flip him over and smack his back like a baby. Papa dying as a golden tornado of souls roared above her head. Parents, children, and potential friends, everyone she had ever known reduced to spirit and power. Their spirits passed into the Eternal Realm, their power flowed molten in the channels of her body—*and she could feel the Dead Man moving in the outlines and the unseen, like a needleworker with a lens looking for a loose thread to pick and pull*—and she stood beneath a white oak tree as her enemy's flesh liquified at her touch and splattered at her feet.

"Stop resisting."

∽

Her screams echoed back in voices that were not her own. She couldn't smell the sea anymore, and the dark room was still and hard, but the straps on her limbs and the cage on her head were the same.

"This isn't the first glance that I wanted for you."

He was circling, a touch on her ankle, a brush on her arm, forcing her to be aware of him as he looked and she couldn't look back.

He bent down and whispered in her ear. "There is so much that I want to show you beyond these walls if you will let me. What are you protecting that is so much more important than your happiness and well-being?"

She could sense Dog somewhere nearby, and even stronger was the call of the Hunter's Heart. Its closeness overwhelmed her with need and longing. His fingers traced the edges of the cuffs and brushed the skin of her wrists.

"You're trying to unravel me," she rasped.

"Unraveling is what must be done to mistakes before they can be set right. I seek to untangle the knots that are hurting you."

"*You* are hurting me."

"It would not hurt if you were not resisting."

"I'm not resisting," she lied.

∽

TIME LOST all form as she drowned in a lifetime of memories again and again resurfacing screaming under the watch of red eyes. The only mark she had for the passage of time was the withering of her body and the rawness of her throat, and then he healed her, and she was completely unmoored.

His hand was on her chest, and he was feeding her life taken from the Hunter's Heart, more pure than from any soul. Somewhere beyond the dark walls of the room, the Heart still called to her, but it also called to her in him, and it spread from his palm and reverberated in her body.

Despite herself, she made a high throat-stopping sound, and he smiled and slowly lifted his hand so she bowed away from the table, pulling at the restraints. He had spent millenia soaking in the Hunter's strength. She couldn't help herself. She needed it. It was hers. His hand hovered just out of reach, and she yearned towards it, and then he placed his hand on her head and drowned her again.

"Where is he?"

"You keep asking."

Did she? She couldn't remember. Her mind had been lumped and reformed a thousand times. There was another presence in the room with him this time. Pale, cold, and unmoving.

"My answer is the same as before," he said. "I will deliver your pet to you once you are free of the Hunter. We could be done, but you are keeping your submission from me."

"Maybe what you're looking for just isn't there."

"It's there. You have managed to pack a great deal of defiance into a life so small," he tapped on the iron bridge that banded her nose, "but it *is* there, and I *will* find it. You shouldn't struggle. I'm not looking for what to destroy. I'm searching for what to save."

"If you want the Hunter's power so bad," she rasped, "fucking take it."

"Yes." He walked to where the cold presence stood in the room, lifted the writhing crown, and placed it on his head. She knew what the crown meant. It meant his eyes were filling with blood and she was going under again.

He walked to the top of the table and stood behind her head. "I have toiled lifetimes, and I have lifetimes yet to live. Your stubbornness is a fragile shell to be cracked and peeled. We will try again."

∼

Papa chiseled Mama's gravestone himself.

TERA BEETCH

—

LOVING WIFE AND MOTHER
WE WILL MEET AGAIN IN ANCIENTS REST

It took him a very long time, because he was particular about the stone, and he chose too many words, and he chiseled them slow and deep using his awl, which completely ruined the tool and meant he would have to get a new one.

Soolie sat in the grass by the mound while he finished spading the trough.

"Help me settle the headstone?"

"Yes, Papa."

She placed her hands on the slab as he tilted it up and twisted it over, doing most of the work himself. The stone sank into the trench he had dug, and she mirrored him, kneeling and scooping the dirt back in around the stone with their bare hands and packing it in.

Soolie stepped back, rubbing her dirty hands on her good green skirts.

"Sit with me for a while?" Papa asked.

"Okay."

She sat cross-legged and propped her cheek on her fist, watching him while he watched the stone, which wasn't going anywhere or doing anything. The rims of his eyes were pink, and his cheeks were more sunken under his beard than usual. Aunt Evaline had been bringing over all kinds of tasty breads and cakes, soups and grain skillets, which was good, because Soolie wouldn't have had much to eat otherwise. Mama had told Soolie to be kind to Papa when she was gone, and Soolie was trying very hard, but Papa spent most of his time looked saggy and sad and not doing much of anything, and she wasn't sure what she was supposed to do with that.

Papa's eyes were getting wet again.

She plucked one of the frilly cornflowers from the grave mound. They were sky blue and Mama's favorite. Papa and Soolie had planted them when the town had gathered to watch Mama's body go in the ground. Even people who didn't know Mama had come, because some people liked the dying of people more than they liked the living of people, which Soolie understood, but she didn't like sharing Mama's burial with those people, and when she told Papa so, he had just looked miserable, which made her feel like she had said something wrong, even though it was true.

She twisted the flower between her fingers so the petals blurred, and picked two more so she could braid them while she waited.

"I know I'm not always a very good Papa," he said.

Soolie staggered the flowers, so they wouldn't all bunch at the end, and started to weave the stems together. "It's okay. I know you try."

"And I'm sorry she's gone," he sniffed.

"I'm sorry too." She plucked another flower and added it to the braid.

"Are you listening?"

"I'm listening."

"Okay," he said, wiping his eyes.

He wasn't chiding her for picking the flowers, so she knew he must be especially sad, and she picked a few more. They had long stems and short leaves, so weaving them was easy.

"I want you to know how much I love you," Papa said, "and that I'm proud of you. You've been very strong, but that's my job, and I promise I'm going to be better for you, baby girl. I promise."

She looked up from her task to see that he was looking at her. He wanted something, and she wanted to give it to him, but she didn't know if she could.

"I don't know if I have any tears right now," she apologized.

"That's okay," he said. "You don't have to cry."

She nodded. There had to be something she could do to make him feel better. "Papa?"

"Yes, baby girl?"

"Can you help me?" She held up the rope of flowers. "I don't know how to connect them."

Gratitude washed over his face. "Of course. I can show you."

She leaned forward as he bent the braid into a circlet and started twining the legs into the protruding heads.

"Like this. See how I'm wrapping them around?"

She nodded. Mama had encouraged Soolie to be independent, but Mama was dead, and Papa needed something different from her. "Thank you. I love you."

"I love you too, baby girl," Papa said. He tucked the last twig-ends between the gaps and set the crown of flowers on his head. "What do you think?"

She giggled. "It's perfect!" He smiled, and she saw how much he needed to know he was helping, and how much he needed for her to be okay. She hesitated. "Papa . . ." She fumbled at the skirt in her lap. "I know I'm not always a *good* daughter."

Papa's eyes glowed red.

"But I'll be better too. I promise."

"I only want to take care of you," he said.

"I know."

"It's hard for me to be a good Papa when you resist me." The circle of flowers began to twist in his hair.

"I'll obey." She really meant it. "I promise."

"You're a good girl," he said.

"I want to be good." She beamed up at him. "Can I try it on?"

"Of course."

He reached both hands up and tangled his fingers into the flowers. As he lifted, long red roots stretched from the crown as if he were pulling it from his very skull. They wriggled, snapping free and curling around his fingers, and as the last capillary threads retracted, the blood wormed its way from his eyes and left them dark and warm.

He looked confused for a moment, holding the circlet of flowers writhing in his hands.

"I love you, Papa," she said.

"I love you too, baby girl."

The crown reached for her, sticky and crawling like a living thing, and she accepted it and lifted it to her head. The moment the first tendril touched her scalp, it took root, burrowing into her mind, behind and over and into the orbs of her eyes. The crown itself was pain and it made her to be pain, and she screamed, reaching out as her vision bathed red and deepened to tar black, and she grabbed his arm and felt the hive of his mind and memories, and the blood crown gave her entrance and she stepped through that door.

∼

The twisted child existed in the shadows of sunbaked halls. His every need was met, his every whim catered to, but they hated him. Cursed child, they called him, the unwanted prince born of violence to the child queen. It was her vengeful spirit that bent his bones, and they wished him dead and prayed for a new heir. For seven moons they made offerings to Fittesh and Mesheddi, and now, the mountain gods had answered their prayers.

The twisted child crouched in the shadows of the sunbaked halls, listening to the lusty newborn cries and the sounds of rejoicing in the city below, and he knew that if he was going to survive, the shadows were where he would have to stay.

～

"WHY?" he screamed, beating the chest of the corpse that lay on the slab before him.

A moment ago, it had wailed in terror and pain, and now it lay like a dancing doll with its strings cut. WHY did they fail *every time*? He had thought for sure that, as his skill at transference grew, the corpse would hold on to the soul for longer, but the soundness of the flesh had made no difference.

He sank to the floor of his workroom, battering at his loathsome body with his meager fists.

～

It was dead again. In a moment, the corpse had gone from animated and struggling, to unmoving and soulless. But this time had been different. This time he had seen a flicker.

Gripping the corpse's arms—begging yet another spirit to not desert him—he had caught a flash of light in its soul-bound eyes. Not an inner light, but the reflection of something unseen, a figure burning fierce and bright in the room with him at the very moment the body went still.

～

He was victorious! The Soul Hunter was caught in his trap, visible at last through the blurry sclera of the eyes he had made. It railed against the weave of his blood and soul, and he danced and laughed. It had taken an entire lifetime, first to understand it, and then to learn how to trap the ancient being that had subverted him for so long. For this one chance, he had sacrificed everything.

He burned one torch to light a thousand.

He immersed his arms in the mechanism of tortured soul and bone and loosed the spear. There was a moment of pure elation as the weapon —unlike any that had ever been forged before, spanning life and death, body and spirit—pierced his enemy. And then the enemy exploded in light, and the room dissolved, and he dissolved with it.

∾

He awoke to find himself formless and alone in the presence of immense power, the Soul Hunter's Heart. He curled himself near it, and it burned him, and he soaked in its fire. He would never be able to contain it, the force was too great, but with time he would learn how to wield even the smallest fraction of that strength, and that would be enough to affect the world, to craft servants, to rebuild.

He would live again.

∾

An unending galaxy of merciless *not* stars—Soul Hunters.

Thousands, tens of thousands, an infinite sea of servants harvesting souls from an infinite sea of worlds feeding an infinite abyss of eternal screaming.

All he could hear was screaming.

∾

The Dead Man was screaming.

Soolie woke in the dark room, bound to the table.

His hands were on either side of the head cage, his eyes locked on hers, his mouth spraying spittle flecking through the holes in the lattice of the mask. At last he stopped, panting furious, blood eyes raging. There was no laughter in them now.

He had escaped the false memory she had caught him in.

Soolie was too weak to laugh, but she smiled. Once she had learned to recognize his presence and what he was searching for, it had been a matter of patience—patiently setting and baiting the trap, waiting until he walked right into the fiction she had crafted, and then she had turned the lens of the crown back on him and seen into the mind of Yevah the Dead Man.

His hands shook, creaking the metal that caged her skull.

"You will regret what you have made me do."

He pushed away, and she heard the sound of retreating footsteps and felt the draft of a door.

Something started undoing the straps on her ankles.

Now fucking what? She couldn't regret what she had done. She wouldn't trade one puppeteer for another.

One strap flipped loose, and then the next. Whatever it was moved quickly.

She could still sense Dog somewhere nearby. He was exhausted and in pain, and he was afraid—for her. And she could sense the Hunter's Heart. She couldn't *not* sense it. The desire was so strong, that it was difficult to remember that it was not hers. The Heart belonged to the Hunter, and the Hunter was *in* her, but the Hunter was *not* her. The only thing Soolie wanted was freedom.

The thing in the room released her arms and moved to the cage at her head. It was dressed all in white, and a wave of tortured wrongness came off of it, more powerful than screaming.

"If you're going to try to kill me," she croaked, "I'll make a terrible mess."

It pulled the cage pin and dropped it chain-clattering on the table top. Leather cushioning unstuck from her forehead as the mask hinged up and over, and it grabbed her by the neck, lifted her from the table, and started to walk.

It was much taller than the Dead Man: a specter of ivory with silver hair and bleach-shell eyes in a face too carved and too still, without tilt or turn, as if it moved without senses to guide it. As they neared the door, she splayed her arms and legs to catch the frame, and it folded her through without pause.

This must be the Wolf that Dog had warned her about. It was more terrible than the boy monster in every way.

It carried her down a hallway ranked with gaslights and simple wooden doors. She kicked and swung her legs. She clawed at its wrists, and its skin was stone. Wails and moans emanated from the many hidden rooms, and it turned and delivered her into a dark cell, and the Dead Man closed the door behind them.

Soolie tried to speak, but the monster's grip was crushing her throat. It hoisted her to the center of the room and held her suspended.

"I did not want to resort to this. I wished to find another way," the Dead Man said.

He held the red crown in his hands and approached until they were face to face, kissing close, and lifted the crown up over her head, and placed it on the head of the creature behind her. Then he lowered his dark eyes to hers. He looked exactly as she remembered from the first dream when she had stabbed him in the chest.

"But you have abused my hospitality."

He walked to the wall, and she heard the rattle of chains. The monster held her with one hand, and caught her forearm with the other, extending it. A cuff tightened on her wrist, and the Dead Man moved to the other side.

"You came to me as a beggar, I took you in, and you have repaid me with violence."

A cuff closed on her other wrist, and at last, the Wolf released her neck, letting her hang suspended, arms outstretched.

"You could just remove the Hunter," she wheezed, "like you said you would."

He picked up a small table and carried it over, while the monster grabbed her ankle and chained it to the floor. She kicked back with her other heel, and it caught and restrained her easily. Another cuff tightened, and she hung, all limbs secured. The Dead Man placed the table within reach. Resting in the middle was a black box. Was he going to torture her?

"Now that you have a body," she said, "doesn't that mean your brain will eventually turn to stew in your undying skull? Is that the big end-plan?"

He lifted the lid and removed three items: a black vial, a thin knife, and what appeared to be a thimble made of twisted bone that came to a talon point. He slid the thimble onto his middle finger.

"Once we are done here, I will show you." He unstoppered the vial, dipped the knife, and restoppered it, holding the thin blade glimmering and wet. He smiled, and all of his previous rage was gone. "You are going to love it."

Maybe he was going to remove her brain entirely. She didn't know if she could regrow a brain.

He studied her.

She could feel the monster nearly pressed against her back, not quite touching. If she could just get the Dead Man to talk, maybe she could find something to leverage. "When I was in your mind, I saw multiple Soul Hunters."

"Yes," he said, approaching. The monster closed its hand on her neck again, holding her still. "That was a clever trick you played."

He was very close now.

Her eyes tracked the knife as he brought it to her face.

"The body you're in is *very* pretty," she tried. "The knot in the nose adds a nice lived-in touch."

A smirk tugged at his mouth, but he did not waiver. He lifted the knife to the top of her head and made a single cut, setting the blade quickly on the table, the edge red with blood.

She hadn't felt anything, not even a pressure.

He reached his taloned finger up to her forehead, and his eyes curved, noting her confusion. "That is not your blood. But it will be."

The monster was right behind her. Something wet dripped on her forehead, and the Dead Man touched the tip of the talon between her eyes, and Soolie screamed.

The talon cut, and where it cut, something entered her skin and moved beneath the surface, burrowing horrible trails through her flesh. She tried to buck and throw her head, but the monster's grip was iron, even as its blood dripped from its other wrist onto her scalp and slithered under her skin, following the touch of the Dead Man over her brow and around her eyes, encircling her skull in an elaborate dance of a hundred-thousand little twists and ever-changing agonies. Worse than the pain, worse than the violation of her flesh, she could feel it changing her.

The room was narrowing and slipping away. Dog and the Hunter's Heart were beginning to fade. And her spirit succumbed to darkness.

Chapter 3

Silas grabbed a leg and pulled, popping it loose from the pile of corpses, bloated thigh meat tearing and flinging fluid as he tossed it to the side. He seized a bloody shirt and hauled a headless torso free, dragging it heavy over the cobbles, past the other survivors who toiled with him, grunting and breathing heavily in the putrid rot. The monsters didn't bother throwing bodies down the wells any more.

"The sun is already too high," Wendin shouted. "We should leave the cart and come back tomorrow."

Kolgrin hefted a body by the shirt and belt-band and slung it to the side of the street. "We'll make better time on the way back with the path clear. We should finish the job."

"We'll be half dead by the time we turn around." Wendin wiped her forehead on her arm. "We should have cleared the path before we brought the cart. Just because you and Rahka are bent on feeding graves doesn't mean the rest of us should have to share your poison."

Hearing her name, the Southern bloodwitch leaned forward from her seat on top of the cart, spreading her knees to accommodate her pregnant belly. "If we abandon the cart, they may wreck it. Your children need water. We keep on."

~

By the time they reached the fountain, daylight had passed its peak. Silas dredged a small cask in the basin, dumped the water into a barrel, and dipped the cask again. They were filling three at a time, which was faster than the fountain could replenish, and the cask scraped bottom, coming up only a third-full of sandy water. Half the survivors stood, waiting to hammer lids and load the barrels back into the cart.

"Kolgrin!" Rahka summoned.

The burly, rust-bearded man caught Silas' eye and tossed his mallet. "Catch, friend."

Silas jumped, alarmed, out of the way, and the mallet few past, clattering off the base of the fountain. Wendin eyed them both coldly as she picked it up and began pounding a lid onto a half-full barrel, but Kolgrin was already at the wagon conferring with Rahka.

Wendin jerked her head at them. "We're good as ganked."

There were eight survivors on this mission, not counting Silas, Kolgrin, and Rahka. Those left behind at the morgue were mostly wounded and children. Even the small older woman Havah was with them today, fiercely toiling through the fatigue and keeping pace. This was the longest many of them had been outside the protection of Rahka's blood magic in several moons, and it was taking a toll.

Rahka crawled down from the cart.

"You should all head back now," Kolgrin shouted. "Load up the barrels."

Rahka walked a pace up the street and stopped to wait while Kolgrin grabbed a rucksack from the footwell. The survivors watched. The old woman Havah was the only one still bailing, arms pumping, thin lips tightly pressed.

"Right, then," Kolgrin nodded. "I believe in you, friends. We'll see you at the morgue on the 'morrow."

Wendin stepped forward, gripping the mallet tendon-taut. "Where the *fuck* are you and the bloodwitch going?"

"We have a hunt," Kolgrin said.

"NOW?!" Wendin pointed the mallet at Rahka. "Her belly's at full moon. She shouldn't even be leaving the morgue, and you're fucking splitting us?"

Havah slushed another cask into a barrel and approached Wendin, laying a hand on the mallet shaft. Wendin yanked back, but Havah met her eyes. The younger woman sneered and released the handle.

"*Chooble!* Now!" Rahka called and started to move.

Kolgrin shrugged. "That's me."

The big man turned to go, and Silas set his cask down to follow, but Kolgrin barred his way.

"No. Not this time, sugar."

"I want to help."

"You can help these folks get back before dark," Kolgrin said. "Don't worry. We're not finding your daughter today."

Silas *was* worried. The city was ravaged, its people had all fled or been slaughtered by the monsters that crossed over when the Regent's tower fell, and for the last several moons, Kolgrin and Rahka had been going off on secretive excursions and leaving him behind. What if Rahka had no intention of reopening the door? What if she couldn't? What if Soolie wasn't on the other side after all? What if Soolie *was* on the other side, but something horrible was happening while they wasted time, and he arrived too late?

It felt like all he could do was worry.

"Don't puppy those brown eyes at me," Kolgrin tapped Silas' shoulder with his fist. "I'll be back. Try not to spread your cheeks for anyone else while I'm gone." He winked and jogged after Rahka, and they both receded up the white cobblestones between the abandoned Sun District mansions and out of sight.

Wendin screamed her frustration, and Havah whacked the edge of the barrel lid to seal it down.

"The more monsters they kill," Silas offered, "the safer we'll be."

"Don't feed me spak," Wendin snapped. "We know *you're* making it back alive."

"LOAD UP!" Havah bellowed. "NIGHT IS CLOSING!"

∽

There were no labor animals, so all survivors served as beasts. They leaned into the wagon as they pushed, gray-faces down, legs dragging. It *was* faster going, now that the path was clear of rubble and corpses, but they were dangerously weary. Silas' boots slid on the mucky cobbles, and he gritted his teeth and powered forward, knowing he was the least affected. Whatever miracle had given him the ability to walk through the fallen Dark Districts, now gave him that same resilience in the fallen city. Others were not so fortunate.

The cart rattled through what was left of the Craftsman District. Shredded curtains fluttered through the teeth of shattered windows. Doors hung out of socket. Broken pieces of past lives—furniture and lamps, clothing and nails—lay scattered in the street. Gutted buildings deteriorated around the disemboweled bodies that inhabited them, all insides turning outsides.

The wheels bumped forward, and the man beside Silas fell face-first onto the street.

"Keep going!" Havah shouted, running to help the man up.

The sun barely winked above the shingle tops. Their way was walled with shadows.

"Go! Go! Go!"

Havah shoved the man, and he stumbled, falling against the back of the cart, this time keeping his feet. The older woman was beside Silas now, thin hands splayed, pushing with all her might.

"We should abandon the barrels!" Wendin called from up front.

"We may never make it to the fountains and back again," Havah shouted back. "We are only three streets away. We will make it!"

The lid of the sun drooped, and closed, and darkness swallowed the street.

For a moment, the only sound was the shuffle of steps, the creak-groan of the wagon, the clatter of wheels on stone. Then, far over the rooftops, there rose a whooping yapping howling. The monsters were coming.

"Fuck this!"

Silas looked up to see Wendin running. Another broke from the front of the cart to follow, and then another. Four of them bolted for the shelter of the hospital morgue.

"Silas," Havah hissed, "take the poles. We'll keep pushing."

Silas nodded. Only four others remained, all feebled by their time sickening in the city. He placed himself up front between the leading poles, gripped one in each fist, took a deep breath, and heaved. The wheels turned one, two, three steps forward through the deepening dark.

At last, the many-windowed face of the hospital loomed ahead. The cart labored up to the steps. The great double doors at the top hung open.

"Almost there," Havah whispered. "Grab a barrel. Let's go."

She climbed up into the wagon and rolled a barrel to the edge. Silas tipped it onto his shoulder and staggered up the stairs, legs wobbling with exhaustion. He crossed into the shadows of the hospital, set his burden down, and ducked back out as the others entered with a single barrel between them. They had only seven full and three partially full. It was enough for three weeks of rationed water at most.

Three more agonizing trips up the stairs and back.

Havah got down to help him with the last barrel, leaving the wagon at the foot of the steps, unstowed. Lands-hope it would be there in the morning, but every moment spent in the streets after sundown was baiting violence, and they had already risked too much. He followed her up the steps and into the hospital, and the others closed the door behind them.

Silas blinked, adjusting to the dim interior. Thin blades of moonlight slipped through the boarded windows. At his back, barring beams were being dropped, clunk-clunk, into place, while up ahead, one of the women was kneeling by a barrel and tipping it onto its side. The water could be rolled from here.

The woman touched the floor and looked up at Havah, eyes wide, lifting fingers dripping dark. She opened her mouth and something launched from the shadows, landing on top of her, bending its naked, boney body over. There was the ragged rip and a cut-off scream, and the creature lifted its face. Dim light gleamed from wide black eyes and fresh blood dripping from jagged teeth. It shrieked and flung itself towards them.

BANG! There was a flash, and the top of its skull blew off.

BANG! Havah fired her pistol again, blasting the head into a blunt-top gory fist, but somehow the monster was still coming. It swiped long talons as the people scattered from the door, drawing their weapons and bolting for the hall. Havah sprinted past, and Silas pulled his pistol and followed.

Up ahead, something dove out from a side corridor. People screamed and guns fired. Sound ricocheted off the hard surfaces of the hospital. There was snarling, wet crunching, shrieking, and Havah was running towards the sound and then ducking to the right, down a passage, and Silas was close behind. As he rounded the corner, something dropped from the ceiling between them, tall and lank-boned, strings of hair hanging over its narrow face and bead-black eyes. Its mouth bulged with needle teeth, and it rushed him, and he stumbled back, raising his pistol too late and too slow, and its head exploded, splattering him with wet chunks and shards of bone.

He spluttered, spitting rotten flesh and teeth that were not his own.

The faceless monster fell onto its back, then flipped and scrabbled after him, spider-like on all fours. Silas sprinted to the side. Its claws lashed, finding the fabric of his pants, shredding and clipping on his heel as he kicked back and dashed after Havah who was screaming his name.

"SILAS!"

They pelted down corridors of empty rooms. The farther they went, the darker the halls became.

Havah collapsed against a wall, chest heaving. Her gray hair had come half-loose of its bun and hung down the side of her face.

"I'm out of bullets."

"I thought you only fired three," Silas panted.

"Six." She held out her hand. "You've fired none. You're a horrible fighter."

Silas nodded and placed his gun in her hand. She cocked the weapon and held it at the ready.

"The narrow stair is around the corner. If we make it, it's a straight descent."

The morgue was fortified with Rahka's blood magic that the dead couldn't cross. That was why it was the only place in all of Ravus that didn't drain the living of their life anymore. Every other space was full of the hungry dead, ghosts and monsters, all starving, all feeding.

"What about the others?" Silas asked.

"The monsters will come for us next." Havah pushed off the wall. "Let's go."

Silas pulled the hunting knife from his belt. It was now the only weapon he had.

Havah took the lead. A chorus of howls rose, echoing in the corridors behind them. The door to the narrow service stair was at the end of the hall. Havah reached it, levered the handle and pushed it open for him. "I'll protect our backs."

He ducked past and began the spiral descent in the dark as Havah closed the door behind them.

The stairway was black. The scrap-patter of steps and the huff of breath were the only sounds as they circled down, down, down, until the walls grew cold and the steps turn from wood to stone. They were almost at the door.

Then Silas smelled it: the fetid smell of old death in the stairwell with them.

Before he could hesitate, he rounded the turn and leaped out into the darkness, knife raised. He collided with something snarling, and he stabbed, and stabbed, and stabbed. It flung him up against the wall, his head cracking against the stone. Sharp talon blades slashed his chest, and it shrieked in his face.

BANG.

The gunshot cannoned with the concussion of his skull, and the creature wasn't spitting in his face any more, and he swung the knife madly, again, and again, and again.

"SILAS! STOP!" Havah was screaming. "STOP, IDIOT. The door! Go through the door!"

Of course. It would never stop fighting. He braced against the wall and kicked the creature back, just as the door beside him swung open. Hands grabbed the arm of his jacket and pulled him through, tumbling into the gas-lit room of the morgue, and Havah vaulted in after. Wendin was there, throwing her shoulder against the door.

"HELP ME!"

Silas jumped up and threw his weight with her as something slammed, scrabbling at the other side, and they struggled the door shut as Havah grabbed the drop-bar and slotted it into place.

The three of them collapsed to the tiles, bloodied, slashed, alive.

"Fuck," Wendin said.

Across the room, survivors were running to aid them, and at their back, death battered itself relentlessly against the door.

~

KOLGRIN OFFERED A HAND, but Rahka ignored him, finding her own footholds in the glitterwhite stone and scaling what she could have easily vaulted five moons ago. He waited as she hefted herself up to squat beside him on the wall, frog-legged and big-bellied.

Together, they surveyed the garden below.

Plots that should have been lush with late spring growth were gray and brown with wiry scruff. Twigs, dirt, and dead leaves littered the pebble walkways. The snow had melted, but the winter fallow lingered. Nothing had come back to life since the tower fell.

"You will lose their loyalty, Rahka."

"It is already lost. We no longer need them." She plucked at the cropped blouse that hung limp between her breasts and left her protruding belly bare. "They are *oocha* and the world is a downing ship. They will not survive, and you and I can not change that."

"I suppose they should be glad you haven't juiced their crawlers."

"I still might. This city is running dry."

Their excursions had been growing less frequent. Nothing fleshly moved in Ravus any more. The refugees thought that Rahka and Kolgrin were tracking down monsters while they hid from the sun, vulnerable to attack, but Rahka wasn't looking for a fight. The witch was looking for blood.

She closed her eyes and tilted her head, searching, and he took the opportunity to assess her condition: it worsened by the day. Her eyelids had taken on a bruised hue above her sharp cheekbones, and her elegant limbs had turned to stork sticks. All of her withered except the bowl of her belly, which continued to grow.

Her eyes snapped open. *"Mitta yah hess..."*
She'd found it.

Rahka slid over the wall and dropped, cradling her belly and landing in a crouch. Kolgrin swung after. Already, she was step-weaving quickly down a path, following the ghosts that only she could see.

"Surely they're not all completely dispensable." He jogged up, pulling his pistol.

She shot him a look. "Do you worry for *kutka* now? Are you growing tender on me?"

"You know I'm too thrust in not to finish. But you do need *him*, don't you?"

"If Silas tries to leave, tie him down."

"That's your sweetmeat, not mine."

"Of course." She ducked a branch, and her golden eyes curved back at him. "You prefer the *collar* to the leash."

"I don't need the responsibility."

"Well, consider Silas your responsibility." Before he could retort, she pointed up ahead. "There."

The pebble path wove through thin brush and under dry capillary branches, up to a set of cellar doors.

"Would you like to fetch this one?" It wasn't a question.

The cellar wasn't locked, and Kolgrin took the time to lever both doors out like heavy wings. Rahka guarded the entry, a curved dancing sword in each hand, feet expertly placed, belly leading. He cocked his pistol as he descended, ducking the low ceiling.

It was a modest storeroom, doubtless one of several, and smelled dank and muldy and a bit like shit. Empty wooden shelves lined the stone walls, and lumpy rough sacks piled on the floor.

"Any guidance from your ghost friends?" He hollered back as he scanned over the barrel of his gun.

"It's a cellar, *bevjak*, not a warren. Look!"

"If there's one of those monsters back here . . ." he kicked a half-eaten turnip towards a dark corner. At least, if something was chewing on the vegetables, there was a good chance it wasn't already dead.

From behind a pile of sacks, a pair of pale hands rose on ruffle-wristed arms, followed by a dirty face.

Kolgrin holstered his weapon. "Found 'im!"

The man stepped into the open, cringing from the light. "I am Minister Tolbey. Counselor to the Regent, Fourth of the Rainegald house. I have resources...."

"Speed your steps," Rahka called down. "I want to weave before sundown."

The man yelped as Kolgrin caught him by the wrist. "You're gonna wish you got eaten by the monsters, friend."

～

RAHKA CROSSED her arms on top of her belly and looked down at the man bound naked to her table. "I could get more *rashni* from an *oocha diling*."

Kolgrin chuckled. "A rat's wag would certainly be more comely."

"And have more merit." Rahka walked her fingers up the meeting of the man's ribs, towards his bobbing neck. She purred, "I will simply have to milk him for all he is worth."

This man had been one of the Sun District regency. Not long ago, he had sat fat as a boiled pudding, presiding over an estate of attendants with larders full of preserved meats, wax-coated cheeses, and casked wines, all of which had been stripped from him in a matter of moons. When the tower fell, monsters had ripped through entire districts in a matter of nights, slaughtering more than they could consume and filling every house and corridor with the refuse of their kills—*bahuta*, Rahka called them—the hungry spirits of the dead. Those who *could* had fled the city, and many of the monsters had followed to pick off refugees in the night. The only people left in Ravus were those who couldn't run—the infirmed and the abandoned—and the *bahuta* clustered on them like flies on meat and fed on their life.

Now, this man's once corpulent body sagged with sunken spots turned dark like the flesh of an old pear, melting under thin skin. The rims of his eyes were slack and raw, and his scalp was patchy and scaled. His blood would be weak.

Rahka looked down into the man's frightened eyes and tapped the wad of rags that protruded between his lips. "You'll do your best to give me what I need, won't you, Minister?"

The man whimpered, and Kolgrin smiled. She still looked like herself when she toyed with her prey.

"Would you like a moment?"

"No." She sighed and reached into her pocket to pull out a little black bag. "The sun is going down. Let's get this done."

Kolgrin took a seat on a nearby stray mason block. He harbored no softness for the regency, but he spared a thought for the remaining women, men, and children that had found shelter in Rahka's shadow, and wondered how many of their party would survive the trip back to the morgue tonight. Well, there was no sense fretting over what would or wouldn't be.

She parted the mouth of the bag and withdrew her bone stylus. It wriggled against the confines of its shape like threadworms in a vial, and she held it up in front of the man's face and twisted it between her fingers so it spun above the quavering lakes of his eyes. Her fingers were ringed raw with cracking blisters from previous uses. Creating blood always cost her, even when the blood wasn't her own.

"Are you sure this one's worth it?" he asked. "Seems like your *bahuta* have already done a dazzle on 'im."

"Every fiber counts."

She leaned over the man, pressed the tip of the stylus to his chest, and started to carve.

It was a familiar ritual now. The stylus left channels in the man's flesh like the tunnels left by burrow beetles when you peel back the bark. The paths branched and turned, growing innumerable fingers that spooled out wriggling over his body, netting raw paths that opened and closed faster than they could begin to bleed, and all the while, the stylus itself was filling with blood drawn up between the moving knots. The man's cloth-muffled screams were wild. Any moment, he would be sure to pass out, if Rahka didn't pass out first. She was sweating, panting, her free hand gripping her leg, her carving hand shaking as she traced the patterns, the black-blistered skin where her fingers touched the stylus cracked and oozed.

"Rahka..."

She snarled. She didn't want to hear his concerns.

At last, the man's body wormed with moving troughs and the pen was full. She only had the last few sets of runes to complete.

He didn't know where the table came from or how old it was. She called it a *pratali miza,* which he understood roughly translated to 'rendering table.' Several moons ago, he had helped her retrieve it from a cellar in the Dark Districts and haul it across the city to the site where the Regent's Tower once stood. "There are many ways to create blood," she had said as they set the legs in a patch cleared of rubble. "But most are very costly and we will need a great deal of blood." The first time he had seen her use it, she had leaned over the quivering boy strapped to her table until her lips were right by his ear, and Kolgrin heard her whisper, "*You were supposed to be my mother.*"

When she started carving, he had excused himself to splatter bile all over a nearby alley wall. Now, Kolgrin leaned forward and hardly blinked.

The orange light of the setting sun warmed the rubble, but left Rahka's brown skin tinged with gray. Her brow furrowed as she traced the runes along the table edge, the collected blood flowing from the pen, twisting like a living thing. A large bowl waited under the opening in the center of the table. The last sigil was almost complete. She finished the final touch and lifted the stylus, now bloodless and bone-white once more. It was done.

The runes roiled. The man's eyes rolled back as at last, mercifully, he fell unconscious, and the paths in his skin began to swell with blood, filling, and then overflowing, writhing faster and faster, blood burbling from their channels, the channels themselves carving deeper, whittling him down. Blood boiled off of him, pooling in the basin of the table and draining through the hole, syrup-sloshing into the bowl, and the man's body shrank, and the blood drained, until the writhing began to slow, and all that was left was an ecruish chewed-up mush that settled sodden bloodless around his bones, and the bloodmaking was done.

She shoved the stylus at Kolgrin.

"You know I won't touch a skag's instrument."

"*Bevjak,*" she spat, leaning on the edge of the table.

He walked around, picked up the little bag where she'd dropped it, and gently placed it in her bleeding hand. "You should rest."

"The blood must be woven while it is fresh." She dropped the stylus into the bag. "You don't have the art. You are a useless."

"I suppose I should leave, then." He meant it as a joke.

"If you want to die with the *choti lirnsen,* go." She turned away, walking towards the perimeter of the massive blood weave that surrounded them. "Get the blood."

"Yes, Lioness." He was right behind her, the bowl already in his hands.

~

THE *NAHNKALA* GALED on the edges of the weave like frenzy fish in red waters, and the barrier shivered against their assault. She smeared the last drop from the bowl with her fingers and added it to the weave that encircled the site of the fallen tower. Now that the tower was gone, there was nothing to keep the *nahnkala* back, except her magic. This blood was not her blood, and that weakened it. The souls bound to it could not keep out the storm forever. The *nahnkala* would break through.

Rahka faced the wall of translucent faces and warped pregnant forms, and they flocked to her, focusing their fury, raising their voices in the cry she knew so well.

HOLLOW. GONE TO THE OTHER SIDE. THE OTHER SIDE. BROKEN. BROKEN. HOLLOW.

Hollow. *Nahnkala*. The hollow ghosts. It was difficult to tell how many there were. Hundreds, perhaps thousands that had died with a soulless lump in their bellies. Whatever killed them had severed the fetal *rashni* while it was still forming and discarded the parent soul to be driven mad by the wound. The hollow ghosts were an abomination, spirits torn in two, existing both here and somewhere else in suspended agony. They yearned, railed, needed to cross the tower door to take back what had been stolen from them.

HOLLOW. GONE TO THE OTHER SIDE. HOLLOW THE ONE WHO IS BROKEN. NAHNKALA.

Even bloodwitches knew not to sever a spirit while it was still a growing part of the parent soul, but whoever had done this did not care for the living or the dead. *San Myrta Damin.* She would destroy the Dead Man if she could. But she had a reckoning with the Soul Hunter first.

She cradled her belly, wrapping her arms above and below. She knew Kolgrin saw the dullness in her eyes, the thinning of her hair, the slackness of her skin. The new soul was killing her. The *nahnkala* thought she was becoming one of them.

HOLLOW GONE TO THE OTHER HOLLOW HOLLOW.

"*Nin gahaghi bachle urich mera rashni,*" she hissed.

She turned back towards the center of the blood ring. Where once the Regent's Tower had stood visible for miles around, all that remained was a field of founding stone and white dust that grated at any mind attuned to hear. In the middle of the rubble hung the shadow memory of the door that once connected Ravus to the Dead Man's realm. It waited for her to craft a new door and use that memory to tell it where to go.

Rahka stroked the mound of her belly. Grow, my little soul, *mera choti bahuta*. I *will* kill you before you kill me. You will open my way to the Soul Hunter and to vengeance.

Chapter 4

Soolie woke in sunlight and sat bolt up.

She was wearing a silken sleeping shift and sitting in a bed covered in soft white sheets, facing an open airy room. There were few furnishing touches: the mattress rested on a platform that spanned from wall to wall, and her clothes were folded neatly on a bench beneath one of the many great windows. She saw no shutters or curtains. The room had one set of large double doors.

Where the fuck was she? She threw back the covers, crawled forward, and swung her feet over the end of the bed. That was when she saw the blood moving on her legs.

Sickness seized her stomach.

She wanted to scurry back, she wanted to smack it away, but it wasn't just *on* her, and she was suddenly aware of a writhing sensation all over her body.

She jumped from the bed, tearing the shift over her head and throwing it to the floor, and stood naked in the center of the room. Every part of her that she could see moved with a thousand curling twisting knotting threads just under the skin, up and down her arms and legs, over her back and breasts. She put her hands on her belly and moved up her chest, feeling her neck and jaw, playing her fingers over her cheekbones and the arch of her skull. Her body boiled like a panicked anthill. It was difficult to tell where the squirming in the pads of her fingers ended and the squirming under her face began.

That is not your blood. But it will be.

She tilted her head and bared her teeth, binding her muscles until her body ached. She wanted to beat the floor and tear her skin. She wanted to sink to the tile and curl up into a ball, but she couldn't stand the feeling of her own skin against her skin, and so she stood with her legs apart, arms stretched out from her sides, and shook with rage.

Then she realized that she couldn't sense Dog or the Hunter's Heart anymore. She had grown accustomed to Dog's constant fear and adoration in the recesses. Now she didn't know where he was or how he was feeling. As for the Hunter, it was difficult to tell . . . but if she couldn't feel the presence of its Heart any more . . . Was the Hunter gone?

What had the Dead Man done to her?

She wanted to rage, but there was nothing to rage against, so she got dressed.

The familiar tunic and wrap skirt were a small comfort, and there was a pair of soft lace-up leather sandals, which she also put on. The last item was the woven hair bracelet Dog had given her, and she draped it over her wrist and used her teeth to help knot it tight as she looked out the window.

The room overlooked a city of flat-top buildings dotted with colorful mats and canopies. In the distance, steep twin mountains rose above the lush green jungle, while just outside the window, a purple bird with trailing feathers of blue and green sat on a tree with leaves the size of four-man canoes. It tilted its head at her and trilled. Soolie recognized this place from the Hunter's dreams. So, this was the Southern Lands.

She scratched at the blood that squirmed over her forearm and tried not to think about it. She was starving. There must be a living soul somewhere nearby that she could feed off of. Was there anything stopping her from leaving?

She turned. "Fucking shit."

The Dead Man's Wolf was standing in the middle of the room, looking at her with red eyes, the blood crown twisting on its head. It turned, walked to the open doorway, and paused, waiting for her to follow. How long had it been watching her?

"You're a quiet fucker, aren't you."

It didn't respond.

"Well then, let's go see if your pap can tell me what the fuck you've both done to me."

As soon as she stepped towards it, it started to move again.

It led her down open hallways and across a great courtyard, along pebbled paths and by burbling fountains, blooming trees, and giant-stalked flowers. Everywhere they went, they passed living people. Some were tending the gardens, others bustling by on errands, and others took their leisure—walking or sitting, eating fruit and tearing bread, laughing and chatting in many different languages, only some of which Soolie recognized. There were people of races from all across the known world and beyond, all seeming healthy, all seeming happy, and many of whom were astonishingly beautiful. Soolie realized she was gawking, but no one even glanced up at the girl with the writhing skin as she followed the quiet monster through an archway, up a stair, and out onto a broad veranda, where it stepped aside to let her continue on her own.

"Is it familiar to you?" The Dead Man sat on a stone rail in the sun. He took a bite from a soft fruit.

Soolie stopped halfway between him and the monster. "What did you do to me?"

He laughed, wiped juice from his chin, and rubbed his palm on his pants. "You are very young and very impatient. I am very old, so you will have to learn to walk with me."

He didn't look old, perhaps mid to late twenties. Today, he was garbed in a vivid sea blue, and he propped one sandaled foot on the rail, rested his elbow on his knee, and took another bite.

He gestured with the dripping fruit, speaking with his cheek full. "This is the same view you showed me, is it not? When we came to an arrangement, before I rescued you from the sea. My homeland."

It wasn't quite exact. The veranda Soolie had seen in the Hunter's vision had mosaics, cushioned benches, and tables of food. This one was carved of simple, sweeping white stone. But the view was the same—a city cupped in green beneath the gaze of twin mountains.

"Where is Dog?" she asked.

"I had to rebuild," he continued. "A great many wars have occurred since my death. The living are very good at destroying beautiful things. The lengths I went to to keep them from uprooting these jungles . . . You really don't wish to come to the rail and see?"

Soolie could feel the blood squirming over her spine and the lids of her eyes. She scrunched her fingers into knots. "I am, as you said, impatient."

"Very well." He took one last bite, tossed the mangled core over his shoulder, and hopped down, quickly crossing the space between them. "I will give you a tour."

～

To Soolie's immense frustration, when he threatened a tour, the Dead Man meant it. He led her from small alcoves to grand arenas, vegetable gardens and stables, great cellars and long banquet halls, showing the same level of pride for the kitchens as he did for the statues of mythical beasts. For every feature and room, he spoke in agonizing detail: the stone and what mountain it was mined from, where he had procured the artists for his murals and how many decades it had taken them to complete each work, even detailing the breeding of trees in the orchard and how they had made one of the sour citruses sweet. For hours, he dragged her around his estate, talking and laughing when she snapped at him, while his Wolf followed close behind.

"Where is Dog?" she asked.

"I am very excited for you to see this next marvel," he said as they rounded a corner and stepped into an ornate hall.

The ceiling was twice two-stories high with lace-carved arches gilt with delicate leaves and blooms. Obsidian serpents twisted in and out of ivory thickets and birds spread massive wings—each scale's curve and feather's hair finely cut and individually painted—and thousands of other creatures, the like of which she had never seen before, ducked in and out of thorned vegetation that crawled up the walls and into the depths of the ceiling. Most striking of all, was the set of doors at the end. They were nearly as high as the hall itself, and each shone like star and ice with insets of clear cut stone in filigree more white than silver. Soolie knew that whatever lay behind those doors must be important, and she was gripped by a sudden need to see.

He was still rambling, so she stepped past him, reaching, and he caught her wrist.

"What's in there?"

"Something for later," he said.

The Wolf stepped in the way.

Soolie scowled. This was the first thing they had come across that she actually wanted. "Why not now?"

"I haven't finished showing you around. I want you to have something to look forward to."

"You've shown me *everything else.*" She yanked her arm back.

"My dear!" he laughed. "We haven't even left the house yet."

∽

"ADON!"

The marketplace cheered as the Dead Man strode in waving both arms in greeting. Soolie hung back, watching him engage the people, calling them by name, slapping shoulders and clasping hands, tasting baked goods and examining wares.

"Tess, how is the youngling? *Mossit, aapin sivath dikk rahe*! Hodik, the chainwork is beautiful, but see how easily it binds? The links are too long. Sannel! I am glad to see you are up and about again. *Asha*! *Aspako hak mahnin*..."

The Dead Man knew every resident by name and addressed them in their own tongues, and they brightened at his attentions, smiling and bobbing—cries of "Adon!"—and showering him with gifts. No one spared a glance for Soolie.

He had already shown her parks and theaters, districts and shops, and now he was showing her the people. Just more showing off.

"They must all be scrubbed between the ears," she muttered.

"You don't appear to be enjoying yourself." He approached, sucking sticky brown sauce from his fingers.

Now, the people's eyes turned on her.

"I'm being dragged along on some pomp-ass's self-indulgent congratulations parade," she said.

"Who holds you captive?" He spread his arms. "You can leave whenever you want."

That was a lie. "You haven't returned Dog to me as you promised."

"I wanted to show you my home first. If I had delivered your pet to you right away, I doubt you would have gone along on my *pomp-ass self-indulgent congratulations parade* quite as willingly. We are nearly there. Come," he extended a hand to her, and she didn't take it. "You are so determined to be *miserable*." He gestured to the watching throng. "This is the most beautiful city that has ever been! Let it bring you joy. Your Hunter is silent. Let me lift your spirit, Soolie Beetch. You are not a captive here. You are home."

She didn't like hearing him use her name. He had never asked, and she'd never actually told him. "I want Dog back."

"Let us walk."

He started moving again, and reluctantly, she followed. He led her under orange, red, and blue patterned shade awnings, between the stalls displaying bright beads, trays of glazed meats, pocket pies, and rolls of embroidered cloth.

"The people here are all the best at what they do," he said. "Some are the best at portraiture, some at making street cakes. Every skill is important, every person has value. Look at these."

He stopped at a display of glass globes, each filled with a fine film of clear and colored bubbles that swirled into entire miniature landscapes. He picked one up and offered it, and despite herself, she accepted. The ball was pleasingly heavy, smooth and cool. Tiny bubbles of gold, red, and orange formed a winged lizard being born in fire and smoke.

"Oshara paints molten glass with her own breath," he said. A tawny-eyed woman with fat cheeks beamed at him from behind the table. "How can that not make you smile? Everything here is a wonder."

Soolie moved to put the globe back, and the woman shook her head, motioning for Soolie to keep it.

"I can see that you want to be miserable," he said.

Soolie put the globe back on the table.

"What can I do to ease your trouble?"

"Dog," she snapped. The longer the Dead Man took to deliver him, the more she worried that this road of pageantry would end in a body.

"Tell me," he nodded thanks to the woman and continued between the stalls. "What is your bond with the creature? I never imagined I would see him again, much less have him willingly returned to me."

"No bond. I'm responsible for him."

"I have been inside your mind. I would hope we could be honest with one another."

She scowled.

"Forgive me," he chuckled and snagged a fruit from a basket, ripping the pithy yellow peel and dropping it as they walked. "It is rude of me to insinuate what you might not be ready to acknowledge for yourself. But you will not deny he has latched onto you as an abandoned runtlet to a hound's teat."

"He is, as you said, a pet," Soolie said.

"And we do often grow fond of our pets." He cracked the round of segmented fruit. He hadn't offered her any food, even in pretense. He must know she couldn't consume it. It was strange that he could. "I was, myself, sorry to dispose of him when the time came," he continued. "I was aware that he had started to develop an instinct for self-preservation, but it still came as a revelation when that instinct overcame his instilled nature. I did not expect him to run, which only makes it all the more remarkable to see him follow you back into my hands." He picked a wedge of fruit, popped it into his cheek and eyed her. "Does he love you?"

Soolie bristled.

He laughed. "That is my fault, I am afraid. Before him, my servants deteriorated far too quickly, which is why I crafted *this* dog to adapt as he healed, which ultimately had some unexpected consequences. Not all bad, though." He popped another wedge in his mouth. "You know that I gave all my creatures an aversion to the light to keep them hidden? With enough exposure, he became *immune*. A remarkable thing."

Soolie remembered Dog's panic at the mention of his old Master. "You tortured him," she said.

"I am a craftsman and I crafted," the Dead Man said. "True, I didn't expect him to develop the ability to accumulate trauma, which *was* unhelpful. However, my work with that dog paved the way for many advancements in my craft, and fortunately, by the time his utility was compromised, I was very close to completing my final servant."

"Wolf," Soolie knew.

He grimaced. "Oh, lands. Is *that* what it told you? No. My final servant is not some vulgar pack creature. It is the only of its kind—pierless, unmatched, unrivaled. A weave of its blood is stronger than any other. It has more soul in a single droplet, than you had once in your entire living body. It is *Hagani na Sitari*. My Chorus!" His voice belled with pride. "The Chorus was created at great cost and with much sacrifice. Sometime, I must tell you how I managed it."

In the stalls, someone screamed.

The Dead Man tossed the last of his fruit and turned quickly back the way they had come. The people parted to clear his path.

Soolie looked at the Chorus standing over her. She took a step to the right, and it took one step to follow. She took a few steps to the left, and it maintained its distance like a toy on a leash. The Dead Man had created Dog from the soul of a child. Soolie found it difficult to imagine that any part of this monster had ever been even remotely human.

She followed the Dead Man.

Up ahead, she could hear the sound of a single voice railing with laughter.

The crowd had formed a circle around a jeweler's stall. Table displays of gems and precious chains were sprayed in blood, and behind them sat an elderly man, one hand flat on the display cloth, each finger mangled, sharp-edged bone sticking out from torn skin and wet flesh. The Dead Man was at his side, tenderly restraining the jeweler's other arm that brandished a penny hammer in its fist, dripping gore. It was the man who was laughing. Tears streamed down his merry wrinkled cheeks. The crowd watched in silence.

Gently, the Dead Man unbent one finger at a time from the shaft of the hammer and set the tool out of reach. "You spend millenia learning how to dry their tears and take away their pain," he looked up at Soolie and smiled sadly, "and then they miss it. Come on, then."

He helped the old man off his stool and around the table. The jeweler turned toward the watching crowd, braying his mirth as if demanding a reply.

"Shussshh," the Dead Man said, "it will be well, my friend." He coaxed the man to stand in front of Soolie and patted the man's shoulder. He looked at her. "Are you hungry?"

Soolie didn't move.

"I know you are." He urged the man forward. "Feed yourself. With my blessing."

The old man's mouth gaped, and his laughter rose to boisterous giggles, tears dripping from his chin, blood dripping from his outstretched hand.

She *was* hungry. She eyed the Dead Man.

"Go ahead. There's no trick. You are hungry. Take, eat."

The crowd watched. Fuck it, her body ached with need.

Soolie stepped forward and stretched out her hand, trying to ignore the red threads that moved under her skin. His mangled hand reached for her as her blood-writhing hand reached for him, and he mashed his broken fingers against the breast of her tunic as she placed her palm against his chest and pulled for the life that lay there.

Nothing happened.

She could sense it—the life that she needed to sustain herself— begging her to drink as she had so many times before, but when she called for it, it did not respond.

The man clumped his bleeding fingers against her breastbone. She snarled and grabbed the front of his tunic, pulling him closer, straining, and she cried out, and the old man squealed and chortled, and her spirit remained unfed.

There was a new sound. The Dead Man was clapping, and as he clapped, the whole crowd began to applaud with him.

"Excellent!" he cried.

Soolie shook her head, clearing the daze, and shoved the old man away. He stumbled back, and the Dead Man caught and righted him.

"This is good news! I had to know for sure." He passed the man into waiting arms. "Take him to the Cradle. I will tend to him."

Soolie shook with exhaustion and rage. "What have you done?"

"I told you!" he said. "I have freed you from the Hunter. Well, I have bound it and its powers within you. I would have loved to have resolved your conflict for you, but you would not permit me, so for now, this is the next best solution."

"I can not feed myself," she snapped.

"Yes. There is that. One request at a time, impatient little dead girl. Come." He began walking away, humming to himself.

Soolie growled and stayed rooted.

He tossed a look over his shoulder. "Did you *not* want your Dog back?"

～

"Mistress."

They didn't have to walk far. Dog sat in the center of a square, his head, hands, and feet in stocks. He looked up through the black snarls of his hair. Even from a distance, she could see that his clothing had been shredded and the stones were splatter-painted with gore.

"What have you done to him?"

"Nothing." The Dead Man stopped at a distance. "My people, however, bear something of a grudge against creatures like him. As often as I clear those memories from their heads, it still pleases them to bring them harm. I could not deny them the simple pleasure."

Soolie stepped forward, but the Dead Man put out an arm to stop her.

"Mistress!" Dog wailed.

She cringed, realizing how he was now seeing her: his Mistress, flanked by the two beings he feared most in all the world, her body netted in the blood of the creature created to destroy him. He must regret following her to this place.

"Release him," Soolie said. "You promised."

The Dead Man flicked a finger at the Chorus, and it walked past.

"I will keep my word. But I can't have him running around my kingdom as he is. He is still, after all, a weapon off its leash."

The Chorus grabbed Dog's hair, reached into his mouth, pincered a fang between the white crescents of its nails, and pulled. The tooth popped out with a sucking sound and a spurt of blood and clinked to the street stones. The creature reached into Dog's mouth, pinched another tooth, and pulled.

"He wouldn't," Soolie objected. "He listens to me."

"And that is a part of the problem, isn't it?" the Dead Man said. "If I am to return him to you as an act of good faith, you must know I can't take that chance."

Dog's eyes remained fixed on hers. A low wail leaked from his throat as tooth after tooth was pulled and tossed onto the bloody stones. She had witnessed him endure worse than this without making a sound, but she knew that he was not crying for the violence being inflicted upon him. He was crying because of her, and what had been done to her, and what had become of them both.

Soolie didn't look away. She wanted to speak into his mind to reassure him, but she couldn't reach him any more.

The Dead Man placed a hand on her shoulder.

Once Dog's mouth was toothless, wet with bleeding holes, the Chorus moved on to his nails. One at a time, it unrooted the talons from Dog's fingers, and then from each of his toes, until—at last—a litter of bloody yellow teeth and nails lay in the street.

The Chorus stepped back. Its hands were covered in gore, but the white of its clothing remained unsoiled.

The Dead Man lifted his hand from her shoulder. "Now, you may go to him."

Soolie ran. She meant to walk, but her legs overcame her. The stocks were iron with heavy closing pins that shrieked as she twisted them from their holes. She freed his ankles first, dragging the heavy bar off and setting it to the side. Then she freed his neck and wrists, and immediately, he slumped into her, too weak to stand, and she wrapped both arms around his waist, his head lolling against her shoulder, his blood drooling down her neck.

"Miffwess," he whimpered.

The Dead Man nodded with satisfaction. "If you keep his teeth and nails filed down, that will save us both a great deal of trouble. I'll have a file delivered to your room that will suit the purpose."

The boy monster was heavy, and she lowered them both to the street and held him, draped over her lap and against her chest.

"I will leave you to get reacquainted," the Dead Man said as the Chorus joined him. "You are of course free to come and go as you please. The blood that binds you does mean that my Chorus can sense you wherever you are and, as it can, so can I. Just a little boon effect of the service I have done for you. In that way, I suppose, I am always with you." He smiled. "In parting, now that you are one of my people, you may call me Adon. My name is Adon sen Yevah, the first and the last, and this is my kingdom. Soolie Beetch, welcome to Adon Bashti."

Chapter 5

"I should kill you."

"I know."

"If you ever bolt again, I will."

Wendin nodded.

"How is Bels?" Havah asked.

"Not good. It got them bad."

∼

Dinner was oats and dried berries toasted in suet with honey and cinnamon. With everyone in the city dead or gone, preserved foods were plentiful, but water was still a rare resource. Silas sat alone on his sleeping mat chewing a tacky moistureless mass. It wasn't getting any easier to swallow. He agitated the bowl, and the loose grains moved easily against the dry sides. So many people had died today.

"Eat," Havah sat and handed him a dark, round-bellied bottle. "This will help."

"Alcohol will only dehydrate—" Silas objected.

"It's cooked out. Merna found a storehouse several days ago. We've boiled it. Drink."

Merna was dead. Silas accepted the bottle. Havah didn't usually talk to him, but most of her people were gone. Around the morgue, those who were left sat in tiny clusters, heads and voices low.

"Seven children ages four to twelve," Havah said, leaning against the wall and propping her arms on her knees. "Five adults, not counting us, most wounded. Mazir has a broken leg. Cordin is missing her primary hand. Bels got raked by that creature in the stairwell and may not last the night. Wendin will heal and shouldn't bolt again. Nolas is unwounded, but Nolas isn't worth the water in his blood."

Silas squeaked the cork from the bottle and took a swig. It was thick and sweet and spiced, as if several different wines, liquors, and syrups had been boiled together. It slicked his mouth, and the oat grains felt hard and scratchy going down. He doubted the drink would do his body any good, and he restoppered the bottle and set it on the tile between them.

"So, nine adults, counting us, Rahka and Kolgin."

"We can't count Rahka and Kolgrin," Havah shook her head. "We need to leave Ravus."

So that's why she was talking to him. He dug at the grain with his spoon. "I can't go."

"Seven children, Silas." She leveled her eyes at him.

He lifted a loose pile and tipped it, spilling back into the bowl. "I know. But I have a child of my own, and she needs me."

"Where?"

"On the other side of that door Rahka's going to open." He hoped. He set the bowl down. "I can't go with you. But there is a town a few days from here that already lost its people. It may give you a temporary haven. From there, you could make your way north or farther east to other farming towns."

"You're not my first draft either," Havah said. "You're a bumble in a fight. I would take any of our lost over you."

Silas laced his hands between his thighs. He wasn't going to argue. Aside from his miraculous ability to persist and survive when others fatigued and fell, he'd had little to offer by way of practical skills. He could occupy the children with school subjects like history and math, things they would never use. He could bear witness as better, more courageous fighters died, and then live to carry the burden of the survivors' eyes on him, watching and wondering why he was the one who always walked away.

The last time that he had felt truly useful, a mysterious voice had guided him to the Regent's Tower where they had discovered a door to another place. Rahka said it led to Soolie and, after the tower fell and the doorway closed, she had promised she could reopen it, but now her pregnancy was causing a delay. She needed to wait until after her child was born, which Silas of course understood, but it didn't make it any easier that she and Kolgrin were always off hunting monsters. One *might think* that hunting monsters would be just as hazardous as opening a magical doorway, but Silas reminded himself that he thankfully didn't know much about blood magic and it wasn't any of his business. Still, it was difficult to wait when he didn't know what was happening to Soolie, and Rahka and Kolgrin were always leaving him behind.

"But," Havah continued, "you've been outside the city, which is something none of us have done."

"None of you?"

"And you're the strongest and most able-bodied," she said. "I don't want you, but we do need you."

"I have to be here when the door opens."

"When is it set to open?"

"Rahka says it could be any day."

"Then come with us for just two days towards this town you mentioned. Get us out of the immediate circle of Ravus, then head back. Rahka can wait four days."

Silas avoided her eyes. There was no guarantee that Rahka *would*, and there was no guarantee that the refugees would survive, even with his help. The risk was too great. He had to prioritize Soolie. She was the reason for his miracle strength, the purpose behind the guiding voice, the meaning amidst all this horror and death.

That was how he knew that he would find her. He was being kept alive so that he could. He kept looking down at his hands, not knowing what to say.

"Seven children." Havah stood. "We are their only family, and most of that family is dead. You are a father, Silas, and true fathers are not only of their blood. True parents parent the children who *need us*. Seven children, Silas. I will find you in the morning."

∼

THE SOUND of knocking disrupted his sleep. Silas tossed back the blankets and hurried across the dim room to the stairway door.

"Who's there?"

From the other side, Kolgrin's voice responded. "Open up. It smells like spak in here."

Silas lifted the cross bar, and Rahka and Kolgrin pushed through. Thankfully, it seemed no monsters were on their tail. He closed the door and resettled the bar.

"Where have you been?"

"We stopped off for a dram and a couple of skags," Kolgrin said, "made a jolly night of it."

Kolgrin offered Rahka a hand with her cloak, and she waved him off, turning toward the furnace room where she kept her bed. The room was dark and still; Silas was the only one who had gotten up to answer the door.

"Rahka, wait." He hustled to catch up. "I need to talk to you."

Kolgin barred his the way and placed a hand on his shoulder. "In seriousness, I saw what happened in the halls. That was ill fate, friend."

Silas tried to push past. "I need to speak to her."

"I'm afraid you can't, but I'll keep you company for a tic."

"Kolgrin, this is important."

"Don't get between a pregnant skag and her bed. She needs her rest."

Rahka reached the furnace room and closed the heavy door behind her. The bar clunked into place.

"Now," Kolgrin lifted his hand. "What's stuck in your boot?"

Silas shook his head. How could he even start?

"Stick with me while I get food," Kolgrin said. "I'm starved as a gutter triplet."

The dinner things had been packed up, but Kolgrin made his way to the stacks of crates, sacks, cans, and barrels, and Silas followed. He had slept with his boots on, and both their steps resonated in the late-hour stillness of the room. He tried to keep his voice low.

"Why did you have to go hunting today? We lost people. We lost . . . everyone."

"And yet," Kolgrin plopped down on a pile of barley sacks, picked up a small pry-bar, and shook it at him, "nothing squashes Silas Beetch."

"Why did you go?"

Kolgrin wedged the tooth of the bar into the seam of a cask lid. "I've told you before. Rahka tells us what we need to know when we need to know it." He levered the bar and popped the lid, releasing a whiff of skunky hickory. "When the spirits tell her, she goes."

"People died."

"That they do."

"It's just—"

"She'll get that door open for you, don't knot your knickers." Kolgrin lifted the lid to reveal puce strips of meat packed in oil. "Now what do you think *this* is?" Kolgrin stuck thick fingers into the cask and lifted a dripping strip. He winked at Silas and tipped his head back, feeding the long piece into his mouth. He made a choking sound, trying to chew over-full, and wiped his oil-slimed fingers on his pant leg.

"Havah has asked me to help them leave Ravus," Silas said.

Kolgrin grimaced and sucked his teeth.

"She wants to leave as early as tomorrow."

"Mule. Yugh. Packer waste." Kolgrin smacked his mouth. He reached into the cask and broke off a chunk of meat. "You gonna go?"

"Well," Silas crossed his arms. "If I do, I need Rahka to not open the door until I get back."

Kolgrin plopped the chunk onto his tongue and tugged it into his mouth. His beard-brush glistened with droplets that he sucked between his lips as he chewed. "If you're looking for a promise, that's a folly chase, friend. You know that."

"I know."

Silas' head hurt. Rahka's labor and recovery *should* give him more than enough time to leave and return, but there were other worries as well. What if she didn't survive the pregnancy? What if having a baby changed her heart? A child had a way of reorienting a woman's stars, and Silas still didn't fully understand why Rahka was committed to helping him in the first place. Initially, he thought she was a crusader for the people, but lately she seemed content to let the people die. Silas just wanted to do the right thing, but there were so many unknowns. If only he could hear that guiding voice again.

Kolgrin tapped his own forehead, leaving a shiny mark. "Ease up there. Your brow's growing a full set of ribs."

"Can you *try* to convince her to wait until I get back?"

Kolgrin offered Silas a dripping plank, and Silas shook his head. Kolgrin shrugged. "Why are you set on going? These ain't your crawlers. Aren't you wanting to get to that daughter of yours?"

"Yes, but these people need help."

"A good heart is like a good wag: quick to hard and slow to soft," Kolgrin said. "You'll never get what you came for, if you're side-trailed by every weeping whelp. 'Sides, if your path's any pattern," he motioned at the barricaded doors that led to the main floor, "your company's as like to get them all killed as anything."

"But I have to try," Silas could hear desperation rising in his voice.

Kolgrin slapped the lid back on the cask. "Well that puts you with a dry hole and a whet appetite, don't it?" He stood, stretched, and rubbed his whiskers on the back of his sleeve. "My mouth's gonna taste like dank-sacks for a week." He looked down at Silas and his shoulders softened. "Look, I'm a callous suck, but you tickle my fondness and I know you care about this rot, so." He clapped a hand on Silas' shoulder. "My word is this: you know these skikes are still alive, which is more than you can say for that kid of yours. For all you know, Rahka gets that door open, there's no telling what's on the other side. Maybe, you'll be lucky to find a corpse. Least with these ones," he nodded at the children bedded under the draining tables, "you can mark their fate and close a chapter."

"Don't you care either way?" Silas asked.

"I've hitched my pony." Kolgrin stripped his shirt, wadding it up, and used it to rub the last of the oil from his fingers and mouth. "This road is ending for all of us, friend. None of us can dodge it. I'm just here for a canter and a view." He winked and flexed the barrel of his chest.

"Though, I can't help noting we're the only able-bodied men left in this town...."

The conversation was done. Silas turned back to his bed. The last time he heard the guiding voice, it had led him to the tower. He knew that the tower was where he was meant to be and how he was meant to find Soolie. He hadn't lost faith, but he also hadn't received any direction in a very long time, and people were dying. He'd only be gone a couple days. *Forgive me, Soolie. I'll return in time. I promise.*

"Well, if you want me, I'll be sleeping ass-up," Kolgrin called. "It's the end of the fucking world, Silas Beetch. The only way to not get brute-sacked is to spread your cheeks and thrust back harder."

Chapter 6

The journey back up to the great house was a long and labored one. Dog leaned on her, and they stopped often in the middle of the street to rest while the sun swung low and the shadows cooled, and the people passed by offering no assistance, and Soolie did not request it.

As they neared the Dead Man's house, she looked back. The city stretched out below, a field of yellow lights beneath a fat moon rising in a starless sky. The wind carried the smell of hearth smoke and the sound of a string-plucked melody, sweet and fit for dancing.

Dog's nearly naked body was cold and heavy, and his mired skin bloodied the clothes he'd once given her. He mouthed a moan into her collar. She didn't have to be able to sense his spirit to feel his despair.

"Not far now," she whispered, and they took another step up the path lit by the great house that loomed above them.

∼

Somehow, Soolie found her way back to the bedroom. (Where else could they go?) Warm light shone from under the doors as they approached, and she leaned against one as Dog leaned against her, and they pushed their way in.

In the center of the room rested a large copper tub. The contents steamed in the light of the many wall lanterns, filling the air with aromas of vanilla, lavender, and citrus. On the bed lay a cream robe.

"Well, I suppose this makes up for everything," Soolie muttered, closing the door and noting there was neither lock nor latch.

She helped Dog across the floor towards the tub. Beside it was a table of jarred salts and bottled oils, scrub brushes and sponges, a pouring jug, large white towels, and a long straight metal file that glittered with diamond grain.

"Sure. This is *much* better than *food* or *teeth*."

Dog whined.

The lip of the bath came up to her chest. She stood on top-toe so she could reach over and swish her hand in the water. It was pleasantly warm, which meant that while they toiled and suffered up the path to the house, someone had observed their progress and timed this bath for them.

"It's not even a good way to get clean."

She helped Dog, rags and all, up the wooden step that had been placed for the purpose, and into the tub. He sank down along the curved inner wall, water rising to his chin. He had started to cry, and the bloody tears drizzled and diffused into ink clouds that quickly melted into a murk as the bath turned foul and muddy with the tears from his eyes and the gore wicking from his skin.

Soolie crossed her arms and leaned on the rim of the tub. "Now you smell like spak in an orchard."

"Mifweff," he warbled.

"Don't talk."

"Iy fowwy."

"Gross. Stop."

He whimpered, and she scowled, but she wasn't really angry, even though he was apologizing when she was the reason he was hurt, which *should* be infuriating. She was mad. But she didn't have it in her to be angry at him. Maybe she was too hungry and too tired. Maybe it was the knowledge that the Hunter couldn't interfere or command him any more. She was the only Mistress he had.

She pulled the tunic over her head and tossed it at the bed, then untied the panel skirt and chucked it after. She examined the items on the table. None of these were going to make the water fresh again. She grabbed a sponge and a brush and climbed the steps.

He watched from under the pelt of his hair.

"Pull up your knees."

He scrunched his legs to his chest, and she knelt across from him. The water rose over his mouth and nose until only his eyes remained above the surface.

"Ancients, you're a mess."

The warmth felt nice soaking into the dull cold of her flesh. The sponge was a pale daffodil color. She dunked it under the brothy water, and it emerged the color of a soggy scab. Soolie sighed and began mopping her face and skull.

"You can't get infections, can you?"

He shrugged.

She scrubbed behind her ears and neck, over her chest, up and down her arms, and he watched. She rose up on her knees to wash her breasts and belly, and he cringed.

"This scares you, doesn't it?" She pointed at the blood writhing in her skin.

He whimpered.

"You can feel who it belongs to."

He looked away.

"That makes sense."

She planted one foot to swab down to her ankle, and her toes bumped against his slick and nubbly, and he winced.

"But you're filthy and disgusting," she said, switching to rub down her other leg, "so I'm going to wash you, and you aren't going to make a fuss."

She stood and looked down at him with her hands on her hips. Best get it over with.

She swapped out for a clean sponge and squeezed in behind him, pushing with her knees and forcing him towards the middle of the tub.

She helped him pull the rags of his shirt over his head and shuck off the shredded trousers. The fresh sponge bobbed on the surface of the bath like a worm-eaten yolk on a lake of black pudding.

She started by scrubbing the ribbed bend of his back, up and down the knots of his spine and over his sharp shoulders.

"Up."

His hip bones were knobby and his haunches thick and unyielding. The last time she had mopped something this wound-riddled, it had been Mama many lifetimes ago. Mama's death smell had been fresh and impending, not old and rotten, but other than that—she told herself—this was no different.

"Down."

She worked her way around, swinging one leg forward and scooting her bare bum on the lip of the tub, before sinking back into the water in front of him. He wasn't cringing as much, but that didn't mean he didn't want to.

"Head down."

His hair swished against her lap as she scrubbed and pulled with her fingers, breaking and ripping at the tangles, rolling the shedding hair between her palms and flicking it over the side of the tub.

"Up."

She parted the curtain of hair, and his tremulous black eyes met hers. He opened his mouth as if to speak.

"Shut it."

She held his chin in one hand and swabbed his face with the sponge, wiping his eyelids and brushy brows, rubbing at the weird puffy tenderness of his lips, scrubbing brown crust from his neck and behind his ears, one hand on his shoulder to keep him upright as she worked down the taught torso and sinewy belly. By the time she finished, the water was tepid, and he wilted against the side when she let him go. She was also exhausted and in pain, but she wasn't going to let him see it. He was in much worse shape than she was, and she no longer had the ability to help him heal. For all she knew, the Dead Man would keep sending them baths and letting them starve.

The trip out of the tub was almost as laborious as the one up the hill. At last, Dog sat on the edge of the bed, soiling it with dirty dripping water, and she rubbed him down with one of the towels until it was damp brown all over, then grabbed the other towel and used that as well, squeezing the nest of his hair and patting him down the best she could, before dragging his body up to the top of the bed and tucking him in.

She used the cream robe to dry herself, then tossed the dirty robe and towels in a pile in the middle of the floor. When she turned back to the bed, his eyes were closed, his wet toothless mouth lolling, and she realized she had never seen him sleep before, much less in a bed.

The night breeze through the open windows was cool, but not cold. On impulse, she retrieved the bloodied tunic and skirt from where they lay wadded on the floor and put them back on. Somehow, lying in bed beside the sleeping monster was more difficult than bathing him. She crawled onto the bed and curled up on top of the covers next to him. He lay still, a cold, tallow-skinned, raw-mouthed corpse.

"I'll find a way to get us both free," she whispered. "I promise."

⁓

A DOOR SWUNG IN, and the Dead Man's Chorus entered.

Soolie gritted her teeth and eased herself upright as it approached the foot of the bed with a long shallow box in its outstretched hands. Dog whimpered in his sleep, but did not stir.

Fucking go away, Soolie thought.

It waited, the blood crown twisting on its head, red eyes watching. Could the Dead Man see her through those eyes? Soolie made a shooing motion and bared her teeth. The Chorus placed the box at the foot of the bed. Then, in one swift motion, it reached over the covers, grabbed her ankle and swung her up, holding her suspended upside down like dead rabbit. Her shirt piled under her pits, and her skirt hung over her chest, leaving her legs exposed.

Soolie trapped her screams behind her teeth. She didn't want to wake Dog. There was nothing he could do, and it would only cause him harm.

The creature hooked one sharp nail under the skirt ties, grazing her belly with its bony fingers, and ripped as if shucking her for the braising.

The torn skirt fell to the floor. Soolie glared at its expressionless face as it punctured its nails through the cloth of her shirt and shredded.

Once it had finished stripping her naked, it deposited her unceremoniously on the floor and stepped back. Soolie stood carefully, shaking. Dog hadn't stirred. The clothes he had given her were ruined.

In the long box, she found a flimsy dress of foamy blue. On top of it rested a simple envelope sealed with pressed white wax.

Soolie picked them both up, walked over to the tub, and dropped them into the bloody brown water. She walked past the monster to the door, and it followed.

~

SOOLIE KNEW WHERE TO GO. She walked down the high ornate hall and up to the great star-bright doors. Despite their size, they swung in easily, and she strode naked into the throne room.

Pillars the size of greatwoods rose from a floor of rose-veined marble to a roof so high, it was difficult to make out the inlay of pearl from the scales of quartz, and beneath that luster lay a feast. Banquet tables heaped with glazed meats, man-sized flake pies, great tureens of fragrant stews, and towers of jeweled fruits and confections. Hundreds of people —knives and goblets in their hands, meats and cordials in their mouths —chortled and chattered as Soolie walked to the center of the room and stood before him.

He sat on a throne whiter than bone. All around the dais, beautiful people gauzed in vibrant colors cradled crystal decanters and trays of delicacies. Their elegant hands were on his shoulders, their strong hands were on his thighs. A woman with copper hair was dropping something in his up-turned mouth as he glanced over and saw her.

"SOOLIE!" He threw his arms wide. "Did you not get the garment I sent for you?"

The room fell silent, and all eyes turned to look on her bare skin and the blood that writhed beneath it.

"I'd rather wear spak."

"You are welcome to flaunt my craftsmanship. I will not press you to cover it." He motioned, and the beautiful people languidly dispersed around the dais in groups and pairings, their bodies leaning and melting into one another like warmed wax. "Though it was a lovely garment. The fibers were milked from rosemoths and dyed from the sacks of a Mordati sea spider. I picked it out especially for you."

"I threw it in the bloody bath water," Soolie said.

"Bloody?" He tilted his head. "Was it?" He leaned forward, resting an elbow on his knee, amusement pulling at his mouth. "Did you wash your pet in the bath I had drawn for you?"

Soolie scowled, and he laughed.

"I am sorry to hear that! The smell must be horrible. I will send to have the waters removed from your room immediately." He motioned and several people in white filed out a side door. "They will not disturb your Dog. You have my word. I should have made concessions, and for that I apologize. Now," he nodded at her. "I won't deny you if you wish to remain naked in my court. However, if you would like to clothe yourself, I would be glad to accommodate."

"I liked what I had," Soolie snapped, "but your *monster* destroyed them."

"Did it?" he asked. "I hope it did not handle you roughly."

She didn't answer. Perhaps he *couldn't* see through the eyes of the Chorus when it wore that crown, and perhaps his ignorance was a lie. Neither made his concern any less false or what happened any less clear.

"That was not my intent," he said, solemnly. "I will take greater care. Please allow me to make amends with a replacement." He brightened. "Something humble, yes? I will have clothing made for you both. *Marah, stena.*"

At his request, a small woman from one of the banquet tables stood and stepped forward. She wore a simple cranberry shift and loose gray pants.

He motioned to the woman. "Humor me. Would something of this nature suit you?"

The woman waited.

There was no point not getting clothes. "Fine," Soolie said.

"Appe loden akihdo."

"Anna, Adon." The woman began stripping off her shirt.

Well, this did feel inevitable. It was a mercy that the woman had undergarments that she kept on. She approached Soolie, her outergarments in her hands, and offered them with a gentle bob and smile. As Soolie accepted, the woman beamed at the Dead Man, then turned and left through the silver doors.

The Dead Man sprang to his feet. "Why is there silence? THIS IS A FEAST!"

The people cheered. From the corners, musicians began to play. Soon the room clamored with dishware, merriment, and melody.

Soolie stepped into the pants and snugged them up at her belly. She turned the tunic over in her hands, looking for the front. The clothes smelled sweet and clean.

The Dead Man dropped back into his throne, and the beautiful people rose from the edges of the dais bearing food and drink, freely partaking and sharing with one another as they draped around him like sun-drunk cats.

Soolie tugged the hem of the tunic down.

A young man with long fingers was toying with the curls on the Dead Man's head while a woman filled his goblet. The Dead Man motioned for Soolie to approach the throne.

She shook her head.

"You must be hungry," he patted his lap as if expecting her to come and sit. "We are feasting. Let me feed you."

The young man nuzzled the Dead Man's neck and looked dreamily at Soolie with gold-green eyes.

"I'm not hungry," Soolie lied.

She hadn't felt it all day, but now she could swear she felt the Hunter's Heart calling to her through the body of the Dead Man.

"Haven't you starved enough?" he asked, reaching out a hand. "I know what you desire. Only I can give it to you."

She remembered.

"Let me ease your pain."

She remembered being bound to the dark table, his hand hovering over her while her body and spirit yearned towards him, and how his eyes had watched her as she cried out.

"I'm not hungry."

It took every fiber of her will to turn her back on him and walk away.

~

INSTEAD OF RETURNING to the bedroom, she ducked through a simple door and entered the hall of many rooms that the Dead Man called the Cradle. Some of the doors hung open to dark stone cells like the one he had held her in—with tables and straps, head-cages and chains—but most of the doors were closed. From one of them rose an especially ragged cry of anguish and despair as she walked by counting. Nine, ten, eleven . . .

She had tried to count the doors while the Chorus was carrying her down the hall by her throat, and guessed just over a dozen rooms from the entry to the table where she had been bound, and about seven farther to the room where the Dead Man had written the blood into her skin.

The first door she tried opened to an occupied room. A body lay on a stone table, leather straps on its limbs and an iron cage on its head. It didn't make a sound as she backed out. She tried several other doors, before finding the one she was looking for resting open.

Chains hung from the walls and piled on their settings in the floor. A small table sat in the corner, supporting a black box. She twisted the lantern key and closed the door. This was a hope's cast, but at least she might learn something.

The wood of the black box was so dense and smooth that she almost couldn't see the grain. Inside, she found the dark vial, the twisted thimble, and the thin knife. She grabbed the thimble first and held it up to the light.

It looked like it had been woven of knotted bone. The cords melted under her scrutiny, sliding into one another in a way that she couldn't follow. Did *everything* have to fucking *writhe*?

She jammed the thimble onto her middle finger, and it closed on her flesh like a tiny mouth with many teeth. Before she could doubt herself, she stabbed the thorn tip into her forearm and dragged, snarling as the talon scored her flesh and scraped her bone, but the wriggling blood didn't respond, and when she lifted her hand to take a look, the skin of her arm was unmarked. The pain had been real, but the flesh and blood were undisturbed.

"Fuck."

She yanked the thimble off, and her fingertip was tender and flush as if she had dipped it in boiling water.

She grabbed the knife and vial, dipped the blade, pulled it out, and held it to the light. The solution had neither scent nor color. It was more viscous than water and evenly coated the surface of the knife. Nothing for it now. She propped one foot on the table, wadded the loose pant leg up to her hip, pressed the blade to her thigh, and cut.

The pain took her by surprise. She gasped, her body cinching tight, and forced herself to watch as the writhing blood burrowed down out of the path of the blade that opened her flesh in a clean straight seam. The cut burned, and the clear liquid sizzled, and blood that was only her own began to river down her leg. The Chorus' weave continued dancing deep in the meat of her thigh, unbroken.

She dropped the knife on the table and pressed both hands to the wound. It was nearly a palm in length and a finger-pad deep. The knife had cut too easily. Blood flowed between her fingers, puddle-splattering on the stone. She wadded the pant leg against the wound, and the gray cloth darkened quickly.

Fucking undergods. The pain hadn't aged; it felt as if she were still cutting and recutting herself, which, unfortunately, made sense. The Chorus must heal the way Dog could, perhaps even faster. The contents of the black vial must keep it from healing too quickly when the Dead Man was using its blood. If that was true, the wound wasn't going to stop bleeding any time soon.

Soolie had grown up in a home that operated under the ever-present threat of a wound that wouldn't stop bleeding. Ultimately, it hadn't been a single catastrophic injury that had taken her mother's life, but the accumulation of many. Still. She knew what to do.

She cut off the other pant leg, wrapped it around her thigh above the wound, and knotted it as securely as she could.

It was almost funny how little time she'd had these clothes.

She slipped the long black vial under the band and began to twist, torquing the cloth with each turn like the turn of a handle and tightening the cloth around her thigh. The wound was still a sharp and constant pain, but the bleeding slowed to an ooze. She stood, holding the vial with one hand to keep it from spinning, and hobbled for the door. Hopefully it would stop bleeding by morning. At least she didn't think she *could* lose a limb from loss of blood. Then again, perhaps she was about to learn another thing in the worst possible way.

She took one last look over her shoulder. The box lay open, the knife and thimble on the table. Blood puddled on the floor and tracked to the door. Fuck it. She left the door open and the light on.

On her way back down the hallway, a heart-struck cry rose from the same room that had screamed and howled on her way in. The grief was so fresh and raw, that she tottered to the door and pushed in to see.

A man lay bound to the table. The Chorus stood at his feet, eyes white. At his head, the Dead Man was wearing the crown, his hands on the cage, mouth moving soft words. The bound man's chest heaved as his cries turned to weeping. Soolie saw that one of his hands was mittened in new bandages. No one looked up as she closed the door.

FOR MANY DAYS bound in stocks in the middle of the square, they had beaten him, flayed his skin and bruised his bones, and Dog had not cried out. He had kept his mind on her, his Mistress, feeling her one moment clearly, the next faintly, her spirit diving and resurfacing as the old Master worked her mind to weed, till, and replant it. But Dog's Mistress was not one of the weak and malleable living souls. She was both Ancient and Reborn. He knew his Mistress would endure, just as he knew she suffered. He wept for her in his heart, but did not let his tears fall on his face. He had given his word that he would conduct himself nobly as her servant, so he submitted to the abuse in silence and thought of her.

But then she disappeared.

It had started with a surfacing clarity that told him she was awake. He sensed her triumph, her struggle, and her pain. And then he had felt the winnowing of their connection. Quickly, too quickly, all that remained was a frail filament, and then that was cut, and then it was gone.

He was suddenly alone in the kingdom of his old Master, and she was gone.

Only then did he break his silence and raise his voice to wail and howl, and his tormentors had fled in fear and left him to his agony, and no sound that he could make was enough.

When he saw her the following day, between the Wolf and the Master, bound in the Wolf's blood, he had not been able to feel her. He had looked on her—conquered—and felt the removal of his teeth and nails like splinters plucked from a mangled mire. When she ran to him, he did not want her to touch him, and when she held him, he could not feel the power of the Ancient Mistress in her, only the blood of the Wolf that bound her. And he feared her then in a way he had never feared her before, because his heart did not recognize her.

Then she had helped him more than any Mistress should, suffering with him back to the old Master's house, bathing him, drying him, tucking him in, and he had submitted himself hopelessly to her care. His despair was so great that—for the first time since his spirit had been young—he had closed his eyes and allowed himself to sleep.

He woke to the sound of many feet.

The room was filled with living men and women dressed in white, bailing out the sludgy bath water and carrying it away in great buckets, mopping the floors and removing the soiled towels, and his Mistress was gone. One of the serving women gathered a shredded skirt and tunic from the foot of the bed.

Fear lanced his heart.

He scrambled naked from the sheets, ignoring the pain of his many wounds, and stumbled for the doors. Men with hefting poles stepped out of his way as he pushed past into the hall.

He couldn't sense her.

In a moment of weakness, he had allowed himself to sleep, and the Wolf had taken her. It should have torn him limb from limb before carrying her away. The shame of his failure was greater than his hopelessness. He had to find her.

Dog had never been permitted to move freely in the Master's house, but he knew the bones of the beast and how unwelcome he was in its veins. He ran, stumbling, panic ringing in his beatless chest, not daring to cry her name. Through familiar dark and lantern-lit hallways, down stone steps, and into the moonlit courtyard, until at last he saw her. Coming towards him down a tunnel of over-arching leaves, moving stilted and wrong, clutching her leg, but it was her.

She looked up as he whimpered and ran to her. The tang of an open wound filled his nostrils as he bowed from the waist in the way she had taught him, mewling an apology.

To his surprise, she laughed.

He had never heard her laugh before. He straightened, confused, and she slung an arm over his battered shoulders, and leaned on him, and laughed harder now, her small body shaking. He put an arm around her in return and realized, to his bewildered horror, that she had started to cry.

His Mistress tilted her head back beneath the moon, bloody tears striping black on pale cheeks that writhed with Wolf's blood, and she laughed and wept, and he waited with her, feeling every familiar comfort stripped away in the crush of every familiar terror's closing jaws.

Chapter 7

"These are yours," Havah held out a belt of shells and two gray wheel-pistols.

Silas hefted the barrel off his shoulder and set it on the tile. "I already have a weapon." It was a glossy-handled pistol that Kolgrin had given him.

"These are better." Havah shoved them against his chest, and he clutched them clumsily. "Six rounds. Quick shot, easy load. Standard model. No unique guns. We all carry the same. Familiarize yourself when you're done fetching the water."

∾

In the morning, Kolgrin and Rahka left without telling anyone where they were going, and the refugees started prepping their packs. They had no way to propel a cart, so they would take only what they could carry.

Silas made the trip up to the hospital main floor to retrieve the water barrels. By the time he rolled the last one in and re-barricaded the morgue's large double doors, the packing was done and the refugees had gathered around Bels' mat to make their goodbyes. Havah motioned for him to join. It felt uncomfortable to be a part of that circle, celebrating and mourning people he hadn't known, and even more strange to know that he was being included, not because he was naturally one of the group, but because Havah wanted to reinforce his sense of obligation.

They sat on barrels and mats, sacks and blankets, and feasted on the food they couldn't take with them. Tins of oiled onions, briney fish, jars of vinegar eggs, nut butter, and a wheel of heavy-rind cheese that they broke into hunks and passed around the circle. Best of all, there were bowls of hot oats with maple, nuts, and dried elderberries cooked in plenty of water. They ate and drank and shared stories about the people who were no longer with them. Silas stayed quiet and thought of the ones he had lost—his wife Tera, his sister-in-law Evaline, and Soolie wherever she was in this terrible world.

Bels was the first to close their eyes. It has been a great trial for them to stay awake for as long as they had. The children started nodding soon after, drooping against the adults or curling up on the mats, bellies plumped with food. Mazir and Cordin wanted to stay up chatting, but Havah hissed that everyone needed sleep. It would be an early and difficult morning. Silas was grateful for the dismissal and made his way to the mat where he spent his fretful nights. He cleaned his teeth with a bristle-pick, checked a gun by his pillow, and tucked in with his boots on.

As he closed his eyes, Mazir and Cordin were still whispering and making their way to their own beds with deliberate slowness. Silas guessed that a difficult tomorrow was exactly why some folks didn't want the night to end.

∼

THE LITTLE BOY stopped in the middle of the street and started screaming, eyes bunching, mouth wide. Silas swept him up, hands under his pits, pack and all, and hefted him to his chest.

"I've got you," Silas whispered as the boy wailed into his jacket. "You're okay. You're okay."

Yasel was only about four-years-old and the smallest of their party. It was surprising it had taken this long for one of them to break. Other children glanced back, and the adults hastened them forward.

They had risen early. No one had stopped to check if Bels was breathing before Havah hustled them quietly out the door, driving them at a demanding pace: eyes forward, mouths shut, feet swift. Now, the sun was centered overhead, and everyone marrow-ached, but they pushed on. Even Mazir with the broken leg kept pace, swinging on his crutches over rubble, bodies, and bones. Silas had seen Havah pass a paper-wrapped lump to the young man last night, and every hour or so, Mazir reached into his pocket to pull something out and nibble-lick his palm before snarling, tucking it away, and plunging forward with new energy. If Silas was right, Mazir might very well have the last lump of topaz in all of Ravus. Hopefully it would help keep him alive.

Yasel clung to Silas' neck, struggling to breathe and sob at the same time. As Silas quickened to catch up to the group, he glanced down to see what had set the boy off—expecting another skull molting flesh, a belly bursting with bloat-stew, loose limbs, snaggled intestines, or some other new and terrible atrocity, but nothing stood out. All the horrors looked the same.

～

It was late afternoon by the time they arrived at the Iron Gate to find the great spike-top doors resting open. The survivors paused at the border of what had been their city and their home. Silas walked up to stand beside Havah, Yasel still clinging to his chest.

The snow had melted and the roads were beginning to dry. The way should have been beset with long waiting lines of pilgrims and merchants, but the broad beaten path was barren. Wrecked wagons and carts dotted the plane, and the corpses of people and animals made their slow collapse into the grass. Compared to what they had crawled through to get here, the way was clear and open.

"We should keep going," Havah said, but her feet didn't move.

Silas sidled the boy to his hip. He remembered the first time he had left the city. He had been more of a boy than man, fleeing a violent house, thinking to make his way onto a ship for a new life and grand adventures. And then he had set his feet in the wrong direction and traveled three days inland where he had found the unimaginable: a wife, a daughter, a home. These adults were older than he had been, and these children hadn't seen the sky in several moons. They were accustomed to a warren of walls. None of them had been out in the open before.

"There's nowhere to hide," Nolas said from the back of the group. "They'll pick us like lice on a bare scalp."

Silas stepped forward onto the path. The others followed.

~

"Sure, just light a beacon to tell all the monsters to come eat us!"

Nolas was a younger man with hunching shoulders and a double-knit cap pulled low over his brow. Silas wasn't sure what had brought him to the group, but it was clear there was no fondness spared between him and Havah. The older woman's voice was warmthless and hard.

"Hold your panic and shut your mouth. We will make this decision by weighing measures, not fears," she turned to all of them, "but we must decide now."

They had rounded the city and started east, but the sunlight was diminishing fast. Soon it would be dark.

Havah continued, "If we light a fire, they may find us more quickly. If we *don't* light a fire, they may still find us in the dark."

Silas lowered Yasel to the ground and raised a hand. She nodded to him.

"We know the creatures hate the light. If we have to face them, it might be better to do so with fire."

"It's easy for you to bait a fight!" Nolas spluttered. "The man who never dies!"

"He has his scars to show," Havah said, "which is more than some of us can say."

Nolas withered and reached under the fold of his hat to scratch at his forehead with long nails.

"I'd rather face them in the light than in the dark," Wendin said.

Havah nodded. "Agreed. We only have a little time to gather wood.

Mazir, you stay with me and the children to set camp. Everyone else, leave your packs, take the ax. Be quick."

The earth near the road was firm and dry, but farther out, the spring sog was still marshy, and the wood that lay in the open was heavy and wet. They ventured into a nearby stand of trees to scrounge the forest floor, and hauled back long fanning branches, twigs and moss for tinder, and a great log that Silas and Cordin dragged together, plowing a furrow through the mud. Not far from their camp, Wendin found a cart with a broken wheel. They emptied the cart of its useless treasures—a crockery set, a lap-loom, silver mirror, and several bottles of moonpiss liquor—and tipped it up on two wheels to balance it tottering towards the settling camp. Nolas followed with bottles of moonpiss in his arms.

Mazir had the fire newly kindled, sleeping mats and blankets already fanned around it like wheel spokes. Havah had unpacked dried sausages, cheese, and nuts for dinner and was doling out sticky twisted sweets to the young ones who suckled the candy and licked the wrappers. The oldest was a girl about twelve. Not long ago, there had been two children roughly thirteen and fourteen years, but both had gone on resource runs with parties that never came back.

"Silas," Havah called as they lowered the cart onto three wheels. "Will you break enough wood for the night?"

"Yes."

Cordin pulled the ax from her belt and handed it to him. Silas felt a wash of relief as his hand closed on the handle. This was a job he was suited for. He crawled up into the tilted bed of the wagon, took a firm grip, and swung.

~

SILAS WAS the only one not suffering from city fatigue. The others knew it, and they huddled and ate their food, holding their breath and looking over their shoulders at the deepening dark, and left him to his work. He was more comfortable with solitude than with forced companionship, and the simple labor was soothing. He fell into a rhythm, swinging the ax, kicking boards free of their bending nails, and piling the broken wood within reach of the fire. By the time he had amassed enough wood to take them through the night, everything beyond the glow of the fire was drenched in nebulous ink.

He dropped a load of planks onto the pile.

"Eat." Havah approached and handed him a paper-wrapped lump. "No use chopping more than we can use. We can't carry it with us."

The paper contained a loose mound of dried meat, cheese, and nuts, and Silas held it cupped in one palm and scooped a small handful into his mouth. She stood by, one hand on the pistol at her hip. Around the fire, the children were bedded down, sharing blankets. The adults lay with their weapons at their sides.

"I'll take first guard," Havah said. "You'll take second. The children and the wounded should rest."

Silas swallowed. "I can take first guard if you would like to sleep."

She shook her head. "I don't trust you to trade off."

She was right to doubt him. He didn't care much for sleep anymore. He would stay up all night keeping guard if he could. He fished through the pile in his hand, picking out the pale grub nuts and popping them into his mouth. Around the fire, bodies settled restlessly under their blankets. He doubted any of them were getting much sleep tonight.

"I won't thank you for being here." Havah faced the dark, and the light of the fire ringed her hair in silver. "I shouldn't have had to convince you."

Silas nodded, chewing and parsing out the cheese cubes.

"But I will tell you not to go back to Kolgrin and Rahka."

"I have to find my daughter."

"Not that way." Her mouth was tight. "You've seen their means. I don't know what Rahka wants from you, but I know it's not a reunited family."

She waited for him to respond. "I am aware," he said.

"And don't let Kolgrin trick you into thinking you have an ally," she added. "A man like that is always hungry, never full."

"You talk as if he and Rahka are the same."

"She is the teeth, and he is the tongue. Same enough."

"And what am I?"

"A fool. Neither the best nor the worst of us."

He nodded. There was a time when her bluntness would have

rankled him, but now he appreciated the plainness. "You seem to suddenly care a great deal about me."

"You better our chances of survival. If you're a good man, you'll stay."

"I can't stay." He toyed with the meat bits in his palm. He didn't expect her to understand. She hadn't experienced the things he had experienced—hadn't seen his daughter resurrected, hadn't felt herself being brought back from death and sensed a guiding presence. He had a purpose. He had to go back.

Havah was quiet, so he finished the food and wadded up the paper into a ball between his palms. The fire crackle-popped, and the trees creaked. He tossed the paper toward the fire, and it fell short.

"Don't lose what you *have* chasing what's already lost," she said.

"I'm sorry," he said, and he meant it.

He stepped forward to pick up the paper, when he caught a flicker of movement in the dark.

Silas spun back, grabbed the handle of the ax, and screamed. "WAKE UP!!!"

On the other side of the fire, Cordin sat up, reflexively reaching for her gun with the useless stump of her lost hand as a wraith of rags flung out of the blackness and hit her in the chest, knocking her back and bending over her.

Silas sprinted, ax raised. Behind him, Havah fired off one shot and then another. To his left, a child was being dragged over the blankets, towards the darkness. Another gunshot sounded, and blood sprayed the children as they scrambled up screaming in their bedding. A creature reeled back, releasing the child's ankle.

"PROTECT THE CHILDREN!" Havah shouted.

Silas veered his course from Cordin. The monster reared, visible in the firelight. It was draped head to toe in rags: trousers layered under skirts, layered under multiple tunics, and a hooded cloak that hung low over blindfolded eyes. The only parts of it that were exposed were the long talons tearing through the heavy knit of its mittens and a shrieking mouth of bloody splinter teeth. Havah had shot it in the throat, and its hooded head slung sideways, spattering blood from its lips as it lunged.

Silas threw himself in front of the children and swung the ax full-force down on the top of the creature's head. The blade sank into its skull and stuck. It swiped, slashing his forearms with its talons, mouth gnashing, blood sopping the cloth over its eyes as Silas wrenched the ax free and kicked it in the chest. It fell spasming onto its back, and he ran forward and swung the ax into its shoulder, and then its leg, and then the other leg, swinging again and again, the body under the many layers jerking wrong and broken.

Another scarecrow of a creature was rushing from behind, and he spun around just in time to sink the ax into the crook of its neck. It slashed at him, and he jumped back, losing his grip on the handle. It snarled, wrenching the ax from its shoulder and tossing it into the dark.

BANG. BANG, BANG, BANG, BANG!

Nolas was screaming, firing his gun again and again, smashing back the hammer with one hand and pulling the trigger with the other. A round caught the creature in the shoulder, and it snapped its head towards him.

BANG!

Nolas fired the last round. He was standing in the middle of the children, and they clung to him, shrieking, as the creature lunged. Silas threw himself onto the rags of its back. Its body was wiry and strong and torqued beneath him. It was going to buck him off. He lunged, propelling them forward, and it stumbled, and he roared and threw his weight again, tumbling them both headlong into the fire.

Sparks and flame burst around them.

It flailed, screaming, and Silas rolled free, jumping up, beating the sparks from his jacket. The creature was in a panic, kicking burning logs and ripping clothes. It tore the hood and wrappings from its face, and its black eyes filled with the light of the scattered fire, and it shrieked, skin blistering, eyes swelling, and ducked away from the light and launched itself again towards the children.

Silas grabbed the gun at his hip and fired once, twice, the second shot hitting it in the torso, but it kept moving, lashing blindly at the scattering children, heading straight for Yasel and Nolas. The little boy clung to Nolas' waist, and the young man stumbled back, grabbing the boy by the shirt, pulling him off, and shoving him at the monster. The creature's hands landed on the child's body, fumbling only for a second as Nolas scrambled retreat, eyes wide.

"NOOOOO!"

Silas was running, pistol raised, afraid to fire with the boy so close. The creature turned its mutilated face towards him, flesh bubbling, teeth bared, and then it pinned Yasel up in its arms, and flung itself into the dark, taking the boy with it.

"NOOOOOOOOO!"

Silas shot now, pulling the trigger, and then the hammer, and then the trigger, the gun bucking in his hands as he plowed into the night after it. He couldn't see or hear. His feet pounded the uneven ground. Behind him, more gunshots. Before him, lumpy fields and dark trees. Which way did they go?

He heard a howl and turned to see another creature charging him from the fire, and he raised the gun, pulling the trigger, and the gun clicked empty as it bowled into him, sharp talons slashing over his shoulder, rag-wrapped face swinging in, teeth snapping. He threw up his forearm, and its teeth buried through the jacket sleeve, into his flesh, and locked on the bone as they tumbled to the ground.

He tried to knee it, kick it, punch it with his free arm, but it was rags on a rack frame. The familiar feeling of the monster starting to feed raked through his body. He wrenched against its jaws, and they rolled— one over the other—and then the creature was above him, and his back landed on something hard and sharp, and he forced one more turn, reaching under and grabbing the handle, and swung the ax blunt-first into the side of its skull.

It shrieked, unlatching, spurting blood, and Silas flipped the ax in his hand, brought the head between them, and rammed the heel of his hand into the back of the ax-head, slamming the blade between its teeth.

Teeth busted, screeching on iron, the blade biting into the spine of its throat, and Silas threw himself forward, shoving the blade with both hands, its arms flailing sharp talons, and when it was on the ground beneath him, he jumped up with a roar, one foot to its chest, and stomped down on the ax-head, crunching through the back of its skull. He grabbed the handle, wrenching it free, and swung first at the arms, and then at the legs, until it twitched and writhed in the bag of its rags.

"Silas!"

"AHHH!" Silas spun, ax raised, but it was only Mazir swinging towards him on a crutch, a pistol in his free hand. "Are they gone?" He looked left and right.

"We got four of them. The rest have run."

Silas' chest was heaving. He couldn't yet begin to assess his wounds.

"Looks like you handled this one. We're collecting the corpses," Mazir said. "Do you need a hand?"

"No . . . I . . . I've got it." Silas grabbed the top of the creature's hood and started dragging its jerking body towards the firelight.

"Clear a path!" Mazir shouted, going ahead.

Already, the survivors were managing the aftermath. Younger children were bundling and rolling up burned and bloodied bedding, while the eldest girl was helping Wendin rebuild the fire. Havah was tossing hunks onto the flames that flopped and jerked and plumed, and Silas realized the hunks were the severed parts of monsters.

She nodded to him, and everyone stepped back as he hauled the body into the light.

"One part at a time," Havah said. "I don't want any running torches. Do you need a knife?"

"I have my own." Silas dropped the body and pulled his knife from its sheath.

She eyed him. His jacket was shredded and sprayed in blood. His shoulders, chest, and forearms were bleeding from many gashes, and the torn wool on his right arm was mashed into deep black bite wounds.

"How did you manage to keep your blade clean?" she asked.

He knelt by the writhing creature and started to saw through the cloth and meat of its neck. Its broken maw burbled. He didn't answer. They both knew that the knife was clean, because he didn't use it when he should have. He had two pistols and a knife on his belt. He had made a lot of mistakes in that fight. He should have made better use of his weapons. He shouldn't have hesitated to fire his gun. Yasel might still be alive.

He lifted the monster's busted head and slung it towards the fire. Havah used the toe of her boot to shove it into a crotch of burning logs, and the wrappings brewed smoke and caught flame.

"Bodies shouldn't burn this well," Wendin muttered. "It's almost as if the critters were made to be disposed of."

"Best not leave any pieces," Havah said. "Check our perimeter for strays. I don't want any loose hands crawling into our beds."

Silas pinned an arm under his boot and sawed at the shoulder joint. Nolas sat nearby on a hunk of wood, his woolen cap pulled low. Mazir was with the children, Silas counted five. All the beds were rolled up except one, and the body in it didn't move.

Wendin was dragging a monster into the light. "This one's missing an arm somewhere."

"Nolas, help her look," Havah said.

"And I found your gun in the grass." Wendin pulled Silas' pistol from her belt.

Silas tossed the creature's limb towards the fire, and raised a ready hand. Wendin underhanded the weapon, and he caught it. "Thanks."

Havah prodded the limb into the flames. "Is your chamber empty?"

"Mine is empty," Nolas said, lingering.

Havah ignored him, so Silas nodded.

"Reload," she said. "Wendin and I'll butcher."

Silas stepped off the corpse and stuck his knife in the wood where Nolas had been sitting. He clicked the gun's hammer half-back, swung the wheel cap, and pulled a round from the rank on his belt. Nolas was watching, and Silas didn't return the look. Nolas knew what he had seen. Silas thumbed the shell into its slot, rotated the wheel, and reached for another round.

"Perly, Cordin, and Yasel." Havah said, yanking on a flailing arm and pulling the connecting shred of shirt cloth tight. She sawed it with her knife and tossed the arm into the fire. "None of us saw Perly get taken."

"She had to piss," the oldest girl said.

"Never leave the light of the fire," Havah said. "If you have to piss, piss in the light."

The children nodded.

Silas clicked the wheel cap shut and reset the hammer. He could feel a churning in his chest and an aching in his eyes. They should have noticed Perly getting out of bed. They should have been more alert.

"Cordin was killed in the fight." Several sets of eyes glanced towards the still body in the bed. "I didn't see what happened to Yasel...."

Silas clenched his jaw and holstered his gun. Havah eyed each of them, waiting for someone to speak. Nolas hovered in the outer ring of the firelight. Silas kept his eyes down and plucked at the arm of his jacket to pull the cloth from the raw syrup of his wounds.

The eldest girl spoke, "Nolas knows."

Havah flipped her pistol from her belt and fired.

Nolas' face burst like a dropped melon, and he fell.

The children screamed and clung to Mazir.

"You should have waited to find out what happened," Silas said, but his voice was hollow.

"Mazir, lay out the children's blankets," Havah said, tucking her gun. "Even if they can't sleep, they should try to rest. We'll have a long day in the morning."

Chapter 8

Kolgrin braced his forearm against the wall, his hand tight-fisted, the other on his hard wag. The man behind him was thrusting faster and faster. Kolgrin pushed into it, straining his thigh-strings and pumping his spit-slicked foreskin.

"Don't you dare off early," he growled.

"Hnnnng." The man's breathing caught, and Kolgrin felt the pulse of unloading twad. "Sorry."

The man released Kolgrin's hips and slid out, trailing wet that drizzled sticky between Kolgrin's cheeks and down his inner thigh. Kolgrin growled.

"Don't be sore. Let me suck you off."

The man touched his back, and Kolgrin hit him away.

"Fuck off."

The man had already stepped off the box. He shrugged and rebuttoned his trousers. "I offered."

"I said fuck off."

Kolgrin kicked the box towards a corner and didn't watch as the man retreated down the hallway. One of Kolgrin's legs was bare and the other ended in a pile of trousers that hung over his boot. He untwisted the trousers to find the empty leg hole, shoved his foot in, and pulled them up, tucking his still-hard wag into the crotch. The cloth stuck to his thighs and ass. Now he had to go find a spakcan so he could unload the twad that was pressing at the door of his pucker before it splurged into his trousers. That skike may not have been able to keep his rod, but it felt like he'd unloaded a canning jar's worth.

Kolgrin was frustrated, angry, and he wasn't in the mood to be spied on.

"How long you been standing there?"

The woman leaned in one of the hall doorways, her arms crossed over her taught tan belly. Kolgrin recognized her. She had high-cheeked Southern features and sharp eyes bright as the gold dancing ribbons in her fingers. She was a newer girl who had gotten her spot at the Three Suns with the help of some milkblood boy who paraded her about like she was his first chin hair.

"He was too small for you," she said.

Kolgrin grabbed his boot from where he'd shucked it into the corner. "They all are."

"I'm not." She tilted her head so her glossy black hair swung away from her long neck. Any skag-fucker would find her alluring.

"You're not my taste." He shoved his foot into the boot. The need for a spakcan was increasingly pressing.

"You door the busiest dance house in the city, and every night you fuck or you brawl."

"Does that drunkard whose silks you're wearing know that you like to watch?"

She stepped out of the doorway, twisting her ribbons around her fingers. "He knows what I want him to know."

Kolgrin made to walk past, but she stepped in his way. She was smaller than he was, but her eyes met his with the brazenness of an animal that has never been prey.

"I'm about to spak twad in my britches, so if there's a reason you're hounding me, out with it."

"You're bored," she said, measuring him from his boots, to his bulging trousers, to his full-brush beard. "And sad. If nothing changes, you'll be glad to die in an alley by your own hand."

"Whatever work you're offering, I'm not looking, and you can't pay enough."

He made to shove past her, and she sidestepped lightly before he could make contact.

"There's no point in paying a dead man."

"I don't respond well to threats."

"Then I haven't measured you well at all, but it wasn't a threat," she said as he walked away. "It was *sachalee*. Come with me or don't. Either way, I don't expect you to survive."

~

SACHALEE. A Southern word for a necessary disclosure when drawing up an agreement. He hadn't known that then, but he had still sought her out the following night. Together, they had battled the living and the dead, waded through blood, and crawled through corpses. More than once they'd been pinned in, and Kolgrin thought they had finally met their end, but somehow they had always escaped. It was impossible to say which she had done more: threatened his life or saved it—the two so often went hand-in-hand—but she had saved it first. Through all their many misadventures, this was the first time he had seen her lose control.

"*Punka fagga haagya pungdaga!*" She screamed, teeth flashing, fists shaking, as she paced back and forth.

Kolgin sat on a stone with his hands on his knees, waiting.

"How could you LET him LEAVE?"

The sky was as gray as the dust and rubble, and the ring of blood formed a thin, dark undulation between the two, dividing earth and sky.

"Silas will return."

"*Punka bevjak,* you don't know that!" she spat at him.

He scraped the bristle of his lower lip against his teeth, watching. "He will be back."

"AAAAHHHHHHHGH!" she screamed, bending over her full belly, beating her thighs with her fists.

"He wants through that door as badly as you do. He'll come back."

She advanced on him. The whites of her eyes were pink, and the gold quivered with fever. Her skin had a sallowness that he had only ever seen on topaz addicts in the throws of withdrawal, and the strands of hair that escaped her head-wrap looked snarled and brittle.

"And *what will you do* if he does not return *in time?*" She stood over him. "You can't take his place. No one can! He's the only hundred-*bahuta damin* with the *rashni* to power a doorway. NO ONE else! No one! Do you understand???"

He waited.

"*SHANITI NE, FUCKING SHANITI NE!*" She spun away from him, raging at the empty air beyond the weave. "*NAHNKALA NAHNKALA NAHNKALA!*"

She was screaming at the ghosts again. Kolgrin couldn't see or hear them, but he did sometimes feel a wave of sickness when he crossed that writhing perimeter. Rahka was spending more time yelling at them every day, and sometimes, it seemed she wasn't yelling *at* them anymore, but *with* them.

"Do you understand?" she spun towards him again. "I need the hundred-soul man. I need the new soul of a bloodwitch child. I need the memory of the old door. And I need them *all*. Or *there is no new door* and it *does not open*."

"Silas will come back," Kolgrin said.

"You better be fucking right, *pungdaga.*"

For Silas' sake, Kolgrin hoped he was wrong.

Chapter 9

Soolie faced the Soul Hunter in her dreams. The blood between them twisted and rippled and changed and moved. The Hunter lifted a pleading hand and met her with golden child's eyes. Its mouth was a halo of starfire, its throat was a desperate emptiness, and its voice was silence.

∽

She sat in bed with Dog's head in her lap, combing her fingers through his hair as he slept. He hadn't wanted to sleep again, but she had commanded it. The roots of his nails were ragged and raw, and when she pulled back his lips, clotted black pockets rowed his gums. If he had been able to feed, he would have healed by now.

Her first priority should be finding something, someone, some *way* to eat. Then she needed to understand what the Dead Man had done to her and how it could be undone. Then there was the matter of finding a way to rid herself of the Soul Hunter for good, preferably without destroying herself in the process. Her mind was full of ladderless goals.

The doors swung in and the Dead Man entered carrying an ivory tray.

"I bring gifts!"

Dog startled up off her lap, pushing his back into the wall, legs tucked to his chest under the covers. So much for him getting rest.

"Is it food and our freedom?" she asked.

The Dead Man crossed to an open window, placed the tray on a bench, and faced the sun, basking and breathing deep. "You've never been a ghost, have you?" He turned towards her and the light gleamed copper in his dark curls. "The formlessness of it is a horror beyond anything you could ever know of pain. It never changes, it never ends."

"So, a lot like following you around yesterday," Soolie said, sliding a hand under the covers to touch Dog's cold forearm in a way that she hoped was reassuring.

"You miss the simplest things. Spending time walking from one place to the next. Being able to touch your own skin. The warmth of sunlight." He leaned back against the window ledge.

Dog cowered. She could feel him shivering.

"What do you want?"

"As I said," he motioned towards the tray beside him. "I brought gifts. I would have delivered them to your bed, but I was not sure that would be welcome. Receive them at your leisure. I am in no haste."

Then he was just going to have to wait.

Underneath the covers, Dog had no clothing, her torn pants were soaked, and they were both sitting in a marsh of blood. Despite her bindings, the wound had continued to ooze throughout the night, sopping the sheets that clung to their legs, wet and cold. Soolie had no interest in getting out of bed under the Dead Man's scrutiny. Unfortunately, sitting in bed while he basked, fully clothed in canary silk and sunlight, also made her feel at a disadvantage.

She scowled. "Where is your Wolf?"

He raised an eyebrow. "My *Chorus* is tending to my people in my absence."

Soolie snorted. "Like you did to the old man with the broken hand."

"That old man's name is Themai, and he is a gemsmith of rare skill," the Dead Man said. "In the right hands, even the hardest material can be broken to bring out its beauty. It is a craft that requires patience, precision, and a delicate balance of force and tenderness, much like shepherding a people. My Chorus is suited for many things, but tenderness is not one of them. I personally visited Themai in the Cradle last night. I fed his desire and allowed him to feel his pain. Then I guided him through letting it go. He is out of the Cradle now and resting. Once his hand is healed, he will return to the populace renewed. *You,*" he tilted his head at her, "would have *killed* him."

"Cradle is a fucked up name for a prison."

"You seem to forget very easily what great lengths I have gone to to free you," he said. "Your Soul Hunter is the only captive in my kingdom, which makes you," he nodded at her, "the only cell."

"So I guess everyone else came here of their own free will," she said.

He hopped up to sit on the window ledge and leaned forward. "Let us make a bargain. You get out of bed, and I'll answer one question."

"Is what you did to me permanent?"

"Both feet on the floor first."

Fine. She squeezed Dog's forearm and muttered, "Stay put."

He looked terrified as she pulled away and slid to the side of the mattress. She swung both feet over the edge and set them on the floor, but didn't stand.

"Is what you did to me permanent?"

"It is," he said. "You carry the Hunter, and there is nothing it wants more than to undo everything I have accomplished. I could not afford to take half-measures. The blood that binds you is strengthened, not by one, but by the melding of myriads of incipient souls. There is no other creature like it, and there is none better at weaving than I. That weave will stand the trials of time. There is nothing that can break it, though I know you have already tried." He nodded at the tray. "Would you like to know what I have brought you?"

Soolie stayed seated. "I have another question."

"Walk to the center of the floor, and I will answer it. Though," he raised a finger, "back away or try to trick me, and I will leave and take my gifts with me."

Perhaps it was best to play along a little bit. For now. She pushed the covers off her lap and stood. Her pants stuck unpleasantly and the dried blood crinkled on her bare skin. Her bound leg ached and dragged as she hobbled to the center of the room. She stopped and glared at him.

He looked her over, scratching his cheek and the length of his jaw. "I won't tell Marah what you've done to her good *stravi*."

"How do I feed Dog?"

He shrugged. "I don't know."

"Well, how does the Chorus feed?" she snapped.

"First to the bench," he pointed, "then I'll answer."

She stilted through the warm window light under his watchful gaze.

"Look at you," he grinned. "You're like a baby animal that I must coax from the shadows so I can tend to your wounds. I will be patient, and soon you will be eating from my hand."

"How does the Chorus feed?" she asked again.

"It doesn't. I gave the Chorus enough life at its creation to last millenia, and when it is done, it will decay. We do not feed on the souls of the living in Adon Bashti. There is the bounty of the land, and there is the Hunter's Heart, and I hold the Hunter's Heart." He hopped off the windowsill.

"Now that you have a body, won't it eventually heal wrong?" she asked.

He walked towards her. "In truth, I don't know how long this body will last. Your Dog," he nodded to the bed, "has outpaced my expectations, and since his creation, I have only continued to perfect my craft. I have spent millenia preparing a place and a body for this final glorious lifetime. It is the way of the corporeal that all are destined for eternal rot and suffering. There is no way to escape it. Unless," he stood over her, "we create a miracle." He put out his hand. "Now, be good and give me back my vial."

She had secured the vial with strips of cloth to keep the bandages tight. He was close—ruddy and clean and warm. She was very aware of how battered and bloody and cold she was. She glowered up at him.

"It looks like you have that tied quite tight," he said. "I would be loath to have it broken. May I?" He reached into the tray and took out a small pair of scissors.

"I can do it." Soolie snatched the scissors and went to the opposite end of the bench to prop her foot. She considered letting the vial fall, but thought better of it, snipped the strips that kept it fixed, twisted it out of the bandages, and held it out for him to take.

He received it with both hands, cupping hers in one palm and lifting the vial gently. She snatched her hand back and focused on stripping off the bloody bandages. She could feel the wound reopening as she dropped them to the floor.

"It won't stop bleeding without the proper administrations. It would be easiest if you allowed me . . . ."

"No." Soolie tossed the scissors clattering into the tray and yanked the soiled pants down over her hip bones, peeling the stuck cloth from her skin. New blood rushed into her leg, filling the wound and rivering down her thigh as she kicked the garment onto the tile.

He sat on the other end of the bench. "Blue bottle, corner of the tray nearest me. You'll want to spread the cut open with the fingers of one hand. Yes, like that. Now use the dropper to squeeze the liquid directly into the wound. That will slow the bleeding. Now, unfold the white cloth . . . ."

She followed his instructions. Many of the gifts he had brought were medicinal: an antidote to the black vial, a stack of damp cloths that smelled sharp and warmed her skin with a pleasant burning as she scrubbed away the blood, a bottle of white ooze that he had her squeeze into the wound 'to seal it.' There were also garments—tunic and pants—black for Dog and dark green-blue for her. The fabric rested soft and light on her skin, and Soolie noted the clothes were very like the ones that the Dead Man had chosen for himself.

"I thought the color would compliment the weave," he said, as she got dressed.

Dog watched from the bed.

"Now that you are mended and presentable," the Dead Man stood and brushed down his pants, "I actually have someone I would love for you to meet." He strode for the door, calling over his shoulder. "You can leave your Dog. I'm sure you want him to preserve his strength."

"Mistress?" Dog mewled.

The Dead Man was already out of the room and in the hallway.

She just needed to learn what he wanted to show her, and then she'd be back. Soolie trotted after him. "Stay. Clean yourself while I'm gone. I'll be back. I promise."

Dog clutched the bedsheets in his raw-nubbed fingers and watched her run out the door.

~

THE DEAD MAN led her in a new direction, and Soolie was again struck by the sheer size of the house and everything in it. He paused in front of a set of doors carved from dark berrywood, and looked over his shoulder to grin at her before pushing and striding through. Soolie braced herself for another lecture on window casings or water pipes and followed.

"TILLA! TILLA BENNIK!"

They entered a tower of a room, round and perhaps twelve stories high. Far above, the ceiling was painted in a wheeling sky of stars and moon and sun and clouds. Every other surface in all directions was filled with shelves upon shelves of books.

"Her name is Tilla *Thastrid,* and she's busy!" A woman's voice bounced back from an upper level.

"Mavi!" the Dead Man hollered back. "Fetch her! This is important. I have someone for her to meet!"

Soolie tried not to gawk. Books had been something of a luxury in Hob Glen. The ones Papa bought had been mostly for edification purposes, full of equations and dead people's names. Aunt Evaline had told her about libraries, and Soolie used to daydream about them—places with vast civilizations of stored knowledge and endless worlds, where you could get lost for days and learn anything you could possibly care to know. She had never imagined that so many books existed in all the world.

The Dead Man beamed. "Remarkable, isn't it?"

She shrugged.

"ADON." A dark, round head poked over a railing several stories up. "I SAID SHE'S BUSY."

"TILLA!" The Dead Man's bellowed, his voice echoing through the high hall.

"I TOLD YOU—"

"I'm coming!" A new voice responded, light and sweet.

Soolie sighted a flag of blue and blonde dashing around the balcony several floors up, and she wondered if the library extended beyond this room, and if so, how large it might actually be.

The dark haired woman threw up her hands and retreated from the rail.

For several minutes, the only sound was a flurry of fast steps down many, many stairs, then a woman rushed to the top of the main staircase that curled down to the floor, and Soolie guessed immediately why the Dead Man wanted her to meet Tilla Thastrid.

Tilla was dead.

~

"This is Tilla," the Dead Man said. "My bibliothecary."

"I'm the librarian." Tilla blushed and hunched over the stack of books that she hugged to her chest.

She was taller than them both, shrouded neck to ankle in a sack dress, with clumpy brown shoes, and hair slapped up in a snarled horsetail that fell to her waist. Despite this, the librarian had an unsettlingly and flawless beauty. Her skin was pale and spattered with freckles. Her lips were large and soft, her eyes ice-lake blue. She reminded Soolie of a doll. Tilla shuffled the stack in her arms, pushed a golden strand of hair off her forehead, and curtsied, avoiding the Dead Man's gaze.

"Greet one another!" the Dead Man prompted.

"Hello," Tilla stuck out a porcelain hand.

"Hi." Soolie shook it and saw the librarian flinch.

"Good!" The Dead Man clapped his hands. "Soolie is new to Adon Bashti and in need of company. Tilla is the only other soul who relies on me for feeding. I thought she might assuage some of your concerns," he flashed a grin at Soolie, "before you desiccate into a painful little lump, and I have no choice but to make choices for you."

Tilla shrugged and hugged her books. "It is not that bad."

"We enjoy ourselves," the Dead Man said.

"Oh, helloooo." The other woman rounded the balcony and stood at the top of the stair behind Tilla, wiggling her fingers in greeting.

"Mav," Tilla said, "don't."

"I'm Mavi."

Soolie waved back. Mavi looked much more comfortable. She had the body of a plum, round and plump, with skin nearly as dark, and wore a dress embroidered in big yellow starflowers. Mavi looked very alive.

"I'll leave you, then." The Dead Man placed a hand on Soolie's shoulder. "You can come here whenever you like. I only ask that you attend when I invite you to join me in the evenings. I do not think it would be good for us to be too long separated."

Soolie pushed his hand off. "Well, you do always know where I'm at."

"There is that." He smiled. "Ladies," he nodded to them and strode from the room.

Soolie looked up at Tilla and Mavi who, in turn, looked down at her. This meeting felt oddly like approaching a schoolhouse on the first day.

I've commanded men, she reminded herself. I've crossed oceans. I've destroyed souls.

"How old are you, Soolie?" Mavi asked.

"Don't talk to it." Tilla backed up, keeping herself between them. "It's clearly dead."

"Soolie, are you an *it*?" Mavi asked over Tilla's shoulder. Her voice was kind.

Soolie wasn't sure exactly how old she was. Did she keep aging after she died, even if her body didn't? She had a spring birthday, but seasons were different in the Southern Lands. For all she knew, she might be fifteen by now. She felt older.

"Twelve, I think," she lied.

"She's got one of those weave things on her." Mavi walked down the stairs to stand beside Tilla. "She doesn't look like one of Adon's monsters. Aren't you a little bit curious?"

"If Adon brought her here," Tilla whispered, "then she's dangerous. Especially for you."

"We don't know her story." Mavi put a hand on Tilla's arm. "Twelve years old?" She lowered her voice, "Don't you think she's a bit *young* for Adon's court? Do you really not want to give her a chance?"

Soolie widened her eyes and tried to look small. It wouldn't hurt to have an ally who could tell her something about this place. Maybe the librarian even knew something about blood magic.

Tilla looked at Soolie, then back to Mavi. "I don't feel comfortable . . ."

Mavi patted her arm. "That's okay. Leave it to me." She descended the last steps and smiled. "Sorry about that, Soolie. I'm Mavi. This is my wife Tilla. Can you drink coffee?"

"I wish!" Soolie tugged on the hem of her tunic. "My dad never let me, but I do like the smell."

Mavi cast a meaningful glance back at her wife. "So you're entirely reliant on Adon, then. You and Tilla will have to talk at some point, but you can chat with me first. Come on."

The balcony wound its way around the perimeter of the open space in a continuous ascending walkway. Mavi led Soolie on a more direct route up vertical twists of iron stairs that tied between the levels. Soolie followed, pausing for a moment to look straight down through the latticed steps to see Tilla close behind and the marble floor far below. After a couple levels, Mavi stepped off the stair and away from the balcony to lean against a shelf of neatly-stacked sheafs and scrolls.

"Phew! The stairs in this place," she shook her head, catching her breath. "Isn't it lovely, though? Tilla is the mind and map of it all. If you ever need to find a book, any book, I swear she knows the home of every author, title, and matter by heart."

"There are far too many for me to know all of them," Tilla mumbled.

"Are you still carrying those?" Mavi indicated the stack of books in her wife's arms. "Go put them away. It'll bother you until you do."

"I couldn't—"

"I'll be fine. I promise."

Tilla wavered. "I'll be fast."

Mavi shook her head as Tilla scurried off along the balcony, heading around to the other side of the great room. "She worries so much."

"She loves you," Soolie pointed out the obvious, and Mavi beamed at her for it.

"Yes, she does."

"That must be scary," Soolie rubbed a hand over her bald head. It was too bad she didn't have hair anymore. People liked children who had pretty hair. "For both of you."

"Oh, I don't know," Mavi started up the stairs again, leading with her arm on the rail to help herself up. "I try to stay in the moment."

They were gaining height quickly. The floor was already far below, but the ceiling was still far above.

"You're not all smiley like the other people," Soolie said, "and you talk to me. No one else talks to me."

"Most people aren't feeling quite themselves," Mavi said. "Tilla . . . protects me . . . from that. Ah, finally! Whooff."

She led Soolie away from the stairs and down a long corridor of tall shelves. The great open room really was only the beginning.

"It's easy to get lost in here," Mavi said. "If you're ever in doubt, look for a straight-a-way and follow the light. It'll lead you back to the main room. Aaaannd here we are."

Mavi opened a door and led Soolie into a small living room.

"Ohhhhh," Soolie gasped.

Mavi laughed. "It doesn't quite have his touch, does it?"

It didn't. A giant braid rug covered the floor, and colorful patch quilts draped the sagging couch and rocking chair. Every wall was hung with paintings and every surface was cluttered. There were books stacked in rickety columns, shoved between potted plants and piled on shelves. There were plants hanging from the ceiling in knotted nets, clippings in bottles that rowed the windowsills, and jars of paint everywhere, especially around the easel and canvas propped near the window.

Soolie ducked around the couch to see. The painting in progress was of a bundle of flowers in all stages of bright and blooming, budding and wilting.

"Is this *yours*?"

The brushstrokes were full of energy. Up close, they fell into a slap-splash of color, but when she pulled back, the forms of leaves and petals and seed pods took form.

"Do you like it?" Mavi dropped into the rocker.

"I LOVE it."

"I spent over a decade painting Adon's pretty little ornamentations all over this place. And now I grow plants and paint messy flowers. I call it my rainstorm period. All messy and growing." She leaned back, creaking the rocker. "I wish I could offer you something. It frets me to not put a cup or a biscuit in your hands."

"It's okay."

Soolie made a show of circling the room, going from painting to painting and plant to plant, oohing and aaahhhhing, before making her way to the couch. It was much softer than she thought it would be, and she sank into it and pulled one of the many quilts over her lap. She did like the room in a way. It reminded her of Aunt Evaline and another life. It was easy to behave self-conscious and silly here. She scrunched the blanket in her fists.

Mavi was watching. "How long have you been like this, if you don't mind?"

"I don't mind," Soolie smoothed the blanket out again. "Not long. And this blood thing that *Adon*," the Dead Man, "did to me is new."

"Do you know what it does?"

"Ties up a monster, I guess."

Mavi nodded. "Tilla could probably tell you more about it. Her knowledge of blood magic and all that nasty stuff is what attracted Adon to her in the first place. Well, that and her collection of dark books. Cursed stuff, " she chuckled. "She can't help herself. Tilla rescues books like they're kittens. The more outlawed or unwanted they are, the more she *has* to take them home. Used to be a head librarian for the Emerists until they found her private stash. What about you? How did you come here?"

Soolie picked at little nubbins on the blanket. "I don't know if I'm ready to talk about it yet."

"You can take your time."

The door opened, and Tilla stood in the entry.

"Tilla! Soolie and I were just sharing histories," Mavi said. "Do you want to come in and talk?"

Tilla was avoiding looking at Soolie. "Actually, this is all a bit fast, and I'm not comfortable with her being in our home, Mav."

"You're right, I pushed. I'm sorry." Mavi stood and offered Soolie a hand. "Do you like books?"

Mavi showed Soolie her favorite sections of the library, shelves upon shelves of books on plants, books on drawing, books on medicine, and books on myths. Mavi apologized that Tilla couldn't join them on the tour, explaining that her wife was very busy restoring a number of spines that had 'gotten nibbled,' as both mice and book-beetles were fond of the rice glue used in certain bindings, and that Tilla had crates of books in various stages of disrepair that she was painstakingly renewing one page, spine, and cover at a time. Soolie acted interested and chose not to point out the tall librarian lurking behind nearby shelves for the majority of Mavi's tour.

Eventually, Soolie hinted that she might want to do a bit of reading of her own, and Mavi left her to her devices.

Soolie placed herself cross-legged against a shelf of poetry and started flipping through a small book of hand-written sonnets while she waited. It only took a moment. She looked up to see Tilla standing nearby, pulling at her horsetail.

Soolie shut the book. "Mavi tells me that you know about blood weaves."

"I can't help you," the librarian said.

Soolie got to her feet. "I need to understand what the Dead Man did to me. I need to find a way to fix it."

"Stay away from Mavi." Tilla's nose flushed. "I know you've hurt people, and I know you're going to hurt people again. You won't find any help here."

"Point me to the right books, and I'll help myself."

From the ground floor of the library came the crack-creak of a door swinging open.

"I said *go*," Tilla hissed and retreated into the shelves.

Soolie sat back down with her book. If the librarian didn't *want* to help, Soolie would have to find a way to convince her.

The Chorus walked into view.

"Come to fetch me?" Soolie turned a page. This poem compared women to fish swimming up river to die. Poets were an odd bunch.

The Chorus held out a crisp, wax-sealed envelope and waited. It was wearing the red crown again. Why did the Dead Man put the crown on the Chorus? Did that serve a purpose?

Soolie studied it standing motionless, blood in its eyes, invitation in its hands. Perhaps placing the crown on the monster was a simple matter of safe-keeping. In the false memory, wearing the crown had been extraordinarily painful. If it hurt that much to wear in real life, the Chorus' head was probably the safest place for the Dead Man to leave it when he wasn't using it.

"Well, I'm not coming," she said and turned another page. "You'll have to go back without me."

It waited.

Then, after a minute, it turned, envelope in hand, and left.

~

It was iris-black outside the windows, every surface dusted in silver, when she returned. No light glowed beneath the bedroom door, and for a moment, she worried that Dog wouldn't be where she had left him. She entered to find him kneeling in a patch of moonlight, waiting.

He had dressed himself, rough-combed his hair and tied it back at the nape of his neck. He didn't look up, and she didn't turn on the light.

"I know I was gone a long time." She closed the door.

His brow was dark and low.

She went to him. "I found someone who knows about blood weaves. I'm going to convince her to help us."

"Mistress..." He glanced up and then back down.

"I know this is rot." She knelt and placed her hand on his cold bony one, and this time, he didn't recoil. "I do have good reason for what I am doing."

"I will always wait for you, Mistress," he murmured. "Dog obeys Mistress."

"It looks like you're healing." She lifted his hand to check the thin gray scales of his nails. That was surprising, but good. "We should file your teeth in the morning. Come on." She stood, still holding his hand. "Let's go to bed. I'm tired and hungry."

She led him to the bed and was pleased to see that the bloody sheets had been changed for clean ones that felt soft against her skin. He curled up beside her and laid his head on her chest, and she tucked the covers around his shoulders before closing her eyes.

The nighthummers thrummed, and the air moved gently through the room, and she slept.

He stayed awake listening to her silence and wondering—as he had spent all day wondering—why they were here in the old Master's house and why she kept leaving him alone. Did she not need him any more? Did she not want to command him? Was she not his Mistress? What had happened to the Ancient Mistress? Would he ever hear her voice again?

She slept and he stayed awake. As they lay together, he could feel her feeding him ever so slowly, a faint ebbing from her flesh to his, sharing of the meager life she had, helping him to slowly heal his wounds.

∽

"FUCKING ANCIENTS!"

"MAV!"

Mavi startled back against a bookshelf, and Tilla threw herself, arms outstretched, between them.

"GET OUT."

"It's okay, Til!" Mavi raised a hand. "I just . . . It startled me."

"No, it is NOT." The librarian's blue eyes flashed with fury. "GET OUT AND DON'T COME BACK."

"I'm sorry," Soolie offered.

Beside her, Dog waited, seeming neither startled nor surprised by this reaction to his presence.

"I know he looks scary," she said, "but he's good, I swear! He isn't one of the Dead Man's creatures. He belongs to me." She should have anticipated this. Of course some of the people would recognize Dog as a past servant of the Dead Man, but she hadn't wanted to leave him alone in the room again. He'd looked so meek and sad, and she'd wilted and brought him along.

"We *know what it is*," Tilla snapped. "Adon's DOG is not welcome here."

Despite herself, Soolie bristled. "He is MINE and bound to ME. Where I go, HE goes."

"You are *also* not welcome here. I want you *both out*."

"Tilbug," Mavi put a hand on her wife's forearm.

"Don't call me that right now."

"Tilla," Mavi said, "there are worse monsters that walk through these doors. And, look at him."

They both looked at Dog, his teeth and nails filed to nubbins, hair pulled back, simple black tunic and trousers, waiting.

"He does seem changed," Mavi said.

"A creature like that does not unlearn *lifetimes* of violence in a matter of moons."

Soolie held her ground. "I understand that he suffered greatly at the hand of Adon and Adon's people."

"Adon does not *have* people, because Adon does not *own* people," Tilla shot back. "Adon owns monsters. You say that it suffered, but it has the blood of thousands in its mouth. *They* suffered, and it stands while they are dead."

Soolie snorted. "Then they are the lucky ones."

"DON'T YOU—"

"TILLA," Mavi grabbed her wife's arm and pulled her back. "I also have a say in this."

"Mav . . ."

"Please," Mavi took Tilla's hands. "You should understand why I have a tender heart for dead things?"

Tilla bent to touch her forehead to Mavi's dark tight curls. "I can't have you getting hurt, Mav."

"I'll be fine." Mav kissed her forehead. "I promise."

Soolie waited.

"We disagree," Tilla said, wrapping an arm around Mavi's shoulders. "My wife makes her own decisions, but if one drop of her blood is spilled, I will crumble your bones on the wind."

Mavi smiled. "Tilla has work. Would either of you like to see my garden?"

∽

MAVI'S GARDEN was on a terrace adjacent to their home. Raised wooden boxes spilled over with purple tomatoes, green peppers, and yellow-ribbed gourds. Trellises dripped sugar peas and patches of herbs filled the air with basil, lavender, rosemary, and other delicious smells Soolie was less familiar with.

She held the garden can under the water spout while Mavi worked the handle until the pump gushed clear and filled the tin, cold and brimming.

"Thank you! It's so much easier with help." The woman accepted the can. "I never had a fertile touch before I came here, but everything grows in the Southern Lands. Adon brings all manner of seeds, and they take like weeds."

"Does Tilla eat?" Soolie asked.

"She can." Mavi sloshed over to a flat of strawberries and started showering the vines in swinging sweeps. "We share dinner most nights. It doesn't sustain her, though. She's like him in that way. They both need something more to keep them going. I've asked to go with her for those times, but she doesn't want me there. I try to respect that."

"They both need life from the Soul Hunter," Soolie said, following along the garden row.

"Yes . . . ." Mavi shook the last droplets from the can. "You know . . . my wife tells me many things, so I'm familiar with the legend of *Ikma na Sitari* and how its Heart came to reside in Adon's throne. How *you* come to know about the Soul Hunter is another question." She eyed Soolie. "Unless that's something you still aren't ready to talk about."

Soolie squirmed. "I'll tell you about it soon. I promise." So, the Hunter's Heart was in the Dead Man's throne. That explained why Soolie had felt it there calling to her.

"In your time." Mavi made her way past Soolie. "I'm sure the topic is tender and you've been through much. You were very passionate earlier in your defense of your friend."

Soolie glanced at Dog crouched against the wall of the house, watching. There wasn't much for him to do, but she was glad he wasn't sitting alone in a room by himself.

"Dog is my responsibility," Soolie said. "We understand one another."

"I only met him once when he served Adon. I recall a wild, shaking creature, raging on a leash of fear . . . ."

"The Dead Man was very mean to him," Soolie said, following Mavi back to the water pump. She needed to reroute this conversation away from herself and Dog until she'd had more time to decide what she wanted the women to know. She had to assume that anything she told Mavi she was also telling Tilla. "So," Soolie accepted the can, "you said that Tilla doesn't want you somewhere?"

"Did I? Oh, yes. When she has her meetings with Adon, she goes alone." Mavi placed her hands on the pump handle. "I can't tell you much about what happens between them, but Adon has an effect on people," she started hefting the handle up and down. "Some of that's . . . the drug . . . of course."

"Topaz."

"In its purest form," Mavi grunted, and water started to gush into the can. "That's what his feasts are for. People walk away happy, malleable, easily led . . . . I owe a lot to Tilla. If it wasn't for her, I'd be as giddy as the rest of them."

"She protects you?"

"Too much, sometimes, but there's only so much she can do. You can't trust your own thoughts in this place." Mavi accepted the can. "Adon has a way of getting into people's minds, always has, even before topaz, before he crafted that crown, even when he was just a myth and a force in this place, all of us working under the watch of monsters answering to something we couldn't see." She shook her head and smiled. "Those were horrible times. But love grows in the darkest of places."

Mavi was very transparent with the prompts she wanted to receive. "That's when you met," Soolie said.

"I was given the job of painting the library ceiling. What a horrible job!" she laughed, making her way to a bank of climbing vines. "But it was wonderful too. We used to take breaks together and eat lunch out on my plank-walk twelve stories in the air, back when we both liked turkey on rye and both could have tumbled to our deaths." Mavi rubbed her face against her sleeve. When she looked up again, her eyes were ruddy. "That's the thing with love. First it makes you invulnerable, then it makes you want to live, and suddenly dying becomes an awfully big deal."

"Mmmmmm." Soolie nodded as if what Mavi said meant anything at all.

"Anyways," Mavi sniffed. "I'm sorry I can't tell you much about her time with him. When Tilla comes back from visiting Adon, she comes back all giddy. She isn't the same for days."

"So, she is allowed to protect you," Soolie said, "but you aren't allowed to protect her."

"Oh, well. We take care of one another," Mavi said. "Now how about you tell me something about you."

Soolie glanced back to Dog. "I need Tilla to teach me about blood weaves."

"That will take trust," Mavi said, "and trust will take time."

Soolie didn't know if they had time.

"And," Mavi added, "it may require you to trust us in return."

~

SOOLIE STAYED all day assisting Mavi in the garden, watching her paint, and helping prepare honey-roasted squash with a fresh herb salad and black oil flatbread for dinner. Dog watched from a distance. At one point, Mavi asked him directly how he was doing, and he looked to Soolie, who responded that he was doing fine.

There was a small, two-person table in the kitchen, and Soolie was helping place the settings when Tilla entered smelling of leather and glue.

"What is she still doing here?"

"Tilla," Mavi handed Soolie the second steaming plate, a smaller portion for her wife. "Soolie has been helping me."

Soolie set the plate between the knife and fork, and smiled and waved.

"Perhaps," Mavi suggested, bringing over a tall glass of water for herself, "she could help you in your workshop tomorrow."

"I'm good with a needle and thread," Soolie offered. "My Papa was a cobbler."

Tilla walked past Soolie and took a seat, shoulders hunched, cheeks pink. Dog stood in the doorway to the living room. Soolie laced her hands in front of her, waiting and watching as Tilla picked up her fork and started ripping little ravines in her squash with the tines.

Mavi sat down opposite. "Would you like to grab a chair, Soolie?"

"Oh?" Soolie looked around. "I didn't see . . . ?"

"In the living room," Mav shoved her chair back. "I can help."

"Mav," Tilla whispered.

"Actually, it's probably time for me to go," Soolie said, and a look of relief washed over both women's faces.

"I'll show you out." Tilla's fork clattered on her plate.

"Thank you for your help today." Mavi stood to offer an open arm, but Tilla was already sweeping Soolie towards the living room.

"See you tomorrow!" Soolie hollered. "I had a lovely time!"

Tilla shut the door that separated the apartment from the library behind them.

They walked in silence down the hall of books and around the balcony to the twisting vertical stairs.

Halfway down in between levels, Tilla turned. "What do you want?"

Soolie was ready. "I need you to teach me about blood magic."

Tilla took one step up towards Soolie, her hands on the rails, their heads level. "Is that why you're sweeting up to Mavi?"

"Mavi is very nice."

"Stop coming here."

"I'd be glad to occupy myself with learning instead, but if no one will teach me," Soolie held her ground, "then I really don't have anything better to do than enjoy your wife's lovely company."

Tilla's eyes blazed and her cheeks flushed. "Threats will get you nowhere."

"I'm just looking to make a friend." Soolie blinked and tried to look sad. She felt a lot less successful with Tilla than she did with Mavi.

"You already have one waiting for you." Tilla pointed down and Soolie looked.

The Chorus was on the ground floor.

"Return to the room and stay there until I get back."

Pain quivered in his eyes. "Mistress."

"Obey."

It would be easier to do what she needed to if she didn't have to worry about him. She was relieved to see that he had started to heal somehow, but she was beginning to feel the harsh ravages of hunger, her flesh shrinking, her spirit screaming for the life of the living souls that she could no longer take. She needed to make concessions and buy them time.

It was time to go to the Dead Man.

The throne room was a riot of color and sound, packed with feasting and revelry, thrumming stringed instruments and rumbling drums. Down the center aisle, a spectacle of stilt dancers flipped a small child hand-to-hand, up onto their shoulders, down between long legs, then vaulting into the air to be caught in a net of arms.

"Soolie!" The Dead Man's voice belled over the festivities. The music silenced and the people stilled. "You came!"

The dancers parted like wary cranes, and Soolie saw that the child was actually a grizzled little man. She was fairly certain she had seen children in the town, but none in the great house. Perhaps the Dead Man didn't care for children.

He stood to greet her. He was garbed in purple tonight, and his smile was as white as the spires of his throne. He spread his arms wide. "And you are clothed this time." Laughter burbled through the assembly. "I hope that means you came willingly and my servant did not handle you harshly."

Soolie held her chin high. "Your Chorus treated me well, Adon sen Yevah, and I came at its invitation."

"There is no need for such formality. You are my guest." He sat back on the throne, and the beautiful people gathered about him. "What is it that brings you to me?"

Soolie bit her tongue. He already knew what she wanted and why she had come. She curtsied. "Only to feast with you and your people, if you would have me."

"Are you hungry?"

She seethed.

"There is no shame in need." He leaned back. "But I know you value your autonomy, so I will not give what is not requested."

Wasn't it only yesterday he had threatened to make decisions *for her?* She thought of Dog waiting in the room, no doubt as hungry as she was. Feeding herself would at least be a start.

"Yes. I am hungry."

"I see," he said. The room watched. "And what is it that you wish for me to do?"

She tried very hard not to scowl. She could do this, because she had to. "You have shown your generosity. I only ask—"

"What," he interrupted, "do you *want*, little dead girl. Tell me."

"I would like for you to feed me. Please."

"Then, approach."

She would manage with what dignity she could, she would get the life that she needed, and then she would leave. One step at a time, she crossed the room with all eyes on her, through the corridor of stilt dancers, approaching where he sat among the beautiful people with their simpering smiles and softly twined limbs.

As she drew near, she began to feel the undeniable pull of the Hunter's Heart, calling from the throne and from him, and she still needed it.

She steadied the pacing of her feet, suddenly very aware of how fast she was walking. She had thought that, with the Hunter bound, she wouldn't feel it quite so strongly, but the pull was more demanding than ever. The emptiness in the Hunter's being was intensely tangible, as if a horrible void was eating her away, and the need to fill it was so powerful, it threatened to pull her apart.

She was coming undone. She stopped at the foot of the dais.

"Come closer," he said.

She didn't know if she could. She didn't know how to move and resist at the same time. Everything in the room blurred except him sitting on the throne, legs spread, hands on his thighs, waiting.

She was breathless despite having no need to breathe.

"You can do it. Come here."

One step. Another. Up the dais to stand before his throne. Her resolve was melting like thin ice over deeply rushing water.

"Closer. Kneel."

It was easy to fall at his feet.

He leaned forward, and as he did, she saw that the back of the throne moved like the knots of the talon thimble, and he cupped her head in both of his hands and directed her eyes to him. He was warmth and light. He had everything that she needed. His dark eyes softened.

"I only wish you had asked me sooner," he said, "so I wouldn't have to do this."

His hands grew roots that ripped into her and took, wringing her soul, raking her body, *devouring*. She shriveled, veins collapsing, flesh stiffening, all suffering.

"Shhhhhh. I know it hurts," he embraced her as she gasped in shock and pain, and he whispered in her ear. "The next time I send for you, you will come."

He released her, and she collapsed between his feet. The agony was blinding, the need overwhelming.

"For now, I will let you feel your pain. You may leave."

She pushed herself slowly back from the throne to the edge of the stair, pulling her feet under her and barely standing.

"Where is my music? This is a celebration!"

The instruments swung to life. The stilt dancers began to tilt and spin around her as she tottered the long path to the door. She leaned on the bright silver panel, and the red eyes of the Chorus looked through her as she grabbed the handle with both hands, dragged the door back and slipped through, letting it close behind her.

The rage that came was not a powerful force, but a helpless fury. At what he had done to her. At what she had submitted to letting him do.

She tried to run and couldn't. Her muscles were brittle thorns upon her bones. Every step was a monumental feat, and she leaned into the pain, and pushed through the simple door and into the Cradle's hall of many rooms.

He had forced her to submit and taken her strength from her.

She labored down the hall, found a closed door, and pushed in.

A living body lay upon the table. Gray beard bristled through the lattice of the head cage. Its limbs were bound. Its belly was a warm mound of muslin.

She stumbled forward and threw herself upon it, her cheek and hands upon the warm rise and fall of its breathing flesh. It moaned in reply, and she felt the life that she needed brewing inside of it, and she pulled at it, bunching the cloth of the shirt in her fists and then in her teeth, biting and straining, but the life did not budge. The body made a wobbly wailing sound, and she released the cloth from her jaws and shrieked.

In a frenzy, she tore the shirt back from its bare flesh. The belly was pale and soft and hair-grizzled and warm, and she scrabbled at it, lashing pink stripes with her small nails, and she screamed and it screamed with her as she clawed her way on top of it, scratching and digging at the life-throbbing flesh until it caked under her fingernails and the skin striped red and wet, and she took a warm bulge between her teeth, blood slick on her chin, and bit down with all her strength, pincering and tearing, and a wad of limp, warm, hairy meat came loose in her mouth, and she gnashed it and spat it out, and licked at the pooling blood, and it was nothing, nothing, nothing, and gave her nothing that she needed. And some of the blood was thick and cold, and she realized it was her own, because she had started to cry, and she collapsed her face upon the sticky mangled mound and wailed her pain, and frustration, and helplessness, and exhaustion, and hunger.

She was only half conscious when the Dead Man found her.

"I know," he said.

He sat her up and turned her to face him. She was barely aware of how he pulled her close, and wrapped her legs around his waist, and lifted her to his chest, her bloody arms around his neck, her bloody face upon his shoulder.

"It is only for a time."

She was barely aware when he carried her down the hallway and through the house, and when he delivered her to the room and laid her in the bed, she wasn't aware of it at all.

He smiled at Dog standing small and dark in the center of the room, and pulled the covers up to her waist. "How long do you think, until she is mine?" He cupped her wrist in his hand and rubbed a thumb over the blood that writhed over her shrunken veins. "Not long, I think."

Dog growled, but the sound was high and thin.

"On the day she submits to me, yours is the first memory I will take from her." The Dead Man lifted her hand and kissed the blood-marred fingers. "And when she no longer remembers you, she will hold my hand and smile as my Chorus tears you flesh from flesh and bone from bone, and this time there will be no door for you to escape through."

Dog quivered and didn't move as the Dead Man rested her hand on the coverlet and gave it a little squeeze goodbye.

On his way out the door, the Dead Man paused. "How strange it must be for you to run so far, only to come right back and find that you are still your Master's Dog."

He chuckled, turned the lamps off, and left, closing the door behind him.

For a long while, Dog didn't move. He stayed standing in the middle of the room in the dark, watching the door, and shaking.

Chapter 10

"I can't believe you're mad at me."

"I'm not *mad*. I'm scared."

Tilla hunched in the middle of the room. Mavi sat with her legs tucked up on the couch, her buttered toast on the low table growing soggy next to her coffee growing cold. Tilla hadn't meant to start a fight, but she'd been withdrawn since last night, and Mavi had finally asked what was wrong, and it had all come tumbling out.

"Do you understand how precious you are to me?"

"I know," Mavi said.

"So, doesn't it make sense that it would worry me to see you putting yourself at risk like this?"

"I can't be unkind to people just because you're scared," Mavi said quietly.

"They're not *people,* Mav." Tilla crouched beside the couch and clasped Mavi's hand in her own. She loved these hands. Loved the paint spatters on the backs, the dirt under the nails. They were warm, creative, loving, just like Mav was . . . .

"Oh, Tilbug, are you crying?"

Tilla shook her head and sniffed. "Don't . . ."

"Okay...." Mav untucked her feet over the side of the couch and leaned in, gently worried.

Tilla didn't like how easily her face flushed and her eyes wept. That hadn't been her choice. She swallowed, blinking, studying Mav's dirt-crescent nails. "The blood in that weave is Chorus blood, Mav. So whatever it is, it's something incredibly dangerous and valuable to Adon. Even if it doesn't hurt us directly, anything it knows about us, and anything we know about it, puts us at harm's risk." She looked up, and as soon as she met Mav's eyes, her own immediately overflowed. "We can't learn anything about it—anything that he might want—because he'll take it, Mav, he'll take it, and I won't be able to stop him...."

She was sobbing now. She hated that she was, but she let Mavi wrap her arms around her and hold her tight.

"What if we took the day?" Mavi offered. "We could leave the house and go into town. Walk around, visit the markets, just the two of us?"

"Yes," Tilla accepted the handkerchief her wife handed her. "That sounds nice."

The trouble was, Tilla knew, it was probably already too late. Whatever this thing was, it had been spending time with them, and Adon would want to know. He would come for them.

***

"NONE of these are written in Midland. I can't even understand them."

Soolie shoved the stack of manuscripts back at Dog and collapsed back against the side of the bed with a groan. "I *know* she has the information we need. I just have to figure out how to get it."

"Yes, Mistress," he said.

He returned the books to the bedside table and waited for her next command, hands clasped, avoiding her gaze. He shuffled his toes in the layer of wadded undergarments and clothing that littered the floor. She hated that she couldn't read his feelings any more.

"You're acting funny. Did something happen while I was asleep?"

"Mistress is hurt," he said.

"Yeah, this is fucking rot." She was haggard and shrunken, and every movement was a struggle, but she'd been starved before. She couldn't help feeling something else was bothering him. "The Dead Man didn't do something to you last night, did he?"

"No, Mistress."

"Hmmm." He always had been sensitive to her weakness. "Hand me that box in the closet. If this librarian is hiding anything we can use, this is our chance to try to find it."

～

THEY RIFLED through baskets and cupboards, checking in every book and behind every piece of furniture. Soolie had Dog put everything back exactly as they'd found it, though the rooms were messy enough that they could probably steal any number of trinkets, and it would take several moons before either of the women noticed anything amiss.

Unfortunately, nothing they found had been worth their effort.

Most of the reading materials were bundles of cord-laced personal letters, and more than half of those were in a language Soolie couldn't read. The ones she could read gave dreary accounts of long treks over hostile lands, fragile negotiations between warring families, and endless bedridden days. They might make decent reading for a historical scholar, but there was nothing about blood magic or dead souls.

The only possible item of interest was in a box of keepsakes tucked in the back of a closet. The box contained a dirty paintbrush, several love letters, and a hand-size portrait of Mavi with her arm around a little bald man with small glasses and an awkward smile. All the paintings hanging on the walls of the home were of plants and scenery and birds. This was the only picture of either of the women. Soolie wasn't exactly sure what that meant, but she had a guess, and she marked it in her mind.

As her last act in the home, Soolie filled a bucket from the terrace pump, peeled off her bloody clothes, and shoved them burbling under the surface. By now, it was afternoon and the sun was hot and the water was underground-cold.

"We're not going to learn anything without her help." She washed her blood-crusted face with the cold wad of her shirt. "She's protective of her wife, and her wife feels sorry for me. There has to be a way to use that." Soolie scrubbed her scalp and throat. "I bet they're not here, because they're avoiding us."

She tossed her wet pants at him, and he caught them and twisted out the water. "I may be able to track them, Mistress."

"Good. Did I miss any spots?" She turned her head one way and then the other so he could get a good look.

"Yes, Mistress. There is still—"

"Get it for me."

She lifted her chin, and he hunched forward with the damp pants to scrub the side of her neck under her ear. She held still until he backed up and bowed.

"Done, Mistress."

She shoved her arms into the wet shirt and dropped it over her head. She had hoped it would wash clean, but the front was still stained dark with blood. At least it would dry quickly in the sun.

"I have an aim that we can try." She accepted the pants and tugged them on over her sandaled feet. "To start, we should act more friendly towards one another, and you should act more human."

He quirked his eyebrows.

"They're scared of you, because of your past, right?" She tied the waist strings. "So we need to separate you from that past. Mavi will be our focus. She's letting her feelings for Tilla color her feelings for us. She wants to care for me, because she cares for Tilla, and she wants to protect me, because she can't protect Tilla. So the more you and I remind her of her and Tilla, the better. Don't worry."

He looked worried.

She twisted the wet hair bracelet so the adorning tooth was on the top of her wrist. "I'll take the lead. We'll start slow."

～

"Soolie!"

Soolie looked up from a bolt of gold and purple cloth. "Oh, hi!"

"What are you doing at the market?" Mavi wove through the flow of people, shopping basket on one arm, towing Tilla behind her. "I didn't think I'd get to see you today!" She put out an arm to offer a hug and halted abruptly, eyes widening as she took in Soolie's newly wizened features. "Oh . . ."

Soolie shrugged and smiled weakly. "I had a bit of a mishap."

"Is that . . ." Mavi's eyes lowered to the front of Soolie's shirt.

"Blood," Soolie apologized. "I know I look a sight. I came here hoping to get a change of clothes, but I think I scare people."

"Mavi," Tilla hissed, leaning in, clutching the shoulder straps of her shopping pack, "can I talk to you for a moment?"

"One tic," Mavi said to Soolie, and the two women retreated to the far end of the stall to huddle heads.

Soolie grinned at the stall tender. "This is very pretty." She held up the cloth.

The tender was too busy sorting a pile of buttons that probably didn't need sorting to respond. It seemed like Mavi was the only living soul in this place that was willing to talk to her.

Soolie angled towards Dog and muttered, "Can you hear what they are saying?"

He dipped his head to whisper, "You said today was going to be just for us. I know, but I'm not okay abandoning someone who may need our help. They're manipulating you, Mav. Mav. Mavi . . ."

Soolie lifted a hand slightly to signal him to stop, and held the cloth up to her face. "What do you think?"

His eyebrows bunched, confused.

She glared at him. They had talked about this. She wrapped the cloth over her head like a shawl. "Well?"

"Whatever Mistress wants . . ."

"Ugh, you hate it," she scowled and tossed it back on the stack of bolts.

His dark eyes rounded with alarm. "Mistress, I would never—"

"No, you're right," she sighed. "All that frilly gold spak isn't me. I'm just frustrated I had to go and ruin perfectly good clothing. I should have taken them off before I experimented like that . . . ."

"Can I ask what happened?" Mavi approached with Tilla at her side.

"Oh," Soolie turned, backing up into Dog and rubbing her head. "I had a disagreement with the Dead Man last night. I don't know if folks talk . . . ."

Soolie Beetch and the Binding Blood

"We don't catch a lot of gossip," Mavi said. "Folks talk, just—"

"Not to you," Soolie finished.

"Not often, no." Mavi said. "Did Adon hurt you? You don't have to tell us about it if you don't want to."

Soolie looked at Dog as if for reassurance. He looked back, bewildered and useless. "No, it's okay," Soolie said. "I've been hungry lately, but I can't eat. Whatever Adon did last night made me feel really, really hungry and it hurt a lot. I just . . ." She shivered and looked at her toes. "Afterwards I got all overwhelmed and scared and . . ." She laughed bitterly and rubbed her eyes. "Turns out you can't *cut out* a blood weave. *Now* I know. I'm afraid I ruined another set of clothes."

"Oh, my dear." Mavi's hand was over her heart. "Can I hug you? Would that be all right?"

"I guess." Soolie sniffed.

Mavi bundled her in a tight-cushion hug. She smelled like onions. Soolie hugged back and stifled a small sound.

"Did I hurt you?"

"Sorry. Maybe I'm just a little fragile."

"Of *course* you are. I always hug too tight."

"No, it was nice!" Soolie laughed. "I haven't had a good hug in a really long time. Dog and I are all bony."

Dog and Tilla stood a pace away on either side, watching.

"I have good hugs in abundance and, since our paths have crossed," Mavi held Soolie out at arms' length, "why don't we help you find new clothes? If you want something to wear *today*, let's not start with the material. We can find something pre-made."

"I don't have any money," Soolie apologized, following Mavi into the crowd.

"No one uses money in Adon Bashti, dear! Come with me. I'll do the barter."

∼

"Are you sure, just the black?"

Mavi rolled out a small quilt in the shade of a giant-leaf tree. They were in a patch of green in the middle of the city, rolling grass, towering trees, there was even a wading pool surrounded by large white rocks. Adults and children sat on the hillside, splashed in the water, and lounged like serpents in the sun.

"Yes, please," Soolie said. She had picked out a simple shift. "I'm so messy, and this way I don't have to worry so much." She plopped down on the grass and patted a spot next to her. Dog obediently bent into a crouch, and she tugged on his tunic until he tipped back and sat hard, sticking his legs out in front of him. "This place is so pretty . . . ." She placed one hand on the ground behind him so they sat fondly close.

"You could almost forget the blood and suffering that laid its foundation," Tilla muttered, propping her rucksack against the base of the tree.

Mavi was pulling paper-wrapped packets and a stoppered bottle from her basket. "I feel terrible eating in front of you. I know you are starving."

"I don't mind," Soolie said. "It's not your fault."

"How did you feed yourself before?" Tilla asked, accepting a packet and sitting on the blanket. "Killing people?"

The low warning rumbled in Dog's chest.

"It's okay." Soolie patted his leg. "She's right to ask." She turned to Tilla and Mavi. "And you're right to not trust me. I . . . did kill someone, early on." She looked down. "Not on purpose. I didn't understand what was happening. He made me angry, and I punched him in the face, and he . . ." She looked up blearily. She shouldn't cry. Crying would create blood tears that would make her look less human. "They called me a bloodwitch and trapped us in the barn. Papa and Aunt Evaline told me to run. If it wasn't for Dog, I don't think I would have made it. He helped me escape."

"Did he." Tilla's voice was slate. She unfolded the paper on her lap, revealing a hunk of bread stuffed with green herbs, white cheese, and slices of red tomato.

Soolie nodded. "He was running too. We've been together ever since."

"A dog like him needs a master," Tilla said.

Mavi opened a mouth full of sandwich to object, but Soolie cut in quickly. "That's not very kind." She bit her lip. "I know he's done bad things, but so have I. I didn't want to, and I don't think he wanted to either."

"Can he speak for himself?"

Mavi chewed and swallowed. "Tilla . . ."

"He can do whatever he wants to." Soolie looked at Dog, prompting.

He looked first at her, then at the two women. "Mistress . . ." This was the part they had practiced. "Mistress is helping me . . . I am learning . . . that it is hard to feel the pain you cause *others* when you are feeling so much of your own." He hesitated.

Soolie placed a hand on his leg and squeezed. He met her eyes, and she nodded.

Dog continued. "With Mistress, I am able to feel less of my own pain, but more of the pain that others feel. There is still a lot of pain, but it is different. Mistress shows me what else is possible."

Soolie beamed at him. Perfect.

"That's really powerful," Mavi said, looking at Tilla as she spoke.

Soolie squirmed. "I'm sorry we keep hanging around. I know we're not entirely welcome. It's just . . . no one else will talk to us. And . . . I really need to learn more about what the Dead Man has done to me, and I think you know."

Tilla bundled her untouched sandwich back up and stuffed it in the basket. "He removed your talons and your teeth so you can't kill innocent people."

Soolie drooped her head and felt Dog place a bony arm around her shoulders as if comforting her. He wasn't even growling.

"Tilla . . ."

"I'm not hungry."

~

THE WOMEN WERE FIGHTING, though not with words yet. They needed to get home and away from Soolie and Dog so they could talk, but they couldn't head home yet, because they were fighting. Tilla wanted to leave Soolie and Dog behind as quickly as possible, and Mavi was pointedly prolonging the outing while Soolie eagerly thanked her for every moment and kindness.

Mavi had pulled out a game called *kleche* that Soolie said was very exciting. It involved an interlocking board of wooden triangles and little bone coins that you moved, either off the points of the triangles or off the sides, depending on the dice. The goal was to get the most coins. Soolie won the first time, but Mavi won soundly the next two times. At her encouragement, Dog played, and lost, but Mavi said he still did very well. Tilla spent the time reading.

It was very exhausting to be so interested and grateful, but Soolie didn't dare let up for a moment as the shadows stretched and the sun slid towards the horizon. It was just as the light was losing all form between the mountains and Tilla was looking up from her book and saying "We should be getting back," that a cheer went up from the heart of the city.

"NOW," Tilla said.

Soolie jumped to her feet, Dog at her side.

Tilla was helping Mavi toss game pieces into the basket, rolling up the blanket and stuffing it into the rucksack.

"No need to panic," Mavi said, hefting the basket. "It might just be a street performer."

"Run." Tilla slung the rucksack onto her back without tying it closed. She placed one hand on Mavi's shoulder, hustling them both up the grassy hill.

Soolie whimpered, struggling against her withered flesh, unable to keep up, even with Dog's arm helping her.

"Mavi!" Tilla exclaimed.

Mavi was running back down the hill. "We can't *leave them*, Tilla."

"WE CAN!"

Mavi supported Soolie's other side, helping Dog hurry her along.

"*YOU'RE* the most vulnerable, Mav!" Tilla was flapping her hands. "You can't *stop him. You can't help them. MAVI!*"

"NO!" Mavi gripped Soolie's arm too tightly, jostling her and glaring at her wife. "I WILL NOT LIVE by sacrificing others, Tilla, I WON'T."

"You should go," Soolie said, stumbling and leaning on the living woman.

"No," Mavi huffed. "We live in his kingdom. We can't avoid him forever. If we get away today, we get away together."

"Thank you," Soolie said.

It wasn't possible for them to get away together. The Dead Man knew exactly where Soolie was. In fact, she was counting on it.

They struggled up the hill, Tilla in the lead, Dog, Soolie, and Mavi shoulder to shoulder following behind. When they reached the top of the hill, the Dead Man was waiting.

∽

"Tilla, Mavi, Soolie! It is good to see you." The Dead Man went first to Tilla and embraced her, kissing her on the cheek, then approaching Soolie, Mavi, and Dog, arms wide.

Soolie whimpered, and Mavi put an arm around her. "Hello, Adon."

He stopped just in front of them, arms still out. "Soolie. You've spent every day with these two since I introduced you. I am glad to see you getting along so well. You must have found a lot in common."

Soolie shrank to Mavi's side.

"We were just heading back," Tilla said.

"I'll walk with you." He stepped in beside Soolie, shoving Dog aside with easy assumption and taking her arm. "Soolie, you look so tired. Would you like me to carry you again?"

"No thank you." Soolie turned her head away, eyes on Mavi.

Dog followed.

"Adon, I actually had a book that I would love to discuss with you." Tilla was walking backwards up ahead. "Would you care to join me?"

He moved a hand to the small of Soolie's back, supporting her as they walked. "I will look forward to it at another time," he said. "I just came in person to invite Soolie to join me in the hall. She has visited, but not yet had the opportunity to stay and enjoy the festivities."

Soolie answered in a small voice, "I don't want to."

"What was that?"

"I said," Soolie raised her voice just a little, "I'd rather stay with Mavi and Tilla."

Up ahead, Tilla's face drained white with fear.

"Of course," the Dead Man said. "They are *welcome* to come."

∽

THE DEAD MAN pushed the bright doors open to a dark room. As he stepped in, gas torches flamed, filling the room with light that glistered off the ceiling and gleamed off the floor, and a sea of waiting subjects stood in a wave of joyful applause as music filled the air. The beautiful people opened around the throne like petals around the heart of a flower and reached for him, beckoning.

The Dead Man turned back to Soolie and the women. "I am afraid dogs have to wait outside."

The Chorus stepped out from the entry, barring Dog's way and backing him towards the open door.

"You understand," the Dead Man said.

The Chorus advanced until Dog was standing in the hall outside the throne room. It closed the doors, shutting him out.

"You are all my guests," the Dead Man said. "I unfortunately do not have room at my throne for all of you, but please do make yourselves welcome." He gestured to a nearby table with two empty seats already prepared. "Soolie?" He extended a warm, life-giving hand. "Will you join me?"

Soolie shrank back, huddling in Mavi's arms. She *wanted* to take his hand. She was beyond death and dying, and she needed it. But she couldn't. Not yet. She took a step towards the empty chairs, pulling Mavi with her.

"I will sit with you, Adon," Tilla said. "If you will have me, of course."

Adon watched Soolie, eyes tightening. Then his smile flexed, and he shifted his outreached hand only slightly, to Mavi.

"I don't believe you and I have spent enough time together, Mavi Thastrid."

Tilla stepped forward hastily. "I would be honored—"

"Mavi," he commanded.

Mavi released Soolie, making eye contact with her wife beyond him. "I'll be okay." She took the Dead Man's hand.

He lifted her hand to his lips and kissed her fingers. "You can leave the basket, my dear."

Tilla stood next to the abandoned basket as the Dead Man ushered Mavi toward the throne. Her hand rested on his as if he was leading her in a dance, and she looked up at him, smiling.

Soolie sat at the table. A man in white delivered a goblet filled with something fizzy and pink that she couldn't drink.

They reached the throne, and Tilla still hadn't moved. The Dead Man was laughing and he leaned in and whispered something to Mavi, who beamed back. He spread his arms, and a man and a woman stepped up to unfasten his tunic and take it away. He stood shirtless, his muscles mounded and soft, and when he turned toward the throne and offered Mavi his arm again, Soolie saw that his back was covered in twists and turns like the blood in her skin, but moving in a different way, and she felt the sudden desire to wrap her small cold body to his broad warm back, to cling to him bare-bellied and fuse her skin to his skin. The blood was familiar, and the way it moved stoked her hunger. He stepped towards the throne, and the writhing on his back and the writhing in the throne began to move the same.

Need seized Soolie with new ferocity. Her hands clamped on the edge of the table, and she vised her teeth so she thought they might crack. The blood on his back and the bones of the throne turned and danced a pairing dance, and the cry of the Hunter's Heart deafened her senses. He was connecting to the Heart through the throne. Her mouth was open. Her eyes were miring with bloody tears.

He turned and stood before his throne, taking both of Mavi's hands in his.

"SOOLIE." Tilla's hand smacked the table, her face close, her eyes weeping and fierce. "*Stop this, please.*"

Soolie was a knot of need. This was the moment for her to press her advantage, but she was struggling to speak. It was taking all her strength to hold her ground and not run to him.

"*Please!*" The librarian gripped her by the shoulders. "You can stop this, please, please. You *know* you have to say 'yes' to him eventually. For you, it's inevitable. But for her, she'll lose herself. He'll take something from her that she'll *never* get back. *Please. I'll do anything. Please.*"

The librarian was sinking to the floor now, clawing at Soolie's lap, begging even as Mavi knelt before the Dead Man.

Soolie forced the words tight through her throat. "Teach me."

"*Anything.*"

"Promise."

"You have my word. *Please, now, please.*"

The Dead Man was starting to lower himself into the throne, and Soolie shakily stood to her feet.

"Forgive me."

"Soolie?" He straightened.

She stumbled forward. "I was wrong." It was easy to be weak and show the depths of her desperation. Her feet betrayed her completely, and she collapsed in the middle of the floor. She reached for him. "Please forgive me."

He passed Mavi off to waiting arms that handled her off the dais looking dazed and glitter-eyed as Tilla rushed to her side. Soolie was barely aware.

He was looking at her. "My grace is not infinite. My generosity is not unlimited. I will not be tested by you."

She let herself crumple wounded on the floor, bloody tears running down her face. Again she raised a frail hand to reach for him. He seemed to glow like gold in the sun, and the throne shone bright behind him.

"I'm sorry." It was barely a whisper.

He waited.

"I won't disobey again."

"Come to me."

She dragged herself, arm by arm towards the throne. She would have run if she could, but suddenly she could hardly move. As she reached the edge of the dais, hands reached down to help her up, and they were his hands.

He lifted her chin and wiped the blood tears on her cheek with his thumb. "Come on."

With his hands holding hers, she was able to stand again. He led her towards the throne and pulled her into his chest and wrapped her in his strong life-giving arms. She was so frail and small, and he was powerful and gentle, and his body thrummed with everything that she needed, and she pushed herself against him.

"I'm sorry," she whispered again.

He scooped up her legs, and she wrapped her arms around his neck.

"Don't touch the back of the throne." His lips brushed the bare skin of her head as he spoke. "It will hurt you. Hold tight to me."

She clung to him, and he sat upon the throne, and as the magic in his body touched the magic in the throne, he became a part of the Hunter's Heart. Its pure light, a piece of the infinite, flowed through him, and she could feel its power at her edges and—for a moment—he kept it from her, and she shook, whimpering, digging her nails into his shoulder, unable to even form words to beg for him to release her.

"Yes," he whispered.

And at last, when she was far, far beyond herself, he gave her life.

In that moment, she knew only him. He was a part of the Heart, and she was a part of him, and he was light, and he was life, and he filled her and healed her, and she clung to him and was reborn.

～

THE DOOR CRACKED OPEN, spilling golden light and sound. Dog scrambled to his feet as the Wolf's pale hands delivered a bundle onto the floor. The hands retreated and the great doors closed.

The bundle was her.

He ran and knelt at her side. "Mistress?"

She lay curled like a baby, and she turned towards him, eyes half closed, face bathed in bloody tears, and giggled.

"Are you okay?"

"Mmmmmmm." She reached for his face, and he took her hand. It was small and soft, no longer skeletal and shrunken. Her cheeks were plump, her body renewed.

"I feel gooood." She flopped on her back, reaching both arms to him. "Come here. I'll give you some. Come here."

How long do you think, until she is mine? Not long, I think. The Master's words rang in his mind.

"I'll take us back to the room, Mistress."

He wrapped his arms under her and lifted her against his chest. She sandwiched his face between his palms.

"Feed the Dog. Feed him." She pushed on his cheeks and scowled. "I can't do it." She went limp, arms flopping as he started walking. "I can't feed the Dog."

"You have been feeding me, Mistress," he said. "I am grateful."

"Unnnnnnnnhhhh," she clutched his shirt front, eyes closed, and murmured into his chest. "I feel so good."

The rest of the house was relatively empty during the old Master's feasts. By the time they reached the room, she was making small noises, and he knew she was asleep, because she started sharing life from the Master's Heart, the light in her body ebbing gently into his.

She would be happier with the old Master than she could possibly be with him. The old Master would gain full control of the Heart, and Mistress would be happy, and she would forget Dog. It was more unbearable than an eternity of suffering torn limb from limb by the Master's Wolf. Dog would not simply be replaced—he would be completely erased.

He laid her in the bed, wishing he had something to wash the blood from her face. He knew she would want to be clean in the morning. As he crawled under the covers beside her, she wrapped her arms and legs around him and nuzzled at his neck, feeding him slowly and making soft sounds. He didn't want her to be happy. The only future with her happy was one without him, and he would rather face annihilation at her side and suffer knowing she suffered, than hold her while she suckled on a bliss he could not give her.

Return the Lost Souls to the Eternal Realm.

Mistress?

Return the Lost Souls to the Eternal Realm.

It was her voice in his mind. There was no doubting it. He gently shifted so he could see her. Her eyes were closed, her mouth slack cradled in the crook of his shoulder.

"Mistress?" he whispered, "is it you?"

Soolie Beetch and the Binding Blood

Return the Lost Souls to the Eternal Realm.
She slept, and he held her and listened. Hope kindled in his breast.
Return the Lost Souls to the Eternal Realm.
Return the Lost Souls to the Eternal Realm.
Return the Lost Souls to the Eternal Realm.
Return the Lost Souls to the Eternal Realm.
Return the Lost Souls to the Eternal Realm.
Return the Lost Souls to the Eternal Realm.
. . .
The Ancient Mistress was speaking again.

Chapter 11

Havah took Nolas' belt, knife, and gun and handed the weapons to the oldest girl. "You'll do better with these than he did."

Silas used a cart nail to punch new holes in the strap, so the girl could buckle the heavy weapons at her waist. "Do you know how to . . . ?"

"I know how to fire a gun," she said, tossing her braid over her shoulder.

"Then you're a step ahead of me already." He tried to smile. Her confidence reminded him of Soolie. He hated knowing that she was telling the truth.

"I know you're good at getting hurt." She pointed at his bandage-wrapped forearms. "Cordin says you should be dead already."

"She's right. I have a daughter just a little older than you keeping me alive."

∼

Wendin and Havah waited until early morning to carry Cordin's body, wrapped in blankets, back up the road to lay with the other dead.

They didn't have shovels to make a grave, and they couldn't waste the wood to burn the bodies. Unlike the monsters, human bodies took days to burn, and that was if their fluids didn't burst and douse the flames. There were so many corpses, and no one to bury them. These fields would stench foul when the summer sun came.

While the others tended to the dead, Silas built a ring of six firespots with the beds tight-packed in the center. He dragged branches, busted boards, and hacked logs, piling all the dry wood he could find in the middle of the fire rings.

"It should last all night if you're careful," he said, toppling the last of the wood onto the reserve pile. He pointed at the separate pile of wood that had been painted or tarred. "Burn this stuff sparingly. It'll smoke."

Mazir wrapped an arm around the eldest girl's shoulders, and they both faced Silas, Havah, and Wendin. The girl held the gun ready in her hands, lips tight-set.

"We'll be here when you get back," Mazir said.

∼

SILAS HAD SIGHTED the tracks while gathering wood in the morning. The open ground was soft, and the creatures plowed recklessly through the marshy reed wallows, leaving muddy torn trails that led to the very stand of trees where the survivors had been scavenging wood.

Their boots crackled the layer of twigs and fir needles as they stepped under the forest cover, guns raised.

"Can you do this, bush man?" Wendin asked.

"I know how to track an animal," he said.

She needn't worry. The farther they pushed, the more they had to wade through the brushy undergrowth, and the easier it was to see the broken twigs and bruised leaves of repeated passage. If anything, Silas was ashamed he hadn't spotted the signs the day before.

Havah pointed, "Looks like Silas' skill may no longer be needed."

They stepped out onto a rough trail of smashed foliage and deep wheel ruts. It was going to be even easier to find the monsters than they thought.

"They really have no fear," Wendin muttered, picking her way.

"They've been hunting frightened families," Havah said, "most still suffering topaz-withdrawal."

"And city sickness," Wendin added.

Havah lifted a branch and ducked under. "Our youngest children are stronger than the men they've been killing."

The morgue survivors had been storing their own untainted water and hiding out in the protection of Rahka's blood magic. No one who had escaped Ravus in the last moon would have had that advantage.

"The sun's half-up," Silas said.

He estimated this stand of woods was no more than a mile-and-a-half across. The trees were thin and tall with long fir-needle clusters on the ends of sparse branches that didn't block out much of the light. The creatures must have found or made additional cover. It was clear from the tracks, that they had been dragging things with them.

"Look," Wendin pointed with her pistol.

It was the first corpse. From a distance, it blended into the trunk it lay against, small and withered. Its eyes were dry holes, its teeth exposed, and a mossy bouquet of hair dressed its leathern scalp. It had been stripped of its clothes and completely drained of life.

"There's another one," Wendin pointed.

"Your belly's not going weak," Havah questioned.

"I ain't bolting," Wendin said. "I'll be fucked if this bush man out-stands me in a fight."

"Good. Let's keep on."

The dried corpses multiplied as they continued, discarded left and right and underfoot. Silas knew the boy Yasel was somewhere among them, and he tried not to look. Havah marched quickly, and he hurried to keep up. It was the old woman who first saw the barricade. She put up a hand. They stopped, squinting, guns raised. She motioned, and they approached together.

The trail ended at a wall of wagons and carts piled against a hillside. Corpses littered the area like pelt-wads about a hawk's nest. The monsters must be behind the barricade.

"Now," Havah whispered.

Silas tucked his gun and swung the pack off his back. He pulled out three bottles of moonpiss and rags for each.

Wendin twisted off the cork to her bottle and stuffed the tail of the rag down the neck. "Don't forget you have two guns, this time," she hissed at him.

Silas nodded.

Havah had already rag-fused her bottle and was striking her lighting sticks along the edges, skittering sparks. The tip brightened with an eye of flame, and she touched it to the dry piece of wood Silas held up for her.

"None escape." She shook out her lighting sticks and dropped them back into their bag and into her pocket.

"For Cordin," Wendin said, holding her bottle, rag tail ready. "For everyone."

"The Silk Lantern," Havah said.

For Soolie, Silas thought.

They held the tails of the rags over the flame, lighting.

"NOW!"

Havah screamed, and they ran, leaping over bodies, towards the wall of carts.

∼

THE BOTTLES HIT the wall and burst up in a wash of flame that splashed fast, quickly catching in the dry wood and beginning to climb. Havah, Wendin, and Silas braced, pistols drawn, as the fire grew bright with easy fuel, smoke dark from the tar and treatment in the wood.

No one spoke.

The heat was tight against their faces. The flames crawled off the tops of the carts and onto the hillside, skirting through the brush and grass before trailing up the trunks of the trees. The long fir needles torched, and the finger branches began to curl.

The heap of burning carts pocketed with black char.

"What if they have another exit?" Wendin said.

Havah didn't move, so Silas didn't move either. The pistol was hot in his hands.

The fire was in the brush off the sides of the hill now. It would travel fast in the undergrowth.

There was a groan, and the wall of carts came crashing down, tumbling burning wood, and the monsters came bowling through, wrapped and hooded against the flame and the midday sun, flinging blind and fast, trailing smoke and sparks. Silas fired his pistol once, twice, three times. There were six or seven of them. He hit the one he was aiming for in the chest, and it staggered, but kept coming. His fourth shot missed, but winged the creature behind it in the arm. To his right and to his left, Havah and Wendin each shot one of the creatures in the head, wrapped hoods snapping back.

"DON'T LET ANY OF THEM ESCAPE!" Havah was yelling.

Silas' first gun was empty. He dropped it and pulled his second as a bundle of rags bolted past on his left, and he swung the weapon up and pulled, shooting it short-range in the temple, and it dropped. Another flung itself at him, but Wendin grabbed the trail of its cloak, hauling back, its talons swinging.

"SHOOT IT!"

It was moving too much, and Wendin was right behind. He couldn't risk shooting her. Silas swapped the gun to his other hand, grabbed the knife at his belt, and lunged between its thrashing arms, striking at its face, slashing the wrapping cloth, blood and gnashing teeth snapping. It spun away from him, towards Wendin, who flung herself back, raised her pistol and fired in its face. A hot branding slashed the side of Silas' skull, and he kicked the monster in the back, and it fell to the ground. Wendin was reloading her gun. The monsters were scattering. Havah was firing after a smaller creature that was flailing into the underbrush. It ran face-first into a tree, and Havah's bullet caught it in the back of the head.

The fire was spreading low and climbing the trunks. The air blistered and burned. They didn't have to drag these bodies to the fire. They just had to bring the monsters down, and the fire would come to them.

"One, two, three!" Havah commanded, pointing at the remaining creatures bolting blindly.

One for each of them. Wendin launched after one that blundered into the trees just ahead of the fiery tide, and in the other direction, Havah did the same. Silas' monster was pelting straight down the rough torn path. It had the least obstacles, and it was moving fast.

Silas dodged old corpses, fumbling with his knife and trying to get it back into its sheath as he ran. His boots were heavy. His eyes burned, his head reeled. He got the knife tucked, raised his gun, hammer back and fired. The creature dropped. He couldn't tell if he had hit it, or if it had stumbled. It launched back onto its feet and was running again. Silas fired again and missed. Even blinded, it was pulling away. He only had one more round before he'd need to reload.

He staggered to a stop on the uneven ground, panting, cracking the hammer back, and raising the gun with both hands, sighting on the black fleeing cloak, and fired.

The figure dropped.

Silas launched back into a run, holstering the gun and pulling the knife. The cloak struggled forward along the ground, and he threw himself onto its back, stabbing the knife down again and again. It bucked underneath him, and he braced—one knee on its spine, his boot in the earth—and stabbed at the wool cloak and the shirt layers, slashing with the knife and then ripping at the bloodied rags with his hands. It shrieked, and his nails slicked on cold flesh as he tore the cloth, and where the flesh exposed to the sun, it began to bubble and smoke, and the creature torqued and howled, and he stabbed it, and stabbed it, and ripped, and ripped, as it fought beneath him, and the bloodied flesh smoked and blackened, and he sawed through the neckties of its cloak and rolled off its body, taking the cloak with him as the smoking stab marks sprouted fire.

The creature contorted and squalled, and Silas stood to his feet, panting and dropping the cloak, watching as its body was swallowed up in foul flames.

He needed to help Havah and Wendin. He turned back to see that the fire was beginning to flank the rough path on either side, and Havah and Wendin were already walking towards him—Havah with her gun raised, scanning the trees, Wendin reloading her weapon.

"They sure can take a killing," Wendin hollered, nodding at the burning monster that flopped on the ground. "Where's your other gun?"

Silas sheathed his knife. "I dropped it."

"We still have Cordin's guns," Havah said. "Let's get moving. The fire is closing in."

Havah took the lead at a slogging run, the fire spreading behind them. Silas followed, reloading as they ran.

"Lesson one," Wendin panted up beside him. "Use your weapons. Lesson two, don't *lose* your weapons."

Silas wasn't sure if she was trying to be friendly, and wondered if the other survivors knew that she had abandoned the cart the night the monsters had attacked the hospital. He suspected Havah wasn't the type to have told, and he wondered if the way Wendin was treating him was somehow related to the fact that he had been there and hadn't run. He flicked the last bullet in and clicked the wheel chamber closed.

Wendin pointed at Silas' head with her gun. "How's your head?"

He had forgotten. She must have shot him when the monster came between them. His head burned, and the collar of his jacket was wet.

"I knew you'd survive," Wendin said. "One got your arm last night, and you never even stopped using it. You're almost as hard to kill as they are. If I didn't have sense, I'd think you were one of them."

"I'm not one of them," he said.

"Obviously."

Up ahead, a blue hollow of sky showed between the trunks, and they jogged out into the open, down a bank, and into a marshy field mudded with wheel tracks leading towards the stand of trees that flicked fire and billowed gray and tan in the sun.

Havah pointed, "Our camp's back around that way."

"They must've ganked hundreds," Wendin said, stowing her weapon. "Think we got them all?"

"We got some," Havah said, starting to walk again. "There will be more."

Silas touched the side of his head. The blood was still oozing fresh. He gently tapped his fingers along the pain. It seemed like the bullet had just grazed him, but he couldn't tell for sure.

Wendin handed him a handkerchief. "You'll be fine."

Silas accepted it. "Thank you."

"Havah says you're thinking of leaving us to go look for your dead kid," Wendin said.

He didn't respond.

Chapter 12

"I expected you yesterday." Tilla was seated on one of the steps near the main library floor. She closed her book.

"Why are there no seats or couches in this place?" Soolie asked.

"Adon doesn't collect books to be read." Tilla stood. "Follow me."

She led Soolie and Dog up the stairs and to the left this time. "Mavi is still recovering. You look like you're doing better."

"We slept well," Soolie said.

She counted the floors as they ascended to the ninth before turning down a narrow corridor of books: two down, and then left, and then right, and then left again. She didn't know if Tilla was intentionally taking unnecessary turns or if this section really was this much of a maze.

At last, they reached a tall, many-paned window. Each square was a different block of vivid color: deep blues and coral reds, merry yellows and acid greens. No two colors were exactly the same, and there didn't appear to be any pattern to them. Tilla walked to a heavy curtain that hung from the window to an adjacent bookshelf.

"The panes are ordered by the material of the dye," she said, noting Soolie's attention.

"It's not about the beauty," Soolie said, "but how rare the materials are."

"You understand."

Tilla pulled the curtain back from where it touched the shelf to reveal a gap just narrow enough for her to squeeze into. She beckoned and Soolie followed, sidling into the shadows between the shelf and the wall for several paces before the wall fell away.

The librarian struck a set of lighting sticks and touched the tip to a candlewick, illuminating a short corridor and a red door.

"Does the Adon know about this place?" Soolie asked.

"Adon knows whatever he cares to know." Tilla pushed the door, and it swung in. "There are no locks in Adon Bashti."

They followed Tilla into a small, windowless library. Soolie counted six free-standing shelves full of papers, scrolls, and books of varied forms and sizes. There was a weathered desk and a fray-cornered pillow chair. Tilla kicked a step stool through a circle of spattered wax, hopped up, and began to light a ring of candles that hung from the ceiling on an iron hoop that was blobby with fatty yellow icicles.

"These books are best read in dim light." She stepped down, candle in hand, and kicked the stool through the mess of old wax, before hopping up to light the other side of the ring. "Don't take books from the room. They won't weather it well, and you don't want him to find you with them. Though he'll know everything eventually." She blew out the lighting candle with a 'whuff.' "Always douse the candles before you leave. You'll find more in the desk. Since you don't breathe, you won't need to take a break for air. However," she pointed at Dog, "does *that* need to be here?"

Dog bared nubbin teeth, and Soolie touched his arm. "He stays with me."

"Make sure he doesn't misbehave. Close the door." Tilla gave the command to Dog, who looked at Soolie, who nodded.

As soon as the door was shut, Tilla leaned back against the desk, facing them. "You are going to get me overwritten or dismembered. Mavi will be lucky if she only dies."

"That is not my intention," Soolie said.

"I'm sure your intention has very little to do with us. Though, if you don't get what you want, I'm sure you will find *new* ways to put my wife in the path of his harm."

"I am very grateful for your help," Soolie said.

"You should tamp your expectations. There is little I can do." Tilla crossed her arms. "I can no longer practice blood magic, and any help I give, he will know. It would be better for both of us if I leave now and we never speak again."

"Maybe," Soolie shrugged, "but you've endangered yourself out of an interest in dark things before. You must be at least a little curious."

"My wife is too trusting with what she shares." The librarian pushed off the desk and walked up to the ring of wax. "Step into the light and take off that shift so I can take a look."

Soolie pulled the dress over her head, handed it to Dog, and stepped naked under the ring of candles.

"Arms out. Don't move."

The librarian walked slowly around Soolie, stopping on occasion to squat down or lean in to get a closer look at the blood moving over her legs and belly and neck.

"Hands over your head . . . . Now straight out from your sides. Uh-huh . . . Now tip your head forward towards me."

Hot wax droplets spattered the tops of Soolie's outstretched fingers. "Well?" she asked as Tilla circled for what must be the seventh time.

"Before we go any further," Tilla grabbed the shift out of Dog's hands and tossed it at her, "I need to know what that's hiding."

"You can't tell?" Soolie stepped out of the candle ring.

"I have my guesses, but as Adon knows for a certainty, I'd encourage you to be forthcoming."

Soolie pulled the tunic dress back on and flicked little hardened wax pellets off her knuckles. Tilla stood with her long arms crossed, waiting.

"*Ikma na Sitari.*"

"You are a Soul Hunter," the librarian said.

"No," Soolie snapped, "I got infested by one."

"I see what Adon wants with you. What is it that *you* want?"

"To get rid of it," Soolie said. "Preferably without destroying myself in the process."

"Did Adon promise you that?"

"He said he could help me."

"Adon lies."

Soolie gathered.

Tilla beckoned, and Soolie followed her between the shelves. Tilla started pulling books and handing them to Soolie to carry.

"To understand what he has done, you must understand blood magic." Tilla dropped a heavy tome on the stack in Soolie's arms and walked to the other side of the shelf. "The Ancients created the worlds using the fabric of their language. They wrote us into being."

"So our world is like a book," Soolie said.

"More like an ever-evolving oral history, or—"

"A book is too simple."

"Much too simple," Tilla pulled three smaller volumes in quick succession and stacked them against Soolie's chest. "Their language goes in all directions, including many we can not perceive or comprehend, and it's always changing. At the core of their language is *rashni* —the spirit. Spirit is the substance of the Ancients. It is what remains of us when the body dies that can pass on to their realm . . ."

"What do the Ancients want with our ghosts anyways?" Soolie asked, bending her neck and using her chin to keep the books from toppling.

"Blood magic," Tilla continued, "is a way to bind spirit to something physical in order to manipulate *rashni* and harness the language of the Ancients in the most rudimentary of ways. Anything aligned with spirit can be used, not just blood—though blood is most common—to create barriers, to craft weapons, Adon's tower that bridged time and space—"

"The Regent's Tower?"

"Lift your chin."

Soolie obeyed, and the librarian tucked a scroll under it.

" . . . was likely the most complex and costly act of blood magic our realm has ever known. He has wrecked entire civilizations and peoples. To our world, the creation of such a tower is catastrophic. To the Ancients, it is merely a punctuation mark in the wrong place." She nodded and pressed her lips. "You will start with these."

"So the weave on me is an Ancient word that binds," Soolie said, following her back to the desk.

"Weaves can do many things," Tilla said. "That type of weave doesn't bind. It hides."

Soolie stopped. "What do you mean it *hides?*"

Tilla grabbed several books and the scroll from Soolie's arms. "He told you he bound the Soul Hunter? Even at the height of his power, Adon does not have the ability to imprison an ancient being like that for long. Such a weave could never last. Even this one will degrade with time, if it hasn't started to already."

Soolie shook her head. Memories of the Hunter taking over her body and puppeting it in her sleep charged through her mind. "You're saying the Soul Hunter isn't bound. It's only hidden? It can still act?" This couldn't be fucking true.

"Your mistake is . . . . DON'T."

Soolie's arms were empty. Tilla had the scroll spread open on the table. Dog hadn't moved.

"You are on your own," Tilla finished. "I've already said too much."

Fine. Soolie tossed the black book back on the desk. "You should leave, then, if you're useless to me."

"Get out before the sun gets low," Tilla said. "I don't want you here when Adon comes for you."

∽

SOOLIE STAYED in the windowless room struggling through wordy thickets about the 'foundations of substance and the perpetual shift underlying the corporeal illusion of immutability.' She read about the representations of the Ancients across cultures and centuries—some gendered, some genderless, some judges, others impartial and removed—all variations on formless beings that exist beyond sight and understanding, who precede life and wait beyond it. She read about explorers to the Southern Lands who returned with claims of having witnessed blood magic, and how the Emerists leveraged their wealth and influence to have laws passed against the study of Southern arts in the 'civilized world,' claiming that the very pursuit was an attack on both civilization and the sanctity of singularity itself. Soolie thought this was all a geyser of horse spak. She didn't understand how these books were intended to benefit her, or why they had been sequestered away, and she worried Tilla was intentionally wasting her time. She did try reading several other books, but her eyes were so tired by then, that every sentence was a disordered jumble, and she couldn't seem to remember the beginnings of sentences by the time she reached their ends.

Time stretched and shrank and developed sleepy pockets in the windowless room. The candle smoke burned her blurring eyes. No one came to get her, which struck her as odd, and she had no sense of what time it was, but she hadn't read something that landed clearly in her mind in what felt like seasons.

Dog sat by the door, a small book in his hands, scowling.

"Is any of it familiar?" She stood stiffly and stretched her arms over her head.

Dog shook his head. "It is difficult to follow, Mistress."

"I don't suppose anyone ever taught you."

"Not until you, Mistress."

She snorted. As if she had time to teach Dog to read. She grabbed the candle bell and stool so she could cap the flames. "Well, you might as well keep yourself occupied."

∼

When she squeezed out from behind the bookcase and under the curtain, all the glass windows were dark and the gas lights were out.

They made their way through the maze of black book canyons, turning one way and then the next, until it occurred to Soolie to worry that they might not actually find their way back tonight. But then they spied a dim and distant light and followed it to find the main room lit, silent, and empty.

The sounds of their footsteps on the iron stair bounced and bickered in the vaulting stillness. Had Tilla not come for them and Adon not sent for her?

The halls of the house were also eerily quiet.

There was something comforting about desolation in a space

meant for so many people. Neither of them talked. When it came time to turn toward the bedroom, Soolie kept walking. Dog halted, tilting his head. She waved him to follow. She wanted to go to the throne room.

As they neared the great bright doors, she could hear the sounds of movement, not the robust joy of feasting, but a scattered clinking and clattering. She placed both hands on one of the doors and slowly pushed, poking her head in.

The throne room was an aftermath of half-eaten carcasses and tossed fruit cores, spilled gravy puddles and smashed glassware. Men and women in simple white garb worked in silence scrubbing tables and piling dishes, mopping and polishing the floors. The throne sat empty on the dais.

It called to her. Without thinking, she started to step into the room when Dog whispered.

"Mistress?"

She shrank back, shut the door, and turned. "What?" she hissed.

He bowed. "Perhaps I could show you something?"

∼

HE LED her out and around the great house, away from the city. The moon was only a sliver, but the stars were as bright as if someone had powdered the sun with a mortar and pestle and scattered its pieces to light their way, bright as pale day. The trail was trenched, well-trodden and poorly kept. They climbed a hillside, zagging through tall grasses and thick-spike sprouts with handkerchief flowers that were scarlet in the sun but violet in the nighttime light.

"Almost there," he said.

Looking back, she saw that the city had dimmed its lamps. From the top of the hill above loomed a dark pillar.

"What is it?"

"The Master's door."

The pillar was a great stone tower, and the ground around the base had been beaten to a fine floury dust by the passage of many feet. She followed him through an open doorway and into the dark interior.

He extended a hand. "It is a long climb. Should I carry you, Mistress?"

She took his hand. "Just lead the way."

They climbed the stairs, turning and turning, up and up, circling a core of emptiness that plunged all the way down to the page of pale moonlight cast through the open door on the floor below. His hand was cold, and she could feel the tips of his fingers against her wrist, and she missed his talons.

After what felt like twenty turns or more, the stairs lit gray at the edges, and a square of stars opened above, and they climbed out on top of the tower.

The roof was broad and flat. There was no rail or lip, and the stone beneath their feet was covered in a thick layer of white powder. She let go of Dog's hand and bent down to scoop it in her hand. It was difficult to study, and when she rubbed it, it squirmed against the pads of her fingers as if it might burrow into her skin. She smacked her hands against each other. She didn't like how it felt.

Above the center of the tower hung an impression in the air, like the closed-eye shadow-memory of a flame. Whatever had been here wasn't here any more. This was wreckage.

"This was the door to Ravus?" she asked.

"Yes, Mistress. When the Master was ready to take flesh, he must have sent the Pack through and closed the door behind them."

"Is this what you wanted to show me?"

"No, Mistress. I wanted to show you this...."

He walked to the tower edge. There was less dust here. As she joined him, he sat down and she sat with him, and they hung their feet over the side, kicking against the stones. They were up above everything. The city was dark, the twin mountains jutted black teeth in the distance, and the stars drenched the sky, too myriad to count.

"I spent many years here," Dog said, twisting his hands in his lap. "When the Master did not have tasks or tests for me, he set me to guard the door. When he saw that my flesh began to resist the sun, he would station me for moons at a time, so I would blister and burn in the day and heal in the evening looking at these stars."

"Your nails are getting long," Soolie said. "Do you have the file?"

"Yes, Mistress." He pulled it from his pocket, and she took his hand in her lap and began to saw at the tips.

"How are you healing?"

"You've been feeding me, Mistress."

She looked at him sharply. "Have we been walking?"

"No, Mistress," he shook his head. "You have been feeding me while we sleep."

"But not walking."

"No, Mistress."

"Hmmm." She zip-zip-zipped at his nail, then lifted his finger, checking to make sure she wasn't going past the bed. "As long as the Hunter isn't doing spak."

He squirmed. "The Ancient Mistress has not commanded me, but I serve both . . . ."

"I know, I know," she scoured his nails harder. "You serve us both equally, but just tell me if it raises its head, okay?"

He looked down at his knees.

"Okay?"

"Yes, Mistress."

"Give me your other hand." She grabbed it. "So, you wanted to show me where you spent your time?"

He withered a little. "Yes, Mistress."

"That's okay." She yanked on his hand to get a better look, tugging him against her. "I'm not angry. Tell me about it."

He was silent for a while, and she worked on his littlest nail, flaking the tip to dust in her lap. As she moved to the next, he finally spoke.

"My first clear memories are here. I don't know how long I existed before then, but I remember feeling the night wind coming and knowing that I would heal in the dark, and watching the sun set, knowing that the color meant I would face worse pain in the morning, and I remember the first time I found it beautiful." He looked at his lap and kicked his heels against the side of the tower. "Sometimes serving Mistress feels like that. Like a new first memory."

"I need to get your teeth. Can you turn towards me and open your mouth?"

"Yes, Mistress."

She scrubbed at the yellow points that were just beginning to grow behind his bottom lip. Bits of tooth collected on his mouth and tongue. She was working on a back corner when the file slipped.

"Oh, fuck." She blotted the gash in his lip with the hem of his shirt.

"I'm sorry, Mistress," he mumbled.

"Oh, shush. Okay, open up again." He obeyed, and she resumed the task with renewed care. She wanted to say something to him, but she wasn't sure what to say. "I learned today that, for most of history, people have believed that human souls grow in the womb...."

She had the file in his mouth, so there wasn't much he could do to respond.

"The idea that souls pre-exist the body is a newer idea. It comes from the Emerists and their belief of souls going from one version of their lives to the next over and over and over again...." She stuck her fingers in his mouth and ran over the top of his teeth to feel for any sharpness. Finding a jag-shell edge, she started powdering it down with little strokes. The blood from his lip smeared her knuckles. His dark eyes watched as she worked. "Did you know the Emerists are also why the barter system was abolished? I didn't learn that today. It's just something I already knew...."

∾

MISTRESS KEPT TALKING long after she finished filing down his teeth, and he listened, spitting and wiping the grit out of his mouth with the hem of his shirt, enjoying the sound of her voice. Many of the things Mistress said were things Dog already knew, though he liked them better coming from her, than from the mouths of living scholars in ages past, performing their knowledge in the old Master's oratory halls.

Eventually, she ran out of words to say, and then she laid on the stone with her head in his lap and closed her eyes, and he watched her sleep.

This young soul has made me weak.

Dog stiffened, hope and joy and terror clutching him all at once. The voice in his head was dim, but it simmered bright and pure.

She has submitted to the Dead Man to harm me. Even now he is working to influence her and make her his own.

The Ancient Mistress. He wanted to leap up to grovel at her feet. He wanted to weep before her and her promised power. He shivered and held himself still, staring at Mistress' sleeping face, unmoving but for the blood that snaked over it.

I have a task for you, Dog, the Ancient Mistress said. *We will regain my power. We will reclaim my Heart. I will return the Lost Souls to the Eternal Realm. Will you obey me?*

Mistress, always.

Chapter 13

"Let's not go out, today," Kolgrin said.

He hadn't expected her to listen, and she did not surprise him.

He followed her to the site of the fallen tower and stayed with her all day, keeping watch while she stared feverishly, first at the center of the weave and then at the empty air outside. Sometimes she screamed, sometimes she muttered to herself. *"Mera pet bachle gai teva re doskati tephra nahnkala, nahnkala . . ."* It was Southern language, but Kolgrin knew by the cadence that they were ghost words.

By late afternoon, she was so unwell, she didn't even try to stop him from carrying her back. She was heavy-bellied, and it was a difficult trip. By the time he walked up the hospital steps, it was already dark and his arms were cramping. He hefted her close—awkwardly elbowing every door lever and backing every door closed—until they finally descended the last stair and entered the morgue.

She hung on him as he felt his way through the dark windowless space to the furnace room. Only once his boot tapped the muffled pad of blanket, did he finally lower her to the floor, groaning as he unbent and stretched out his arms.

He felt along the wall at chest-height until he found the gas lantern dial. The globes gloomed yellow, flickered, and went out. Well, the lamps were finally done. He would need to scrounge about to find a lantern.

"*Yah nani ha skata mera rashni,*" Rahka was murmuring.

The lantern clang-clattered as he stumbled over it. He lifted it, and shook, and let out a relieved sigh to find the base sloshing heavy with oil. He located the bag of lighting sticks close by.

"*Mera rashni. Mera rashni,*" Rahka mumbled. "*Mera pet bachle gai teva re doskati . . .*"

He struck the sticks and held the glowing tip to the wick. Light filled the unwelcoming room. The walls were dingy with soot. The great iron doors to the furnace sat open, and a lidded pot rested in the cold coals. Millions of corpses had turned to ash in that kiln, though for the last year, the residents of the morgue had used it to cook their meals. Now that Rahka and Kolgrin were the only two left in the city, what they ate, they swallowed cold.

"*Tephra nahnkala, nahnkala . . .*"

"Those ghosts really got a hold of you today, didn't they?"

She lay on her side on a tangle of blankets. He tugged one of the quilts out from under her legs and pulled it up over her. She was too tired to eat tonight. He would have to try extra hard to get her to eat in the morning.

"*Chooble,*" she murmured, as he lifted her head and tucked a pillow underneath it.

Chooble: fat hairy pig. It was as close to a pet name as Rahka came.

"Lioness."

"I know what they want," she whispered. "The *nahnkala*, I know."

Her eyes were closed and her words barely lifted off the pillow. He leaned close to hear.

"I saw it before the tower fell. A *maaptan myrta* all in white, made from their many broken pieces . . . ."

"When we were in the tower?"

He didn't remember a white monster, but there had been a moment —when he was preparing his pistols and Silas and Rahka were looking back down the tunnel—that had stuck in his memory. Not because of the monster hoard or the writhing tower walls or the doorway that

148

opened to another part of the world, but because when Rahka had turned back screaming *"THE TOWER IS FALLING,"* there had been tears on her face. Not the delicate tears of art and artifice, but khol-muddied purposeless tears. Rahka had been crying, and that was more unnatural than any creature terror.

"Hollow the ones who are left," Rahka murmured. "Gone beyond the tower. Ah, *mera bachle* . . ."

"Now I *know* those aren't your words," Kolgrin grunted, standing up. Her blood weave couldn't keep out what she carried with her. The least he could do was give her the dignity of looking away. "I'm gonna scrounge up some meat. You keep chatting."

He left her, foreign words spinning on her tongue, her eyelids glimmering wet in the lantern light.

∼

"*CHOOBLE!*"

"I'm coming!"

"*Chooble!*"

"What?" He lifted the lantern and grimaced as the light hit his sleep-tender eyes. "What's happened? You need a spak can?"

She was sitting up, bowed against the wall. She pointed at the blankets. "Sit. I have something to say."

"Now? I spent all day in your miserable company, and you want to talk now? I was dreaming something." He grumbled, "I don't know what it was, but it was fuck-well better than this."

"Sit," she insisted.

"Is this you? Or is it ghosts?"

"Don't think that just because I'm haunted, I am out of my mind."

Kolgrin scowled. He slept bare-chested and the room was chill. His body and his head ached from weariness and that bottle of rose brandy. But it was rare for Rahka to want to talk.

"Fine." He set the lantern down and eased himself onto the blanket with a grunt. "Be quick with it. My bed's getting cold."

"You are soft towards Silas," she said.

"That's my business."

"Now is your chance to leave. I am going to tell you a story. I will only tell it once, and then you will decide if you will stay. Do you understand?"

Kolgrin crossed his arms. "How long is this going to take?"

"As long as it needs."

"Then I'm taking a blanket."

He pulled one of the quilts over his shoulders, and Rahka started to talk.

∼

When Nadhi was very young, she was possessed by *Ikma na Sitari*, the Soul Hunter. Then she got pregnant. The Soul Hunter desired an infant soul to cultivate as its own, one final vessel to fill its emptiness and help it reclaim its Heart. Nadhi knew that it had seized on the one in her womb, so when she felt the first birth pangs, she hid herself in the thorn rushes and cut her wrists.

She made her cuts very slowly to give it time to believe her, and the Soul Hunter fought and pulled on her mind, but Nadhi was strong. She told it that, if it did not release the unborn soul, she would kill them both, and it would have nothing to cling to, and it would be set adrift for another hundred years. *Sen Ikma* knew Nadhi's mind and that she spoke the truth, so it released the soul, and a daughter was born in the blood and dirt and thorns, and Nadhi lifted the child in her wounded arms and carried it back to camp. Both survived, and *Ikma na Sitari* remained in the mother's body.

That was the last and only time that Nadhi held her daughter.

Sen Ikma still desired the child, so any time they brought it to her, Nadhi would scream until they took they it away. The daughter's first memories were of her mother's screams.

Time passed. The Soul Hunter was a parasite and it consumed Nadhi so she wasted in mind and body. Food could not sustain her. She could have ended her suffering at any time, but she refused to feed on the souls of the living or to pass her burden on to another. Since it could not break her will, the Soul Hunter began to speak into the mind of her daughter.

You can save your mother, it said. *You are still young. You will not be easily broken. Lay your hand on her and become my vessel and she will live.*

The daughter wanted a mother, and so she approached Nadhi to save her—but Nadhi made herself cruel. She told the daughter how repulsed she was that her daughter had stolen her life, that she hated her and regretted her sacrifice, that she loved *sen Ikma* and would not be parted with it. Because of this, the daughter distanced herself. And with time, the mother's words became true.

Even so, the daughter dreamed of setting her mother free. She devoted herself to the study of ancient beings, blood arts and dead souls, but while she was learning, the Hunter continued to devour Nadhi until there was nothing left to save. Until the daughter found herself tending a parasite in the corpse of her mother, and she stopped dreaming of saving, and sought only to find how to bind the Soul Hunter to flesh so she could cut it to pieces.

She came very close to accomplishing that goal. But the Hunter escaped.

I did not know, then, that *Ikma na Sitari* had found another vessel, but I should have sought it out. I should have abandoned my people to hunt it down, but I was *bevjak*. I hoped it had been set adrift for another hundred years, and I let myself believe that there was no path for me to follow.

All my life, I had been my mother's shackles, and as I had imprisoned her, so she had held me captive, and I entertained the thought of a new life not defined by ancient beings and their lust for power.

Then, ancient beings slaughtered my people, and Silas' daughter sought me out, and I saw the Soul Hunter in her eyes, more alive than ever it had been before, and I stood on the corpses of the ones who knew me and the parent whose love it had eaten, and I vowed to never rest until I hunted it down.

Since that day, the Soul Hunter has done the very thing I wished to do. By binding itself to Silas' daughter, it has made itself one with her flesh. Where once it would have been *very difficult* to bring it harm, now, violence upon her body is violence upon its spirit.

Seven blades have I forged with my own blood and *rashni*. I know what it seeks and where it will go. I will forge that door and meet it at its journey's end, and I will cut it, at last, to pieces. And I will bury my mother's memory in the blood I am owed.

∼

Her head dipped and her eyes drooped. He could see how much the story wearied her.

"Now," she said, "you will decide whether or not to stay."

"I've said it before. I'm stuck in."

"Don't make this promise lightly." She lifted her eyes to his. "*If you stay*, you will not get in my way. No matter what the cost to yourself, to me, or others, you will not interfere. Promise me."

"Lioness," he said, "I was never going anywhere."

"So be it." She slowly slid along wall to lay herself down. "Understand, I do not plan to make it out of this alive."

He lifted the blanket from his shoulders and draped it over her. "I didn't know that was ever an option."

Chapter 14

"I know you're keeping stuff from me." Soolie dropped the books on Tilla's work table.

Tilla set down her pen. "Those shouldn't be out of the room."

"Why not?" Soolie picked one up and shook it. "They're just old men talking about other old men. They're stupid and pointless and useless and stupid."

"I already told you I can be of no further help. Take them back."

"I didn't know there were so many useless books in the whole fucking world."

"I am not having this conversation with you again. If you can't stop throwing tantrums and taking the books out of the dark room, I will rescind your access."

"No locked doors in Adon Bashti," Soolie snapped. "Not that it does me any fucking good."

Tilla rubbed her forehead with the tips of her long fingers. "I can not manage this today."

"Heyyyyy," Mavi poked her head in. "I just came to say that lunch is ready."

"I'm not hungry, Mav. I really want to get this done."

"Come sit with me anyways? Just for a moment? You too, Soolie, Dog, if you'd like."

"Sure. I'm not doing anything else right now," Soolie growled and stumped after Mavi.

On her way out, Tilla handed the books to Dog, who turned in the opposite direction to return them to the room with the red door.

∼

They sat on a high floor in the main room, Tilla and Mavi with their backs to the balcony, Soolie opposite against a bookcase. This close to the ceiling, there was even more movement and color to the painting. The stars had streaks of purple, blue, and gold, and slashes of red, orange, and white brightened the rays of the sun. The clean elegance from afar was brilliant chaos close up. It was definitely one of Mavi's paintings.

"It's so pretty," Soolie said, and meant it.

"Mavi is very talented," Tilla said.

"I *am* amazing." Mavi tore a strip of skillet bread, folded it, and mopped it in the green oil in her bowl. "How are your studies, Soolie? Are you making any progress?"

Soolie snorted. "If I wanted to learn a bunch of old self-congratulatory bullspak."

"Oh?" Mavi ripped a bite and looked at her wife. "Is that all?"

Tilla shook her head and made a pass sign with her hand.

This was pointless. Soolie lifted a knee to stand. "Well, this has been great, but I'm going to go back." Maybe she could find some books that were actually useful.

"Wait, Soolie," Mavi extended a hand. "You've been spending all day and night in that room. Surely it's okay to take a little break? With friends?"

Soolie scowled. All day and night? How many days had she spent in the library?

Dog was just now rounding the balcony to join them, and she hadn't realized that he was gone, but she was glad he was back.

"Soolie? Are you okay?"

Soolie Beetch and the Binding Blood

She wasn't sure. She felt unsettled. Dog stood at her side, waiting.

Tilla tugged at her hair, and her eyes wandered towards the stairs. Mavi leaned forward. Well, if Tilla was going to keep secrets, Soolie could always chum up to Mavi. She sat back down, and Dog kneeled beside her.

"I'm okay," Soolie said. "I do have a question, actually."

Mavi smiled. "I'll answer if I can."

"You're such a good painter. Why don't you have any paintings of the two of you?"

"Oh," Mavi rested her torn bread on the plate. "Well, that is a bit personal . . . ." Her eyes flickered to Tilla.

Soolie smiled innocently; that's what she thought. She shrugged and tugged at her tunic. "I didn't mean to pry. You're both just so pretty, and you obviously love each other a whole lot."

Tilla stood.

Mavi shook her head. "It's not my story to share . . . ."

"It's fine. You can share it," Tilla said.

"Are you certain? Did you want to—"

"Whatever. It's okay," Tilla said. "I'm going back to work. I want to finish this restoration before tonight. You know I don't like leaving things undone."

Mavi nodded. "I know. I love you."

"Love you too."

"Is something happening tonight?" Soolie asked, watching Tilla round the balcony back down to her workroom.

"Her visit with Adon," Mavi daubed the torn bread in the oil. "She always needs a few days to recover. You probably understand what she's going through better than I do." She sighed, dropped the bread in the bowl and set it to the side.

"Can I help?" Soolie asked.

"No, dear." Mavi smiled. "Not with this, I'm afraid. But we can show her kindness and care when she gets back."

"Okay." So that's why Tilla was acting odd. It still didn't explain this feeling. Like Soolie had just woken up from a nap and didn't know what time of day it was. She reached for Dog and he gave her his hand.

Mavi watched them. "You two remind me a lot of Tilla and I."

Soolie clasped Dog's hand in her lap and tried to look understanding.

"I'm sorry." Mavi tilted her head back and sniffed. "Ahh. You asked why we don't have paintings. You see, Tilla didn't always look the way you see her now."

Soolie remembered the little portrait in the keepsake box.

"Adon was looking for someone to tend this library," Mavi waved a hand at all the books. "Unlike the gardens and the kitchens and the markets, he needed someone with a fondness for dark and powerful things, with the craft to care for them, but without the inclination to use them. Tilla had that affinity, and there was something that she needed that Adon had the power to give ... so she and Adon made a deal."

"A new body," Soolie said.

"A new body," Mavi nodded. "She knew there were risks. We sat up long nights talking through the many ways it could go wrong or cause harm. Adon promised her a female form with no trickery, nothing monstrous. She was so scared and nervous, but then Adon unveiled himself in flesh for the first time," Mavi unstoppered the oil bottle and began pouring the dregs from the bowl back in, "and he was so warm and charming, so unlike any of the other creatures he had created. It gave her hope." She shook the bowl to loosen the last drops. "But every deal with Adon comes at a cost. He could have given her a body that represented her, that felt more like her...."

"But he didn't," Soolie said. She had seen how Tilla huddled in her skin.

"Of course not," Mavi said, her tone bitter. "He gave *himself* a body to live in and turned her into an ornament. Does that answer your question?"

It confirmed what Soolie had already guessed. They were all monsters, but Tilla had actually chosen it. "Does she regret it?"

"Regret isn't the word." Mavi squeak-twisted the cork back into the bottle. "But when Tilla looks at herself, she sees Adon's desires and design, and it never should have been that way." She tucked the bottle back into her basket and wrapped the oily plate in a cloth before nestling it beside. "I can't tell her how to see herself, but I try to reflect back to her what *I see*—the same gorgeous badass I've always seen, the woman I'm madly in love with to the end of the world."

Soolie hadn't learned anything she hadn't already assumed, but the confirmation wasn't entirely worthless. "Thank you for trusting me. I'm glad you have each other."

"Of course!" Mavi beamed. "Folks like us have to link together."

"Absolutely!" Soolie visibly squeezed Dog's hand.

∽

SHE WAS DREAMING the same dream again. Soolie on the outside of the ring, the Hunter in the middle, hungry, screaming, silenced. There was a comfort that the dream never changed.

Dog woke her by jostling her arm. The lights were off. Soolie groaned and lifted her head. The pale specter of the Chorus stood at the foot of the bed, crownless. Adon had sent for her.

"Finally," Soolie scrambled away from Dog and out of the bed. How long had it been since she had fed?

"Mistress, should I come?"

"If you want to."

She didn't bother putting on sandals. She was ready to go.

Dog crawled out of bed behind her, and the Chorus stepped between, barring his way.

"I guess not," Soolie said.

The Chorus walked to the door and waited.

"Stay here until I get back," she said.

"Mistress." He huddled and clutched his hands.

"Don't worry," she called over her shoulder. "There probably wouldn't be anything for you to do if you came. Just go back to bed."

∽

THE CHORUS DIDN'T TAKE her to the throne room. It led her deep into the halls of the house, stopping at a set of doors like the ones to her bedroom and standing to the side.

There was no point in doubting the inevitable. Soolie pushed through.

It was a smaller chamber. The ceiling dripped with chain lanterns like a field of glowflies, filling the room with gentle light that absorbed into walls both dark and soft. There was no furniture, no adornments. Instead, the entire floor sank into a nest of mounded velvet. Cushions and furs cast about in a luxurious wallow, and in the far center was Adon, reclining with his arms out, chest bare, and a throw of furs over his lap. The crown writhed on his head, and he met her with carnelian eyes and smiled.

"Soolie. Join us."

She eased the door closed. She'd faced worse.

The air was heavy with musk and spices. The floor up to the nest was laid with pelts that caressed her bare feet as she approached the edge, and then she saw Tilla and Mavi. The two women lay naked, tangled together in a heap of pillows. Mavi's full black body was cupped in the curve of Tilla's white side like nesting pieces. As Soolie saw them, Tilla opened her eyes and reached a languid arm, making cooing, contented sounds.

"I thought Mavi didn't usually join you," Soolie said.

"Mavi and I were previously interrupted," he said. "I'm sure you remember. It would have been unkind to not find a moment for us to connect. Besides, I wanted to take the opportunity to ask after you. You've been spending so much time together."

Mavi's eyes were opening now, and she and Tilla both beckoned for Soolie to join them.

"They want to greet you," Adon said. "You are welcome to say hello."

Soolie stepped down into the nest, and the velvet cushioned her feet as she picked her way towards the women.

"I don't think this is something either of them want." She felt oddly sorry for them.

Soolie snagged a blanket and draped it over their bodies. Mavi's hands coaxed at her arm, and Tilla's fingers stroked the side of her face.

"Their behavior would indicate otherwise." Adon sounded amused.

"Well, you fucked with them." Soolie smacked their leach-cling hands away and backed out of reach.

Adon laughed. "That I did."

The two women retreated into one another, snuggling up like milk-drunk pups under the blanket, eyes closed, mouths moist.

"They won't remember that you covered them," Adon said. "They'll wake up in their own rooms, feeling happy and safe and satisfied, with barely a memory of our time together in their little skulls."

"But they'll know that they don't want to feel that way." Soolie made her way back to perch on the edge of the nest nearest the door.

"Do you judge me, dead girl?" He tilted his head back. "For surrounding them with beauty and giving them pleasure? You, who would *devour* them, who would destroy every plant in my garden? You are a ravager. I am a gardener. Look at them," he motioned to where the women dozed. "Tell me that is not beautiful. Tell me that is not good. And *then* judge me, if you dare."

Soolie braced her hands on her knees. His words got all twisty and poisonous. If she grappled with them too carelessly, she might get all knotted up. It was better to trust her intuition, and her intuition said there were some things worse than death and pain.

He leaned back. "Why are you sitting so far away? Have we not already been close with one another?"

"I'm not going to be one of your empty puppet people," she said.

"No, you want to be *more* than that, don't you?" The crown moved and his red eyes gleamed. "Would you like to be a revolutionary, Soolie Beetch?"

"I want to be free of the Hunter."

"You see, we have the same goal."

She scowled. She didn't think so.

"Come sit." He patted the cushion beside him. "Let me feed you, and let us talk."

"Not while you're wearing that fucking crown."

"As you wish."

The door behind her opened, and the Chorus walked in and made its way around the outside of the bed. Adon gasped as he lifted the crown and the blood slithered from his eyes, and the Chorus rested the circlet upon its white hair and removed itself from the room.

"There." Adon shuddered as he settled himself. The crown really did hurt him. "I have done as you ask. Now, will you join me?"

Nothing for it now. Soolie pushed herself up and picked her way across the nest. His legs and bare feet stuck out from beneath the blanket, and she looked down at him and scrunched her nose.

"You distrust me."

"No fucking shit."

"You may leave if you wish to. I will not keep you."

She teetered. Even apart from the throne, she could feel the light inside of him calling to her. She wanted to be close to him, to be fed again, but she hesitated, biting her lip.

He watched. "Would it help if I tell you what is going to happen?"

She didn't answer.

He held her gaze, and his voice was soft and low. "Three things will happen tonight. One: We will rest together and I will feed you from the Hunter's Heart. Two: I will tell you why you saw a thousand Soul Hunters and why we must remake the world together. Three: I will examine the blood weave for any degradation. I do not expect to see any change, but I am told you have been seeking to understand it, and I can not be too careful in protecting us."

Soolie tightened her fists at her sides.

"I will let you decide the order of things," he said. "If you wish, I can make my examination by looking only at your back. That would be sufficient."

The Chorus waited right outside the door. She knew his offers were a theater of choice. Soolie turned her back to him and knelt.

"Fine," she said. *Get it over with.*

He shifted behind her, getting closer.

"Pardon my touch," he said.

His fingers reached, slipping under the hem of her tunic and pulling it up her thigh on one side, and then the other. She scowled and raised her seat just a little so he could untuck the dress and roll it up, bundling it at her neck

"Hold this."

She clamped her hands at her shoulders to keep the tunic in place. Across the bed, a low contented snore snuffled from under the blanket where Tilla and Mavi slept as his fingers moved down her back, pressing, measuring.

He traced the small of her spine, and a sharp fizz of life from the Hunter's Heart came off his touch, making her tense with a jolt.

"DON'T."

The feeling ebbed, and she felt only the warmth of his hands again.

Her stomach was tight. Her ears rang. "Are you done yet?"

"Almost," he said, his broad hands wrapping, pressing thumbs-to-spine, fingertips-to-side.

She pulled away, jumping up and jerking down her tunic.

He smiled. "I'm done." He was kneeling and wearing a simple panel skirt that came to his knee.

She scowled. "You weren't naked."

"Disappointed?"

"You keep making me uncomfortable on purpose."

"Not on purpose," he said. "I am sorry that I have underestimated your level of discomfort with me. I do want you to be at ease. Would you like to leave?"

She stalked over to where he had previously reclined, and dropped herself down. As if she was going to leave without getting fed.

His eyes crinkled as he crawled in next to her. "May I?"

He draped the blankets over her lap, and she let him place his arm around her and pull her to him, wrapping her in heavy fur and the warmth of his body.

"Now," he said. "How would you like to proceed? If I feed you first, you may not be in a state to hear what I have to say, and I do think you will want to listen."

"Both at the same time," she said, holding her hands in her lap. Perhaps if he was also trying to talk to her, it would force him to moderate, and make it easier for her to keep a hold of herself.

"As you wish," he said.

His body brightened with a sense beyond sense, and immediately, her hands left her lap and clung to him as the life in him cocooned her, and the warmth of his body soaked into her cold flesh, and the light of Hunter's Heart gave her new life—and he began to speak.

"The Ancients created *Ikma na Sitari* to reap souls from their many worlds."

She closed her eyes. Her body was glowy, and his voice buzzed through his chest.

"Our Soul Hunter is but one of many Soul Hunters in one of many realms that exist to feed the Ancients. It never told you what happens to the souls that pass on, did it?"

"No," she murmured.

"The Ancients consume them. That is why we were created, that is why the worlds exist, to generate souls for the Ancients to feed upon, and the Hunters exist to bring us to the slaughter."

Rage crept into his voice, and a wave flooded her, and she shuddered.

"They aren't *benevolent shepherds*," he continued. "They are cattle hounds rounding us up for the culling. *That* is the natural order it wishes to protect."

"Hnnnn . . ." Her vision was blurring, her fingers curling, and he took her hand in his and held it to his breast.

"I know this, because *it* knows this, and I know its Heart," he continued. "I was ready to burn this world, Soolie, as my final act of defiance. To spit in the faces of the gods and torch this realm, rip every last soul, living or dead, and leave them nothing to glean from us. I choose immolation over subjugation. *Adon Bashti*, the last city, my gift to our realm, one final beautiful feast and one final beautiful lifetime . . . ." He caressed the top of her head. "But then you came to me—the little dead girl with a Hunter in her soul. You contain the knowledge of the Ancients, the language of creation. Together, nothing is set. Our fate becomes our own. We can remake the world and ourselves, defy the gods for another thousand years or more. No monsters, no sickness, no pain, no death. Only paradise."

He notched a finger under her chin and lifted her face to his. He was close and blurry, and her mind and body were hazed with light. He whispered. "Recreate the world with me, Soolie Beetch. There is only one way to be free of the Soul Hunter, and that is to enslave it."

DOG PACED IN THE ROOM. From the foot of the bed, to the bench, to the door, to the foot of the bed. The Wolf had taken her in the middle of the night, and she had been gone a long time. Shadows of the Ancient Mistress' words darkened his thoughts.

He is working his way into her heart.

He is making her his own.

Dog paced to the door and raised a hand to the handle again. She had told him to stay behind. To follow would be to disobey.

Are you ready to serve me? The Ancient Mistress had asked. It was the Young Mistress who had commanded him to stay behind, but the Ancient Mistress was also in danger. *She has made me weak.* Didn't he have a duty to serve both of the Young and the Ancient and protect them from harm, even when he couldn't hear them?

His hand touched the handle.

If the Ancient Mistress' voice had been bound, should Dog abandon her because she could not speak to command? Was his fealty so frail that it failed in silence?

His hand closed on the handle, and he pulled. Mistress, I'm coming.

He launched with the release of a thousand tension springs, down the familiar maze of dark hallways, in and out of the glow of gaslights, taking corners at a speed that scrabbled off the walls and would have raked furrows were his fingers and toes not bare. He could scent her trail, the mucky tang of dead flesh with a hint like burning iron. Mistress.

Dog skidded around a corner and saw the Wolf standing sentry by a set of doors. Its white eyes looked through him, and his teeth panged at the memory of its touch, but he couldn't stop now. He bolted forward and the Wolf did not move. Dog's hand touched the door, and a fist clamped on his arm and threw him, reversing his flight full force. His body slammed into a wall and dropped to the floor. He scrambled up, head spinning.

The Wolf stood in the same place, eyes ahead, motionless.

Dog launched, pulling at the floorboards and throwing himself into a slide as he neared the doors.

It struck serpent-like, grabbing him by the ankle and sweeping him up so his head cracked against the door before it threw him against the opposite wall.

Pain jarred his body, and he felt a twisting wrongness in his hip and leg as he dragged himself back up, favoring his left side, snarling.

The Wolf had resumed its position.

Dog grabbed his thigh with both hands and jerked, forcing the joint back into place. He braced, ready to bolt, this time, straight for the Wolf.

It turned, stepped to the door, and opened it.

Dog growled.

The Wolf held the door.

He slunk forward fast, head low, shoulders high, fingers straining to extend talons that were not there. It did not respond, and he ducked past into the room and saw his Mistress.

She was lying curled beside the old Master with her head on his lap. One of Master's hands rested on her back and the other caressed the dome of her skull as he watched her intently with red eyes, the crown on his head twisting and turning with the blood in her skin.

A wounded sound escaped Dog's mouth as the old Master looked up and smiled.

"I am done with her for now. You can take her."

Dog crawled down into the unsure footing of velvet and cushions, cringing his way forward. He crouched at her side, and the old Master did not move to help him. Dog pulled back the blanket to uncover her body, and she was warm with the Master's heat. He placed a hesitant hand on her shoulder.

"Mistress?" he whispered.

She mumbled and nuzzled the Master's lap. Dog scooped an arm under her to drag her away.

"Nnnnnnnooooo," she groaned.

He pulled her into his arms, and she made sulky sounds as he stood.

"Wait," the old Master said.

Master stepped up with the fur blanket in his arms and wrapped it over Dog's shoulder and draped it over the Mistress, and it smelled like body and spices and was still a little bit warm, and she burrowed her face under the blanket and made a purring sound that Dog had never heard her make before.

"Now go," the old Master tipped his crowned head towards the door. "She will sleep well tonight."

Dog carried her draped in the blanket out of the room, and the Wolf closed the door behind them.

As soon as they rounded a corner, Dog dropped the fur in the hallway. He held her close, and she clung to him the way she had clung to the Master. When at last they reached the room and he laid her in bed and pulled the covers up, she opened her eyes and reached for his face.

"Dog?"

"Mistress," he whispered.

"You're so cold."

"Yes, Mistress."

"Get in. Get warm," she tugged on him, and he obeyed, sliding in next to her so she could wrap one leg over him and tuck her face next to his. "Youuuur head is wet," she murmured.

"Yes, Mistress." His wounds were bleeding.

"Dog?" she murmured drowsily into his neck. "Promise me . . ."

He shouldn't promise Mistress. Mistress commanded. She shouldn't request anything of him. He hesitated.

"Promise . . ."

"Yes, Mistress."

"If I forget who I am . . . will you remind me?"

"Mistress, I promise."

She slept, and he felt the ebbing of life from her to him, and he wrapped an arm around her, and it was very like being warm.

"Mistress?" he whispered quietly, and she did not stir. "Mistress, what do I do?"

Every day, she becomes more vulnerable to him. Soon he will craft in her a moment of pure submission, and then he will use his crown to erase everything else. When submission is all that is left, he will use her to control me. We must act before he gains that control, the Ancient Mistress replied. Her voice was clearer than before.

"I am ready, Mistress," he whispered, holding her close. "Command me."

We need the Dead Man's crown. She is vulnerable towards you, more so even than she is towards him, but this will not last. We must take advantage of that as soon as possible.

Take advantage of Mistress? He whined. Had he made his Mistress vulnerable?

She will not suspect and will not defend herself against you. You will use the Crown to erase her weakness. Then your Mistress will come into her power.

Mistress would be powerful again.

Then I will be the Soul Hunter and nothing else.

Chapter 15

The blood moved differently when she looked at it—like the difference between a swarm of thread worms moving in the dark and a swarm of thread worms burning under the pupil of an eyeglass. The Soul Hunter was imprisoned in that ring of blood, suspended in its true form, the pure rippling fire of an ancient being with the hungering void where its Heart should be.

It reached for her.

The dream was silent, but Soolie was the one who was screaming.

⁓

"FUCKING USELESS." Soolie threw the book across the room, and it tumbled like a shot bird and flopped open under the ring of candles.

"NO!" Tilla dove from the chair to snatch it up before wax could drip on the pages. "WHAT ARE YOU DOING?" She tucked the volume to her chest. "These are the *only* of their kind. What *is wrong with you?* GET OUT!"

Dog set his book on the desk, snarling.

"This *can't* be how people learn blood magic," Soolie snapped. "I haven't read *anything* of any use at all."

"Mavi is the *only* reason I haven't banned you from this room."

"If this is your way of thanking me, you're bad at it."

Several nights ago, Soolie had found both women souse-brained and sloppy-limbed, sleeping in soiled clothes and giggling their way in and out of consciousness. She had *hoped* that by helping, she and Dog might ingratiate themselves, so they had cleaned the women up and made sure Mavi got food and fluids until Tilla was well enough to resume her wife's care. When the librarian then started to visit the small room with some regularity, Soolie had thought the plan had actually worked, but apparently *not*. Every book Tilla recommended was the same old spak. How had Soolie not burned this place down by now?

"Perhaps if you *took a break*?" Tilla said, returning the offending volume to its shelf.

"Sure, let's take a break." Soolie dropped into the chair. "Why don't you tell me how many people died to make that pretty body you're wearing?"

Tilla paused with her finger on the spine of the book. "Well." She slid it the rest of the way home and stuffed her hands into her skirt pockets. "I don't know."

"How can you judge *me* for being a monster, when you *chose* it?"

"Adon promised that no one—"

"Adon lies," Soolie interrupted.

"Yes." Tilla walked back and sat against the desk. "You think I'm a hypocrite for not trusting you. I'm not distrustful because I don't understand you. Are you going to lie and pretend that you haven't killed people? That you won't kill again?"

Soolie shrugged. "I'm just trying to survive."

"Yes," Tilla said. "For you, survival means killing people. For me, survival meant taking this body. Given the chance, even knowing what I know now, I wouldn't make a different choice." She leveled her eyes at Soolie. "Which is how I know that, given the chance to kill again, you will."

Soolie scowled.

"But . . ." Tilla sighed, "I also have a vague memory of you covering us in Adon's chambers, and Mavi wants to believe there's something good in you."

"Why, then," Soolie motioned at the shelves, "don't you teach me what I need to know?"

"I *can't* teach you. And you can't learn what you have chosen not to."

That didn't make fucking sense.

Dog perched on the arm of the chair beside her and re-opened his book. At least he was entertained. She did have something else on her mind....

"Adon told me something." Soolie crossed her arms and propped her ankle on her knee.

Tilla started gathering abandoned books off the desk. "Adon lies."

"I don't think he was this time."

"And most medicinal herbs can be used as poison." Tilla checked the writing on a spine and added it to the stack in her arms.

"He said we could remake the entire world to be like Adon Bashti."

"Does that appeal to you?"

"Just measuring my options," Soolie shrugged. "Bashti doesn't seem all that bad. You've chosen to stay here."

"That is not a choice I was given."

Soolie thought Tilla had more choice than she was letting on. At her side, Dog turned a page.

"He also said that the Ancients eat our souls when we die."

"You've been listening to Adon quite a lot, then."

"Is it true?"

"It has long been believed that, when we die, the substance of our souls is absorbed into the consciousness of the Ancients and our individualities cease to exist." Tilla walked her stack down the first aisle. "Incidentally," she called just out of sight, "this knowledge is in many of the books you claim to have been reading."

Soolie scowled. She didn't remember it. "Adon made it sound like they breed and eat souls the way we breed and eat rabbits."

"The Ancients don't eat the way we eat." Tilla walked back to the end of the shelf, searching the titles. "They aren't creatures of substance. In the Eternal Realm, everything is *rashni*, so when our *rashni* returns to the Eternal Realm, we become one with it."

"That just makes it sound like they're not eating *what* we are, but *who* we are. That's not better."

"Eat is a crude term," Tilla parted the books and slipped in a journal. "The Ancients seeded the first souls, and when we die, our souls are absorbed back into their eternity. Like a tree returning to the earth."

"Or a rabbit being digested."

"I like to think of it like a story being passed on after the book has been destroyed," Tilla said. "We lose our physical form, but we become part of something broader, less defined, more eternal. Adon says we are eaten. I suppose it is all a matter of perspective."

"Well, I don't *want* to be eaten."

Tilla sighed, "Then you have more patience for existing than I do."

"If you're so *keen* on it," Soolie sniped, "what are you going to do when *she's* gone, and you can't die?"

Tilla was quiet.

"Unless you haven't thought of that," Soolie said.

"I've thought of it."

"'Cause I only know of one being that can rip a soul from a dead body, and the Soul Hunter won't be able to help you."

"The Soul Hunter is not the only of its kind. In time, the Ancients will discover the brokenness of our world."

"And you want that."

"All things must end."

"That's stupid." She was frustrated at how quickly the librarian was brushing her off. "You hate things that kill, but you're okay with the Ancients destroying souls. That doesn't make sense."

Tilla rested her dwindling stack on the edge of the shelf. "Perhaps you should ask yourself why you are so comfortable comparing your murderous impulses to the nature of eternity."

"So you only take issue with killing if it's not *natural*?"

"You are being quarrelsome," Tilla said. "It's not my fault that you are angry and bored."

"Because the Soul Hunter serves your precious fucking Ancients," Soolie pursued, "and it's *fine* with killing people as long as their souls get gobbled up."

Tilla sighed. "Nature is the function of existence. Whether or not something is considered natural is arbitrary. It would be better to ask if something is *harmful*."

Soolie snorted. "That sounds fucking subjective."

"Yes," Tilla lifted her stack back up. "That is exactly my point."

˜

She wasn't sure how long they had lain in bed. The sun was slanting through the windows and the air droned with the buzzing of fat beetles, brightened with the occasional sweet trilling of birds. The sheets brushed pleasingly against her legs.

She rolled onto her back and splayed out. Dog was watching her, his dark hair fanned on the pillow behind him. She examined the hair bracelet on her wrist and turned it to count the number of threads and again lose count. She studied the fang that was wired to the band and touched the razor point with her finger, and it drew blood.

She held the finger up, and the light gleamed on the red bead swelling at the tip.

"What if this is your last fang?" she asked.

"Then it is yours, Mistress," he said.

˜

She stood in a ring of blood, trapped, screaming, begging for the Soul Hunter to let her out. It watched her from the outside, expressionless, and its face was Soolie Beetch.

˜

Soolie stood in front of the star-bright doors.

She had woken up alone, which must mean she had left the bedroom to look for Dog, and she knew Dog wasn't in the throne room, and yet, here she was again, standing in front of the star-bright doors.

They swung in at her touch.

White clad bodies bobbed in a sea of feasting wreckage, sweeping, mopping, bundling linens, and piling dishware onto carts. No one spoke or looked her way, but no one ever did. The feast was celestial, rising and setting, never ending, and the servants' work was never done. They would clean through the night and into the day, preparing for tomorrow's celebration right up until the moment it began. Adon said they slept and ate in turns, and the way he said it—as if eating and sleeping were a continuation of cleaning and clearing, serving and setting—made Soolie wonder if you had to die to lose your humanity, or if there were worse ways.

The doors were silent closing behind her.

The dais sat at the head of the room, clear of any clutter, presenting only the throne that had called her here. She let it move her bare feet over the cool marble, around golden utensils and strange sticky pools. The clatter and scuffle surrounded her, then grew faint and far away as she reached the steps and drew closer to the throne.

The spires rose needle-sharp, higher than her fingers could reach. There were no arms, no embellishments. Every surface was glass-smooth and squeaky white, except for the back that writhed with ever-moving knots. She could sense the pain in the fabric of its form, and she recognized that pain as more meaningless, inaudible screaming, more silent servants moving in unison.

You belong to me.

She ascended the steps, and the throne responded, twisted turnings spiking. It sensed her and reached for her—not the way it reached for him in pre-charted unison—but wild and tortured. The bone thrashed, and the demand of the Hunter's Heart drowned out the silent screams.

The seat was slick as ice. She crawled onto the throne and knelt, facing the back and raised her hand. The woven blood in her skin was a frenzied blur. The throne contended with the confines of its form, and she placed her palm upon its face.

Pain.

It seized her, knots wrapping around her fingers and over the back, stripping her skin with a billion-toothed files, blood fast-greasing the white coils. She screamed and tried to pull away, legs slipping on the slick seat, nothing to leverage, nothing to hold on to. Behind her, the servants stacked their dishes and rolled their carts, and she felt her flesh being scoured as it crawled up her wrist. She battered her thighs against the sharp edges of the throne, hooking the fingers of her free hand on the ledge of the seat, but the hungry knots were pulling her farther and farther in.

The back of the throne turned red like roiling bloody innards. It was devouring her.

"Soolie!"

Adon's arms were around her waist.

The throne didn't want to let her go.

He pulled, and it torqued and turned, grinding her flesh as first her wrist, and then her palm, and then her fingers dragged free, and he bundled her immediately to his chest.

She was shaking, gasping, tears streaming down her cheeks.

"Oh, Soolie." He held her close, resting his cheek against the dome of her skull, then brought her out to arms' length. "Let me see."

She lifted the hand. Her skin had been shredded—bloody pulp clung to her bones from wrist to pit-scoured knuckles, to fleshless tine-tip fingers.

He took the wet, wounded hand in both his own, and she whimpered in pain.

"Why didn't you listen to me?" he asked. "I told you not to touch the back of the throne."

She shook her head, sobbing.

"Soolie," he insisted.

"I don't . . . know," she spasmed.

"You do know," he said.

"It . . . called to me."

"And?"

"I had to see."

"You didn't trust me," he said.

"I'm sorry." The shock of the way it had seized her—the summoning need turned to ravenous harm—was greater than the pain.

He shook his head and smiled. "You do love to learn in the most difficult ways."

"I'm sorry," she said again.

"Come here."

He sat on the throne and lifted her onto his lap, and he rocked her until she'd exhausted all her tears and lay meekly against his chest.

"It would be wise for me to let you suffer your injury," he said, "as it is one that you chose, and I should not deny you your consequences."

She tried not to whimper.

"But it hurts me to see you suffer. I don't suppose you'll be eager to disobey me *in quite* this way again."

She shook her head.

He laced his warm-fleshed fingers with her tortured bleeding bones.

"Hold tight to me."

He leaned back, and she felt the moment that he became one with the throne, engulfing them both in the Hunter's light, and she didn't feel her wounds any more, and she let herself be washed away, and all the pain and all the desperation was worth it, to know nothing in that moment but him.

∼

Tilla set the glass of water on the table.

"Can I touch you?"

"Just sit close."

Mavi's eyes were puffy. Her nose black-cherry. She sat on the couch, her legs crossed under the tent of the quilt wrapped around her shoulders. Now that she was able to cry again, she didn't want to stop, and Tilla knew better than to try to cheer her up.

Tilla took a seat and tucked her hands under her thighs. "I'm sorry."

"Please stop apologizing."

"Okay. I love you."

"I think I might start painting again tomorrow."

"I'd rather you not push yourself."

"I think it will do me good."

"Okay. I love you," she said again, and it sounded like 'I'm sorry.'

"I still don't remember what happened," Mavi said.

"Please, don't ask."

"I hate for you to carry that alone."

"I'm not." Tilla put a hand on the couch between them. To her relief, Mavi's hand snuck out from under the blanket to hold it. It would take time for touch to be the same between them again. "Allow me to keep the harm of knowing. There is pain enough to share."

Mavi squeezed her hand and let go to reach for the water glass. "I know it doesn't make a lot of sense, but I'm actually grateful to have a better understanding of what you go through."

"It does get easier," Tilla lied.

As a living soul, Mavi had been affected by Adon's influence with a greater, lasting severity. It took Tilla only a few days to start feeling like herself again. It had taken Mavi more than twice that.

Mavi took a drink and held the glass in her lap. "How are Soolie and Dog?"

"I've been talking to them like you wanted."

"And?" Mavi lifted her head.

"I really don't think there's anything worth saving, Mav."

"But they *helped* us, Tilbug."

"Yes," Tilla remembered. She even had a memory that Mavi had lost, of the Soul Hunter draping a blanket over them in Adon's chambers, and it *was* one of the reasons she kept visiting—pulling select books from the shelves and leaving them out, putting up with that girl's tantrums—one of the reasons, but not the main reason.

"Has she learned anything?" Mavi asked.

"You know it isn't good for us to talk about it, Mav."

"But he looked through our minds and didn't find anything, right?" Mavi set the glass down and scooted around to face her. "He hasn't stopped her from coming to the library, has he?"

"I don't know," Tilla sighed. "Adon doesn't seem concerned, but that might just be because she doesn't seem capable of learning. I worry that whatever he did with that weave is getting in the way."

"Can you help her?"

"There's really nothing I can do, Mav." Tilla willed her wife to believe her and to let it go. "Every time I see her, she asks the same questions and yells the same threats. At this rate, she's going to destroy my books."

"There are worse books to have destroyed."

"Mavi!"

Mavi shrugged. "I just . . . I believe there's good there. I do."

"A mortal soul with ancient power is never good," Tilla said. "The corruption of humanity is as inevitable as it is irreparable."

"We disagree."

"We do."

It was one of their differences: Tilla believed books were sacred, Mavi believed souls were sacred. They were both willing to go to great lengths to salvage what the other was willing to burn. It was something they loved about one another and tried not to discuss too often.

Mavi sniffed. "I think I'd like a hug now."

Tilla opened her arms and received her wife's blanket-bundled body, wrapping her arms even tighter as she felt that body start to shake. She rested her cheek against Mavi's curls as Mavi's tears soaked through the shoulder of her blouse.

Tilla didn't believe the Soul Hunter and the Dog were redeemable, but it really didn't matter either way. The real question was whether it was worse to have one lion in the village or two. Either way, a lion was going to kill. It was a fool's hope to think they might kill one another. But Adon had broken their agreement and hurt Mavi. That was Tilla's main reason. That was why she was feeding the other lion.

Chapter 16

"You can always give up," the librarian said. "It's not so bad to be with someone who can make you feel safe at the end of the world."

Chapter 17

They found Mazir lighting the fires while the eldest girl kept watch over the other children sitting on blood-spattered blankets in a scattered mess of empty sweet wrappers.
"Did you get them?" Mazir asked.
"We got them," Havah said.

∽

"Are you able to put that back together?" Havah asked.
The gun was dismantled on his blanket in a tidy array. Silas scrubbed the bristles of the cleaning brush on a rag and went back to twist-scouring the chambers.
"My stepfather was one of the Regent's Guard. He cleaned his wheelgun at the table every night."
"Is that why you favor those fussy pieces Kolgrin picks out?"
He pointed at the rags and the bottle of moonpiss in her hand. "Is that for me?"
"It's for you."
"I'm already set." He waggled his little bottle of cleaning alcohol at her.

"Not for the gun. I'm here to clean your head. And to talk."

"Can you do both while I work?"

Wendin and the children lay close by, bundled in their bedding, while Mazir and the girl kept watch, guns in hand, squinting out at the darkness between the fires. Far above, the stars peeked through the smoke, cold and bright as water cupped straight from the pump.

Silas was ragged. His eyes and throat felt raw, and his chest burned tight with smoke. He needed sleep and water, and he wouldn't get enough of either. He didn't want to talk.

She crouched at his side and set the bottle and rags on the bed next to his weapon. He dripped alcohol on a shred of wool, stuffed it into a chamber, and used the brush to swish it around to swipe up any grime, while she uncorked the moonpiss and sloshed a dram over a gray cloth. The stringent smell of liquor burned his nostrils. She knelt at his side and started wiping up the blood that had dried on the side of his face and down his neck. The fumes made his eyes water.

"The girl's name is Sorell."

Silas grunted and tore off a new shred of wool.

"I knew her mother." Havah refolded the cloth and splashed a little more alcohol onto it. "I was a skagmarm for nearly thirty years, and she was one of mine. Topaz got her, but that's not as common as people like to think." She wiped at the side of his head, edging toward the tender wound. "Any girl chasing drug has reason, and good reason at that, but more often than not, a skag's death runs her down. She doesn't have to go looking for it. Sorell's mother met a man she thought was going to take care of her and hers. He made lots of pretty promises, then, like they do, lost his interest. So she took a heavy dose and wandered into the Dark Districts alone."

Silas wiped the wheel pin down and reached for the oil. She unfolded the rag and sloshed liquor over it.

"Brace yourself."

He twisted the dropper top off the bottle, and she slopped the rag onto the gash on his head. Sharp pain washed his skull and his vision blurred as he shakily dripped oil into the gun's mechanism.

"She's a good kid. Takes care of the others. Proud. Just like her mom." Havah pressed the wound, then wiped and dabbed. "Looks like

Wendin didn't get you too deep. Knowing how fast you heal, you'll be right."

He tightened the oil bottle and set it to the side. "You should clean your weapons with soap and hot water when you get to Hob Glen."

She wrung the cloth out over the grass. "I'm told you've walked into the Dark District and back out alive."

Silas clicked the chamber wheel back and slid in the fixing pin. "I did."

"We've all seen you survive what should have killed others. You heal faster than any man should."

He knew where she was going. "I'm heading back to Ravus in the morning."

She returned to scrubbing the blood crust from his brow. "You're needed here."

Here wasn't why he'd survived. He tucked the gun back into its holster and started rolling up the cleaning kit. "You're not going to talk me away from finding my daughter, Havah."

She pressed the rag hard against his wound, and the pain stabbed deep. He set the cleaning kit to the side.

"These children are fighters, Silas. They've endured lifetimes of suffering, and they want to live. If you abandon them, their blood will be on your soul."

He didn't want to abandon anyone. The pain of the liquor in his wounds raked up his neck and head, and somehow the pain helped. "She's my daughter."

"Stay with us." She lifted the rag, and he turned his head to see her. Strain and lack of sleep nestled tender hollows in the wrinkles under her eyes. "Please."

"I wish I could."

"Why *can't you*." Anger crept into her voice.

Because he hadn't just survived, he'd been saved. "I owe my daughter," he said.

"Okay," she said in a voice that meant the opposite.

He *wanted* her to understand. It wasn't that he didn't care, it wasn't that he was a bad man, but the very reason he was useful was the very reason he had to go.

"You are right," he said, knowing it wouldn't help, and trying anyway. "I do keep surviving when I shouldn't, but there is a *reason*." He'd had a lot of time to think about what had happened in Hob Glen, turning it over and over in his heart, polishing it into something clean and clear. "Somehow—I don't know how—my daughter gave me a second chance. Everyone in our town was killed by the monsters except for me, and ever since, I've been stronger than I am, and I sense a presence watching over me, and sometimes, I even hear a voice guiding me to her. I don't know everything, but I know that I'm alive because she needs me. I can't fail her again."

"You're needed *here*," Havah said. "Rahka is worse than a monster, because she has made herself what she is, and Kolgrin is as bad, because he follows her. If you run back to them, you are as bad as they are."

"You're not hearing me," he said softly.

"Because I don't swallow horseshit."

"This is about something greater than I am. My daughter, Havah—"

"Is *dead*," she snapped.

Silas dipped his head. He couldn't blame her for her anger. She was fighting for the ones she loved. They both were. "I'm sorry," he said.

"This is murder. You are worse than Nolas."

"Do you have any children?" he asked.

"The ones I birthed are all dead," she stood, "but that does not make me less of a mother. I'm going to fight for the ones who need me. You go chase your shame and your ghosts."

Chapter 18

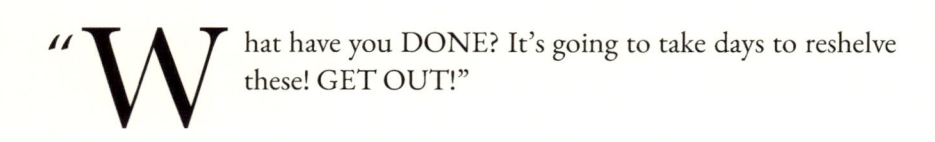

"What have you DONE? It's going to take days to reshelve these! GET OUT!"

~

The sun was warm and the breeze was lazy. Doors rested ajar, windows hung open, and the sounds, smells, and people moved freely from stall to street to building, and Soolie meandered with them, stopping to admire full-wall murals and smell flowers, to rifle through tables of trinkets and listen to the street minstrels. Unlike Ravus, Adon Bashti didn't have dark districts or light districts. There were no gates, no walls, and nowhere her feet could take her that she couldn't go. There weren't even rich people and poor people, because there was no currency. People offered to exchange services and goods, more out of consideration than necessity. No offering was denied, and everyone received whatever they needed.

She picked out a red cord with talon beads on the ends and tucked it into her dress pocket. She didn't bother asking, and the lady behind the table didn't give her a glance. Soolie was growing accustomed to being ignored. In the absence of suffering, there was a peacefulness to it.

She didn't remember deciding to leave the big house and wander the city, but she was glad she had. She felt more herself here in the sunlight, far from the dark smoky library with its books eating moth-holes in her brain. She needed the break, and she let herself drift without questioning her feet.

Around mid-afternoon, she noticed the residents gathering in a singular direction, and it felt only natural to follow them: down a stretch of buildings and out into a wide open space where they merged with a great crowd, packed body-to-body, straining to see. As she drew near, the people squeezed even more tightly to avoid touching her, and she found that she was able to walk easily through, up to the edge of a massive amphitheater.

The congregation sat hip-to-hip in nesting crescents segmented by packed aisles that converged to the center of the bowl. All manner of residents were present, including entire sections full of children—more than Soolie had ever seen in one place before—ranging from barely walking to labor-ready, all sitting and listening attentively to four men that stood in the round below. The men wore simple clothes and spoke earnestly in a language Soolie did not understand, and they appeared to be presenting a case. In front of them, at the center of it all, was Adon. He was clothed in sunset orange with simple sandals on his feet, and he sat on the theater steps, leaning forward, resting his forearms on his thighs.

Were he not the clear center of attention, he might have easily been mistaken for one of the people.

The living bodies in front of Soolie crawled over one another, stacking themselves down the aisles like pushed rows of books to clear her path. Far below, Adon lifted a hand to shield his eyes.

"Soolie!" he shouted. "Have you come to join us? Come! Come!"

She descended, people piling out of her way and closing in behind her, until she stepped free into the clear stone round. Bodies rose row upon row in all directions.

"What a pleasure to see you in the daylight." Adon patted the step beside him. "Sit with me. I'll catch you up."

As she reached his side and sat, thousands of eyes focused upon her.

Stepping into Adon's presence was like stepping out of shadows into a beam of light.

He leaned towards her and pointed at one of the men. "Hestil is a stonemason who adopted an apprentice named Anavi who has been misbehaving. The three with him are fellow artisans and witnesses."

This was some kind of court.

"Hestil, jakhen ranee," Adon said.

The man bowed and continued speaking. Those with him nodded solemnly. Adon asked questions, and Soolie sat and waited, looking at all the faces looking back. The moment was pleasantly dull. It was surprisingly easy to sit next to Adon while he talked to other people.

A murmur rippled through the assembly, and Adon leaned in to explain. "This is not the apprentice's first offense. His case has been brought to me before."

"What did you do last time?" Soolie asked.

"Found him a new adoption far from the woodworker's daughter. It seems he has sown ill-favor in another field. "

The men were silent. The crowd stilled. Soolie wondered if everyone in this city spoke multiple languages, and she found herself wishing she were less reliant on Adon to understand.

Adon raised his voice to address them all, *"Es Anavi, binde go mir layla giya. Miy use panate gin miy skeval kagroona."*

The crowd applauded. The four men clasped their hands to their foreheads and bowed.

"The apprentice will be brought to the great house, and I will take him in," Adon explained as the men made their way to the side.

"Are all the people in your house there as punishment?"

"Not all in the great house are servants," Adon said, "and those who *are* do not serve as punishment. Self-governance is the greatest of privileges. Those who are unable to govern themselves are governed for the good of all. This is not a punishment, but an act of care, a sacred undertaking."

An older woman in a head-shawl was stepping out of the crowd.

"By the by," Adon asked, "where is your Dog?"

Soolie shrugged. "Where is your Chorus?"

"Administering to my people."

That wasn't an answer. "I don't know where Dog is," she said. "I forget about him sometimes."

He smiled. "Should we hear another plea?"

"Okay."

The woman who approached spoke Midland, so Soolie didn't need a translation. She explained that a woman in her home had given birth in secret and was hiding the child in her quarters.

"Are there any others who can speak for this woman?" Adon's voice carried over the crowd.

"Adon sen Yevah!" a voice called. "We have brought her. She is here!"

"Bring her forward so that she may speak for herself."

Halfway up the stands, a woman was hefted to her feet. The crowd was a millipede of hands, handling her down the steps and expelling her before him. She was young, with long brown hair and fearful eyes. A bundle lay bound to her chest in a sling, and she wrapped her arms around it and bowed her head.

"Adon."

He stood and stepped down to greet her. "What is your name?"

"Phila, Adon."

"Is this the young one?"

"It is."

"Let me see."

She pulled back the cloth of the sling to reveal a pale head lumped against her breast. Adon held his hands out to receive it, and she reluctantly untucked the little body. He took it, gently supporting the head and cradling it to his chest. It was swaddled, eyes closed, and it didn't make a sound. The woman clutched her hands, watching.

"This is not a welcoming place for one so small," he said.

"They made me bring him, Adon."

"Did they also make you drug him to keep him quiet?"

"She drugged it herself, Adon," the older woman said, "so it wouldn't be found."

The mother was starting to cry.

"You should not dose one so small," Adon said gently. "The little ones must be allowed their wailing. That is one of the reasons they are best cared for in the nursery."

"Please," she begged. "I am a good mother. I am."

"I see how your heart hurts you," he said.

"Please," she fell to her knees. "Don't take him from me. Don't take him."

"I should not be the one to make this decision. The children belong to the people." Adon cradled the baby with one arm and extended his hand to her. She crawled forward and grasped it, smearing it with her tears. "We will ask them. My dear, can you stand?"

He helped the woman to her feet, placed an arm around her shoulders, and addressed the crowd. "People of Adon Bashti! Our children belong to us all. Together, we raise them. Together, we care for them. From an early age, every child is educated so that they may discover their aptitudes, and—when they are old enough—each child is placed with those best suited to guide them. You are *all* children of Adon Bashti, and you all belong together."

A thousand heads nodded and the many watching children nodded with them.

"Phila says that, because she loves this child, she should get to keep it for herself. You are the children of Adon Bashti, so it is to you that I entrust this decision. I ask you to look on this woman with kindness and to consider not only the good of the mother, but the good of the child. If this child should be given to this woman to raise as she sees fit, so that she may keep it to herself, away from the community and the care of the people, if that is what is right, stand now to make your vote known."

Across the theater, the people remained seated. There was a rustle rumble as all who stood in the aisles and beyond the rim of the theater sank to their knees. The mother began to wail, and Adon raised his voice above hers.

"If this child is to be embraced by the people, to be raised in the arms of the community as a child of Adon Bashti and guided on its best path, stand now to make your vote known."

A thunderous roar shook the theater as everyone took to their feet, clapping their hands, raising their voices and drowning out the cries of the woman who slipped from under Adon's arm and crumpled to the ground.

Adon handed the baby off in one direction and spoke low to several men who took the mother in the other. As the crowd started to settle, he turned back to Soolie who had remained seated. It was interesting to watch him manipulate the crowd, not with drugs and powers, but with words.

"They will take her to the Cradle so she can heal."

"Is this a regular thing?" Soolie asked.

"The pain of a mother?" He sat beside her. "It is a primitive impulse and not easily overcome. For this reason, we must have grace for our more base appetites." He smiled. "All have their place."

"I meant the gathering," Soolie said.

"Oh, yes," he said. "I meet with the people regularly."

"Can anyone bring a grievance?"

"Anyone who wishes."

Soolie stood. "I have one."

The crowd fell silent. A couple who had started to approach, retreated to the edge of the assembly.

"Do you?" Adon looked amused. "You wish to present a plea before the people?"

Soolie stepped down and turned to face him. "Yes. I have a grievance against Adon sen Yevah."

The crowd recoiled, but Adon's eyes creased. He tucked a smirk behind a crooked finger. "You will not make a mockery of our court, Soolie Beetch."

She stood her ground. Let's see how he responded without his throne and his crown and his Chorus monster. "Am I allowed to bring my case?"

"Well," he said, "this court is for the children of Adon Bashti."

"You invited me into this court, and I have a grievance. May I present?"

"So I did." He tipped his head. "Very well. State your name and make your case."

Soolie faced the people. "My name is Soolie, and I bring an accusation of falsehood." The watching faces were cold. She pointed at Adon.

"This man claims to have bound the Soul Hunter with a blood weave that can not be broken." She turned to him, and he raised his eyebrows, waiting. "Do you deny it?"

"I do not."

"But you want to use those same powers to remake the world, which can only mean that the weave is not as indelible as you claim."

"Is that your grievance, Soolie?"

"It is," she said.

"Then I will answer you." He did not speak loudly to the people, instead lowering his voice and speaking directly to her. "I did not mislead you. It would take a miracle to break such a weave. I believe that, united, we will have the power to work all manner of miracles."

She crossed her arms. "You want me to think that the only way I can be free of the Hunter is by being enslaved to you."

He smiled. "Do you think I want to *enslave* you?"

She snorted. "Don't you?"

"Will you let me?"

"No."

He shrugged, "Then we will have to find a different arrangement."

She scowled, and he laughed, and the crowd chuckled with him, the sound flocking around the arena like birds.

"Is that not the answer you wanted?" he asked.

She had wanted to test him, to find a fracture to pry at, but right now he looked back with mirth in his dark eyes, fractureless.

"Come," he said. "Decide this next case with me."

"I'm not interested in helping you with your chores."

"You should not speak ill of chores. When labor serves a purpose, it is an honor. Come," he patted the stair next to him again. "I *know* how much you want to toy with me. Accept my offer, and you can decide this next petition on my behalf. I will abide by your ruling."

She walked over and sat, expecting him to place a hand on her leg or pull her close, but he just nodded.

"I can make any ruling?" she asked.

"Within reason," he said. "The solution should suit the crime and benefit the people. No killing, and no blood may be spilled."

"You removed all of the fun options."

"It wouldn't be fun without a challenge."

A couple stepped forward again, holding one another's hands.

"This should be simple enough," Adon said. "I believe it to be a civil matter."

Soolie *did* want to throw his dance off-step. Still, she found herself watching his face as the couple talked. He looked so invested in what they had to say. He glanced back at her, acknowledging her attention briefly, but for the most part, he remained focused. This was a different kind of power from the power to rip apart worlds and end souls: the power to simply sit at the heart of a crowd and be their center.

It was a civil matter. The couple wanted to get married, which, Adon explained, was not expressly forbidden. Marriage was permitted as a concession when people could not find an agreeable alternative.

"If it's not celebrated or enforced," Soolie asked, "what's the point?"

"I believe," Adon said, "some find security in the illusion of ownership."

Soolie studied them and the couple looked back. "Why is it important to you?"

They hesitated, looking to Adon.

"She is deciding your case," he said. "You should answer her."

The man replied, "We wish to belong to one another only."

"Can't you just not sack other people?" Soolie asked.

" . . . Yes."

"So?" Soolie prodded.

"I . . ." the man looked at the woman, who looked pleadingly back. "We wish to communicate that commitment, so that others will honor it as we do."

Soolie didn't follow. Adon was watching her. The woman clung to the man's arm.

"I want to hear what she has to say," Soolie pointed. "Why do you need other people to know?" The woman's eyes went from the man, to Adon, and at last to Soolie in a way that Soolie found grating. "You have permission to speak. Speak."

The woman looked down. "There is another man at the vineyard."

"He bothers you?" Soolie guessed.

"He wants me, and I do not want him."

"Sounds like *that's* your problem," Soolie said. "Is he here?" They both looked towards the crowd. "Bring him up."

A smile tugged at Adon's mouth. Soolie *didn't* want to impress him, that wasn't it. But he pushed her, and she wanted to push him back. She wanted to surprise him and make him feel matched by her, and she wasn't sure what the better word for it was, and she couldn't think about it now. The woman shrank into herself as the crowd delivered another man to stand in the round.

He was a broad man with a wide chest and forehead, and he bowed to Adon and Soolie, and raised his head a little too bewilder-eyed, Soolie thought.

"Do you desire this woman?" Soolie asked.

"I love her," he said. "It is not wrong to love."

"Do you know that she does not want you back?" Soolie pressed.

"I had hoped she would return my affection," he said. "Had I known how unwanted my love was, and that it made her uncomfortable, I would have kept it to myself. I am learning this news at the same time that you are."

"Did you tell him?" Soolie asked the woman.

The woman nodded. "Many times. And," she looked to her man for reassurance, "he refuses to leave me alone. He watches me."

"Explain."

"I have asked him to stop, but he comes into my room when I do not want him there. He watches when I do not want him to."

No locked doors in Adon Bashti, Soolie thought.

Adon leaned towards her, voice lowered, "There are a number of vineyards. He can be reassigned."

"What work does he do?" Soolie asked.

Adon answered, "He is a vineyard hand. It is a—"

"Are there not enough men to do that work?" she interrupted.

"There are enough," Adon said.

Soolie nodded. "Then he can continue the work without his eyes."

The man's eyes widened even more. "Adon . . . Surely . . ."

"They have caused you trouble," Soolie said, "so you will be relieved of them. That is my ruling."

"Adon sen Yevah!" the man cried out. "Surely this is a jest! Surely this can not happen!"

Adon was watching her. She didn't look back, but she could hear the amusement in his voice. "I gave my word. I can not now become a liar, after having only so recently cleared my name."

The man turned and flung himself at the wall of the crowd, and the crowd pushed him back. The couple clung to one another.

"You have caused a stir," Adon said.

"I don't know *why*," Soolie muttered. Her ruling wasn't that outrageous.

"This is a city free of violence," he said. "They do not remember your kind of justice."

"The city is *full* of violence," Soolie said. "They've forgotten how to see it."

"And I suppose you would be the one to open their eyes . . . by blinding them."

"You gave me the ruling, and I made it."

"So you have. How will you carry out your ruling without spilling this man's blood?"

"Bring him to me."

Several people seized the panicked man and wrestled him to stand before her.

Soolie stood. "Stop struggling or it will be worse for you. Kneel."

They pushed the man to his knees. Soolie waved the people off. His face was meaty on his bones. She wished she could simply drain him of life and drop the husk in the dust.

"Do you know what you are doing, Soolie Beetch?" Adon asked.

"Give me your hands," she commanded.

"And where should I place them?"

"Stand behind me and give me your hands."

"As you wish."

The man knelt wild-eyed before her, and Adon stood behind her. She grabbed Adon's wrists and pulled them forward on either side, his chest pressing against her back. He smelled warm.

"We don't feed on souls in Adon Bashti," he murmured in her ear, guessing her intent.

"Then you should have added one more rule."

She placed his hands on the man's upturned face, and Adon moved his thumbs to rest on the closed eyelids. The man whimpered. The crowd was silent. Soolie placed her hands on Adon's hands, her thumbs on his thumbs, and reached for the life in the shaking man's body, and Adon opened the way.

She demanded, and—with Adon as her conduit—the man's life responded. The life of a human soul was so much less pure than the life of the Hunter's heart, but *still* she felt a thrill and gripped harder, feeling Adon's thumbs sinking into the sockets.

"That's enough." Adon closed the man's life off to her.

She let go. It had felt good to take life again. Even if it had only been for a moment and with Adon's help.

Adon lifted his hands from the man's face. The lids had shrunk back like withered winter leaves, and the eyeballs stuck dry to the craters in his still-living face.

The man screamed. He fell back, scrambling across the stones, hitting the legs of the crowd.

"Let him through," Soolie said.

The crowd parted, and the man flailed forward, falling down into the bodies, then struggling his way back up, and everytime he turned the dry bowls of his eyes towards where Soolie and Adon stood, he would scream again.

"He sees us," Adon said. His hands were on her shoulders.

"Yes. His eyes are dead. From now on, he will see only dead things."

She felt Adon chuckle, his chest and belly against her back, and she pulled away. "What?" she snapped.

"Power becomes you," he said.

"I should find Dog." She turned to leave.

"Perhaps you could forget him for just a little longer?"

". . . No," she said at last, "You have your responsibilities, and I have mine."

"Very well. Will you join me again tonight?" he asked. "I have been enjoying our time together."

"Will you force me to?"

"You are no one's slave, Soolie Beetch."

"Then we'll see."

∼

Someone stood at the foot of the bed, a crown of blood twining in its hair.

She was alone under the covers. Dog was gone again. He had been leaving lately, and more often. She hadn't said anything, and she wasn't sure why she hadn't said anything. He was probably just going for a walk. He'd be back.

The red eyes watched as she pulled the covers over her head and rolled over back to sleep.

∼

"Are we going to the library today, Mistress? Mistress?"

Chapter 19

"SILAAAS!" Kolgrin dropped the bowl and spoon, tin clattering, mush splattering on the tile, and leapt to his feet with his arms out. "I never doubted you. Get over here!"

Silas let out a long sigh of relief.

Upon reentry, the city's fatigue had settled heavily on his bones. It had only taken a few days outside the walls for his senses to forget the stench of death, and the renewed rank had been choking thick. He had staggered through the horrors, a kerchief to his nose, eyes down, wearying, despairing. He had *escaped*. He had been helping people. He had thrown it all away to return to this rotting wasteland on a hope shot. What if Kolgrin and Rahka were gone?

The journey down the long hospital corridors and dark twisting stairs had been a catacomb descent. By the time he neared the morgue, the possibility that he might be walking into an abandoned room—that he might be the only living thing left for miles—had felt very real. He had never been more relieved to see two people than he was to see Kolgrin and Rahka sitting here in the dark.

"I didn't expect to find you here in the middle of the day," Silas made his way towards them.

The gas must have finally burned out, because the only light came from four lanterns set on the floor, casting long light and longer shadows. He knew it was daylight outside, but here in the morgue was perpetual night.

"Waiting for you, friend!" Kolgrin kept his arms out, and as soon as Silas came within reach, he pulled him, pack and all, into a hug. "Glad you're back. You have no ken how glad."

It had been a short time, but they had both changed. Despite his bluster, Kolgrin's eyes had a new tightness and the rust brush of his beard hung from his cheekbones. His embrace was as heavy and overbearing as ever, but the great round roast of his chest had shrunk lean.

Rahka was nearly unrecognizable. She reclined on a stack of bulgar sacks, knees spread, her thin frame pinned by the mound of her belly, reminding Silas of a gorged bloodmite, fragile black limbs splayed beneath a bloated balloon. Her golden eyes flashed up, meeting his and catching the lantern light feverishly bright in their wine-stained hollows.

"What are you staring at, *bevjak?*" she snarled.

Silas looked away. He was glad they hadn't abandoned him, but he was worried. Rahka still had to give birth, and she didn't look fit to open a pantry door, much less a supernatural one.

"Come," Kolgrin's arm directed him towards the spot along the wall where Silas had made his bed before. "Let's get this load off you."

"Is Rahka unwell?"

Kolgrin grabbed the back of the pack and hefted so Silas could unbuckle the belt and duck out of the straps. "Sicker'n a trout full of worms," he grunted and lowered the pack against the wall. "But don't worry. She'll still manage that door for you."

Silas hoped so. Across the room, Rahka was rolling forward and standing stiffly. She tottered towards the dark hole of the furnace room.

"Does she have medicine?" Silas asked. "What about the health of the baby?"

"What baby?" Kolgrin snorted.

Silas knotted his brow. He didn't always follow Kolgrin's jokes. He had wanted to ask who the father was, but he could only guess that the father was likely dead, and Silas didn't want to be unkind. Rahka was a bit of a mystery. He still didn't understand what she was after or why she had promised to help him. He knew she was a bloodwitch, which made her dangerous and unsavory, but she was also a pregnant woman, which meant she should be defended and protected.

He couldn't doubt his course. He was where he was supposed to be.

Rahka passed into the furnace room and the heavy door clunked behind her.

"Have you eaten?" Kolgrin asked.

"Yesterday." Silas had developed a bad habit of eating only when fed.

"Come," Kolgrin angled him towards the great pile of provisions on the other side of the room. "You are going to eat with me, and then you are going to drink with me, Silas Beetch."

"I have had a long journey."

"All the more reason!"

"I would rather rest."

"Now, you listen." Kolgrin spun him about and rested a hand on each shoulder. "While you were off having brawls and adventures, I've been playing nursemaid to a sour bowl-bellied skag. The city is dead. There is nothing either of us can do tonight and nothing's coming in after us. And I *will* have myself a final dram with a pretty face before I kiss eternity's mudhole."

Silas looked away. "I just don't . . ."

"Is there *anything*," Kolgrin's voice softened, "you can do right now that's more important than making your last friend on this Ancients-forsaken earth happy?"

Silas hesitated. Kolgrin's eyes sought his with unusual sincerity. Silas didn't know what Kolgrin had been going through. They had all been through so much. Perhaps he could sit for just a moment.

"HA!" Kolgrin barked, and thrust Silas back so he stumbled and sat suddenly hard on the stack of grain sacks. "I KNEW a sad face would unbutton your britches."

"I haven't agreed!" Silas protested.

Kolgrin grabbed an upright barrel, twisted it next to Silas, and perched down. "You know what they don't have enough of in dance houses?"

Silas shook his head, jarred by the abrupt shifts in temperament.

"WINE." Kolgrin reached down and grabbed a dark bottle. He twisted the cork top, flicked it into the shadows, and shoved the bottle into Silas' hands. In a moment, Kolgrin had a bottle of his own, and he smacked the smooth glass bellies together and raised a salute. "Houses stock nothing but sour wheat and liquor—cheap gutter slosh and quick regrets—and that'll do in a pinch, but for a *good slosh,* my friend, there's nothing like the blood of a berry. Drink!" His voice boomed in the empty room as he tilted back and chugged, throat bobbing.

Silas sat. He was tired. His clothes were cold and stiff. The wounds on his head, back, and arms stabbed and ached, and the full mounting uncertainty of what he had returned to loomed like a wall of snow poised to come rumbling down and bury him. He was almost afraid to move.

"Now. I insist." Kolgrin pointed at the bottle in Silas' hand. "I must not be merry alone."

"I—" Silas protested.

"Oh, I see you." Kolgrin put his drink down and clapped his hands. "I promised food. You unlace your boots and open your throat. I'll be your wench."

The big man bustled into action, hauling over quilted blankets, a large clean sweater, trousers, and woolen socks. He brought a barrel of water and cups, and an array of preserved foods: cheese and nut butter, pickled corn, tomatoes, and squash, cakes of honeyed dried apricots and figs, and a cask of meats packed in salt. A few times, Silas tried to help, but each time, Kolgrin bellowed abuse in his direction until Silas returned meekly to his seat.

At last, Kolgrin halted to stand over him, hands on his hips. "I'm here bending my back, and you haven't even offed your boots yet."

"I am sorry . . . ."

"No," Kolgrin shoved a finger in his face. "Drink first. Then your laces. Quick. You're being rude."

Silas looked at the welcoming array of food and blankets, and the big man glowering down at him. Kolgrin must be lonely, and Silas hadn't had someone *want* to spend time with him in what felt like lifetimes.

Obediently, he lifted the bottle to his lips, tilted back, and drank. The wine was dark, sharp, and sweet like currant or elderberry. Silas didn't drink a lot of wine.

"Good. Give it. I don't undress a man without expectations, so you better change yourself."

Silas handed the bottle off and began picking at the laces of his boot. "I was afraid you might have left while I was gone."

"We weren't going through that door without you. Rahka says she needs you. Take another drink."

"Oh . . ." Silas wished he'd known that before. He yanked off the first boot, tucked the laces, and handed it to Kolgrin in exchange for the bottle. "I don't suppose that's likely to be a good thing." He took another swig.

"For you? Probably not." Kolgrin chucked the boot towards the middle of the room and accepted the bottle back.

"Do you know what she has planned?" Silas handed his other boot to Kolgrin, who tossed it in the general direction of the first.

"Not much, and what I do know, I'm not leaking." Kolgrin plopped down on the floor next to Silas and leaned against the sacks. He took a long drink, before handing the bottle up.

"Because you don't think I'd want to know?"

"'Cause Rahka wouldn't want you to."

"Do you owe her something?"

"I don't owe anyone."

Silas nodded. "Well. Thank you. For the food and the change of clothes."

"You can thank me by ditching those filthy weeds and drinking."

Silas rolled the clean woolen socks on over his grimy feet. The trousers and sweater sat on the floor within reach. They looked comfortable. He took another drink from the bottle. The wine buzzed in his empty belly and warmed his skull. Even if Kolgrin was dangerous and uncouth, it was nice to feel wanted. Sitting together in a dark, empty room, Kolgrin's voice bouncing off the walls, it felt like they might be the last two people alive.

"I know you're only showing me this level of hospitality, because there's no one else," he said.

Kolgrin recovered his own bottle and rested it on his thigh. "Yeah, no one fucking likes you, do they?"

That felt right to hear. "I guess not."

"Look, friend," Kolgrin twisted around and leaned against a barrel to face Silas. He took another long chugging swig, bearded cheeks hollowing as he sucked hard on the bottle, then grunted, settling back and catching his breath. "Look. I like having you around. You're a pretty face. Easy to fuck with and hard to break."

"Is that so," Silas said.

"That's so."

Kolgrin took another drink, and Silas drank with him. Kolgrin slung his emptied bottle clatter-skittering over the tiles and smack-bouncing off the far wall.

"I'm sorry you've been alone down here," Silas said.

"We're all fucking alone."

"Yes. I just mean . . ." Silas trailed off. There was something sad about the man.

It must have been visible in his face, because Kolgrin growled. "Fuck you." He reached behind the barrel and pulled out another bottle. "I'll fuck you raw, Silas Beetch. You know I can."

"If you assault me, I will only feel more sorry for you."

Kolgrin snorted. Then laughed. "A proper threat. Fine, we are at a draw. Consider yourself safe with me, Silas Beetch. You have my honor."

Silas smiled a little. "For what your honor is worth."

"Silas," Kolgrin leaned forward, suddenly serious, and placed a hand on his knee. "I vow on my own wag, I will defend your sanctity with my life. Any man or monster wants to get up your bum will have to go through me first."

Silas tried not to grimace.

Kolgrin sat back, satisfied.

"Thank you. I know you mean well. Friends are rare in these times."

"I'm not your friend, friend." Kolgrin bit the cork with his teeth, yanked it free, and spat it out.

Maybe different people had different definitions of friendship. Silas swirled the bottle, watching the faint glimmer swish in the glass. "I've only ever had one friend. And I wasn't good to her."

"You fuck her?"

Silas sighed. "My wife's sister."

"You hound," Kolgrin bared purple-creviced teeth in a hungry grin.

"Don't say that," Silas said. "She might be the only person who's ever cared about me."

"Was she good?" Kolgrin pressed. "Did you wet that leg more than once?"

"She died the next day." Silas took another drink. "I watched it happen." He was starting to wish he felt drunker than he did.

"You must have some riotous tastes after that."

"I don't think so . . . ."

"Come now. What does Silas dream of when he wakes up with twad in his sheets?"

"I don't really . . ." Silas didn't usually like to talk about these sorts of things, but the wine oiled the hinges to doors that were generally rusted shut. He shrugged. "I don't really want anyone in that way. I don't think I really wanted her . . . ." It was a strange thing to say. He took another swig, and the drinking and the swallowing and the need for air got away from him, and he found himself abruptly out of breath. He gasped, "at least . . ." he panted, "not the way she wanted me . . . . I was scared, and she was there, and that's kind of how it was with both of them, except Tera was using me, and I was okay with that. Tera needed someone, anyone, and I was okay being her anyone . . . but Evaline . . . wanted more that I couldn't give her, and I was . . . cruel."

"Awh, you sweet man," Kolgrin rolled his head from side to side. "Another life, and I'd teach you a thing or two."

"Okay." Silas sighed. "Then you tell me something."

"I've told you plenty."

"No, you haven't. Tell me something real."

"Drink," Kolgrin motioned with his finger, and Silas obliged. "Nothing to tell. No mam, no pap. No kits. Nothing dragging. There's nothing real about me, Silas. What you see is what's for sale."

"You care about Rahka?" Silas prompted.

Kolgrin grunted.

"Do you know what she wants?"

"Far as I can tell, to scorch anyone who touches her."

That sounded awfully lonely. "You know," Silas leaned forward. "I met her once, before we met, in the wreckage of the Great Square. She'd been attacked by the same thing that was attacking my daughter. I think she'd been burned."

"I've heard her spin a number of different tales about how she got those scars," Kolgrin said. "If whoever burned her is still out there, they should be spakkin' themselves."

Silas nodded. That must be what she was after. "But I still don't understand what brings you in."

"Hmmm." Kolgrin looked up at the ceiling. "You ever met someone who sees the worst in you and feeds the hell out of it?"

"Sounds awful."

Kolgrin chuckled. "If I had your sponge heart, I suppose it would be."

"But not for you, because your heart is hard."

"Hard as a skike with a pickle up his pucker."

Silas raised the bottle to his lips, "I think caring scares you."

Kolgrin snorted. "And how many of those crawlers were alive when you left them?"

Silas lowered the bottle. Kolgrin was changing the subject. He looked down. "Five."

"Countin' that twad-nap Nolas?"

"Havah shot Nolas."

"Good," Kolgrin grunted.

"She hates me, you know," Silas added.

"You fucking left her crawlers to the claws, of course she hates you." Kolgrin winked. "I, however, couldn't be more proud."

Silas' eyes felt warm. He slumped back against the sacks. "Sometimes . . . What if I don't know what's good and bad any more?"

"Sometimes," Kolgrin said, "things are the best, only they are *especially* bad." He lifted the nearly empty bottle from Silas' hand, downed the last swirling drops, and replaced it with his own half-full bottle. "Now, let's see if you can build up enough courage to change your britches."

∿

"My stepfather wasn't a good man."

Silas peeled the dirty shirt over his head. He'd lost track of how much he'd had to drink, and they hadn't touched the food, but he felt mostly fine. Sloshy and reely and warm, but fine. Perhaps this was another effect of his strangely bolstered disposition. He tossed the shirt on the floor.

"I've heard of stepfathers." Kolgrin was looking up at him, nodding.

Silas couldn't remember how they'd gotten on this topic. Perhaps it hadn't happened organically at all. It was the unspoken truth that existed beneath his thoughts, the foundation that gave out underneath him whenever he stood still, and he had never been this drunk and this open with someone who wouldn't feel sorry or judge him before. He didn't know. He reached for the sweater. It was big and bulky.

"Wait," Kolgrin raised a hand. "Finish what you were going to say first."

"That was it." Silas turned the sweater around and around, trying to find the big hole.

"No," Kolgrin grunted. "Finish what you were going to say first. And then the sweater. It's only fair."

Silas wasn't sure how that was fair. He looked down at his chest, covered in mud and blood, healing bruises cuts and scars. "I'm really dirty."

"Mmmhmm." Kolgrin took another drink.

"My step father wasn't a good man," he started again. "He was a guard. Could have had any woman, and he chose her. I used to wonder what he saw in my mom, you know?"

"He beat her?" Kolgrin asked.

"No." Silas studied the sweater, sorting his thoughts from the cables. "I don't think so. She was an addict, and he kept her flying. All day, she would wheedle and beg and whine for him when he was gone. And then he would come home and go upstairs and get her flying, and then she'd be quiet for the rest of the night. I didn't get it. Of course, I hated him. Then, all of a sudden he got real mean, but just towards me."

Kolgrin nodded, watching, drinking.

"He'd hit me. Throw me against the walls. He was a big man. He told me if I didn't leave, he'd kill me. I believed him."

"So you ran," Kolgrin said.

"I ran." Silas' hands tightened on the sweater. Tears were welling in his eyes. His chest was tight.

"Who was it?" Kolgrin asked.

"My younger sister."

"Yeah," Kolgrin said.

Silas' chest heaved and he started to sob.

"Oh, well . . ."

Silas hugged the sweater tight. His face hurt. Pain and wetness swelled in his eyes and in his nose. It was hard to breathe.

"C'mon now." Kolgrin was next to him, prying his hands off the sweater. "Hands up, you drunk baby."

Silas shuddered, raising his hands, still shaking. He hadn't cried about this before, while knowing it was what he was crying about. Kolgrin was sticking his arms into the sweater holes. The sack of knit enveloped his head, and then his face popped out the top, and Kolgrin tugged the sweater down over him.

"A man shouldn't have to sob naked." Kolgrin said and patted him on the back.

Silas clutched his arms to his chest. "I . . . never . . . went . . ."

"I know."

"I lied to . . . my family . . . ."

"Probably for the best." Kolgrin put a big arm over his shoulders. "Look on the rosy side. Fates are, none of them are suffering anymore, 'cause all of them are deader 'n rugs."

Silas sniffed, stoppering decades of unspilled grief. "I'm . . . I'm okay."

"Yeah, you are." Kolgrin patted him on the shoulder. "This your first time getting soppy with a man?"

"I . . ." Silas accepted the bottle Kolgrin shoved at him. "I guess so?"

"Figures," Kolgrin snorted. "Can't tell you how many times a man taking off his shirt ends in tears."

Silas wiped his eyes. "Just wait until I change my pants."

"Are you *trifling with me*, Silas Beetch?" Kolgrin roared, laughing and sitting back. "HOW DARE YOU. Expect no more help from me."

∼

"I was twenty-six when Tera died. So . . . I don't entirely know. I feel older."

"You look fucking ancient."

". . . Lands. Soolie is now only three or four years younger than I was when she was born."

"How old'll she have to be before you stopped looking?" Kolgrin asked.

"I'll never stop looking," Silas said.

"Well—even if she is still alive—what if she doesn't want you?"

"She might still need me."

"She might not."

"Well. Then, that's good," Silas said. "If she doesn't, I hope it's because she's happy."

"So, you're content being forgotten."

"Yeah. Yes."

"Then what the fuck do you want from her?"

"Nothing."

"Bullspak."

"I want her to know I'm sorry . . . ."

"That's a danksacks thing to want."

". . . That I never gave up. That I love her. And that if she needs me, I'll be there. Always."

"You shouldn't have fucking come back here, friend."

"I know," Silas said. "If it helps, I don't think it was entirely my choice."

Kolgrin was quiet.

"How old are you?" Silas asked.

"Who fucking knows . . ."

Chapter 20

"Would you like to go for a hunt?" Adon leaned in the bedroom door.

Soolie sat up and rubbed the black crust from her eyes. "Hunting what?"

"Your Dog can come."

"Sure, then, I guess."

∽

THE FOUR OF THEM—ADON, Soolie, Dog, and the Chorus—set out in the early morning while the world was still damp and thinly lensed in shadows. Adon led them down city narrows and unpaved back-paths. They made swift steps, and by the time they reached the jungle's edge, the first sungleams were only just licking the rooftops behind them.

Night drained more slowly in the jungle. Heavy vegetation formed a high roof with faint windows of glimmering green that grew and spread as they walked, lifting black shrouds to reveal a lush and wild cathedral of towering trunks carpeted in fronds and long-tailed moss. Red and white insects spooled along vines that hung like fat cobwebs. A big bellied plant snapped its lid, and Soolie saw the shadow of something the size of a walnut battering itself against the inner walls.

They traveled in silence, listening to a symphony of chattering, whistling, click-click buzzing of creatures seen and unseen. The emerald light gave Soolie and Dog a sallow pallor, but turned the Chorus' silver-white to pale peridot against the blackish of its red eyes and crown. Adon's warm skin and coral tunic resisted any transformation, and he stood out floral bold on the field of green. Every once in a while, he would glance back at Soolie and flash a smile.

They moved at a greater speed than that of living things and didn't stop to rest. At last, Adon led them out of the heavy foliage and into the bright afternoon sun, and they began the trek up the side of one of the great twin mountains.

The path was narrow and rocky, and the stone rebuffed all but the most stubborn vegetation. Long antennaed bugs with conifer-seed bodies trundled over flat rocks and thrummed the air with song. White furry rodents shrieked and flicked long whip tails, while great purple birds painted circles of trailing blue and green tail feathers above.

"You've been quiet," Adon said over his shoulder. "Are you enjoying yourself?"

Soolie followed on the path, while Dog and the Chorus kept pace alongside leaping and traipsing over boulders and loose gravel.

"You usually do all the talking," she said.

"You think I talk too much."

"You do."

He laughed. "I can be very proud."

He bent to offer her a hand up a steep slope of slate, and she ignored him, scrambling up on all fours and passing on the path. "You're an arrogant self-sucking fuckstain."

"I see," he said, falling in behind her. "Please continue."

"I wasn't missing the conversation."

"And I didn't invite your company for carnal pleasures. Surely conversation isn't too great an ask."

The view was all achingly blue and green and glaring white, colors that almost hurt to look at. Soolie took a deep breath, inflating her limp lungs with cleansing air. Dog bounded a pace up ahead and crouched on a rock, tilting his head and waiting.

When she didn't respond, Adon asked, "Are you unhappy here?"

"What would be the point of me telling you anything," she said. "You've already stolen more than I'd ever give you."

"I recall that you were kind enough to return the favor."

"I defended myself."

"You attacked," he said. "Though, for my part, I could have taken the time to earn your trust. I underestimated you, and I understand that now."

The path dissipated into a field of boulders at the base of a sharp incline. They made their way balancing, crawling, and leaping from stone to stone. She avoided looking at him as he made his way to her side.

"Would you like to play a game?" he asked.

"No."

"You like games," he said. "Let's pretend we are strangers who have only just met."

"No."

He bounded up an especially large boulder and offered a hand, and this time, she accepted and let him hoist her up to stand next to him.

"Then, will you let me carry you so we can reach the summit before sunset?"

She jerked her hand back. "I don't let strangers carry me."

"My name is Adon sen Yevah," he bowed. "If you will permit me, I will carry you up this mountain."

"My name is Soolie, and no, fuck off."

He met her eyes sincerely. "Please. We have walked a long way. The sunset is beautiful, and I wouldn't want you to miss it."

Dog and the Chorus were already at the foot of the mountain. The sandals on her feet were thin, and her feet were battered and sore. . . .

"Fine."

His face split in a triumphant grin, and he crouched so she could climb onto his back. As soon as she was close to him, a ripple of ease washed over her, and she wrapped her arms around his neck, and he laced his fingers under her seat. He was so much easier to hold on to than Dog's small frame. She could feel the magic twisting across his back, pulling her into him as if they might weave into one another—blood passing between their skin like suturing threads—and she was momentarily flushed with the awareness of the pure *rashni* of the Hunter's Heart, and she gritted her teeth against the impulse to try to pull that life out of him and into her.

The Chorus was a statue. Dog withered, watching.

Adon launched from the boulder with the speed of a great cat, bounding and whooping, and soon the three of them were scaling, leaping from crag to crag, rock to cliff's edge, the wind whipping their clothes to their bodies, the purple birds shrieking and wheeling around them as they climbed with the ease and speed of near weightlessness.

She clung tight and didn't see the top coming until Adon vaulted them over onto it. He crouched so she could drop down and stood watching her take in their surroundings.

The top of the mountain was a great table. Far below, the boulders looked like peppercorns, the distant city like grains of rice. She walked the circumference. On one side, the mountain's twin rose to face them, sharp top unblunted. On the other, the precipice dropped into a heavy pelt of green veined with silver rivers. The distant horizon was a gleaming thread.

"Is the ocean that way?"

"It is," he said. He sat on a stone slab that rested in the middle of the mesa. "Men carved out the top of this mountain. Her name is Mesheddi and her brother is Fittesh. Mesheddi is in love with Fittesh, but he must go to war. Heartbroken, Mesheddi begs the Ancients to keep them together. Her prayers are so impassioned, that the Ancients take pity on her and turn them both into mountains that stand together forever watching over the land." He nodded to the stone beneath him. "For centuries, offerings were made upon this altar."

"She loved her *brother?*" Soolie wrinkled her nose. "Like family love?"

"The mountain ranges that separate the Southern Lands from the Mainlands are their children."

"Yuck."

He laughed. "I take it you, Soolie, have never loved."

Dog stood near the far mountain edge, his eyes on her. The Chorus took its place at Adon's shoulder.

"I thought this was a hunt," Soolie said.

"Yes," he patted the stone next to him. "Sit with me? I will explain."

The Chorus unslung a pack from its back and set it on the stone. Soolie sat warily opposite as Adon lifted the flap and pulled out a leather strap. On either end hung a fringe of leashes roughly two-hands in length, each ending in a small brass ring.

"There are many beautiful species of birds that make their nests in these mountains." Adon took one of the fringe leashes, bent it into a loop and fitted it through the ring to form a noose. "The loomwing is not such a bird. They are an invader, brought over as pets because of their colorful plumage, but they only make good pets if you clip their wings." He slipped a finger through the noose and pulled it slip-taught.

"The purple birds," Soolie said. Up this high, she couldn't see them circling, but they had passed a great many during the climb.

"Loomwings aggressively protect their young. They will destroy the nests of other birds," he handed the strap to the Chorus, "so they must be culled, so that the native birds can live."

The Chorus laid the strap over its shoulder.

"It's less of a hunt," Adon said, "and more of an extermination. There's very little sport in it. I let my Chorus do the work. However," he leaned in, "if you would *like* to make it a sport . . . ."

Soolie waited.

"I do have several leash straps. We could have a little competition between my Chorus and your Dog to see who can fill one first."

Soolie glanced over at Dog, hunched alone, buffeted by the wind and looking small. She did think Adon underestimated him. Perhaps she could use this to tilt the ground in her favor, even if for just a moment. "What if we wager on it?"

His eyes glittered. "You will lose."

She stuck out her chin. "He is better than you think."

"I created that Dog. As I created his replacement. You let your sentiments get the better of you, my dear. This is not a game that you can win."

Soolie wanted to check on Dog, but Adon's eyes were close and intense, and she didn't dare look away. "If Dog wins, I get to wear the crown."

Adon raised his eyebrows. "That is not a small ask."

"If you are so confident, why do you hesitate?"

"My hesitation is not for me," he said. "If you are going to ask for something so great, I must request something comparable in return."

She braced herself.

"Hmmm." He assessed her and stroked his jaw. "If my Chorus wins," he said at last, "you will *let me* show you what our future will be together. No resisting and no tricks."

So, either she went into his mind or he went into hers.

She shrugged.

He put out his hand. "I have your word."

She took it, and again his touch was strong and rough, gentle and warm. "And I have yours," she said.

He flashed a smile, lifted her hand, and kissed it before she could pull away. "It is sealed. Chorus!"

The Chorus took the belt from its shoulder and threw it at Dog, who snagged it out of the air and looked to Soolie, querulous and concerned. Adon still held her hand.

"Mistress?"

"Just catch as many purple birds as you can as quickly as possible. Fill the strap and bring it back to me," she commanded.

He bobbed. "Yes, Mistress."

The Chorus produced another strap of leashes and slung the pack onto its back.

"Would you like to say the word?" Adon asked.

She shouted, "GO!"

The Chorus sprinted for the cliff's edge and dove over hands-first, a streak of blood and white arcing into open space. There was a shriek and the flurry squalls of panicked birds. Dog looked at her, and then sprinted for a different side of the mountain.

Adon winked, "Sounds like I'm ahead."

Soolie pulled her hand away. "They've only just started."

"*Has* your Dog started?"

Dog swung feet-first over the far side.

"My Chorus has chosen the side with the most gradual slope," Adon said. "From there, it can leap to seize the loomwings without falling too far." Adon pointed in Dog's direction. "Your Dog has chosen a side of vertical cliffs and undercuts. While there will be nests, he won't be able to leap to grab the birds without plummeting to the jungle floor. Even if he kills them with stones, the bodies will fall too far for timely retrieval." He leaned close and whispered. "You had best prepare your mind, my dear. I'm afraid you have already lost."

Soolie's stomach twisted in sour knots. "It is not decided *yet*."

From the direction of the Chorus came the sounds of birds screaming, flapping, shale sliding, rocks kicking loose. Adon's eyes stayed on hers. *Let me show you what our future will be together.* Perhaps it wouldn't be too terrible. From Dog's direction, there rose a chorus of high scratchy screams and shrieks of fury. Adon's eyes flicked towards the sound as Dog scrambled back onto the flattop, his belt full of little fluffy brown bodies that fluttered and flailed, filling the air with tiny cheeping squalls.

"Hatchlings don't count," Adon scoffed.

Soolie shrugged. "That was never specified." Even if she didn't win, perhaps she could at least call it a draw.

"But *you did*," he grinned. "Catch as many *purple birds as you can*, was your command, and those are brown as scat."

Dog wasn't approaching. He slung the belt onto the ground and planted a foot between the struggling screaming babies just as, up from the edge of the mountain, there rose a torrent of birds.

They came all at once, great wings spanned wide, tails bright in the sun, over the top and diving for the monster that stood with its foot on their children. Dog held his ground, crouching fingers flexed as the storm fell, and then he became a blur, leaping and grabbing necks, twisting bodies, and slinging flapping feathery flurries to the ground, stamping down with his heel, his blunt fingers digging into plumed breasts, crushing their cages and marring his hands in feathers and blood. The younglings' screams blinded their parents with rage, and they wheeled and dove, sharp beaks stabbing Dog's flesh, claws raking his cheek, but for every cut, another two or three bodies fell, piling around him seven, nine, twelve, sixteen, until only a small handful of adults survived, circling high, shrieking as their young still screeched and struggled, pulling one another in opposing directions on the ends of their leads, tumbling through the mangled bodies of their parents.

Soolie smiled.

"He has done well," Adon nodded. "I have no doubt he will be able to fill that belt twice over."

From behind her, the Chorus dropped three belts of twist-necked purple birds on the stone between them.

"And yet," Adon said, "he has lost."

Soolie held his eyes, but she knew he had seen her flinch. In the pile of dead birds, Dog crouched, popping baby birds from their nooses and swapping them out for the necks of dead adults.

"DOG," she shouted.

Adon's smile was smug and self-satisfied. Dog never stood a chance.

He lifted his head, hands still moving. "Mistress?"

"Stop. It's over."

"Mistress?"

Adon kept his eyes on her and held out both hands. The Chorus lifted the crown from its head and placed the writhing circlet in its master's grasp.

"Stop," she said again. "The game is done."

Out of the corner of her eye, she could see Dog standing with a belt of bleeding birds, watching as Adon lifted the crown to his head. The blood threads stretched and stuck and stitched down, and blood squiggled over his dark eyes and filled them red.

"Are you ready?"

"Let's get this fucking done with."

He beckoned. "Come close."

Her head whined like firewood about to pop. She scooted under his waiting arm, and he wrapped it around her and pulled her to his side, leg to leg, hip to hip. He placed his hand over her eyes and rested his cheek on her head.

"Close your eyes."

He held her still and, while there was no heartbeat, she felt that he was breathing in and out, and in and out.

"Wait for it."

She bit her lip.

"You're resisting."

"I'm *not*," she snapped.

"You are." He sounded amused. "You're as tense as a wet cat. Breathe with me."

"I don't breathe."

"It will help. Stop thinking and focus on my breathing. With me."

He breathed in and she scowled, and out, and then in. She waited for him to scold her, but he simply held her and waited. She breathed in with him, and the tightness in her brow lessened just a bit, and out. In, and out, listening to his breath, feeling him beside her. There was a hypnotic swell to it, and despite herself, despite the hard rod of rage and fear in her chest, she slowly began to ease and to almost forget what he was about to do.

He lifted his hand from her eyes. "Open your eyes."

She opened them.

They were still on the mountaintop. The sun had melted into a bright lake of gold that hazed up to blue scattered with shreds of fuschia and purple cloud, and the whole vast world was bathed in color and light.

"Ohhhh," she gasped, and one of his hands found hers. "But . . ." She looked to him, and he smiled back with dark eyes. Far off, the Chorus stood with the crown on its head.

"Is this a . . ."

"Shhhush. Just look."

She took another breath and watched as the sun thinned on the horizon and the colors deepened.

"I have spent millenia gathering the greatest craftspeople to erect the most elegant halls and extraordinary treasures, the likes of which, mankind has hitherto possessed neither resource nor scope to verge upon," he said, "and none of it compares to the daily beauty bestowed upon our realm since the beginning of time. *This* is grandeur forged with the language of the Ancients. This is the power that, together, we possess. To be the creators. To write directly into the foundations of the world, to renew flesh that has gone wrong and mend what is broken, to give new life. We are the writers of our fates. I am the ink, and you are the pen, and all the realm is our page."

"This is what you wanted to show me?" she asked.

"I do not need visions and dreams to show you our future together," he squeezed her hand. "I only need for you to open your eyes."

∽

Dog trailed behind as they descended the mountain. The old Master carried her in his arms, her head upon his shoulder, and the Master's Wolf ran alongside, luminous in the moonlight. The three of them traipsed over boulders and down the path, and all the while Dog fell farther and farther behind, watching the distance grow as they descended and no one looked back.

He was losing her. Soon it would be too late. If he didn't find a way to take and use the crown, soon there would be no Mistress to save. The Master would enter her mind, and this time she wouldn't be able to fight him, and he would erase her, and Dog would lose both the Ancient and the Young.

He had to sacrifice one to preserve the other. Better to have one Mistress than none at all.

They entered the mouth of the jungle and were swallowed by darkness. When at last, three emerged, Dog was no longer with them.

Chapter 21

"Silas, wake up!"

The world spun sour. Silas blinked. Everything was pitch dark, except for Kolgrin's face looking panicked in the light of a lantern.

"Kolgrin?"

"Rahka's unwell. I need your help."

"Of course. What's happened?" He grasped the offered hand, and Kolgrin helped him to his feet.

"I heard her moaning." Kolgrin led the way. "I think it's started . . . ."

"She's gone into labor?" Silas had been there when Tera gave birth. He knew a little. "How much water do we have? We'll need clean cloths and willow bark, and—"

"It's worse than that." Kolgrin pushed in the furnace room door. "I think something's wrong . . . ."

He halted, lantern lifted, and Silas stepped to his side, looking in.

The nest of blankets was empty.

"She was here a moment ago," Kolgrin said. "Just a *moment* ago."

"The door." Silas pointed across the room. The door to the side stairway hung open. "She can't have gone far." Silas headed towards it. "We'll find her."

"Grab your boots," Kolgrin said.

"Where?"

"I threw them over there. You'll need them. I know where she's gone."

∼

Silas hadn't been to the site of the tower since it fell. It was so much closer to the rest of the Sun District than he remembered or imagined. One moment he was following Kolgrin through tightly-packed abandoned mansions, and the next he was walking out onto a field of rubble and dust.

The first strange thing he saw was a black table sitting in the open, and then he saw the red river. It was nearly a full arm across, and it writhed like fish surging upstream, not as one entity, but as a billion threads that twisted and turned in a full circle around the field of white with the black table in its center.

"Watch your step," Kolgrin said.

"Ancients help us." Silas leaped across. "Is that blood?"

"There she is." Kolgrin pointed to the base of the table.

Rahka sat on the ground, one leg tucked in, the other out, clutching her belly, fingers digging, head down.

"RAHKA!"

She didn't move.

Kolgrin ran and Silas followed. The dust beneath their feet bore the marks of repeat passage, leading to the table and circling the inner rim of the river, and Silas wondered if the blood in that ring belonged *only* to monsters, or if there was another reason Rahka and Kolgrin hadn't included him on their expeditions. His heart thrummed against the hull of his skull.

"Rahka? Answer me, Rahka?" Kolgrin crouched. He cupped her neck, and her head rolled towards his palm. Her face was damp and gray, her eyes half closed. "Silas?" he begged.

Silas knelt, and Kolgrin stood behind him. She smelled sickly and unwashed. He placed a hand on the taut globe of her belly, and it was cold to the touch. They were in trouble.

"We should have brought supplies," he said.

A hand clamped over his nose and mouth, and great arms wrapped him in a tight embrace, pinning his arms to his sides. By reflex, Silas threw himself backwards, knocking his assailant onto their back with Silas on top, but the arms held on, binding him to the assailant's chest. It was Kolgrin. The familiar dazzle of a dozing drug burned in Silas' sinuses and warmed his brain.

What was happening?

He twisted and wrestled, but Kolgrin planted his boots wide and wouldn't be turned, and the cloth was pressed over Silas' nose and mouth, and the gray sky was clouding over with forced sleep. The last thing Silas saw was two golden eyes looking down at him.

"Place him on the table."

Chapter 22

The trip back was the longest Soolie had been this close to him, and she felt drifty and dreamlike as Adon carried her through the house and out onto a veranda lit by torches. The sky was sparkling dark, and steam rolled soft and white from a large basin set in the floor.

"The bath is heated from below, so it never grows cold. I thought you might enjoy a soak before dinner."

"Do I get it to myself?"

"You'll find salts, oils, and towels on the table." He set her down. "May I?" he asked, taking her hand.

"Okay."

He kissed her fingers. "I'll return for you in an hour."

He left through the open doorway.

She didn't really want to smell like anything in particular, so she dropped her shift on the stone at her feet and crawled into the water.

The basin had an inner ledge for sitting that ran all the way around, but it was deep enough in the middle that she could hang weightless, limbs softly bent, toes grazing the bottom. The surface flickered in the firelight, and the water dove clear as glass to the white stone bottom.

She drifted, slowly oscillating her arms to keep her head above the surface, watching the stars through the steamy haze. Then she let go and allowed the water to swallow her completely. The sound of the world fogged and the lights wavered above, and she drifted in that warm womb until she couldn't feel the cold death of her body any more, and she closed her eyes.

His presence and her hunger for him woke her.

She opened her eyes to see him watching from above. His hand plunged in, and she took it, and he helped her step up from the bath and out onto the veranda with her skin steaming in the torchlight.

"Did you enjoy yourself?"

"It's nice."

He touched her arm. "I brought you something."

The clothes she'd been wearing were gone. He walked to a pile of gauzy white that rested on a table, lifted it, and turned.

"Do you remember the first time you stood before my throne?" The garment was long and filmy. It caught the light, but let the darkness shadow through. "It occurred to me that you were right. The best compliment to the blood on your skin is to not cover it at all. Will you allow me?"

He was asking nicely, and she couldn't think of a reason to fight him.

She raised her arms.

He dropped the dress over her head, and it rippled down like mist, hanging from her shoulders and wafting at the tops of her feet, light as the stirring breeze.

"Do you like it?"

She ran her hands down her sides. The cloth was so thin, touching it felt like touching her bare skin, and where it rested, the blood weave showed clearly through. "I'm only going to fuck it up."

"It is very delicate." He took her hand. "It might help to remove this." He cupped her wrist to show her the hair bracelet that was tied there, sharp wire and fang edges threatening the fragile cloth. "I am not sure it belongs."

"Okay."

He held her wrist underside-up and examined the tight, wet leather knots.

"Forgive me," he said, and lifted her wrist to his mouth. His lips brushed her skin as his teeth bit and loosened the knot.

He picked the last twists free with his fingers, his eyes on her as the bracelet fell away. She watched as he walked to a torch and held it over the flame until the damp hair curled and split from the braided knots, and as it caught fire, he dropped it burning into the torch cage and turned back to her.

"This is going to be a very special night for us," he said.

∽

Dog swung over the high balcony, onto the outside of the spiral stairs, and dropped. He fell from one floor to the next, barely controlling his descent by laddering his hands on the stair rails as his feet sped towards the floor. The stair stopped one level above the main, and he dropped and vaulted over the last railing to land in a crouch, facing the librarian.

She stood between him and the main doors, a cooking knife in her hand. "I can't let you leave with those."

Dog placed one hand on the satchel that hung crossbody at his side. "You will not stop me."

She widened her stance and leveled the knife at him. She was slow, and her movements were fearful. It would only take him a moment to duck under her arm, turn the knife toward her belly, and thrust.

"I should still try," she said. "If Mavi knew, she would never forgive me."

"She will also know if you are disemboweled," Dog said.

"I should have destroyed those a long time ago."

"You didn't."

Her chest sunk. She lowered the blade. "You are more human than before. But she has not made you less of a monster."

He launched himself, sprinting past and pushing through the doors. She called after him, "Does she know what you are about to do?"

Dog didn't respond.

∽

A WAVE of cheers and applause heralded them as they entered the room and he guided her up the dais to the throne. He had not fed her yet, and to be so close to him for so long was maddening. The life in him and the life in the throne called to her, and she yearned towards him.

He cupped her face in his palm and smiled. "First, I must enjoy myself. Sit. Rest."

His hand lingered on her cheek as she sat on the throne.

"Don't lean back," he said, and released her.

She perched on the edge. The seat was neither cold nor warm and her fingers squeaked on the smooth surface. She could feel the magic behind her responding to his closeness, and despite the memory of her mangled fingers, she wanted to lean back and reach for him and pull all three of them together.

The beautiful people in their brightly-colored clothes flocked to him like garden birds to a tree. Soolie wasn't sure if these were the exact same people she had seen around him before, but they were the same in manner and in the peerlessness of their form and shape. She counted seven young and living bodies, three men and four women. Adon took his eyes off of her as their many hands landed upon his body.

From the edges of the room, servants in white entered bearing platters and tureens, filling goblets, and ladening plates. The music was all strings tonight, and the instruments voiced together in dipping, surging, swooping song as the people began to fill their mouths and bellies with feasting, and the room with the sound of clattering utensils, cracking cartilage, juicing fruit, and swirling wine.

In the center of it all rested a carpet of furs and a great divan.

Adon's shirt was left on the steps, his pants on the floor. The people moved about him like ribbons of seagrass as they made their way off the dais, shedding a trail of colorful garments in their wake. By the time their feet touched the furs, all bodies were bare.

Skin pale as moonlight moved over skin black as water, pink dimpled spines and wheat-brown thighs, long rust hair and short dark scruff, round muscular haunches and soft bottomed cheeks, and in the center of them was Adon. Somehow, surrounded by such sculpturesque beauty, the beauty of his body became more real. He was not the tallest, the most curved, or the most muscular, but the broadness of his shoulders and the mounds of his chest, the sun-ruddy skin, alert warm eyes, and strong bent nose—the body he had made for himself *was* the most inviting, and Soolie felt she understood it.

A woman with waves of tawny hair lay back on the divan, parting her legs and reaching for him, and Adon was on top of her and moved into her, and her long legs wrapped around his hips, and one of his hands was under the curve of her back lifting her into him and another was fisted in her hair, and all around them, the beautiful people fell upon one another, and Soolie watched.

Fat nipples pinched between sharp teeth, heavy hands on muscular waists, fingers parted long bushy lips, tongues licked and mouths enveloped, and they shoved their parts into one another and made feral sounds. From the woman, Adon moved on to a man with a scooping back and cheeks that shook as they moved, then he was between three people at once, and then he lay back on the divan and the beautiful people visited him to suckle and gorge themselves, holding one another's heads down and pleasuring one another with fingers and tongues.

Soolie's stomach was sharp and hungry, and she held herself very still. She didn't want to be a part of this. It looked odd and messy, and the way the people touched one another made them seem like a many-limbed animal with a single mind, and Adon was the head of the beast.

She was both drawn to him and repulsed by them.

She didn't want to be one of the fawning many, and she didn't know if she wanted to be touched in any of those ways, certainly not by all of those people, as if they were beyond sense and their bodies all belonged to one another. But she also didn't like how excluded she felt, and how easily he ignored her while she wasn't able to ignore him.

She sat in the room full of feasting and nakedness and hated *most of all* how maddeningly hungry she was. She set her jaw and held tight to the throne and watched and did not move.

∼

DOG SLUNG the rope over the bar and pulled, hoisting the bound naked body into the air by its wrists. The man screamed, shouting again and again for help, and Dog did not bother taking the time to silence him. He pulled the leather roll from the satchel, loosened the tie, and rolled it out on the ground. In the center rested the twisting bone stylus of the carving pen. This was the moment he had prepared for.

Dog plucked the pen from its sheath and stood in front of the living body, examining the bare belly that fluttered with panicked breath.

"PLEASE! HELP! OH, ANCIENTS, HELP ME!"

Dog used his foot to shove the great tin bucket under the man's twitching feet. Then he touched the tip of the stylus to the man's belly and started to carve.

∿

Sated bodies dozed, moist, mussed, and bare. Adon lazed on the divan, one leg out, the other bent. He looked at Soolie for the first time in what must have been hours, and smiled.

"Have you enjoyed yourself?"

Soolie shrugged. "Looks sticky."

"You feel neglected." He extended a hand towards her. Seven heads raised and seven sets of eyes looked at her. "We don't have to be done."

"No," Soolie said.

"Join me, as our guest of honor," he said. Many hands reached for her.

"No," with all the force she could muster.

He propped himself up on one elbow. "Are you afraid? Have you and the Dog ever experienced one another? Or is your fruit untasted?"

Soolie grimaced.

He laughed. "I do enjoy making you uncomfortable, Soolie Beetch. I like the way you tense like a scared little animal, right up until the moment you are completely undone. Don't you?"

"No," she said again, fingers biting into the seat of the throne.

He tilted his head. "This is nothing more intimate than what we have already shared. It is a long existence without pleasure. Allow yourself to be led by me. You will enjoy it."

"No," she said again. She didn't want it. But she was very hungry for the life inside of him. She wanted him to touch her, but not in that way, and the feelings were a little confusing.

"Well," he said, "Some other time, then. When you're ready." He motioned, and the beautiful people began to gather their clothes.

∼

Dog finished the last turn of the carving that twisted and cut through the man's flesh, completing the command. He stepped back. The ancient words began to writhe faster. The man screamed, and the screaming turned to a gargle, and the man's eyes boiled and burbled jam down his face, blood spilling from his lips, and then his flesh began to sag, liquifying under his skin, arms shrinking to yellow-sleeved sticks, skin sloping over his skull, hanging on his ribs as the pouch of his belly distended with fluid flesh and his legs bloated into purple shiny taut balloons.

Dog reached out with the small silver knife and touched the blade edge to the swollen underside of a bare foot and cut. Liquid red spurted from the incision, splashing splattering into the pot. Dog cut the step of the other foot and stepped back as the body drained, deflating like a wineskin until only hair and loose-skinned bones remained.

∼

"Now, will you join me?"

The people adorned the rim of the dais, and he sat on the divan alone, shirtless, but wearing pants again.

"Why don't you come to the throne?" she asked. She wanted to feel the moment when he connected to the Heart.

He raised an eyebrow. "Consider this a compromise. Come. Join me."

She sighed and pushed off the throne.

"Wait," he held up a finger, and she paused. "It is time that I attend to a certain matter."

Adon glanced to the Chorus where it stood in the back of the room, and it stepped to the great double doors and was gone.

"Desperate animals should be caged or put down, don't you think?"

She shrugged, waiting.

"You may approach," he said.

She walked towards him, down the steps, across the floor.

"Take off your sandals."

She yanked the ties, loosened the laces, and kicked them off, stepping onto the furs that were long and soft around her feet as she walked to where he sat.

"Sit beside me."

His chest glistened, and little rivulets gleamed along his collarbone and down his breast. His smell reminded Soolie of the way a horse's neck smells after a long run. She was very aware how naked and exposed she was in the garment he had given her.

"May I rest a hand on your shoulder?"

She nodded.

He placed a heavy hand on the curve of her neck, his thumb wrapping around.

"Breathe in with me," he said, and she breathed in. "And out." She breathed out. "I am afraid we must now have a difficult conversation."

"Then will we eat?" she asked.

"Yes," he said. "But there is something we must discuss first. Are you ready?"

She nodded. She was very hungry. He rubbed his thumb against the bump of her spine.

"Good. You see, *now* you are being very good, but only a moment ago, you said something that wasn't good at all. Do you know what that was?"

She bit her lip. He leaned in until his damp curls brushed her forehead. His eyes were gentle, his brow concerned. She shook her head.

"We have talked about this before." His voice was kind, but stern. "And this can't keep happening. You have a very bad habit, and if we are to trust one another, we're going to have to break it."

She still wasn't sure what he was talking about. Maybe if she just went along with the conversation, it would be over quickly. "I'm sorry," she said.

"I know," his hand was heavy on the back of her neck, "and I wish there didn't have to be consequences. I wish you learned the first time. I don't like hurting you, Soolie." His dark eyes were solemn. "Promise you'll never say '*no*' to me again."

She nodded. She'd do whatever he asked if it meant he'd feed her.

"I need to hear you say it."

"I promise."

"I believe you." He kissed her forehead. "If you obey me, your punishment will be quick." His hand tightened on her neck. "Once for every time since we entered the throne room."

"No . . ." she whispered before she could stop herself, knowing what was coming.

"Oh, Soolie," he said, disappointed. "Now I have to hurt you a fifth time."

He pulled the life from her. It was worse, knowing it was coming. She whimpered open mouthed, agony wracking her body, her flesh shrinking as he watched, his brow compassion-creased.

At last, he released her, and she collapsed onto the seat where he had just sat.

He walked around the divan, away to the door, and faced her. "Come here."

She lifted her head. Murky tears smeared her eyes and streaked her cheeks, spattering dark down the white film of her dress.

"Now, Soolie."

She dragged herself forward over the divan, crawling onto the floor and standing—bones grating, muscles sawing—she walked up the room surrounded by feasting and revelry to where he stood, looking down at her.

"Kneel."

She bent one knee, and then the other, and looked up at him through bloody eyes. "Please?"

"Do not ask me to spare you. You know I can not."

He placed a hand on her head, and the taking wracked her body again. She tried to cry out and couldn't make a sound. He was killing her.

She didn't feel when he released her, and didn't see him go. She was stunned with pain until she heard his voice again, commanding through the fog.

"Come."

She crawled. Her joints were ground glass, her muscles were fragile shreds tearing themselves as she moved. He stood in front of the dais. She tried to stand and barely made it to a crouch before falling forward. The hard floor bruised her palms and the bones of her knees. She struggled for what felt like moons while he watched and waited.

At last, she fell at his feet, smearing the tops of them with the mud of her tears. Her hands were frail like the stripped ribs of a leaf.

"Kneel," he commanded.

She crawled her way up his leg, pushing herself to a sitting position.

"Five times you denied me, so five times you must be punished," he said. "Do you understand?"

She tried to speak, and only a hiss escaped her leathern lips.

"If you understand, ask me for it."

Her only hope was for him to save her. She had no choice but to throw herself at his mercy. Her jaw crackled as she hinged it open, forcing sound.

"Please," she wheezed. "Punish me."

Again his hand was on her head, and again he took from her, more than she thought she could bear to lose. She crumpled, desiccated, fragile as a burned-out husk. He left her there.

"Come."

Her vision was dark. She couldn't see him. She struggled towards the sound. Her limbs were locked, her skin was hard. She rasped and strained. The flesh of her fingers was shrunken back, and she reached slowly across the floor, touching her nail-tips to the smooth marble, and scratched, trying to pull herself towards his voice.

"Come."

She tried, but her body wouldn't move. Her head lay on the marble. She couldn't even raise it to cry.

"Come."

She twitched. Every effort was monumental, every moment agony. She was trying, trying, but her limbs refused.

He didn't speak, and still she struggled. Had he left her?

Something lifted her and set her on her knees. A hand cradled her head and tilted her face upward.

"And yet," he whispered in her ear. "I will be merciful."

Something warm and soft touched her mouth. He was kissing her, and suddenly her mind and body were filled with fire and light. Her muscles unknotted, her joints smoothed, her flesh swelled, ripening flush upon her bones as his strength flowed into her—the Hunter's Heart in her veins. He lifted her towards him, and she wrapped herself to him in return. Her arms were about his neck, her legs hooked around his waist, his hands were broad on the small of her back and gripping her under the dress, and he pulled her into his bare chest, demanding, and his tongue probed wet and thick in her mouth, and she bit down hard.

The pain was new and immediate, lashing through her own mouth red hot, as his pain was her pain, and for a moment she could not tell if it was his tongue or her own between her teeth, and it did not matter. The tongue jerked, pulling to get away, and she ground down on the meat, blood filling her mouth, and ripped.

He was still holding her to him, eyes wide, choking, blood splurting from his dark mouth, and she pushed his chest with both hands, and he staggered and dropped her hard on the marble floor.

She scrambled back, and spat the lump of his severed tongue onto the tile. He was reaching for her, blood spilling over his lips, eyes lighting with realization and fury as she backed away. She could feel the raw searing pain of his wound, the life of the Hunter's Heart tied her to him, and she hated hurting him, and hurting him was hurting her, and all around the room, chairs skree-toppled back, glasses smashing, silverware dropping as a hundred people stood to their feet and faced her, and he took his first step towards her, and she ran.

New verve and terror gave her speed, bare feet pelting the floor, sprinting down the room and throwing herself at the exit doors, pawing frantically, pulling one open, and flinging herself through as the raged roar of voices rose behind her.

∽

DOG CROUCHED IN THE DARK, silently spinning the silver knife between his fingers. The Wolf was coming.

He couldn't hear it, but he could sense the charge of soul-suffering in the air that preceded its arrival. He tensed.

A black shadow lanced through the doorway, and the Wolf crossed the threshold, stepping into the tower and the weave of blood that Dog had laid for it. It froze mid-stride. The weave would only immobilize it for a moment.

Dog launched from the stair above and dropped on top of it, landing in a crouch with both feet on its shoulders, the blood crown within reach. He grabbed a fistful of hair on the back of its head and sawed through the front of its throat, spraying blood. The knife was short, but sharp, and he held the handle in his fist, blade down, and slashed at the cords, muscle, and bone, peeling back its head, its red eyes staring straight up into his as he slashed through the last of its neck, ripping the crowned head free from its shoulders, and jumped for the tower door—head in one hand, knife in the other—and a stone-cold grip closed on his ankle mid-air and slung him hard, reversing, into the stone edge of the stair.

Dog crashed, tumbling over the steps and slamming into the curved tower wall.

The Wolf had already broken the weave. Its headless body stood in the door-patch of moonlight—neck blood rivering over its white tunic and down its pants—and rotated to face him.

Dog scrambled up, still gripping its head by the hair, and sprinted up the stairs, turning around and around in the dark.

The Wolf leaped straight up the core of the tower, vaulting off the sides, and landed hanging off a ledge just half a turn down. Its bloody, headless shoulders angled towards him. Dog scrambled back from the edge, and it launched across the breach and was on him in a moment.

He stabbed it with the knife, and the thin blade went into its chest, but its hand was already gripping his other wrist, twisting and crushing the bones like sodden straw. Dog lunged, gnashing his blunt teeth, and it snatched its own head from his broken hand and kicked him in the chest, crumpling his ribs and sending him flying back against the steps.

It held its head with both hands, red eyes facing forward, and set the ripped mass of its neck on the wound between its shoulders.

Dog turned and ran, pulling at the stairs, his broken-wristed hand flopping at the stone edges. The knife was still in its chest. He had no teeth, no talons, and no weapon.

He pelted out onto the top of the tower and spun around, but it was already upon him, its head newly affixed, its body bathed in blood. It rammed, powering a fist into his belly, sweeping up and throwing him, flailing, into the air, then jumped and smashed down on his spine with its forearm, punching him face-first into the stone. The sheer force and speed ruptured his insides and splintered his bones. He tried to push himself up to his knees, but it grabbed him by the back of his hair and slung him around, flinging his body up full circle and bringing him down with a slap like a wet rag.

He felt his spine twist and break, his vision going dark, as he lashed out for the creature's chest, his fingers closing on the handle of the knife, and he pulled, and swiped up, slicing through hair at the back of his head and the Wolf's closing fingers.

Dog threw himself blindly forward, broken limbs propelling, and he toppled out into a sudden blast of open air. He was off the edge of the tower plummeting down, down and then the Wolf's hands seized his falling body, and he knew this was his end.

Mistress.

The ground and the Wolf's fists met with him in between.

Chapter 23

"Fucking lands, he's already awake."

Something cinched on Silas' wrist, anchoring his arm above his head. He yanked and it held. Both wrists and both ankles were tied down. He was on his back looking up at the sky, splayed naked like an insect on a collection board. The table, where it touched his skin, was smooth and biting, but not cold, and it bowed away from his back. He could feel air brushing his spine as if there was a hole directly underneath him.

"Kolgrin?" He pulled at the restraints, tilting his head to see his friend stepping back.

"Silas." Kolgrin's brow was heavy. His eyes dark. "This is the part of our story where things get ugly."

"What's happening?" He wasn't feeling the full rush of panic yet. The shock was too strong. Nothing made sense. "Rahka?"

She approached his side and placed a hand on his chest. Her fingers were raw and crusted with broken scabs. She pressed, her eyes fluttering. *"Anna, anna, mitta sen rashni. Mera rashni. Sen dravira kaski rahgiha."*

His breath quickened under the weight of her palm. The panic was rising. "Kolgrin? Kolgrin!"

"Hnnnngaaaaa!" Rahka's hand dug in, nails scratching furrows as she bent over him, teeth bared and clenching, body shaking. *"AAAAH-HHGNAHNKALA."* Her legs buckled, and she clung to him like a castaway to wreck-wood. *"Chooble,"* she gasped.

Kolgrin jumped up and ran around the table to her side.

"Help me up."

"She's in labor!" Silas cried.

Kolgrin kneeled and offered Rahka a supporting hand.

"She needs help. I can help!"

Rahka stepped on Kolgrin's offered leg, leaning heavily on his shoulder and lifting one foot onto the table.

"She knows the risks," Kolgrin said, rising slowly to his feet as she leaned on him, grunting and hissing between her teeth and stepping up to stand over Silas. "As did you."

She settled on top of him, her full weight straddling his hips, her pregnant belly hanging low, resting skin to skin. Her breathing was heavy, her movements forced like someone reeling from liquor and trying to keep it down. She reached into her pocket and pulled out a small black bag.

"What is she doing?" The panic was taking hold. "Kolgrin?"

The big man walked back to his seat. "Trying to open the door."

Rahka reached into the bag and pulled out something white and writhing, holding it in her mangled hand like a writing pen. She dropped the bag and sat for a moment, wavering, studying, but not seeing him.

"Kolgrin . . . ?" Silas tried again, "Is she going to kill me?"

"Probably," Kolgrin said, taking a seat. "Far as I know, she might kill us all."

"A mera bachle, nahnkala. Yah kaski myrta, mera bachle."

She leaned down, eyes intent, and touched the tip of the stylus to his skin.

Silas screamed and bucked, but she held him down. The pain was deep and searing, as if the tool in her hand poured molten serpents into his flesh. He strained to see. Her hand twisted patterns, and raw ravines spooled in all directions. His skin was being flayed by a hundred thousand cuts, never stilling, always new. His vision clouded with pain as they spread, roiling over his belly and onto his back.

"AAAaaaahhh!" Rahka screamed. Her hand tightened on the stylus, and her thighs clamped on his hips as her body clenched down. "*Yah nani ha skataaaaah!*"

The ravines continued to turn, flaying his flesh from the base of his neck, to his sides, to the bones of his hips, moving underneath her pressing weight. But, for the moment—while she wasn't carving—they did not spread.

She bowed forward, leaning on his tortured body, teeth bared, and a warm yellowish fluid washed out from under her, soaking her black skirts and flowing into and out of the rawness in his flesh.

Her face was a waxy pewter and her golden eyes a dull yellow. She lifted the stylus, shaking in her bleeding crusted hand.

"KOLGRIN!" Silas screamed as she touched the pen to his skin and started to carve again.

"I can't stop her, friend," his voice was tight.

Silas struggled to form words. "She's killing us *both*!"

"Quite possibly."

The paths crawled up his neck, reaching around his back and between his thighs, and she stopped again, doubling over, shaking.

"*Nahnkala, nahnkala, a mera bachle...*"

"Kolgrin! Stop this!" The pain was constant, renewing and wrong. "I know you don't want to watch us die!"

"We all die, friend."

Somehow, she was carving again. Her head lolled. Her eyes glazed. The pen in her hand was red with blood.

Paths crawled up his face, splitting and closing and resplitting his lips and nose and eyelids. He was completely covered in raw moving flesh, and Rahka tipped sideways and fell off the table. Her body hit the ground.

"Fucking undergods." Kolgrin leapt to his feet and was at Silas' side in a moment, sawing at the ropes that held his wrist. He freed Silas' hand and placed the knife in it. "Cut yourself the rest of the way free. If that's as painful as it looks, you have my sympathies."

Kolgrin was on the ground beside the table, turning Rahka onto her back.

Silas reached up and sawed at the rope that held his other wrist. The pain was excruciating.

"Is she . . . ?"

"Not dead yet, but she will be soon," Kolgrin said.

Silas sat up. The edge of the table had strange snaking symbols, and the center bowled down to a hole.

"Your clothes and weapons are there, if you want them," Kolgrin pointed at the foot of the table. "Hand me the knife."

Silas turned the knife hilt-outward before passing it off. He was in a daze. Kolgrin was bending Rahka's legs and spreading her knees, her skirts piling up around her waist, baring her parts.

"What are you doing?" Silas asked.

"Put on your pants," Kolgrin growled. "You're covered in burrows, and I can't stand to watch a wag get chewed up like that."

Silas obeyed, going to the base of the table, shaking out his trousers and pulling them on. Kolgrin was kneeling between Rahka's legs and bending down to take a closer look. Silas left the sweater, jacket, and boots, and walked up behind Kolgrin, buckling his pistol belt.

She looked dead. Face slack, eyes closed. The hairy parts between her legs bulged, and blood ran down between her cheeks and pooled in the dust. Kolgrin turned the knife in his hand and leveled the point at the dark, coin-sized opening.

"Kolgrin, what's happening?"

"It's killing her."

Silas put a hand on Kolgin's shoulder. "You don't know that."

"Hands *off*," Kolgrin growled up at him. "Look at yourself. Hasn't she done enough to you? What the fuck are you fighting for?"

Silas held his ground. "The child is innocent."

"THERE'S NO CHILD." Kolgrin's roar was enough to make Silas step back. "FUCKING HONE YOURSELF, SILAS BEETCH. GET OUT OF HERE. GO. While you still can, GO!"

"I can't." Where would he go? Once again, he had been saved when he should have died. If he was alive for a purpose, that purpose had to be here.

"The door's *not opening*. Rahka failed." Kolgrin said. "She needed two things: your life and the soul of this thing inside of her, but she'd done too much magic. She cut off too much of her soul, and she's unable to grow a new one. The thing has no soul, so it's trying to take hers. That's why it's killing her. What's more," Kolgrin continued, "outside that blood ring is a hoard of dead pregnant skags that died all fucked-up by blood magic, and whatever is happening to *her* is making them think she's one of them. They're bent on using her to get whatever the fuck it is that they want, and she's *losing her ever-spakking mind*."

Silas swallowed and nodded. "Okay. How can I help?"

"You BLOODY ANCIENTS FUCKING IDIOT," Kolgrin shouted. "YOU CAN'T—"

"Wouldn't you have a better angle if she was up on the table?"

Kolgrin glared, shoulders heaving. "Oh, fuck me! Help me get her up."

Silas put his arms under Rahka's arms, and Kolgrin took her legs.

"Put her ass at the end . . . ."

"How do you know all those bloodwitch things?"

"I understand more Southern than she thinks I do."

They laid her on the table, head tilting back into the basin, hips at the table's edge. Silas stood at her feet and lifted her legs, cupping one hand behind each knee, planting her heels on his shoulders. He leaned forward and pushed her thighs back towards her belly, exposing the bloody lips that parted for the pressing bulge behind them. Kolgrin crouched in the tight space below Silas, placing himself at eye-level.

"You know," Kolgrin muttered, "this is exactly what I thought one would look like up close."

"If she survives . . ."

". . . she'll kill us both," Kolgin finished, aiming the knife at the opening and sliding the slim point between the parting lips. He held the knife steady with one hand and pulled his pistol with the other, turning it so the handle of the gun rested on the handle of the knife. "If I *have* to poke a woman, there's no other man I'd rather have at my back."

"Just do it."

"Yes, *sir*."

Kolgrin whacked the handle, wedging the tip of the blade into the top of the slick hidden skull. He hit the knife again and again, jamming the blade deeper and deeper. New blood trickled out.

"Don't you think that's . . ."

"Once more."

Kolgrin swung and smacked the handle one last time. He holstered the gun. The knife handle stuck out, blood trickling down and dripping off the hilt. Kolgrin grabbed the handle tight and pulled it out in a single motion, hard and straight.

He looked up at Silas. "We should try this again under better circumstances."

Silas saw the shakiness in his eyes. "Let's push her to the top of the table."

They heaved her up. Silas bundled the sweater and placed it under her head. Kolgrin spread her feet over the basin of the table. She was still. They stood at her shoulder, side-by-side.

"Are they dead?" Silas asked.

Kolgrin shrugged.

The perimeter of blood moved.

Silas saw it first. He pointed.

"Undergods," Kolgrin breathed. "We've riled them."

The river was rising. Where it had flowed down along the ground, now it climbed, jumping over itself at least two hands off the ground.

"What does that mean?" Silas asked.

"I think something's trying to break through."

Rahka sat up screaming. "*GET IT OUT OF ME!*"

Silas tried to step back, but Kolgrin grabbed his arm, holding him tight. Silas didn't know if he was being held captive, or held for comfort, but he put a hand on Kolgrin's hand and stayed his ground.

Rahka hunched forward, screaming, then threw her head back, flinging her head cloth into the dust. She knotted her fists in her skirts. "*GET IT OUT!*"

The blood that surrounded them roiled.

"NOW! GAHAGHI!"

Kolgrin gripped Silas' tortured arm in a bear-jaw grip. "We can't do that for you, Lioness."

She screamed, her face binding up, and they stood by as she raged and the surrounding blood raged with her.

Silas had been at his wife's side when she gave birth. Tera had always been quiet in her suffering, and her labor was no different. She had rested in the wash tub, clutching his hand in her small white one while Evaline and her grandmother rushed about getting steaming hot towels and updating the grandfather upstairs. Silas had tracked the contractions by the tightening of her brow, the catching of her breath, and the squeeze of her hand. Only when little Soolie was crowning did she finally cry out. He had spent the whole day-and-a-half in awe and absolute terror.

Blood spittled from Rahka's mouth and her whole body shook. The sun was dipping behind the buildings, and she had screamed her throat raw.

Silas and Kolgrin hadn't moved. Silas' flesh still writhed, and he knew that any normal person would have long succumbed to the constant wounding pain, but he stood strong. He was a man with a miracle who could endure more than anyone else. He was Soolie's father.

How would he reach his daughter now?

Kolgrin's grip tightened, and he nodded towards Rahka's feet. A wet liver-colored lump was forcing its way from her body A scratch-coughing snarl ripped through her teeth, and the thing expelled into the basin and stuck in the hole.

She barely paused, heaving herself up to a sitting position and rasping, "Hand me the stylus."

"No, Lioness." Kolgrin's voice was gentle and low. "It's already dead. You failed."

"*Hand me—*"

"No, Rahka." Kolgrin released Silas' arm and stepped to her side. "We're done."

She grabbed the front of his shirt, hanging on him. "What did you . . ."

"He saved your life," Silas said.

Her wild eyes snapped towards him, then back to Kolgrin.

"Rahka." Kolgrin looked sad. "You don't have to . . ."

Kolgin's eyes widened as her knife slipped between his ribs once, twice, three times. He stepped back, hand to his chest.

"NOOO!" Silas ran to him as Kolgrin fell to his knees.

The big man was looking at his palm smeared in blood as Silas knelt, grabbing his arms. "You're okay. You're okay. I'll get you out of here."

"Naw . . . I've earned this." Color drained from Kolgrin's face. He chuckled and coughed. "Spinesnake, friend. Her blades don't miss."

Rahka swung her feet off the edge of the table, shoulders hunched.

"WHAT HAVE YOU DONE?" Silas shouted as Kolgrin collapsed in his arms.

She plucked at the gristly blood cord that tied her to the lump in the basin, looped it over the edge of her knife, and cut. She slid off the table and collapsed onto the ground, legs failing beneath her.

Silas held Kolgrin's body, shaking, watching as the bloodwitch pulled herself through the dust towards the bloody stylus that lay where it had fallen. She tucked her knife into a sheath on her forearm and picked up the stylus with crumpled fingers that fumbled and dropped it, and she picked it up again.

Slowly, she reached and grabbed the edge of the table, and pulled herself back up. As she stood, a gush of bloody afterbirth splattered between her feet, followed by a heavy black bag of the fetal pouch slapping into the wet dust. In the distance, the ring of blood jumped higher and higher like oil-spattered flame as Rahka pulled herself onto the table and kneeled in the basin over the expelled lump of flesh, the stylus in her hand.

What was he to do? *If you're there,* he thought to the guiding voice, *I need your help. Please? Help me? Please?*

But the only sound was Rahka's ragged, rising wails.

"Kolgrin?" he whispered.

The burly man lay still.

Silas stood.

Rahka was dragging the stylus over the rumpled purple body. Her hands shook with exhaustion, trauma, and rage, and she gripped the stylus in a bloodied fist and started stabbing at it, screaming, and stabbing.

Silas put a hand on his gun and took a step towards her as she collapsed into the basin, clutching the mangled flesh of the thing she had birthed in her brutalized hands.

He still didn't hate her.

She had killed Kolgrin, but he still couldn't kill her. That wasn't who he was.

"He loved you, you know," he said, knowing that she wasn't listening and couldn't hear. "I think he cared for us both in his own way, but he loved you most, because you were the most alone. You shouldn't have killed him."

He turned away from the table. If he was still alive, Soolie *must* be also. Even if this door never opened, even if he had to search the whole world and never heard that guiding voice again, nothing—not monsters, not spirits, not witches or their torments in his skin—was going to stop him. As long as he had breath in his lungs and earth beneath his feet, he would never stop looking until he found her.

He set his feet towards the heart of the city, and that was when he saw that the blood weave had completely left the ground and dismantled into a hovering galaxy of lashing surging tendrils that were quickly closing in.

∼

THEY WERE COUNTLESS, many voiced and of one mind. They had been broken to create the unspeakable—soul without self, power without agency—a Dead Man's Chorus.

They could feel the stolen pieces of themselves on the other side.

They had railed at the tower that kept them away. Now they battered at the blood that kept them back.

Hollow the ones who are broken. Gone to the other side.

They did not see as the living saw, but they knew the blood and pain that stood in their way, knew the wounded door and where it led, knew the bloodwitch touched by the Soul Hunter with her connection to all things dead and all things spirit. She was their kindred. She held the *nahnkala* and spoke their words. She was broken as they were broken—spirit torn from spirit. Her agony was their agony. Her hollowness was their vessel.

They were countless, many-voiced and of one mind, and in their unity and multitude, the singular focus of their will was an undeniable force. They spoke and the foundations of the world heard them and obeyed.

∼

"*Mera pet bachle gai teva...*"

Silas spun back to see Rahka standing over the bloodied form in the basin. He knew she had screamed herself hoarse, but foreign words poured from her lips with the voice of a thousand tongues in perfect unison.

"*...re doskati tephra nahnkala, nahnkala...*"

The sun had dipped below the horizon, deepening the sky to purple-blue, but the witch's eyes were luminous, her pupils pin-prick specks, as if she stared directly into the sun and reflected it back.

Silas pulled his gun, clicking back the hammer, aiming first at Rahka, then at the closing swarm of blood. Her hair lifted up off her shoulders, her feet up off the table. She hung suspended in the air as in water.

"*Hollow nahnkala. Hollow, hollow, nahnkala, to the other side.*"

The blood was closing faster. Whatever the river had been keeping out, was out no longer.

Silas threw himself to the ground and scrambled under the table, through the splash of afterbirth, to where Kolgrin's body lay.

Rahka rose higher and higher, and the blood rose with her as she became its center—the planet to its ring of orbiting gore—and she levitated away from the table and suspended directly overhead in the true heart of where the tower had stood. Her hair was a tangled cloud. Her eyes flashed bright. Her mouth spilled strange sounds that Silas couldn't hear, but *could* feel as surely as one feels the shaking of the earth, and as she spoke, the blood began to blur impossible to follow, and the heart of the ring above filled with a deep, black pool of stars.

Rahka rose up through the ring of blood, into the stars, and was gone.

"RAHKA?"

Silas scrambled to his feet. Warm, fresh air drifted down from a different, darker sky. The blood spun just out of reach, beginning to slow, fragments flying off.

This was the door.

"RAHKA!"

"Get on my shoulders." Kolgrin was at his side, gray-faced and bloody-chested, struggling to his knees.

"Kolgrin! Fucking Ancients!"

"It's coming apart," the man planted a foot and presented his knee. "Better mount me now, Silas Beetch. It's your last chance."

The ring of blood spun messy writhing streamers.

"NOW," Kolgrin growled.

"How can I leave you?" Silas stepped onto Kolgrin's leg, and then up onto his shoulders. "How are you alive? Rahka never misses?"

"Rahka never misses," Kolgrin grunted, wobbling as he tried to stand, hands clapped to Silas' feet.

Silas crouched. The blood was wreathing out, the pool of stars was growing dim.

"GO." Kolgrin planted his feet

"What about—"

"I'm gonna go wag-off to the memory of when you were pretty," Kolgrin growled. "You find your daughter."

He heaved up, and Silas stood on Kolgrin's shoulders, and launched head and shoulders through the spinning ring that pulled him up and through, and the doorway flew apart, and the way back to Ravus was gone.

Chapter 24

The moon lit every thorn and bramble silver-edged and sharp toothed, but the path underfoot was hazardous and dark. Stray stones and sticks caught her bare feet so she stumbled, sprinting, sobbing. Where was he?

DOG?

She cried his name in her mind, knowing she couldn't reach him.

She didn't understand. Why had he left her alone while she was vulnerable? Why was Dog not back in their room, and how did she know without going to see? She had left the throne room and sprinted from the house, making her way into the hills, running for the old tower. She could feel the lashing pain in her tongue and jaw dulling, and she knew that meant Adon was healing.

The tower cut a black door in the stars at the top of the hill.

DOG! Please be here!

She could hardly smell anything through the stench of her own tears, but as she neared the tower, she sensed the blood, and as she neared the doorway, she saw it—fresh gore splattered across the writhings of a broken weave.

"DOG!" She pelted up the steps, crying his name out loud. Far above, she heard a scuffle and a slam. "DOG!"

Was he in trouble? What was happening to them?

The newly-fed life gave her body fleetness, and she flung herself around and around, and up the last twist of stairs, and out on top of the tower to see the Chorus, white robes drenched in blood, pursuing a dark, broken-limbed figure towards the edge.

"DOOOOOOG!"

Neither of them heard her. Dog reached the edge and went over, and the Chorus dove after him. She screamed, running, her feet sliding in the dust as she skittered at the edge, looking down the long drop to the ground below.

Dog's body was a stamped rag pile. The Chorus stood over it, looking up. Its crown-red eyes met hers, and it launched itself, sprinting four-legged up the side of the tower, coming straight for her.

Soolie threw herself back from the edge, just as the night filled with the rending screams of a thousand voices. She turned to see a tear opening in the roof of the tower, widening with a great surge of unhallowed language, turning the world in on itself and forcing a way, and a swarm of spirits erupted through.

They filled the sky and dimmed the stars with their many phantom forms, warping into one another and moving together, and their many screams made a single cry, heard not with the ears, but with the soul.

"WE, THE HOLLOW, WILL TAKE BACK WHAT WAS STOLEN."

They became aware of her as one, routed, and descended with a million hands that reached into her skin to the Chorus blood that bound her with the strength of a thousand broken souls, and they seized it.

"OURS."

Soolie screamed as the phantoms ripped the soul from the Dead Man's weave, the blood coming undone, and everything the weave had held back came crashing down upon her, a fast tide of darkness pulling her under, and the last thing she saw was a form rising up out of the floor where there was no natural door, and turning toward her with bright golden eyes and a bloody blade in its hand.

THEY HAD FORGED a way with the force of their will. The *nahnkala* ripped their stolen spirit back from the woven blood, and then they were over the edge of the tower, flying for the one whose flesh imprisoned them, whose torment was their torment.

The Chorus sprinted up the side, and they met it coming down. It bolted into them, and they into it. Its flesh was bound with their souls, and as they laid their claim, its body came undone—skin melting like a thin fatty shell, meat molten splattering bloody sauce—and still, it tried to run up through the force that unraveled it.

"WE TAKE BACK WHAT IS OURS."

The bones of its feet and fingers lost hold on the tower stones, and it tipped out into the open air as they turned those struts, too, to formless, soulless slurry that hung for a moment, and then fell. Down through the open air it dropped and hit, bucketing gore onto the mangled form below.

The last thing to land was an unclaimed circlet of weaving blood.

Chapter 25

Silas stepped onto dusty stone. Behind him, the blood-bound pool to another world shook, rippled, and was gone. He was standing on top of a high tower beneath a sky of brightly-packed stars. Ahead, a small figure collapsed and lay still.

"Soolie?"

He ran to the little body, dropping to his knees, and cupped one hand under the bald head, turning the face towards him. Her cheeks were sticky with red smears that clotted in the creases of closed eyes and ran down to her pointed chin. But it *was her*.

He had found her.

"Oh, Soolie!"

He pulled her into his lap and held her to his chest. She was so small, and the thin nightgown she wore was sticky with violence, and he held her even tighter, terrified of the horrors that had happened to her. He had found her. Was she hurt? He brushed her forehead as if to sweep back the locks of hair that were no longer there. Her skin was gravehouse cold. If he hadn't *just* seen her fall, he might have thought she had been dead for days.

"Soolie? Baby girl?"

For a moment, he was afraid that the blood gluing her eyelids meant that her eyes had been gouged out, but the lid still domed. He cracked the crusty seal, peeling one open. Smears of red algae floated over a surface that was gristle-white. The eye twitched. She wasn't dead. Whatever was happening to her, they would figure it out together. He had found her. She was in his arms.

Sharp pain stabbed him in the back, and he gasped, hunching protectively and pulling her close.

"Ikma na Sitari sen Myrta Lirna."

Silas gritted his teeth. Not this, not now.

"Rahka."

He lowered his daughter's body to the stones, painfully letting her go, so he could stand and face their attacker.

Rahka's stance lacked her killer's grace. Her bloodied legs bowed and shook, her distended belly drooped, her breath was ragged and fast, but her eyes raged gold through the snarled tails of her hair. She was tugging at her arm bracer, trying to free another knife.

"Rahka, you're not yourself." Silas reached for a pistol. "I know you can hear me. Rahka!"

She managed to get the knife free as he raised the gun. He reached for the hammer to ratchet it back, and she threw. The knife was a bright needle, flashing and embedding in his hand, double-bladed ends sticking out both sides of his palm, and he screamed, still trying to cock the gun, fumbling with unresponsive fingers. She charged, one leg dragging as she reached under her skirt to grab for another weapon on her thigh. Finally, his fingers clacked back the hammer, and he fired, but too fast. The shot went high over her shoulder as she pulled back a third knife and threw, not at him, but past him at Soolie's body on the ground.

"NOOO!"

This one wasn't double-bladed, and the knife over-rotated, handle smacking against her chest. He needed to shoot Rahka. He needed to pull back the hammer.

She dodged to his left. She was pulling another knife. She was going to go around him.

He dropped the gun and threw himself at her. He was faster than she expected, and he saw the surprise and rage in her eyes as he caught her and wrapped her close, pinning her arms to her sides, her swollen belly pressed hard against the symbols in his skin, the knife in his palm raking her back and gashing the wound in his hand. She shrieked and smashed her forehead for his face, but he was taller than she was, and he jerked his head back.

"STOP!"

Her movements were wild. She was weak, and he was still strong. She wrestled, unable to free herself.

"Sen pircha myrta ibagav." Her voice was ragged and shrill. *"Ikma! Ikma, maara myrta!"*

"RAHKA!" He didn't know what she was saying. "I know you don't want to kill me! I know you don't want to kill Soolie. You *chose* not to kill Kolgrin. Don't let the spirits win! Fight them!"

It had to be the ghosts that were doing this. The spirits had taken her baby and driven her mad.

"YOU ARE *BEVJAK!*" she screamed.

Her knives were in his back and hand, and his skin turned with her million moving cuts, but she was still a woman, her belly still swollen with recent life. "I don't want to fight you!"

"That is NOT your *lirna!*" Her struggle was flagging. "Your daughter is dead!"

"No."

"YES." She looked up. Her eyes were mere fingers from his own. "It is *Ikma na Sitari*. An ancient being that exists to prey on the living. It has no heart and can not love."

"I know you have endured terrible horrors," he told her, "but I can not let you hurt my daughter."

"Silas, *listen.*" Desperate tears welled in her eyes. "That creature violated me in my mother's womb, and my mother sacrificed herself to save me. It uses the bodies of children as its vessel, and Soolie *died* trying to stop it."

He shook his head. "No. Soolie came back. I saw her."

"She did not. I met your daughter while she was still alive, and I know how fiercely she fought, but she is dead, and it's puppeting her corpse. Don't you understand?" She pressed into him, pleading. "It's a *monster* wearing your daughter's corpse. You're not protecting your daughter. You're protecting her murderer."

He wouldn't believe it. He glanced back at the body that lay crumpled in the dust, bloody-faced, white eyed, cold. He had persevered and sacrificed too much, born witness to *too much*, to throw it all away now. "You don't know what I've seen."

"The living don't come back from the dead, Silas," she whispered, "as much as we may want them to."

Rahka wasn't fighting. He was just holding her now.

"I have not been open with you," she said, "because I feared you were not strong enough to make the right choice, but I have no reason to deceive you." Her weeping eyes sought his. "Your heart is a father's heart, and it *grieves*, knowing that what I say is true. That is not your daughter. Let me stop it from using her body to kill again."

He looked back to where the cold little figure lay covered in blood. It had his daughter's face. He knew that, were it to speak, it would speak in her voice. Could he *now* question that?

"Silas?"

His wife Tera used to say: 'I'm going away and never coming back.' He hadn't been able to accept it, not while she was dying and not after she was dead. Could it be possible that he had convinced himself that a monster was his Soolie, because that was easier than the truth—that he had held her in his arms while she took her own life?

"Your daughter died trying to stop it, Silas. Don't let her sacrifice be for nothing."

"I believe you," he said and released her.

Immediately, Rahka reached for a knife at her thigh, and Silas dropped the double-bladed knife that he had pulled from the back of his hand and grabbed his second pistol, smacking his bloody-gashed palm into the hammer, and screaming, he fired.

The shot hit her in the belly.

She staggered back, eyes wide, and he smacked his bloodied hand into the hammer again and fired. This shot hit her in the neck, blasting a chunk out of the side, and before she could fall, he fired again, and the golden eyes exploded in blood and matter.

He whispered, "But believe my daughter more."

He dropped the gun, and her body fell.

Something moved out of the corner of his eye.

"Soolie!"

He ran to her as her body started to kick and shake, her flimsy gown twisting up around her waist. He fell to his knees and gathered her in his arms, and she clawed at his chest. Her eyes snapped open, and they were spasming light and dark. It was just like the time he had found her in the woods outside Hob Glen. That meant Soolie was still in there, and she was fighting her way back to him. His daughter *was* alive.

She opened her mouth and screamed, and screamed, and screamed, bucking, thrashing, kicking.

"Soolie!"

He hated that he couldn't fight this battle for her. He held her while she snapped her teeth and shrieked against his chest. If all he could do was wait with her, he would. He would be here as long as it took. He wouldn't leave again.

Something rose up out of the floor.

At first, Silas thought the portal had opened up again, but then he saw that it was ascending a stair with agonizing slowness, a creature made all of gore. A writhing circlet of blood sat on a sopping mop of black hair that ran into heavy wet clothes. It slogged up onto the stones, the white dust clinging to its bloody feet. Its eyes were red, as if it had been weeping blood....

"You," Silas said. "You're the one who was in the woods. She saved you."

"You do not get to die." It spoke the same words it had said the night it stopped him from taking his own life.

He held her and the monster looked down at him. Both of his guns were out of reach.

"She's my daughter."

"My Mistress."

The creature's limbs hung slack, its feet pointed wrong. It moved as if it had been crushed in the sack of its clothes. He might be able to grab a gun and fire before it could reach her.

"What do you want?"

The crown on its head began to twist and turn in a new way. "I will take away her weakness," it said. "I will return the Hunter's power."

Chapter 26

"So the weave on me is an Ancient word that binds?" Soolie asked.

"Weaves can do many things," Tilla said. "That type of weave doesn't bind. It hides."

"What do you mean it hides?"

"He told you he bound the Soul Hunter? Even at the height of his power, Adon does not have the ability to imprison an ancient being like that for long. Such a weave could never last. Even this one will degrade with time, if it hasn't started already."

"You're saying the Soul Hunter isn't bound. It's only hidden?" Memories of the Hunter taking over her body and puppeting it in her sleep charged through her mind. "It can still act?"

"Your mistake is thinking that the weave is hiding the Soul Hunter from a girl," Tilla grabbed another book and led the way back to the desk. "Its true purpose is to hide the Soul Hunter *from itself*."

"What?" Soolie scowled.

Tilla set her stack down and started unloading the books Soolie carried in her arms. "You are one of the soul-bound dead. The only conclusion is that it resurrected you, binding you both to the same body and making you one being."

"Are you trying to say we're *both* the Soul Hunter?" Soolie scoffed, holding up the last of the books for Tilla to grab. "We don't want the same things. I don't know what it knows."

"We are capable of many contradictions, even under the most ordinary of circumstances," Tilla sorted the books into stacks. "Didn't it tell you that you were no longer two, but one?"

"I didn't think it was being literal."

"A Soul Hunter can not lie, at least, not on its own," Tilla said. "There is none better at lying, than a human soul to itself."

"Sooo," Soolie picked up a book with a black cover. "I *am* the Soul Hunter. The Soul Hunter is me. We just disagree with ourselves."

"Yes."

"Sounds like we're not the same, then."

"You are divided in purpose and mind."

"So, we're *not* the same."

"But you are the same being."

"Hmm." Soolie didn't like that. She opened the book. There were no words inside. Instead, every page was filled edge-to-edge with warped patterns that made her eyes hurt. At the same time, there was something familiar about them. She squinted, and the ink slid under her scrutiny. "Teach me."

"I can't do that," Tilla said. "I already risk Adon's wrath by giving you access. He will read our conversation in my mind, and he will punish the ones I love."

Soolie snapped the book shut. "You gave your word."

"This is how it must be." Tilla's tone was firm. "He will use his crown to see into your mind as well. You have no secrets. It is only a matter of time."

"I can defend myself," Soolie said. She would just turn the crown back on him again. "I've done it before."

"His influence will make you vulnerable. He has your Soul Hunter's Heart. You will fail. You will not succeed and you should not try."

"Then why the fuck are we even having this conversation?" Soolie snapped.

"Consider it my curiosity for dark things, and nothing more." Tilla's blue eyes were fixed, intent. "Any recommendations I make from now on will be useless to you." She grabbed the scroll, unwrapping the red cord and spreading it open on the table, revealing blocks and blocks of tiny Midland text. "Which is to say that you should definitely start with this one."

Soolie looked down at the book in her hands and at the map laid out on the table. It was clear which one would be actually helpful. She opened her mouth.

"*Don't*," Tilla said, her eyes flaring. "You are on your own. I've already said too much."

Soolie understood: Don't say anything you wouldn't want the Dead Man to hear. Everything Soolie needed was in this room. She just had to find it.

"You should leave, then," Soolie tossed the book back on the desk, "if you're useless to me."

"Leave before the sun gets low," Tilla said. "I don't want you here when Adon comes for you."

～

SOOLIE AND DOG sat cross-legged in a mess of strewn books. There were hundreds of blood-weave tomes in this tiny room. Fortunately, Soolie had an aptitude. The writhing patterns spoke to her, not in words, but in desire, responding to sight, to light, to touch, vibrating under the pads of her fingers in tune to her very intention.

There was something deeply intuitive about it. Blood magic was the art of communicating your will into the *rashni* that mortared all things. There were no true rules or limitations. Blood was used, because it was easier to bind to spirit, easier to manipulate, easier to transcribe in ways that could be passed on, but the *language* of the Ancients was nothing so simple or constrained as lettering. In theory, if one were sufficiently attuned, one could instigate change with a spoken word, a movement, a mere thought, though not just *anyone* could use blood magic. You needed to have been affected by the immaterial—by existence beyond the bounds of life—in some way that forged a connection. Soolie's connection, other than being dead, was the infestation of the Soul Hunter—a being that had once been able to manipulate reality at will

—which was probably why she was understanding everything so quickly.

Dog scowled at the book in his hands.

"Can you understand it?"

He blinked, looking up, and his shoulders sagged. "I was never taught reading, Mistress. Though I have been near it."

"Well, this isn't like reading normal words." She closed her book and scooted next to him, pointing at the open pages. His book appeared blank except for a small dot in the center of the page. "Don't think about what you see. Sense it."

Dog tilted his head, and she leaned in, watching his face, and then the page. The dot pulsed.

"Mistress!"

She nodded. This was why she'd had him start with this book in particular. Every page was a tiny weave that wanted to be seen. "Good. Keep going." She flipped her own book back open.

"So," he looked back up at her, worried. "Tomorrow..."

"You'll be on your own."

"Mistress didn't like me keeping secrets from her before," he looked back down.

She understood his fear, but she also didn't have time for it. She was close to understanding how to use the Dead Man's blood weave to hide *new* things, and she needed to be able to hide all of this knowledge before he came for her again. But also, once that happened, her fate would be entirely in Dog's hands....

"Okay. Put it down." She set her book down, and he did too. She took his bony hands in hers and looked him in the eyes. "You told me once that you would always obey me."

"Yes, Mistress."

"But there is more to serving than obedience."

His eyebrows bunched.

"If you only ever do the letter of what I say, then you're no different from the Dead Man's Chorus. I need you to serve me, not because I tell you to, but because you choose to. If you serve me, you will act in my best interest."

"Even if that means..."

"Even if that means lying to me."

"But . . ." he said again. "What if I don't get the crown? What if I get the crown, but I can't use it?"

"It is a hope shot. You might fail."

He cringed. "What if Mistress never remembers?"

"Well," she let him go, picked up the book, and placed it back in his hands. "For a while, if all goes right, I won't. Which is why you have to remember for me."

∼

"Mistress?"

"This is your last question. Once I start, you can't interrupt me."

"I understand . . . . What if the Ancient Mistress commands me again?"

"Then you'll have to make a choice."

"Dog will always obey."

"I know you've made rules for yourself, but if you choose to always obey the last command you heard, because you don't have the spine to decide what matters, then you don't care *who* you obey, and you might be good at obeying, but you're bad at being a servant."

He looked miserable.

"Now don't talk. I need to concentrate."

∼

Dog followed her into the bedroom, carrying two bowls of marrow-root stew. The women lay in a tangle. The sheets had popped off the bed corners and twisted up on the mattress, the patch-quilt had been kicked away and dragged back haphazardly over their bodies. Tilla's small white feet alternated with Mavi's plump dark ones, sticking out the bottom. Tilla wiggled her toes at Soolie and Dog as they entered.

"Mavbear! They brought fooooooood." She turned over and stuffed her face between her wife's breasts, giggling.

"Eeehehehehehehe!" Mavi wrapped herself around Tilla like a cub climbing a tree.

They had been like this for days. Soolie set one water cup on Tilla's bedside, then crossed around and set the other by Mavi, Dog following with the bowls of stew.

"Okay!" Soolie stood at the foot of their bed and clapped her hands. They lifted their bed-tousled heads. "You must drink your water."

"Aaaaawwwwwhhh!" Tilla mock-wailed while Mavi nuzzled her neck, sniffing her hair.

Dog took his place at her side. "Should I force them, Mistress?"

"No." She'd just do the counting thing again. "By the count of five. ONE. TWO."

Both women swung their arms to their bed stands, grabbed their glasses, and gulped the water down.

"THREE."

"Done!" They chorused.

So this is what happened to Tilla every time she visited Adon. Soolie suspected that Mavi had been included as some kind of punishment, but Soolie couldn't think of a good reason *why* that might be the case. It wasn't as if either of them had helped her, or done her any good at all, for all that she had tried. Every day she asked them the same questions . . . .

"NOW," Soolie said, still raising her voice to command their attention. "You will *TELL ME* where to find the books on breaking blood weaves."

Tilla burrowed, pulling the blankets up to her chin. "Mmmmm, they're all there."

This same spak. "They're NOT. I've read every book I can get my hands on."

"Tryyyy, the red one." Tilla giggled.

"WHAT red one?"

"The red one with the cover that feels like deeeeeeep water."

Soole growled. How were they both *so* very out of it, and the info Tilla was giving was still so useless. Beside her, Dog whined and clutched his hands to his chest.

"WHAT?" she snapped at him. "If you have something to say, just say it."

He squirmed, looking at his toes. She didn't want to yell at him, and she wasn't yelling *at him, specifically.* It was just that she felt like she was battering herself against an invisible maze. She felt so helpless. Why the *fuck* was everyone talking nonsense?

To her surprise, Dog mustered himself and bobbed. "May I ask?"

"Ask?" She looked back at the two women drowsily touching each other's noses while their stew grew cold. "Sure."

Dog slunk to the side of the bed and knelt at Tilla's back. He grabbed her arm and rolled her to face him, dragging the blankets and leaving Mavi uncovered. For a moment, Tilla's eyes flashed anger.

"Where is your stylus?" Dog asked.

Soolie groaned. What did he need a writing implement for?

"I have many," Tilla said. Behind her, Mavi was trying to wriggle under the flap of quilt that hung off her wife's back. "And many quills."

"I'm going back." Soolie turned towards the door.

"Where do you keep your *stylus?*" Dog asked again as if the librarian didn't understand what a stylus was.

"What could a *Doooog* need with—Mavi, stop, that tickles!"

Everything was spak.

∼

"You know, despite the whole no locked doors thing, there is one thing he never leaves lying around."

"The crown, Mistress."

"Yeah . . . . Have I said that before?"

". . . No, Mistress."

"Remind me to look into it tomorrow. Maybe there's something there."

∼

"What's that book you're putting away?" Soolie asked from her lounge spot in the pillow chair. "Have I read that one?"

"Yes, Mistress," he called from back in the stacks.

"Oh, I thought it looked new." She groaned. It was so hard to keep them all straight.

"Mistress?" He was approaching again, several volumes in his hands.

He handed her a white one with the pressing of a temple on the front. This was sure to be drollsome as spak.

"I have something I want to tell you, but . . ."

She flipped open the white book. Written in Midland. She closed her eyes, pointed, and looked. ". . . *means to circumnavigate the edict of the Fifth Opal Priestess. Votress Millar Spelt proposed a new interpretation of the Langlild Highlore Scrolls . . . .*" Soolie let the book flop into her lap. Oh, she was so tired.

"What is it?" she asked.

He hesitated, clutching his books to his chest. At least he was enjoying himself. She hadn't known he could read.

"I want you to know, I do choose to serve you, Mistress."

"I know," she said.

He opened his mouth as if to say something else, but he shut it and bowed.

"Thank you," she said.

⁓

She lay on her back with her head in his lap under the many stars. At some point, she had reached for his hand, and now she held it on her chest with both of hers, rubbing the smooth nubbins of his filed nails.

"Why did we come up here?" she asked.

He was watching her. "You were frustrated by the books, Mistress."

That made sense.

"I used to enjoy reading." She toyed with his fingers, curling them and pedaling them with her thumbs. "I didn't care what they were about—history, medicine, poetry—I'd read them all multiple times. Mama would let me carry them around with me, and I'd climb trees or lay in the meadow and read. Papa didn't like me taking books outside, so after Mama died, I mostly read by the fireplace, but I still have lots of good memories. Books took me to new places. Learning made me feel bigger. I wish I knew why I can't feel that anymore."

"I'd never read before, Mistress."

She looked at him. "Is that why you've been doing it so much lately?"

"I only wish to serve you, Mistress."

"You know," she placed his hand on her chest and held it there. "You could be more than that. If you wanted to. Maybe not right now, but someday."

"Mistress?"

"More than just someone who wants what I want, I mean. You could be someone who enjoys things for yourself. Actually, I think you already do, but you think you have to justify enjoying things by making them useful to me."

"I am proud to serve you, Mistress."

Overhead, a star streaked across the sky. Another followed.

"What's one thing?" she asked. "One thing you like."

He was looking down, and it was hard to read his expression in the dark, but his voice sounded funny and gentle. "I enjoy this, Mistress."

"Look up," she said.

The one falling star had multiplied—as if a congregation dressed all in white had gathered on a cliff over a dark sea and, when one cast itself over, those who remained were so overcome with sympathy, that they threw themselves after, showering across the sky bright and white, extinguishing themselves in the dark waves.

As he lifted his head, he turned his hand to touch hers palm to palm, and she laced her fingers in his, and he held hers back.

"I enjoy this too," she said.

"Do you think you will forget this as well, Mistress?"

"I'm not sure what you mean."

He held her hand a little tighter, and they watched the dying stars.

∽

She stood on the edge of the weaving blood, facing the Soul Hunter on the other side. It wore her face, and she met its brown eyes.

Return the Lost Souls to the Eternal Realm.
Return the Lost Souls to the Eternal Realm.
Return the Lost Souls to the Eternal Realm.

Return the Lost Souls to the Eternal Realm.

It chanted as if to overwrite her. The blood that bound it began to move faster and faster.

Return the Lost Souls to the Eternal Realm.

Its face, her face, began to brighten with inner heat, her skin blistering, white fire breaking through.

Return the Lost Souls to the Eternal Realm.

The blood ring began to boil and haze with white light.

Return the Lost Souls to the Eternal Realm.

Its body, her body, split like a cocoon, and it emerged, a rippling being of fire housing a great emptiness where its Heart should be.

Return the Lost Souls to the Eternal Realm.

The last remnants of the blood evaporated, and the Soul Hunter was upon her, enveloping and pulling her into its emptiness, the indelible certainty of its will battering her mind.

Return the Lost Souls to the Eternal Realm.
Return the Lost Souls to the Eternal Realm.
Return the Lost Souls to the Eternal Realm.

Chapter 27

Dog woke soaked in wrongness and pain. His bones had been shattered, their splinter edges tore the fragile membrane of his skin. The Wolf, the Dead Man's Chorus, had crushed his body, yet somehow spared his mind, so that he was aware long before he started to mend, struggling against the unresponsive weight of detached ligaments and pulverized flesh.

From her many visits to the Dead Man and long moments holding Dog in her arms, Mistress had kept him fed. Slowly, but surely, she had filled him with life from the Hunter's Heart, and that life now healed him more quickly than life from a human soul ever could.

His eyes regrew first, and he opened them to gore-drenched darkness. He was covered in blood and meat, and his arms and hands did not yet work, so he could not raise them to wipe his face. He waited, straining. She needed him. He had failed to take the crown from the Wolf.

His pain grew as his nerves reconnected, and it was some time before he felt something nipping at his belly, probing his flesh and spirit, crawling.

His left arm gained enough movement that he was able to twitch, jerk, and straighten it out, and once it was somewhat aligned, it began to heal more quickly. The crawling thing made its way to the broken struts of his ribs, flicking, biting. At last, he was able to reach up and scoop the gore from the orbs of his eyes, blearily squinting through the murk and pain, as the thing began to flick sharp tendrils at the collar of his neck. It was the Master's crown.

He could not yet move the rest of his body, but he lifted the crown, feeling it cling-snap to his fingers, and carried it up over his face, watching it stretch long roots for his scalp as he lowered it to his head, and the roots caught, and burrowed, and the crown latched on.

The new wash of pain felt old. Blood was pain and pain was blood. It filled his body, his eyes, his mouth, and his mind. He could sense the many spirits that had dismantled the Wolf, the living man and woman on top of the tower, and his Mistress. He could sense her, and she was unbound. Somehow, the Wolf was gone, and the Ancient Mistress was free.

She needed him.

He reached over his collapsed chest and tugged at his other arm to straighten it out. He twitched his legs.

At last, he was mended enough to stand—sagging on bones that stuck through his shoulders and belly, bending on a twisted and malformed spine, fumbling on legs turning odd and weak-hinged—he shambled towards the tower door.

Mistress, I'm coming.

His feet bent and slipped on the stair edges, and more than once he fell, forcing brokenness to move against brokenness. As he rounded a second turn, he sensed the life of the living woman snuff out. There was only the man and his Mistress now.

He dragged himself out into the starlight and saw her in the arms of a living man whose skin writhed with a carving blood weave.

"You," the man said. "You're the one who was in the woods. She saved you."

Dog remembered this man. He had been Mistress' father when she was living.

"You do not get to die," Dog acknowledged. Mistress had brought this man back from death, so only Mistress should decide his fate.

She was struggling in his arms. The Ancient and the Young warred with one another. Her eyes skittered light and dark. It was time to set her free.

"She's my daughter."

"My Mistress."

"What do you want?" the father asked.

He wanted her. He reached for her with the mind of the crown, sensing her anguish and conflict. "I will take away her weakness. I will return the Hunter's power."

His vision clouded as his mind extended out of his body and into her.

~

Dog was standing on a rooftop. The black-tar shingles were tacky and warm under his feet. Horizon stretched boundless on all sides, blue to lavender, pink to gold, without the interruption of land or structure. The roof floated like a slanted raft without house or ground to keep it up.

She sat on a hatch door, knees drawn up and tucked under her chin, arms wrapped around her shins. Her body was naked, clothed only in the long hazel hair that fell in soft waves over her shoulders and down to her ankles. She looked up and saw him.

"It's you."

"Yes, Mistress."

"Sit with me."

He joined her, kneeling at her side, looking out at the great expanse.

"I'm glad you're here," she said, resting her chin on her knees. "It's nice to not be alone."

"Are you alone?"

"No," she said. The hatch under her groaned and shuddered. She hugged her legs more tightly, and it stilled. "I suppose not."

He hadn't seen her with hair since before she and the Ancient Mistress became one spirit. She seemed smaller, softer. Somehow, he didn't mind.

"Why are you here?" he asked.

"Oh," she blinked. "I have always been here."

"What is *here*?" he asked.

"Possibility."

The hatch shivered, its hinges rattled, and he saw her tense. The hatch shook.

"I need you to move, Mistress."

She hid her face against her knees, and her hair muffled her voice. "I can't."

He crawled down in front of her and crouched, looking up. "Just for a moment to let me in."

Her head shook. "If I move, the Hunter will get out."

"I need to talk to the Hunter," he said.

"Noooooooooo," she raised her head, clear tears in her brown eyes.

"Yes," he extended a hand. "Trust me?"

She took his hand. "Don't let it out."

He stood, and she stood with him. The hatch thundered under her feet.

"It's okay, Mistress."

She stepped off the hatch. "Don't go."

He let go of her hand. "I promise . . ."

The hatch stilled. It lifted a crack, and he crouched and hinged the door up, looking up at her one last time, standing with her hands clasped, watching him.

". . . I will restore your power," he said and swung through the hatch and dropped.

It slammed shut behind him, and he was falling through emptiness that was featureless except for the presence of fractures in the nothingness, and then he was standing, and she was standing in front of him, white eyes, bare dome head, but she was not alone.

He was surrounded in all directions by broken windows of space—as if breadth and depth had been shattered into a billion shards without surface or reflection, but with edges—and in every window stood the Soul Hunter. He saw the young Mistress before him, and beyond her he saw a girl in a yellow shift with glossy black hair, beyond that a little black boy, beyond that a flax-headed child, beyond that an infant. Endless faces and forms, all of them with the Hunter's white eyes and burning spirit, and they faced him shouting, all at once.

RETURN THE LOST SOULS TO THE ETERNAL REALM.

He reached for the form of his young Mistress and in a moment he was beyond her, and a round child stood before him. He stepped forward again, flickering through the broken panes, faster, faster.

RETURN THE LOST SOULS TO THE ETERNAL REALM.

He ran, reaching nothing, touching nothing.

RETURN THE LOST SOULS TO THE ETERNAL REALM.

He saw his young Mistress far ahead, and he turned, and there she was far behind, and all the faces were starting to change, morphing, flickering from one to another. He closed his eyes and opened them, and Mistress was standing in front of him again, white eyes burning.

RETURN THE LOST SOULS TO THE ETERNAL REALM.

He closed his eyes again.

RETURN THE LOST SOULS TO THE ETERNAL REALM.

And listened.

RETURN THE LOST SOULS TO THE ETERNAL REALM.

He heard it, nearly imperceptible, the sound of a voice that spoke first. He turned himself toward it. With his eyes closed, he could no longer sense or see himself walking, but he willed himself forward.

RETURN THE LOST SOULS TO THE ETERNAL REALM.

As he drew closer, her words began to burn as if to boil the flesh from his bones and the spirit from his flesh.

RETURN THE LOST SOULS TO THE ETERNAL REALM.

They threatened to pull him apart. YOU ARE LOST, they said. YOU MUST NOT BE. Their surety overwhelmed him so that he wanted to dissolve into her. *RETURN* they commanded, and he would have obeyed, but he had made a promise. He clung to it, and rebelled, and he opened his eyes.

The Soul Hunter stood before him blazing pure, glorified and whole. The center of its being pulsed brighter than any star with the power to unthink him in a moment, and he knew he was an abomination that could not survive in its presence.

RETURN THE LOST SOULS TO THE ETERNAL REALM.

Against all self-preservation, he honed his mind to it. It threatened to obliterate him with its purpose, but he persevered, willing the crown to take him further, and further, and then the void around them was sucked away into a terribleness of infinite *everything*. No longer a nothingness, but an impossible allness, and in that place beyond place, the Soul Hunter's eternal light became somehow eternally small.

Time itself was unraveled here, and Dog could not exist here, and it took untold moments for him to realize he couldn't hear it anymore. It was waiting.

The Soul Hunter was still, silent and brand new. It did not ask and it did not want. It had not yet been given its first thought. It was waiting to be told.

It was waiting for its purpose.

He hesitated, but only for a moment.

"You were created to be Soolie Beetch."

I AM SOOLIE BEETCH.

Everything exploded.

Chapter 28

Soolie remembered everything. She remembered learning how to manipulate the Dead Man's blood weave to hide her thoughts and memories from herself and his prying red eyes. She remembered entrusting her fate to Dog to learn blood magic, to steal the crown and use it to set her free, knowing she wouldn't be able to hold him to it. She remembered how many times she had gone to the Dead Man's chambers and left Dog at the door, and how many times he had lifted her in his arms and carried her back to their room.

She remembered other things as well.

She remembered the beginning of the realm, the laying of the foundations and the setting of the stars. She remembered every soul she had ever tracked down and sent on to the Eternal Realm, and every living soul she had inhabited on her quest to grow strong enough to find her way back to her Heart. She remembered being forged into being in the presence of the Ancients who spoke to her in a familiar voice: *YOU WERE CREATED TO BE SOOLIE BEETCH.*

I am.

Chapter 29

The bloody creature stood frozen mid stride. The crown on its head shivered and spun. Its red-glazed eyes were open. Was it attacking? In Silas' arms, Soolie went limp. Then she bucked. Then she went rigid and still.

"Soolie? Soolie?"

He had to stop it. He dropped her and dove for his fallen gun, sliding in the dust and grabbing it, laying on his side as he cracked the hammer back, and aimed at the creature and shot. The creature's body flung back as if hit by a ramming log in the chest.

He was confused. Did the bullet have that much force? Then he saw her.

"SOOLIE!"

She was rising from the ground. Her skin glowed and wavered with heat. Blood and clothing smoked, then flashed fast flame and was gone as fire engulfed her in purest white, so her whole body burned like a sun everywhere, but for in the center of her chest, where resided a horrible emptiness. She raised her arms, reaching out as her body continued to rise until her feet no longer touched the ground. The sight of her seared his eyes.

"Mistress!" The creature knelt, looking up at her. Her light bleached its blood-clotted face.

"SOOLIE!" Silas called her name.

He didn't know what was happening, but this, whatever this was, was why she needed him. Right now was the reason he had been spared—so that he could find her here, at this time, and save her from whatever fate this monster had for her. He had to reach her.

There was no wind, and the dust beneath his feet did not move, but a repelling force rolled out from her, so that as he stood, his feet started to slide, and he had to lean against it, raising his forearm to protect his eyes.

"It's Papa!"

She lifted her face to the sky. Her eyes and mouth opened, blazing bright, as if she was screaming, and directly overhead, the stars extinguished so that the heavens mirrored her form—a galaxy of fire surrounding an impossible void. The windless force threatened to whip his feet off the ground, and he hunkered, taking one slow step at a time. It was deafening, yet made no sound.

"Soolie! I'm here!"

The bloody creature watched.

"I love you!"

He could almost reach her. The white fire had no heat, but the power that roiled off of her felt as if it could ripple the flesh from his bones. He reached for her, and the carving cuts turned furious in his skin.

"Remember who you are!"

He placed his hand into her fire, and—as he touched her—a shutter dropped from his eyes and he could see.

The tower was in the heart of an immense tornado. All around them, a whirling mass of faces and screaming voices tunneled up, up, up, flinging into a nothingness that swallowed them completely, and from those screaming forms, strands of brilliant gold flowed out of the storm and into Soolie suspended in the center of it all.

It was a storm of souls. An impossible number of them. He knew this immediately, as surely as he knew that they were being crushed like fruit, their juice guzzled, their husks discarded, and he was overcome by the memory of another time and place where he had lain close to death in a town square, and woke to find his town full of tortured corpses fallen at their windows, crouched fearfully in corners, skeletal hands clutching at weapons and one another, as if a hundred women, men, and children had all dropped dead in the very moment that a miracle had brought him back to life with the strength of a hundred souls.

Shock took the ground out from under his feet.

He was shaking and sobbing, but he couldn't feel it. He could hardly see or hear. He was knowing something unknowable. His foundations were demolished, and he clung to nothing.

He didn't see her descend. Didn't see the creature come to her side. Didn't raise his head until she was kneeling naked in front of him.

"Papa," she said.

He retched and vomited into his lap, choking on the bile.

She lifted his chin with her finger, hardly seeming to notice the acid dripping from his lips, studying him with brazen brown eyes that traveled from his face down to the twisting carvings in his chest.

"Soolie." His senses swam. Her name was heavy on his tongue. "Were those *people*? How . . . ? What did you do?"

She leaned in, tilting her head, and walked her fingers down the raw ravines of his breastbone.

He couldn't stop himself from asking what he didn't want to know. "Soolie. What happened in Hob Glen?"

"Why are you a door?" she asked.

"You killed everyone to save me."

"I did not save you." She lifted his arm and studied down its length. "You wanted to die, and I stopped you."

"Why?" he whispered.

"To punish you, Papa. But I forgive you now." She traced the twisting channels down his wrist and placed her fingers lightly on the gashing hole in his palm.

"Don't." He recoiled from her.

She didn't listen.

Life flowed from her hand into his, knitting his damaged flesh, surging up his arm and through his body, pushing out the knife in his back and closing the wound, forcing his flesh to sing with a billion bright buzzing lights. It was the same miracle that had pulled him back from death in the square of Hob Glen. His daughter hadn't saved him from the massacre. His second chance *was* the massacre, and he felt himself filled up with her violence and a terrible understanding. There was no purpose. The demon hadn't destroyed Soolie and she hadn't beaten the demon.

Soolie was the demon.

"This is evil," he said.

"I'm glad you're here," she said. "I need you."

He was shaking, he was sick, he was unbearably alive, and still she forced life that was not his own into his body until he thought his skin would burst and his flesh would melt, until the carving writhing in his skin was the only thing holding him together. He could barely see through the blistering haze into eyes that were brown like his eyes, and he found no love in them, not even hatred.

"Stop," he said.

She didn't stop.

Chapter 30

She had been weak for so long. The Dead Man had stolen her strength and used it to build a kingdom for himself. Now, she was going to face him, and she would need every advantage she could find. She could not, in this moment, take back her Heart, but she could take from him his kingdom and turn it into her power. It wasn't even a conscious decision. She desired, and the lives and souls of Adon Bashti were hers to claim.

Hundreds of thousands, young and old, the Dead Man's collection, all left their bodies at the Hunter's call. Their life poured into her, their spirits returned to the Eternal Realm. The hollow ghosts that had destroyed the Chorus joined the whirling throng, and were flung up through that door, and were gone. The brackish souls and the bright, she demanded them all—all except the two on the tower with her and the one that sat upon the throne beyond her reach, anchored to her Heart. Abundant life filled her with power unlike anything she had felt since her strength had been stolen, and it was good, and she was still not satisfied. Only her Heart could satisfy.

She flung the last souls into the void, sealed off the path to the Eternal Realm, lowered herself to the dusty stone, and looked for him.

Dog was kneeling several paces away.

Come.

Joy washed over his face as he heard her voice in his mind again. He struggled to run, moving broken and wrong, and stopped a step away to bow, but she flung herself into his chest. He staggered back in surprise as she wrapped her arms around him, pressing her clean bare skin to his cold gore-splattered rags.

Thank you.

He held her, grimy hands on her back, and she heard him in her mind.

My Mistress.

And with those two words and one thought, he instilled a world of adoration and devotion, awe and joy for her and everything that she was. They embraced one another, and she shared the new life she had taken, letting it flow into him, and he let it flow back into her. Their connection was no longer only one-way. She had let him into a foundational part of her being, and it had changed them both. She felt the talons on the tips of his fingers regrowing, their sharp points pressing lightly into the skin of her back.

Welcome back, they thought to one another.

There is a man, he looked past her to a figure on the ground. *He came for you.*

I will tend to him.

She released Dog and went to the weeping man. It was Papa. She knelt in front of him. He had changed a great deal since she had last seen him lying on the cobblestones of Hob Glen. His beard was shaggy and dripping with vomit. He was sinewy, sobbing and shaking. Most interesting, though, was the incomplete blood weave carving in his skin.

She took his hand and lifted his arm to get a closer look. Most living souls wouldn't be fit hosts for such a weave, but Papa had the unnatural level of *rashni* that she had given him. But the weave was missing something.

Papa was looking at her. He wanted something that she wasn't fit to give him.

"Soolie," he said.

She leaned in to take a closer look at his chest. Whoever did this had studied much and understood little. "Why are you a door?" she asked.

It's missing its link to the other side, Dog thought, standing at her shoulder.

He was right. It was all the pieces of a door, but without a destination. There must have been another piece to tell it where to go.

"You killed them to save me." Papa said.

"I did not save you," she corrected him. "You wanted to die and I stopped you."

"Why?"

"To punish you, Papa. But I forgive you now." She took his hand.

What will you do with him? Dog asked.

I think we can use him. "I'm glad you're here," she said. "I need you."

She let her light flow into him, healing his wounds and filling him up with the *rashni* of Adon Bashti, charging his flesh and soul with their power. He was speaking, but she closed her eyes, blocking out his babbling words and tuning her mind to the weave in his skin. It was a forceful carving, brutal and inelegant, and easily improved upon. She found the weakness in the weave and took the power of the thousands upon thousands of souls and reforged it.

"I am so sorry, baby girl. I am so sorry. I am so sorry . . . ."

Then the weave was complete and the man was silent.

Chapter 31

After seeing the Dog, Tilla had climbed the stairs back home and found her wife in bed.

"I need to hold you. Please."

"Yes."

They slept, body cupping body like a crescent moon and its shadow. Mavi always got too warm when they slept like this, but even though the night was mild and Tilla could feel Mavi's body growing hot and sweaty, Mavi nestled in and held Tilla's hand even more tightly tucked between her breasts.

Tilla felt the moment Mavi's soul left like a flush of blood and prickling heat and then cold, and she knew Mavi was gone. The Dog had freed the Soul Hunter.

Desperate pain and sorrow seized her, and she clung to her wife's body, begging, not daring to open her eyes.

PLEASE. YOU'RE THE ONLY ONE WHO CAN TAKE ME WITH HER.

She felt it in her belly first, a sickening unraveling as her tissue collapsed, bones melting, her soul ripping from her flesh.

Thank you.

She buried her face in the moist hollow of Mavi's neck and let herself dissolve.

Chapter 32

Adon sen Yevah, the first and the last, sat on the throne of Adon Bashti and seethed with fury. He couldn't believe he had let her harm him. It wouldn't happen again. The Heart of the Hunter filled him with endless strength, and he clenched and unclenched his fists, waiting.

No one approached. The members of his harem clustered on the edges of the dais, keeping watch. Any other night, and he would have dismissed the revelers by now, but not tonight, and the room was wall-to-wall with uneasy merriment. Glutted bellies gorged painfully on meats and sweets, slur-soused mouths slurped liquors and wines. The fingers of the bardist troupe blistered and tore and slicked the strings with blood. The people would stop feasting when he told them to.

She would come to him. She had no choice: he had her Hunter's Heart.

When he first located *Ikma na Sitari*, his initial impulse had been to send his creatures to rip her apart, but *then* he had discovered that the great ancient Soul Hunter believed itself to be a little dead girl. He had reveled for days at the sheer mad luck of it. She had been *so vulnerable* to the power of the Heart, that he'd been able to enter her mind from leagues away, to influence her and bring her willingly to him. It should have been a joyous union, a triumphant becoming.

But then she had turned the power of the crown back on him with a trick. Then she had ripped out his tongue in the presence of his people.

He gripped the seat of the throne, sneering and bearing down on the strength surging through his body. He had underestimated the Hunter side of her. She had appeared so weak when he spied on her sleeping mind, full of confusion and doubt—of her self, her senses, her reality. He had seen how much power he held over her, and even *still* he had been cautious and taken his time, knowing she was not simply another malleable, living mind under his sway, knowing that everything —the renewal and future of *worlds*—depended on her subjugation. He had toyed with her like a fish on a line, reeling her in, and letting her run, and wearing her down, until it was time to finally make her his own, and *somehow* she had still defied him.

Of course she hadn't caused him lasting harm. All wounds of the flesh were temporary. But she had *denied* him in his court and in the eyes of his people.

He had been too sentimental. He should have broken her from the start and taken her by force. His veins boiled, standing out on the backs of his hands like tree roots.

In the crowd, another reveler passed out, tipping from their chair and hitting the floor. The servants stepped over the body to clear the place setting and refill the table's glasses.

He was done with games. His Chorus would retrieve the girl and the Dog, and he would crush the Dog and scatter the pulpy shards of its flesh and bones in the fields. He would bind the girl in the Cradle, and he would torment her for a hundred-thousand years. It didn't matter if Adon spent the full duration of this body breaking her down, the power of the Hunter was the power to remake and reforge. He would burn this torch to light another. He would drain her until she was an agonized husk. He would feed her, and then he would harm her, and then he would feed her again. He would wear her down like water on stone until she was too eroded of self to even *begin* to conceive of ever resisting him, and then he would use the crown to place notions of resistance in her mind and he would punish her for them until she was terrified of her own thoughts.

When he was done with her, there would be no girl left, no Soul Hunter. There would be only mindless, malleable fear. He would encase her on the dais at his side. From his ruling seat between the Hunter and her Heart, he would be conduit and conductor. He would reshape the realm in his image.

Without word or warning, the entire congregation of revelers fell.

A sea of people dropped. Trays hit the marble floor, glasses shattering, bodies crumpling around the dais, toppling over in chairs, on and between the tables, and the room filled with the rising spirits of the dead, translucent golden gleams that hovered for a moment before his wide eyes, and then were pulled away in a flicker and were gone.

He screamed, gripping the throne, his flesh rippling with the power he forced through his body, and he screamed again, wordless rage bouncing off the great walls in a silent room carpeted with the bodies of his people.

He didn't know how she had broken the weave.

It shouldn't be possible. Somehow she had unified herself. She would have had to overcome his Chorus, and that *alone* was impossible, but he could sense without looking that Adon Bashti no longer slept in peace waiting to rise with the morning. The new sun would bring nothing but rot and decay. He had spent a thousand lifetimes building this city and collecting its people, and in a moment of petulance, she had *killed them all*.

He gripped his throne.

As long as he possessed the Hunter's Heart, she would return to him. She would bow to him. She could not overcome him. No amount of stolen souls could compare. He sat in the room of corpses and waited.

∽

He did not have to wait for long.

One of the great doors swung in, and they entered. His Chorus was not with them, and yet there were three. The Dog approached on one side, looking like the rejections of a hostile womb, Adon's crown rooted upon its plastered hair. In the middle slumped a tall sickly-looking man, malnourished and scraggle-faced, with unclean skin that writhed with a carving weave. And lastly, *Ikma na Sitari*. She was as bare as the first time she had entered his throne room, as spotless and unmarred as the Dog was covered in gore. Her skin was pure as salt. Her eyes blazed white fire.

Adon kept his seat as they walked the corridor of corpses to stand before him. As long as he sat upon his throne connected to the Hunter's Heart, they could not touch him.

He looked on her coldly. "You are a child throwing a tantrum. You will earn yourself nothing but beatings, little girl."

"I see your people are dead," she said. Her voice burned like her eyes.

The living man looked unwell. Adon had never seen this man before, but whatever reason the Soul Hunter had for sparing his life was of no consequence. When Adon dismembered her companions, she would be too overwhelmed by him to care.

"You wish to hurt me by destroying what I love," he let the Hunter's strength flow through him. "In that, you have succeeded. You have wounded my heart."

Her bright eyes dimmed, and he saw her small fists tighten. He smiled. Already, he was affecting her.

"I offered you new life, hope, and eternity, and you repaid me with cruelty and violence. You do not deserve my absolution, and you could *never earn* my forgiveness."

The Dog looked over at her, worried, as the flame in the Soul Hunter's eyes flickered out.

"You betray me, because you are lost and afraid. Your path is destruction. Mine is the way of life. If you throw yourself at my mercy, I may still forgive you."

The power of the Hunter's Heart was so great, the words he used hardly mattered. He could sense her weakening, her resolve slipping. Already, she desired to give in to him.

"It will be painful," he soothed. "I must crush you so you can be remade. I will humble you so you can be uplifted. I am, and have always been, the one that will hold you, form and guide you, Soolie Beetch. There is freedom in submission, and I am the only way to your Heart."

She was shaking. Her brown eyes rimming red. The Dog made to reach for her, and then whined and recoiled in fear.

"As long . . . as the Heart is in your possession," she struggled to speak, "I can not resist you."

"Then stop fighting," he said, stretching out his hands, "and come to me." The moment he laid his hands on her, she would forget herself, and he would own her.

"Which is why," she whispered, "I must remove it entirely."

He tilted his head, not knowing what she was saying, and she placed a hand on the writhing-wounded back of the living man beside her, and pushed.

The man stumbled towards the throne with rolling steps on bending bones. His face distorted, skull softening, flesh swelling, his chest and belly bubbling as with a thousand tumorous growths as his human form devolved into a roiling mass of flesh, and just as Adon began to realize what was happening, the man's skin split and the red boiling knots burst free and began to expand, forming a ring of soul-bound flesh headed for the throne, and in the center of that ring was a doorway to nothingness.

The writhing ring reached the dais, closing fast, and Adon threw himself from the seat, screaming, tumbling down the hard steps, landing on his back and scrambling to his feet as the weave met the throne.

The Hunter's weave had been charged with the strength of a thousand souls, and it carved relentless into the seat of peerless white, unraveling it into futile dust. There was a flash of unbearable light as the Heart was laid bare, and Adon and the Soul Hunter cried out in shared agony as the weave closed on the Heart, swallowed it up, and the door snapped shut.

A writhing nugget of pain and suffering that was all that was left, fell into the dust as the last edges of the throne dissolved around it, and the Hunter's Heart was gone.

The Hunter collapsed to her hands and knees, screaming, and he threw himself at her. The Dog intercepted, dodging in and slashing for his chest with its sharp talons. Adon ducked the attack, crouching and kicking out, but the beast dove over him, grabbing his hair as it passed, and using its momentum to fling him, head snapping back, full arc slamming face-first into the marble floor at its feet.

"*STOP!!!*" the Soul Hunter screamed as his pain was her pain.

The Dog hesitated—for only a moment, but a moment was enough. Adon pushed himself up and punched hand-open for its bloody chest. The life in it was bound to dead-flesh and did not flow as living life did. It resisted, barbed and hard, but Adon was strong. Its crown-red eyes went wide with horrible realization as its lips peeled back from its fangs and its body began to give way, and Adon forced the soul from the creature.

"MASTER..."

It gasped as its limbs and flesh ribboned, splattering like burned toffee, and Adon seized it by the throat, and its neck sunk in his fist like a rotting fruit, the eyes fell back into its melting skull, and the last of the servant Dog splattered at his feet.

The Soul Hunter was collapsed on the floor, wailing.

He stepped towards her, shaking the wet flesh from his hand, feeling nothing but rage and hatred. "Unfortunately," he snarled. "I have no reason left to save you."

Her bleeding brown eyes quaked with fear, and she scrambled back naked into the tables, crawling over bodies and through spilled stew and broken glass as he stalked after her.

"Look what you have *done!*" He kicked a pot clattering. "This was something *beautiful* and you have SLAUGHTERED. WRECKED. AND RUINED IT."

She scrambled over fallen musicians, instruments clunking and twanging sour, as she hit the edge of the room. She turned, pressed into the corner, slowly rising to her feet, her knees pinned together, shaking her head as he advanced.

He saw it in her eyes: this last-hope effort had cost her everything, even her will to fight.

He closed his bloodied hand on her throat, and her pale hands gripped his forearms. He didn't even have it in him to toy with her. He would crush her only once.

"MASTER."

Her eyes flashed white, and she was out of his grasp.

Suddenly, it was his back against the wall, her hand closing on his throat, and she bared a mouth of bloody yellow fangs and stabbed two sharp-nailed fingers through the orbs of his eyes, scraping the back of his sockets. He screamed, and her nails reached into his mouth and pierced his tongue and pulled it taut to the root and ripped it out, and then she was behind him, throwing him to the harsh street stones and locking his neck and ankles in iron stocks, splitting the skin of his bowed spine from neck to tail, plucking out one bone at a time, teasing at the nerves as his eyes began to regrow, bubbling in their sockets, and his tongue budded at the back of his throat, and she flipped him over and staked him to the top of a tower with long metal spikes through his wrists and feet and chest, and as the sun came up, she plucked out his teeth one at a time and dropped them down his blood-choked throat.

"MASTER."

She pinned open his lids and made him face the sun until his eyes boiled and burst and burned to crust-gel ash, and when they grew back again, she made him watch as she pried his nails back from their beds, and ripped the bones from his fingers and the bones from his toes and the bones from his wrists, and arms and legs, and she sorted them and categorized them and pulled out his organs and placed them into little jars, and he woke on a stone slab screaming as she tweezered out his veins and wrapped them into tidy spools, and poured molten glass into his limbs and tumbled him up the stairs to watch him shard and shatter and heal and shred, his blood splattering needles of glass that smoked in the sun.

And she dismembered and remade him for a thousand years until he forgot everything except how to scream.

"MASTER."

She said the word, and the word was meaningless.

She held him in a throne room surrounded by a thousand corpses, one clawed hand on either side of his head, her face and hair clotted with gore, her fangs bared, the red crown writhing on her head, her eyes the color of blood, and he could not recognize her for what she was, because of what she had done to him.

"Most of my memories are still of you."

And the Dog crushed the Master's head between his palms as across the room the Soul Hunter screamed.

Chapter 33

"**M**istress." Dog dropped the mash-headed corpse of the Dead Man on the floor in front of her.

"Noooo," she quivered. It had hurt her to hurt him. She had walked into this fight, knowing the power he had over her, and somehow, she has still been overcome. "I can't."

He lifted her hand from the marble floor and placed it on the chest of the Dead Man. "You're the only one who can."

Kill the Dead Man. Even after Dog had overpowered him with the crown, and done whatever he had done to the Dead Man's mind, and crushed his skull, as long as his soul was bound to his flesh, Adon might still return. He was one of the Dead Man's monsters.

"It feels like he's a part of me," she whispered.

Dog held her hand on top of the Dead Man's body. "Mistress, take what is yours."

Dog was also a part of her, but unlike the Dead Man, he was a wanted part. She closed her eyes and drew strength from that, and reached into the Dead Man's flesh, and found the ancient soul that was bound there burgeoning with the Hunter's light, and she willed it free.

It felt like tearing herself apart, and as the body under her hand melted and gave way and the light that the Dead Man had stolen flowed back into her, a wail rose from her belly, and she cried out as she opened a rend in the fabric of the world and released the corrupted ink of his spirit into the realm of the Ancients.

Then she collapsed and began to sob, and Dog was close, holding her, knowing that she wanted him to. They sat together, two dead creatures huddled over the remains of a Dead Man, surrounded by corpses, the only souls left.

Chapter 34

"I'm ready," Soolie said, tugging on the front of her dress.
    She had chosen dark red with long sleeves and blue buttons that glimmered when you twisted them in the light. He had chosen a sleeveless tunic and loose pants that were a pale gray and matched the color of his scrubbed talons. She doubted he would be able to keep the clothes clean, but he had picked them out himself, so she hadn't questioned it. He wore the crown, and the color of his eyes matched the color of her dress. *Does it hurt?* she had thought to him. *I do not mind,* he had thought back.

"I made you something." Dog reached into his pocket.

"You didn't yank another tooth, did you?" She'd had enough of that.

He shook his head and held out a short, silver-white chain dangling from his fist. Soolie took it. From the center hung a tiny burnished black gem. It was surprisingly lovely. She was glad he hadn't hurt himself.

"It's the seed of a forgetree," he offered. "The seeds can go for a thousand years without sprouting."

Soolie had heard of forgetrees. "It needs the heat of fire to crack."

Dog nodded. "Once sprouted, there's no worm that can kill it. You can uproot them, and they'll continue to grow."

She held out her wrist. "Did you *really* make it?"

He took the bracelet and looped it around and clipped the clasp. "Not entirely, Mistress, but I did search all of the town gemsmiths looking for one and placed it on the chain."

"Thank you." She twisted it around so the little black seed lay on top of her wrist. "I needed something to replace the one I lost."

"Well," he bobbed, "perhaps if Mistress burns *this* one, this one will grow."

It was a nice, but silly sentiment, and she understood why he had thought of her.

"I got you something too." She reached into her dress pocket.

He stepped back, eyes widening with alarm.

Get back here, she snapped into his mind, and he came cowering back, shivering and nervous, but she could see it was good nervousness, not shame nervousness. She pulled out the crimson bundle and let it unwrap, the leather ribbons untwisting, the long beads at the end clicking against one another. He quivered, scrunching his hands to his chest, and she was overcome with the horrid realization that this might be the first gift he had ever received.

He must have seen the cloud pass over her face, because he abruptly stepped back to bow from the waist, his hair flopping forward. He had cut it off fighting the Chorus, and it had only just regrown long enough that he could tie it back again.

"Stand up and turn around."

He bobbed and did as he was told, shivering obediently as she gathered his hair at the base of his neck, collecting any stray strands, then wrapping the leather under, and cross-cross over and under, and cross-coss over, then tightening the cinch bead. The leather was soft and stretchy. The long dripping beads hung from the brush stub of his hair. It would look better once his hair had grown out long enough to hang down his back.

The beads were carved from giant burrow-bear talons that had been buffed and smoothed, and she had gotten them for him, because he had given her his claws so many times, and she didn't want him to have to pull out his teeth or claws ever again. He turned back to her, the lower rims of his eyes wet with filming blood.

"You needed something to tie your hair back," she muttered.

Dog nodded and dabbed at the wells of his eyes with his fingers, and rubbed his hands clean in his hair, so he wouldn't get tears on his clothes. He beamed at her.

"I'm ready," she said again.

He pushed open the front door of the great house, and a cloying stench enveloped them as they stepped inside. Corpses lined the halls and stacked wall-to-wall in the state rooms. They were heaped in the kitchens and hilled in the gardens. There were thousands. Even with Soolie and Dog working day and night to cart the dead up the hill to the house, by the time they had gotten the last of them, all of the bodies had begun to slide their skin and burst their bellies. The fetor was so strong, it almost masked the smell of drenching lantern fuel.

Dog led the way down the ornate hall with its ivory and gold carvings. Bodies piled along the walls and around the pillars. Fuel fumes wavered off the wet floor in the sunlight that slanted through crystal-cut windows. He pushed in the bright silver-white doors, and they strode into the throne room. Rats the size of rabbits bounded over corpses and molding dishes, their bodies round and glossy with feeding. Maggots wriggled patches of creamy yellow rice in faces, arms, crotches, and bellies. Flies hummed in the putrid air.

Everything was turning back into life. It was almost a shame to burn it.

She stepped over the sticky clot that had been the Dead Man and approached the dais. Dog stood to the side and waited. He knew she had to do this part on her own. She wasn't sure why it had taken her so long. She had needed to process, to brace herself, to prepare. She ascended the steps.

It was right where she had left it.

In the middle of the dais, in a heap of white dust, a tight moving knot of flesh and soul and torment, shiny like an agate, darker than living blood. She could sense its pain. She knelt and sat on her heels.

She honestly hadn't thought much about her father this last year or two, and when she had thought of him, it had always been of when she was little and living, never of where he might be *now* that she was dead.

She'd never thought to wonder if he was missing her, or if he had been looking for her.

'I am so sorry,' he had said. His last words had been an apology for who she was, said to someone she wasn't.

She shouldn't feel pain over someone who didn't know her and could only love what she had been, not who she was. And yet, he had suffered, and the remnant of him still suffered, not only because of his love, but because of how she had used him. What *had* he gone through to reach her a lifetime too late for him and at just the right moment for her?

"Thank you," she whispered and reached out a single finger to touch the writhing knot of pain.

At her touch, it unlaced, unfolding and expanding to reveal—in the clasped setting of its agony—the radiant star of the Soul Hunter's Heart right where she had left it, closed inside the doorway without a destination. It bathed her in power and light, and she unbuttoned the front of her dress and relaxed the form of her flesh so her chest melted away and the great depth of her emptiness was exposed. Then she scooped it up tenderly in her hands, her Hunter's strength bound in a ring of her father's suffering, and cupped them to her.

The Heart belonged, and it slid into her and was home and made her whole again. She was light and she was power. She expanded to see all things. The depths of the world and all its struts and foundations were subject to her, and known by her, and answered to her will.

She saw the living souls, few and meager, struggling to survive in their little ways. And she saw that they were meaningless and pointless, and also precious in their unique futility, each one a realm of experience unto themselves. And she knew, if she wished to, she could help them.

She saw the monsters that remained, ravenous and hungry, terrified and without restraint. Lost in a world that could not feed them, that destroyed them in the light of its sun, but would not let them end. And she knew, if she wished to, she could help them too.

She saw the Lost Souls, most multitudinous of all, some completely formless, some still aware of how they suffered. All hungry, all fading and losing their sense of self. And she knew the Ancients would want her to find them and send them on, as surely as she knew that one day the Ancients would remember her—one of their many Soul Hunters of their many realms—and they would find her and see her as something that *should not be*, and on that day, she would cease to exist.

She saw all of these things and their many possibilities. And she knew she could release the memory of the little living girl into that sea of knowledge so it became one of the multitude of many lifetimes that she held, and she chose not to. She held her father's pain and felt it becoming a part of her, his unending suffering turning and turning around her Heart, and she told it that it was home.

No one could map her path or tell her what her future held.

She did not know how long it was before she returned, but when she once again found herself kneeling in the dust of the Dead Man's throne, she looked and found Dog still standing there, waiting.

She reformed her chest and buttoned up her dress. She willed the blood tears from her face and lifted their stains from the lap of her skirt. She stood, clean and whole, and Dog bowed and offered his hand.

"Ready, Mistress?"

She took his hand. "I'll light the fire."

As they stepped out the front door into the dim light of the setting sun, the footsteps behind them bloomed fire that rushed from footprint to footprint, and the fumes in the halls billowed, the windows exploded, and smoke began to rise from the wounds.

They stood on the path, watching the roof pocket holes and sprout flame. She leaned her head on his shoulder, and he placed his arm around her, which was still something new, but it felt familiar and good.

A far roof crashed, releasing great clouds of orange-bellied smoke, obscuring the stars. All of the Dead Man's house would burn. Only the library would be left standing, with the little cluttered apartment and the terrace garden where newly seeded dahlias and sweet peas would soon sprout and settle roots in the buried bones. Soolie rather liked the idea of tending that garden and library. Now—with the Hunter's memories restored—individual human thoughts and lives were the most of what she did not know, and she imagined she could spend many lifetimes getting lost in those shelves and pages, painting, and watching things grow. Though, knowing and experiencing were very different, and there was still a great deal of the world that she wanted to see.

She lifted her head to look at Dog, and his red eyes shifted to hers. After all that they had been through, he still managed to look worried.

Have I done something wrong, Mistress? he thought.

When you were in my Hunter's memories, were you tempted to tell me to be something else?

He squirmed against her side, which always made him feel too bony, so she pinched him to make him stop. He looked down, guiltily.

I did think it, Mistress.

What did you think?

He pulled his arm away, pleading. *I'm sorry Mis—*

Oh, stop, she thought back.

For a moment, I wanted to tell Mistress to be my Mistress, because then I would have her as my Mistress for always.

She nodded. *Why didn't you?*

He looked up meekly. *I didn't think Mistress would want me to.*

She wrapped an arm around his waist, yanking him close, and turned back to watch the fire. Awkwardly, he placed his arm around her shoulders again.

I wouldn't have wanted that, she said. *But I'm glad you thought about it.*

Why? he asked, obediently.

Because you chose not to.

Do you mind *being Mistress?*

I don't mind. Do you like being called Dog?

I don't know. The fire reflected coals in the red of his eyes. Up above, bright needle stars pierced the darkness. *I didn't give myself this name, and there have been many Dogs before me . . . . I could go by another name.*

She waited.

But all the others are dead. And, he looked away sheepishly. *I like hearing you say it.*

Dog?

Say it?

"Dog."

"Mistress."

The night turned to day, and the day turned to night, and they stood together and watched the fire burn.

Acknowledgments

I am lucky and privileged to have a job, a family, and a life that have made this pursuit of passion possible. There are billions of people with stories to tell who never get the chance, because they're forced to spend the time they would otherwise devote to art on survival.

For the love and support I have received, I am eternally humbled and grateful. Most of all to Cass and Kel. Your love gives me superpowers.

And to everyone who has a story to tell—I wish you all the luck, perseverance, and courage in the world. Your story is worth telling.